Estelle scrunched _____. The small cavern for _____ was large enough for only one body. From this new angle, Estelle could see that the blood soaked the blouse over the woman's left shoulder, and her sandy-blond hair was a mess of blood and dirt. Without moving the corpse, or without moving the car, there was no way to see the victim's face.

"Estelle," Linda whispered.

"What?"

"That's Janet."

"What do you mean?"

"I recognize the blouse and jeans," Linda said. "That's what Janet was wearing this afternoon when she stopped by the office." When Estelle didn't respond, Linda added, "Mike's Janet."

"The primary appeal of this series continues to be its evocation of daily life in a small New Mexico town."

—Booklist

Previously published Worldwide Mystery titles by
STEVEN F. HAVILL

CONVENIENT DISPOSAL
A DISCOUNT FOR DEATH
SCAVENGERS
RED OR GREEN? (in *Deadly Morsels*)
BAG LIMIT
DEAD WEIGHT
OUT OF SEASON

STATUTE of LIMITATIONS

STEVEN F. HAVILL

W🌐RLDWIDE®

TORONTO • NEW YORK • LONDON
AMSTERDAM • PARIS • SYDNEY • HAMBURG
STOCKHOLM • ATHENS • TOKYO • MILAN
MADRID • WARSAW • BUDAPEST • AUCKLAND

For Kathleen

STATUTE OF LIMITATIONS

A Worldwide Mystery/March 2007

First published by St. Martin's Press LLC.

ISBN-13: 978-0-373-26593-0
ISBN-10:   0-373-26593-X

Printed in U.S.A.

Acknowledgments

The author would like to thank Frank Cimino, Vincent Mares, Bill Patterson and Royal Quint.

Posadas County, NEW MEXICO

ONE

ESTELLE REYES-GUZMAN scrunched down into the sofa, a large pillow clutched to her chest, face buried in the pillow's soft corduroy to stifle her laughter. Across the room, her two small sons sat on the piano bench, elbow to elbow, creating a remarkable coordination of sound and story. The oldest, six-year-old Francisco, provided the music as his nimble fingers danced on the keyboard. Four-year-old Carlos narrated. He held a large children's book open on his lap, and even though he couldn't read the words, Carlos had heard the story so often that he knew it by heart, using the pictures as his cue.

In the story, a sweaty, dejected *javalina*—the ubiquitous wild pig of the southwest—shuffled across the bleak desert at high noon. Even the towering cacti provided no shade from the sun that blistered his tender hide. The plodding, monotonous bass notes of the piano accompanied the little pig as the scene unwound in Francisco's head and through his brother's narration.

The little pig looked up, squinting into the sun. As he did so, a triplet of high piano notes, as light and quick as the wink of sun reflecting from a discarded can, made him flinch. He wiped his brow with a colorful bandana and heaved a great sigh, and even as Carlos said the words, "I'm sooooo hot and tired," Francisco's fingers executed a weary *glissando* that wandered down the keyboard. Both boys giggled.

Their mother, the sole audience member for this particular

performance, suppressed a laugh, not wanting to distract her sons even though they had performed this particular story so many times that everyone in the household knew it by heart. Still, each performance brought new discoveries. And this time, Posadas County Undersheriff Estelle Reyes-Guzman savored the moment for herself.

The Christmas season had brought a rare visit from her husband's aunt, Sofía Tournál, from Veracruz, Mexico. Sofía was a favorite of the two little boys, perhaps because she was so skilled, in her own dignified, quiet way, at drawing them into lengthy conversations that challenged their agile little minds. Estelle loved her aunt dearly and treasured her visits.

After a day of non-stop visiting, baking, and cooking, often as a triumvirate with her mother and Sofía, Estelle was ready to draw into herself for a few minutes. Used to long moments by herself, in company only with her own thoughts, Estelle felt the constant onslaught of holiday cheer coaxing her toward dark, quiet corners. Ever perceptive, Sofía had whisked Estelle's mother off to an early Christmas Eve church service, leaving Estelle alone with her husband and the two boys. With the children fully engaged, Dr. Francis Guzman had taken a few minutes to escape into the sanctuary of his office.

Estelle nestled on the sofa, shoes off, an afghan fluffed around her shoulders, absorbed in the remarkable mixing of story and soundtrack by her two sons. She was further lulled by the aromas that filled the house, especially from the large cauldron of *posole* on the kitchen range. The tangy chile and spices fought with the remnant fragrance of the final batch of tiny sugared pastries that Sofía had conjured.

There were no telephones in the desert world of the story-book *javalinas* that Christmas Eve. When the phone jangled, it wasn't a sound effect. Estelle groaned and refused to move. By the second ring, six-year-old Francisco Guzman had interrupted the story flow, matched the telephone's pitch on the piano, and mimicked the jangling telephone with a trill in unison.

"Telephone, *Mamá*," he bellowed without missing a beat.

"Thanks, *hijo*," Estelle sighed. She shifted around on the sofa, and by the time she reached across to the end table and picked up the telephone receiver, it had jangled twice more.

"Guzman," she said, and watched as the two boys huddled in whispered collaboration over the book. Francisco's hands curled together in his lap, trapped by the conscious effort not to touch the keys while his mother was on the telephone.

Estelle listened to a moment of silence—almost long enough for her to guess that it was a telephone solicitor calling—before a voice on the phone said hesitantly, "Is this Estelle?"

"Yes?"

"This is Eduardo," the caller said, but Estelle had already recognized the husky, diffident voice of Eduardo Martinez, now several years retired after a long tenure as chief of police for the Village of Posadas. Eduardo had kept his school zones safe over the years, always happy to turn over any case more complex than shoplifting to the Posadas County Sheriff's Department. More than one village resident—including some of the Sheriff's Department deputies—assumed that Eduardo was simply lazy. Estelle knew that was far from the truth. Eduardo had his own strong beliefs about what constituted law enforcement and had no trouble determining when his tiny department needed help.

"Well, Merry Christmas, sir. It's good to hear from you," Estelle said. She pushed herself out of the deep sofa, unwound the afghan, and walked toward the kitchen.

"Did I interrupt at a bad time?" the chief asked. In the background, Estelle could hear a television show, muffled conversation punctuated with bursts of canned laughter.

"Not at all." She glanced at her watch and saw that it was ten minutes before seven. Her mother and Sofía Tournál would be returning shortly from the early Christmas Eve service at the tiny mission in Regál, a stone's throw from the Mexican border twenty-five miles southwest of Posadas. Her husband was working on some secret thing back in the master bedroom, away from the prying eyes of their two inquisitive sons.

"How's Essie?" Estelle asked. Eduardo and his wife, Essie Martinez, were like two peas from the same pod—short, rotund, gentle folks, who had created a large brood of short, round children who had then produced classroomsful of grandchildren.

"Oh, she's fine. She's off at church, I think. We got the family here for the holiday, you know, and they all went." He laughed weakly. "It's quite a crowd, these days. Say—" and he hesitated "—is your husband home, do you think?"

Estelle heard something else in Eduardo's soft voice that touched off an alarm. "Sure, he's here. Are you all right?"

"Well, I think so," and once more Estelle heard the hesitation. "But if he's there, maybe…"

"Just a second." She was at the master bedroom in five strides and rapped a knuckle on the door. "*Querido?* Eduardo Martinez is on the phone for you."

"I'll pick up in here," Dr. Guzman replied. "Come on in."

As Estelle swung the door open, her husband had already turned away from the large computer screen that dominated the desk in the corner. He picked up the telephone extension beside the bed.

"Eduardo?" he said into the phone. "What's going on?" He listened, his fingers drumming a slow roll on the nightstand. After a moment, he reached out and picked up a pencil, then scooted a small note pad closer. "Okay." He listened again, turning to look at Estelle. He shook his head slowly, then turned back to the pad. "Okay, Eduardo, this is what I think we'd better do. You've been taking the Coumaxium right along?"

What should have been a simple "yes" or "no" answer became a wandering dissertation, and Francis fidgeted, finally interrupting. "Okay. Look, where are you right now? It doesn't sound like you're home."

Again Francis waited for the explanation, and Estelle saw her husband's forehead pucker as his frown deepened. "I think you should just wait right there, then. You're at the motel by yourself?"

Estelle sat down on the bed, intrigued. "Then this is what I think we'd better do, Eduardo," Francis said. "I think we'd better bring you on over to the emergency room. That's going to be the fastest." As Dr. Guzman listened, he looked over at Estelle and then rolled his eyes heavenward.

"No, no...I don't want you to do that," Francis said quickly. "Pop a couple of those aspirin you just bought. That's the best thing to do right now. Take a couple and then just sit down and relax, okay? I'm going to have an ambulance swing by there to pick you up."

His patient said something that made Francis grin. "Yeah, well," the physician said, "I know it's an expensive taxi, Eduardo, but sometimes..." He paused as Martinez launched into another string of excuses. "How about this," Francis said, and he had to repeat himself until he was sure that Eduardo was listening. "I'm pleased that you think you're feeling better, but how about this. I'll swing by and check you out. How will that be? I have to go down to the hospital here in a little bit anyway, and it'll only take me a minute to duck around by the motel. I'll be there before you know it."

After another moment of listening, he rose, moving closer to the nightstand. "Yes sir," he said. "False alarms are a good thing. But we need to make sure that's exactly what it is. Let's be sure about this, Eduardo. Stay put, all right?"

Estelle settled into one of the leather chairs beside the computer table. "It isn't a bother, Eduardo," Francis said, and sighed in exasperation. "Just stay put, take a couple of aspirin, and wait for me. Don't go driving off somewhere. Not even home. If I get down there and find out that you've driven off somewhere, I'm going to be pissed, Chief. Okay?" In a moment, he switched off and exhaled loudly. "Denial is a wonderful thing."

"What's he doing at the motel?" Estelle asked as Francis punched in the auto-dial for dispatch. With a minimum of words, he ordered an ambulance, dispatched to the Posadas Inn. As he did so, he gathered his wallet and keys.

"It's only a half-dozen blocks from his house, and it has a traveler's-aid vending machine," Francis said as he hung up. "He was looking for some aspirin, and that's not so easy to find on Christmas Eve. The motel is closer than the convenience store. He said that he couldn't get his breath, and then when he sat down and tried to relax, he felt as if someone was sitting on him." Francis put an arm around Estelle's shoulders as he headed toward the door. "Before he went to the motel, he was home by himself, so that tells us something. He didn't feel good enough to go out with the family." He glanced at his watch and shook his head. "He says that last year when Essie fell and broke her hip, they called an ambulance and it cost 'em six hundred bucks for a ride across town."

He paused and turned, encircling Estelle in a full bear hug. "It'll just take a few minutes, *querida*. We'll get him over to the ER and hang some wires on him to see what's going on." They stood silently, caught up in each other's arms. "Gilbert and Sullivan have a nice concert going out there."

"It's delightful," Estelle said. "They're still doing the old standbys, but Francisco says he has a new story that he wants to play for Aunt Sofía when she and *Mamá* come home."

"Well, don't let him start until I get back," Francis said.

Estelle followed her husband into the living room, where he scooped a lightweight windbreaker off the back of the sofa, walked over to the piano, and bent down so that his head was between the two boys. He whispered something that brought conspiratory giggles. Estelle walked her husband out to the car, ignoring the cut of the wind and the occasional mist of icy rain. There would be a trace of holiday snow on the San Cristóbal peaks by morning.

"*Padrino* is still coming over?" Francis asked as he slid into his SUV. "You guys baked enough this afternoon for an army. We need someone to help us chow our way through all those calories."

"He promised that he would," Estelle replied. She leaned through the window, and their kiss was a quick token. "Thanks for keeping an eye on the chief," she said. "I hope everything is okay. We'll see you in a bit. Be careful."

Dr. Guzman backed the SUV out of the driveway and turned south on Twelfth Street, his affectionate wave belied by the expression of preoccupied concern on his face and the snarl of the engine as he floored the gas pedal. Estelle stood for a moment in the front yard of their sprawling, much added-to home, enjoying the chill of that December night. Light curtains of mist slanted through the wash of each streetlight and drew halos around the Christmas lights on porches and rooflines. The tropical disturbance hundreds of miles south had pumped the dank air northward, but the temperatures had refused to cooperate by chilling the mist and rain into snow.

The neighbors across the street had set out *luminarios,* using the traditional paper bags and candles. The bags sagged from the dampness, with half of the candles drowned. One of the bags had sagged against the lighted candle inside and flamed briefly, then subsided into a puddle of charred paper as the little bonfire winked out.

For another minute after her husband's car disappeared down the street, Estelle remained outside, listening to the piano music that drifted out from the house. As the chill was beginning to seep through her sweater and she was turning toward the house, she heard the ambulance siren off in the distance, and that ran an icy finger up her spine. She stopped and watched as a large silver Mercedes whispered down the street and then into her driveway.

"This is good," her mother said in Spanish as Estelle helped her out of the car. "My daughter stands out in the rain, no hat, no coat. *Los Dos* have more sense," she said, referring to her two grandchildren inside.

"The rain feels good, *Mamá*," Estelle said. "How was the service?"

"The service was just fine," Teresa Reyes said. "You should have gone." She nodded toward the house as she navigated around the car's front fender, Estelle at her elbow. "It wouldn't hurt them, either. You go inside now."

Sofía Tournál took Teresa's other elbow. "We actually saw a little snow in Regál Pass," she said, her Mexican accent thick and elegant as she diplomatically changed the subject. "Just enough to grace the trees."

"As long as it doesn't stick on the highway," Estelle said. "We don't need a string of tourists ending up in the ditch. I was beginning to be a little concerned about you two."

At that, Teresa hesitated at the front step and turned toward her daughter. Perhaps she had heard the last notes of the siren as the ambulance sped south toward the motel. "You're not working tonight, are you?"

"I hope not, *Mamá.*"

"Well, then," Teresa said, as if that settled all matters about snow, Regál Pass, and tourists. "They decorated the church with a mountain of juniper boughs this year. I thought I was going to sneeze through the whole service. You should have seen it."

Together they maneuvered the three low steps of the front stoop, and four-year-old Carlos greeted them at the door. Francisco remained at the piano, now playing a slow, simple, and immensely sad piece of music. Sofía Tournál stepped inside, head cocked as she listened, eyes narrowed critically. Francisco finished the piece, looked up at his great aunt, and beamed.

"I haven't heard you play that before, *hijo,*" Sofía said.

"Mrs. Gracie gave it to me yesterday," Francisco said matter-of-factly. Whichever of Mozart's early works his piano teacher had found for Francisco, Estelle saw that the sheet music was not in evidence on the piano stand. If Mrs. Gracie had been impressed with the little boy's almost instantaneous absorption of the music, she hadn't commented when Estelle had picked him up after his twice-a-week lesson. "We'll just see," was her favorite comment. Over the years, Mrs. Gracie had no doubt mentored many children whose momentary passion for music would veer away in some other direction, leaving the piano silent. But Estelle knew that in this case, the wait was unwarranted. For little Francisco to abandon his music would be akin to abandoning his most cherished, closest friend.

"He was probably about your age when he wrote that," Sofía said.

"I think so," the little boy replied soberly. He played a chord so softly it was a mere kiss of the keys, then slid off the piano bench and carefully closed the lid.

Estelle had started to close the front door but stopped when she saw a shiny new Blazer idle to the curb in front of their house. "Here's *Padrino*," she said.

"Well, we all timed *that* with perfection, didn't we?" Sofía said. "And I see Francis had to leave. His car is gone."

"Not for long, I hope," Estelle said.

Sofía held up both hands in mock self-defense as the two boys careened past her, their grandmother, and Estelle to plaster their faces against the glass of the storm door.

As he ambled up the front walk, former sheriff of Posadas County Bill Gastner saw the boys waiting. He stopped, a wonderful beetle-browed scowl darkening his heavy features. Shaking his head in disgust, he waved a hand in dismissal and started to turn back toward his vehicle.

That brought howls of delight from the boys. Francisco unlatched the door and plunged outside. In a moment, Gastner was escorted into the house, a child glommed onto each hand.

"Ho, ho," he said. He managed to extricate himself and reached out toward Sofía. "Did you guys go to Regál?"

"Yes, we did," she said, and returned Gastner's hug.

"Brave or dumb," he said. "One of the two." Teresa had already covered half the distance toward her rocking chair, and she leaned against her walker. Gastner crossed to her and escorted her the remaining steps. "How's Teresa?" he asked.

"Teresa's fine," the elderly woman said. She lowered herself into the rocker with a sigh. "That's a wonderful shirt."

Gastner looked down at the expanse of cozy blue flannel. "Something, huh?" he said. "Every once in a while, Camille hits the mark," he added, referring to his eldest daughter. "Usually, she sends me health-food books, or some damn thing like that."

Estelle appeared from the hallway where she'd gone to hang up coats, but the telephone cut off her greeting to Gastner. She veered to the kitchen to take the call.

"Unplug the damn thing," Gastner called. "Christmas Eve is off-limits."

"That's right," Teresa grumbled with surprising vehemence. "I try to tell her that, but she won't listen."

The Sheriff's Department beeper on Estelle's belt chirped simultaneously. She picked up the phone, at the same time turning on the portable hand-held radio that sat in its charger by the telephone.

"Guzman," she said, and she couldn't help glancing at the clock and seeing that barely nine minutes had elapsed since she had answered Eduardo's call.

"Hey," the quiet voice of Sheriff Robert Torrez said. "Do I need to send Irma over?"

Estelle hesitated an instant, bringing herself up to speed with the sheriff's cryptic conversational habits. Irma Sedillos, Bobby's sister-in-law, worked as the Guzman family's *nana,* bringing order to a frenetic household. With Sofía Tournál visiting and always more than willing to babysit the two boys, Irma had taken a much-deserved vacation for Christmas Eve to be with her immediate family. The sheriff's question meant that Estelle's few moments of familial bliss were over.

"No. We're covered," she said. "What's up, Bobby?"

"A couple of minutes ago, your hubby called 911 dispatch for an ambulance at the motel."

"Yes, he did. For Chief Martinez."

"Okay." If the sheriff was surprised, he didn't react. "About thirty seconds after that call from Dr. Francis, someone at the motel called dispatch to report some kind of incident, maybe an assault. One victim down. I don't know who called. Maybe the desk clerk, I don't know. I'm headin' that way now. Mike Sisneros took the call, so he'll be about there by now. He was a couple miles south."

"I'll be right down," Estelle said. "Essie and the family are all at church, by the way."

"Okay," Torrez said. "I'll take care of that when we know what the hell is goin' on. You sure you're covered there?"

"Yes. I'm on my way."

She placed the telephone gently back in the cradle, then looked up to see Bill Gastner regarding her.

"It's Eduardo Martinez," she repeated. "But…" She covered the rest of it with a helpless shrug.

"Uh-oh," he said quietly, and his heavy features sagged. "Dead?"

"Maybe."

Gastner didn't ask for elaboration, but shrugged back into his jacket. "Mind if I ride along?"

"I could use the company," she replied, already heading toward the hall closet.

"We'll be fine," Sofía called from the living room.

"Poor Essie," Teresa Reyes said, proving once again that her octogenarian hearing was as keen as ever. "Not such a merry Christmas for her."

"We'll be back as soon as we can," Estelle said, crossing quickly to her mother for a quick peck on the cheek.

"We know how that goes," her mother said.

The drive from one end of Posadas to the other took no more than a few minutes, especially with Bustos and Grande avenues nearly deserted. Just before they reached the Interstate, Estelle slowed and swung into the parking lot of the Posadas Inn, once part of a well-advertised national chain but now a weatherbeaten relic of its former self. High on its pedestal, the neon sign announced FREE T.V., RESTAURANT, AMERICAN OWNED.

This time the mist played kaleidoscopic halos of red, blue, and white, slanting across the parking lot of the Posadas Inn and muting the harsh, flashing lights of the emergency vehicles. Estelle pulled her unmarked county car to a stop beside the bulk of the ambulance. Twenty yards away, a group hunched around a figure partially covered with a bright yellow rain slicker. The body lay close to the curb, a pace or two from an older-model sedan with out-of-state license plates.

Estelle had never thought of Eduardo Martinez as a small man, but the lump under the slicker could have been mistaken at a distance for a child.

"Shit," Bill Gastner muttered, more to himself than anyone. She glanced at him as she pulled on her black baseball cap. His big, rough face was set in a scowl, teeth clenched to make his already square, prominent jaw all the more pugnacious. His comment wasn't directed against the weather. He was looking at the same thing that had made her blood run cold—a yellow plastic crime scene tape that delineated the area around Eduardo Martinez's body.

TWO

THE RAIN BEADED ON the plastic cover of Deputy Mike Sisneros's Stetson and drizzled off the brim. He kept the aluminum lid of his clipboard nearly closed, protecting the pages inside. As Estelle approached, he took a couple of steps away from the group to meet her. "I don't think they can do much for him," he said. "They're giving it the old college try, though. Somebody at the motel initially called in a fatality, but he's hangin' in there."

Turning in place, Estelle looked out across the wet, shiny asphalt of the parking lot. A cold, wet place, not the least bit friendly, she thought. After a moment Estelle saw her husband rise to his feet and steady one of the IV bag supports as the gurney was hoisted up onto its wheels. In a few seconds, the EMT team whisked Eduardo Martinez to the ambulance. His face, partially concealed by the oxygen mask, looked like wet alabaster. Dr. Guzman climbed into the ambulance, one hand locked on the chief's.

Estelle felt as if she'd swallowed a pound of lead. The last time she had seen Eduardo Martinez, a chance encounter during a county commission meeting, he had smiled like a cherub, full of good cheer and excitement about the holidays.

Sisneros interrupted her thoughts. "This vehicle is stolen out of Hickory Grove, Indiana," he said. He nodded at the Dodge sedan. "Registered to a Harlan Wilson Waid, 229 Sunset

Terrace. Reported stolen from an auto parts store parking lot sometime during the evening of 12/21."

"That's three days ago," Sheriff Bob Torrez said.

"That's right," Sisneros said, as if the correct arithmetic was a surprise. "That's all we got on it right now. No who, no why." He snapped the clipboard closed.

"I don't care about *this* car," Estelle said. "Where's Eduardo's vehicle? He didn't drive down here tonight in a stolen car. What's going on?"

"That's just the point. I don't know," Sisneros said. "I don't know what happened. I'm thinking the best guess is that whoever stole this piece of shit in Indiana drove it this far and then took the opportunity to grab himself a new set of wheels while Eduardo was inside or something. That's what makes the most sense. I don't know why he came down to the motel in the first place."

"No one actually saw what happened?" Estelle asked. She glanced back at the ambulance. Her husband, satisfied that the EMTs had everything under control, was stepping down, ready to follow the ambulance to the hospital in his own vehicle. Had Francis seen the chief's car leaving the parking lot? If not, they had missed crossing paths by only seconds.

"This is as far as we've gotten, Estelle," Sisneros said. "But we wanted to jump on the possibility of the chief's car being stolen as quickly as we could. He wouldn't have walked down here from his house. Not in this weather. Anyway, Tom Pasquale headed south on 56 as far as the border crossing. Regál is closest if someone wants to hightail it into Mexico."

"We got the roads covered," Torrez said, cutting Sisneros off impatiently. "East, west, north, south…between us, the State Police, and the Border Patrol, it's covered. This had to happen just a few minutes ago, so whoever took the chief's car…*if* someone took his car…they ain't gonna go far."

"Or they might be lounging in a motel room, watching television," Estelle said.

"Well, the chief's car isn't here, and he is," Sisneros said.

"Eduardo called us at home," Estelle said and glanced at her watch. "About fourteen minutes ago now. He was feeling ill, but he didn't want to go to the hospital or have Francis call an ambulance for him. Francis did anyway, and then headed over here to check on him, to see what was going on. Apparently the chief had been home by himself. Family at church." She looked across toward the sidewalk, and then the short distance to the main entrance. "Who called dispatch, do we know?"

"The motel desk clerk, most likely," Sheriff Torrez said. "But we don't know that, either. All we got is that dispatch had a man call it in. Didn't leave his name." He leaned with both hands on the head of a stout aluminum cane, ignoring the rivulets of water that matted his curly black hair and then ran down his swarthy face. He looked miserable. "He told dispatch that there was a man down out in the parking lot. Then he hung up. That's what we got at the moment."

"I rolled in first, then your husband, then Pasquale," Deputy Sisneros said. "I saw right away that it was the chief lying by the sidewalk and rendered what assistance I could. I saw that this wasn't his car, and the first minute I had the chance, I called it in."

Estelle nodded in approval at Sisneros's quick thinking. A junker car with out-of-state plates, the spare tire, keys in the ignition, no one around other than the chief…

"Tom got here, and then the ambulance," Sisneros said. "The only thing that makes sense to me is that somebody was after a new set of wheels. Especially now that we know this one's stolen." He nodded at the dilapidated Dodge. "They're sitting here with a flat tire on a stolen car. Eduardo rolls in, and bingo.

They find a new Buick as a Christmas present, with a victim who isn't going to resist much, or at all. There's no sign of a struggle...no wounds or anything like that."

There were a dozen routes that someone could use to slip out of Posadas County, but anyone unfamiliar with the bleak, rugged country would most likely stick to the main highways, taking their chances with the thin police coverage on a Christmas Eve.

Estelle slipped under the yellow tape, approaching the spot where Eduardo Martinez had lain. The chief had fallen to the tarmac on the driver's side of the decrepit sedan from Indiana. Whether Eduardo had struggled with his assailants, or simply been so preoccupied that he had left his keys in his own car while he went inside the motel, was a puzzle. But in the chief's delicate condition, a struggle wouldn't have lasted long.

"Did the desk clerk see where the chief parked?" she asked. "Did he see any of this happen?"

"We haven't had a chance to talk with anyone inside yet," Sisneros said. "But I don't think so."

"Why do you say that?"

"Well," and he stopped, looking back toward the small portico that spanned the front entrance, a structure just large enough for a single vehicle to pull under. He shook his head dubiously. "Unless the clerk stepped outside, he wouldn't be able to see this spot. That little wall of the foyer would block his view. There aren't more than a handful of guests, and they're all parked down at the other end, around the corner. No way to look out and see anything."

"Something wasn't blocked," Estelle said. "Somebody saw something...some reason to call dispatch to report a man down." She continued around the abandoned car, a four-door K-model Dodge sedan many miles and years past its prime. She paused at the front fender. The right front tire was the tiny space-saver unit intended for limited, short-distance use as a spare. She circled the Dodge slowly and saw that the keys hung from the ignition.

"Call the county barns and have someone come out and pick up this vehicle," she said to Sisneros. "There's not much we're going to get from the outside, but the interior might tell us something."

She paused and looked hard at Sheriff Torrez. He hadn't budged, as if his cane had become rooted in the asphalt of the parking lot. In late October, during a confrontation when everything that could go wrong had, Torrez had taken a .223 bullet through the rump, at the same time suffering nasty fractures of his right forearm and right leg. A souvenir of that same incident, a white, half-inch scar marked the right side of Estelle's upper lip.

In early December, Torrez had returned to work on a part-time basis, shuffling about with an awkward walking cast, out of balance with both arm and leg encased. The casts had been removed in time for the holidays, but Estelle knew that the sheriff had pretty much ignored the ordered physical therapy—regardless of threats, cajoling, and bribes from his wife, Gayle.

"Someone needs to go over to the hospital," Estelle said. "If there's a chance that Eduardo can tell us something…and maybe Dr. Guzman saw something when he arrived. We need to follow up on that." She knew deep in her heart that the odds of that weren't good. If Francis had seen two desperate men charging out of the lot, he would have said something already. But Sheriff Robert Torrez didn't need to become an added complication for them by puddling in the cold rain. Something as simple as wearing a cap would have helped, but Bobby Torrez had taken being miserable to a new art form. Sending him to the hospital would at least keep him out of the weather.

"Yep," Torrez said, and his quick agreement surprised Estelle. "And I'll take care of lettin' Essie know," he added. "She's gonna want to be with him." He turned to Bill Gastner, who had been standing silently near the passenger door of Estelle's sedan. "You want to ride over with me, Bill?"

"Go ahead. I'll drop by the hospital after a bit," the former sheriff replied.

Torrez nodded dubiously. "Merry Christmas."

"You be careful," Gastner said.

Bob Torrez managed something that could have been mistaken for a smile. "That's all I've been doin'," he said as he turned and peg-legged back toward his pickup truck.

Another Sheriff's Department unit jounced into the parking lot. "Mike, now that Jackie's here, I'd like another sweep of this area," Estelle said. "Any little thing. You know the drill. I'm going inside to talk with the desk clerk. Maybe we'll get lucky."

"Yes, ma'am."

Estelle beckoned to Gastner to accompany her. "Let's go have a chat," she said.

Three other vehicles were parked in the side lot beyond the lobby and office, a scattering of travelers too tired to press on, so travel-weary they were willing to spend Christmas Eve in the efficient, sterile motel rooms of the Posadas Inn. An older model van was first in line, and Estelle detoured far enough out into the lot to see that the other two vehicles were a small sports car with a ski rack on the trunk, and a white pickup truck with contractor's side boxes and headache rack.

As she and Gastner entered the lobby, Estelle saw the night clerk in animated conversation, cell phone affixed to the side of her head, her back turned to the door. Miranda Lopez, the daughter of one of the medical-records clerks at Dr. Guzman's clinic, was a strikingly pretty girl with angular features accentuated by too much makeup. Estelle knew that Miranda was a high-school student, and no doubt was taking the opportunity to earn extra bucks during the holidays by working the long, odd hours that no one else wanted.

With her tangled black hairdo, curvaceous body poured into tight jeans, and a white, tucked-waist blouse that left three inches of flat belly and a diamond navel stud exposed, it would be difficult to mistake her for a him.

Miranda turned, saw Estelle and Gastner, and quickly cut off her telephone conversation.

"Miranda, is Mr. Patel here?" Estelle asked.

The girl nodded vigorously. "I called him. He said he'd be right down?" Her voice was clearly teenaged and as feminine as the rest of her. Estelle wondered who had told the sheriff that a man had called dispatch...or if someone had just made an innocent assumption.

"You mean he's coming from home? Or is he here on the premises?"

"No. He was home, like when...," and Miranda trailed off doubtfully. "What's happening? All the ambulances and stuff?"

Estelle smiled sympathetically but ignored the questions. "You're working by yourself?"

Miranda nodded.

"Did you see Chief Martinez earlier this evening?"

Miranda nodded again and bit her lip. "Is that what...?"

Estelle gave the girl a few seconds, but the nod was apparently going to suffice, the question and thought left unfinished.

"You obviously know him, then. Did you talk to him?"

"He wanted to buy some aspirin?" Miranda said. She leaned over the counter and pointed down the hall beyond the ice maker. "That vending machine right there?" Miranda's voice was a soft singsong, marked by her tendency to make sentences into questions, the tail end of the phrase rising like a little check mark.

"Did you see him buy aspirin?"

Miranda nodded. "He wasn't feeling so hot, I don't think. He asked if he could use the desk phone."

"He just came in, bought aspirin, used the phone, and that's it? When did he go back outside?"

"Well, I had to give him change? He was all...I don't know...all kind of like confused, and stuff? He almost lost his balance, like when he went back out the door?" Miranda glanced outside. "He used the phone to call a doctor, I think. But then he kind of just wandered, you know? Is he okay? I was worried about him. And that *girl* was so pregnant I thought maybe she was having her baby or something. I thought maybe the ambulance was for her."

"Which girl is that?" Estelle asked. "There was a girl with him?"

"No, no," Miranda said. "I mean earlier? The van people? They checked in a little while ago."

"Ah. Okay. Did you happen to see what kind of car Chief Martinez was driving?"

Miranda shook her head. "He just came in? I guess he was parked along the side, there? I didn't see him until he came inside, though. I mean, I was talking on the phone, and turned around, and he was just like, there?"

"So you couldn't see his car? You didn't see where he parked?"

"No. I couldn't. I think he parked, like down there?" She gestured vaguely toward the north.

"After he used the phone, and then left, did you walk over to the door?"

"No."

"Do you have any idea what happened after he left?"

"No…and then the police cars came, and the ambulance. I looked out the door then. They were all down at that one car."

"Did you call 911, Miranda?" Gastner asked.

The girl shook her head, a quick little *I didn't do it* expression.

"You've been here by yourself all evening?" Estelle asked.

"Sure," Miranda said. "I called Mr. P, though, 'cause of the people in the van. He said he was coming down a little bit later? And then this happened, and I called him again. So he should be here pretty soon. You want me to call him again?"

"I don't think so," Estelle said. "But no one from here called 911? No one that you know of?"

"Well, *I* didn't. That's all I know. I didn't like know anything was wrong and stuff until all the cops started showing up? I mean, maybe one of the guests saw something out the window. You think?"

"We'll talk to them," Estelle said. "Did you happen to see the owners of the little blue Dodge sedan that's parked over around the side?"

"I don't think so. Well, maybe…I'm not sure. One guy, he like came to the door? It looked like he was going to come inside? And then he didn't? He was talking to someone else?"

"What did he look like, Miranda?"

"He was like a big guy, you know?"

"Tell me what you mean by big."

"Well, he was just *big,* like *huge.* He had on this funny little cap. All peaky and stuff?"

"Like a welder's cap?" Gastner asked gently, but Miranda just looked puzzled.

"He pulled the door open a little? And then it like sounded like someone yelled to him outside. I think he went back down the sidewalk?" she said.

"And you could hear someone else talking?" Estelle asked.

"You said it sounded as if someone called out to him. This big guy in the funny cap?"

"I think so. Oh, and he had this real long ponytail," Miranda said, a trace of pride creeping into her voice. "When he turned and stuff, I could like see it? It hung right down his back." She pivoted and reached around to touch her own back with her thumb.

"Anglo?"

Miranda nodded. "I think so."

"Did you see this man, or anyone else, talking with Chief Martinez? In all this coming and going?"

"No. I think he like came in afterward?"

"The chief did, you mean?"

"Yes."

"How long afterward?"

Miranda shrugged. "Just a few minutes, I think."

"Let me make sure I understand you, Miranda. The big guy comes to the door, starts to open it, and then changes his mind when someone yells to him. Just a few minutes later, Chief Martinez comes in, buys some aspirin, uses the phone, and then goes back outside. That's the way it happened?"

"Yes, ma'am."

Gastner leaned on the counter and regarded Miranda impassively. "When you say 'a few minutes,' young lady, what do you mean? Are we talking, say, *two* minutes? Five minutes? Ten minutes?"

"I…," Miranda started to say, and stopped.

"Just take your time," Gastner said gently. "Relax, take your time, and remember what you were doing. Remember what you saw. We have all night."

Miranda looked down at the computer keyboard, frowning. "Okay," she said. "Those people in the old van—she's the pregnant lady—she and her husband had just gone, like to park? That's when this guy comes to the door? The big guy with the ponytail."

"Seconds later, you mean?" Gastner prompted.

"Like, *just seconds*. The van was parked right there by the door, and they started up and like swung around?" Miranda pointed to her left. "I mean like, right away, they're gone and this ponytail guy is at the door." The words came in a rush, as if she had finally warmed up to her role as key witness. "Like he would have had to almost step out of the way when the van pulled around. And *then,* this ponytail guy just like changes his mind and leaves. He walks off *that* way?" Miranda pointed to her right. "That's when the chief came in, just after that."

"How long would that be?"

"Like just a little bit."

Gastner smiled encouragement. "If you started counting from the time when Ponytail left to when the chief entered, how far would you get?"

Miranda closed one eye, the opposite eyebrow lifting. Estelle watched as the girl replayed her mental tape. "I think I'd like get to thirty, maybe?"

"That soon. Just thirty seconds?"

"Yes. It wasn't very long and stuff."

Estelle frowned at Gastner. "That's why he chose to park along the side, rather than pulling under the portico. The van would still have been in the way." To Miranda, she said, "I'd like the room number of the van folks. May I see their registration card?"

The girl hesitated. "She was *really* pregnant?" Her hand drifted down to her own flat belly. "For a minute I thought all the ambulances and stuff was for her." She slid the card across the counter toward Estelle. "They're in 110? That's the room down at the end. That's where Mr. P said they should go."

"I beg your pardon?"

"I had to call him, 'cause they said they didn't have any money and stuff? And she wasn't feeling too good?"

Estelle looked at the card. "He filled this out? The man did?"

"Yes."

Neat block letters filled the card. "Todd Willis," Estelle said. "Las Cruces." She glanced at Gastner. "Why does that name ring a bell?"

He shrugged. "No bells in this old head."

"They seemed like nice people. I was kind of afraid that she was going to have her baby like right here in the lobby," Miranda said.

"Are you up on first-aid procedures?" Gastner chuckled, and Miranda flashed a quick, nervous smile.

"Not hardly."

Estelle continued to examine the card. "They *both* came into the lobby to check in?" she asked without looking up. Miranda glanced first at Gastner and then at Estelle, as if unsure whether or not to answer the question.

"I think they did 'cause they couldn't pay. Like maybe they thought…" Miranda let the rest of the thought trail off.

"Good technique," Gastner said.

The door behind Miranda opened, and a dapper, swarthy man in razor-creased tan slacks, white shoes, and salmon-colored polo shirt stepped into the office.

"Mr. Patel, good evening," Estelle said. She reached across the counter and shook the man's hand—his return grip so light and limp that it wouldn't have supported a pencil.

"Hey, Adrian," Gastner said. "Good to see you."

"Miranda tells me there has been a problem," Adrian Patel said precisely, with just a hint of rolled rs in his speech.

"Yes, sir," Estelle replied. "Chief Eduardo Martinez was

just taken to the hospital. We think with a coronary. It also appears that his vehicle may be missing."

"You mean all this while he was here at my motel?" Patel asked.

"Yes. Apparently he came into the lobby to purchase some aspirin. There's a possibility that he may have had a confrontation with someone outside, in the parking lot. But we don't know yet."

"This is all most unfortunate." Patel heaved a deep sigh. "A confrontation, you say? With a guest?"

"We don't know."

"Ah. What may I do for you, then?"

"For one thing, sir, we need to talk to two guests who might have seen the incident. We understand that they're in Room 110, down at the end."

"Ah," Patel said, and nodded. "Yes. We have those from time to time. Sometimes a bed and a meal may make a world of difference to them."

"Yes, indeed," Gastner said.

"I should think that they would still be in their room at this time," Patel said. "Should you need to talk with them."

"Just a couple of quick questions would be helpful," Estelle said.

"I will remain here," Patel said. "Should you need to talk with myself or Miranda again about this, you will feel free." He nodded as if to add, *and that's that.*

"We appreciate your help," Estelle said. She paused, regarding Miranda. "They didn't call 911 from the lobby. Is that correct?"

"No, ma'am," Miranda said promptly.

"And not from their room?"

"I don't think so. The panel here lights all up and stuff if a phone line is in use?" Miranda said.

"Okay. Thanks."

Once outside, Estelle stood under the portico, hands thrust in her pockets. "Interesting," she said.

"Yep," Gastner agreed. "Interesting *and stuff.*"

"The young couple can't afford to pay for a room, but they have their own cell phone and van."

"These are the times we live in, sweetheart. And stuff."

"That new baby is going to have an interesting life." Estelle grinned. "And if you're going to talk like that, you have to have a bare midriff, sir."

He looked down at his gut. "Scary thought."

Estelle hunched against the drizzle, breathing the clean, wet air outside, relieved to be clear of the aroma of carpet cleaner and disinfectant. The two of them walked back to the county car and then drove the length of the motel toward Room 110.

THREE

THE VAN WAS PARKED with its tires cocked against the concrete curb. If the occupants of Room 110 had pushed aside the light-proof plastic curtain, their view outside would have been of the van's blunt, rusted, and dented face. Estelle pulled the county car in behind and perpendicular to the vehicle, stopping just far enough away that she could both read the tattered license plate and watch the yellow door of Room 110.

"That old boat has seen some miles," Gastner said. He leaned back in the seat and cocked his head, looking at the ski-laden Toyota. "Oklahoma skiers," he said. Two spaces farther down, the white utility truck was parked facing out, its doors clearly marked with magnetic signs. "And a Deming plumber."

Estelle nodded as she reached down to turn the radio up a bit, never taking her eyes off the van. The back windows were plastered with an array of stickers, most from national parks. The registration sticker on the license plate was valid. She keyed the mike.

"PCS, three ten."

"Three ten, go ahead."

"Ten twenty-eight New Mexico four niner seven, Baker Edward Charlie."

Dispatcher Brent Sutherland responded before the computer had a chance to search the NCIC brain. "Three ten, four niner seven, Baker Edward Charlie should appear on a 1972 Ford

Econoline van, color green, registered to Paula Ann Hart." He spelled the last name. "Fourteen thirty-seven Mesa Park, Las Cruces. Negative twenty-nine."

"Ten four. Thanks."

"Three ten, be advised that the occupants of that vehicle were the subjects of a complaint earlier this evening."

"Ten twenty-one," Estelle said, requesting a change from radio to phone. She hung up the mike. She turned and raised an eyebrow at Gastner, who shrugged.

"Who the hell knows," he said. Estelle had her phone in hand when it rang.

"Guzman."

"Estelle," Sutherland said, "you might want to talk with Jackie Taber about that van. She responded to a complaint at…just a sec." Estelle could picture Brent leaning forward to read the log. "At the Prairie Rest B-and-B over on North Tenth. Apparently the young couple driving that van stopped there looking for a room. They claimed that they didn't have any money."

"What was the complaint?" Estelle asked. Asking for a room was hardly grounds for a complaint.

"Ah, nothing really specific. Mrs. Melvin—that's Rachel Melvin, the owner? She called here and said that there was something suspicious about the couple…couldn't put her finger on what it was. She wanted the police to check them out. I logged that call at 18:04."

"They were up front about not being able to pay for the room?"

"Jackie didn't say anything to me about that when she called in."

"But they left the premises of the B-and-B when requested to do so by the owner?"

"I guess so. You might want to talk with Jackie, though. She talked to them a few minutes later over at Pershing Park. It looked like maybe they were going to camp there."

"Okay. Thanks, Brent. And by the way, did you log the caller's name for the 911 involving Chief Martinez?"

"No, ma'am. He hung up on me. He reported a man down at the Posadas Inn, then just hung up."

"But the caller was a man. You're sure of that?"

"Yes, ma'am."

"We'll be out of service for a few minutes with the owners of that van, Brent. Bill Gastner's with me, and the sheriff went over to the hospital with the ambulance."

"Right." Sutherland sounded relieved. Estelle was reasonably sure that Bob Torrez hadn't informed dispatch of his intentions. She clicked off the cell phone and glanced up as a sweep of headlights flashed in the rearview mirror. A white, older model Ford Bronco nosed in and stopped. "Let's see what Jackie has to say," Estelle said.

She got out of the car and joined Deputy Jackie Taber on the walkway in front of one of the service rooms, where the narrow overhang would provide some protection from the weather.

"Nice night," Jackie said by way of greeting. She was a large young woman, square through the shoulders and thick through the waist. "Good evening, sir," she said, as Bill Gastner ambled up to join them.

"Well, it was," Gastner said.

"I'm really sorry about Chief Martinez," Jackie said. "It doesn't look good for him."

"Nope," Gastner said, and let it go at that. Estelle glanced at her old friend. Gastner and Martinez had been friends for decades, and with the village-county consolidation of public safety services, the two colleagues had met a dozen times in the past month.

"Brent tells me that you had occasion to talk with the owners of this van earlier," Estelle said, and the deputy nodded.

"That's why I shagged down here," Jackie said. "I'll go back and help the guys sweep in a minute, but I wanted to tell you—" she nodded in the direction of the old van "—they stopped at the B-and-B over on Tenth," she said. "They told the owner that they didn't have any money, but asked if they could stay the night. I guess Mrs. Melvin didn't like the looks of them."

"Rachel Melvin doesn't like the looks of anybody who's younger than sixty," Gastner observed.

"That's true, sir," Jackie said, and a smile ghosted across her round face. "When we talked, she didn't want to open the front door far enough for me to step inside, either. She said that the young couple inquired about a room and told her right up front that they were short of money. She said that they both came to the door, and that surprised her, since the girl was obviously pregnant and quite a ways along."

"And that's it?" Estelle asked.

"Mrs. Melvin said that she told them they should check in Lordsburg. That she didn't have a room available."

Gastner chuckled. "Lordsburg? She didn't recommend that they come down here to the motel?"

"She didn't say, sir. But it doesn't sound like it."

"No room at the inn," he said. "How goddamn biblical."

Estelle looked at the former sheriff with amusement, then at the deputy. "You talked with them?" she asked the deputy.

"I talked with Mrs. Melvin first, and established that nothing had happened that would constitute probable cause for a stop. They asked for a room, told her they didn't have any money, and went on their way when she refused. Mrs. Melvin admitted that they were perfectly polite and not the least bit pushy. She only *grudgingly* admitted that, by the way."

"Why bother calling the SO, then?" Estelle asked, knowing the answer even before Bill Gastner voiced it.

"Because she's an old biddy," he said. "And she wouldn't recommend this motel because Adrian owns it. Part that and part that her sister owns the one she's talking about in Lordsburg."

"Maybe so," Jackie said. "But I saw the van a few minutes later, parked on Pershing, over behind the park. I'm sure that they saw me approach." Jackie pushed her Stetson back a bit. "Since Mrs. Melvin had told me that the woman was pregnant, it seemed prudent to make sure that they weren't in need of medical attention, so I stopped to talk with them. They're a young couple from Las Cruces."

She slipped a small notebook from her blouse pocket and thumbed pages. "Todd Willis and Stacie Hart." She closed the notebook. "And she's eight months pregnant. Or nine."

"They're married?" Gastner asked.

"No, sir. They said not. Maybe living together."

"Bound for?"

"Apparently headed for Tucson to visit Miss Hart's relatives. The van belongs to her sister, who's letting them use it for a while. Their own vehicle broke down. License and registration bears that out."

"Huh," Gastner said. "So we're only two hours from Las Cruces, even driving in that old heap. And Tucson is just four hours farther down the pike. Why did they leave Cruces so late in the day that they'd need a motel in the first place? Especially if they were short in the funds department?"

"I didn't ask them that, sir."

"Maybe the girl just became uncomfortable," Estelle said.

"Maybe so. Who knows why people do the damn things that they do."

"When you talked to them, Jackie, did either of them get out of the van?"

"No, ma'am. I approached them and we spoke through the driver's side window."

"Did Miss Hart appear in distress of any kind?"

"She looked bedraggled," Jackie said. "They both did. She's *huge,* though, and she kept shifting on the seat as if she couldn't find a comfortable position."

"*Ay,*" Estelle said. They heard the scuffing of a door opening and Estelle stepped away from the side of the building and looked down the sidewalk toward Room 110. A young man in jeans and sweatshirt stood framed in the doorway, one hand on the jamb, one on the knob. He saw Estelle and gave her a questioning look. "Let's find out," she said.

"Hello," the young man said as the three approached. He held the door open further. "Come on in out of the rain."

"Thank you," Estelle said. "I'm Posadas County Undersheriff Estelle Guzman, sir. This is Deputy Jackie Taber and Bill Gastner."

"Todd Willis." He turned and nodded toward the bathroom. "My fiancée is in the bathroom."

"Is Ms. Hart all right?"

"She's fine. We're tired, is all. She'll be out in a minute."

"Mr. Willis, I'm interested in two things. First, did you call 911 this evening?"

A flush crept up his pale cheeks. Estelle watched as he appeared to debate with himself about what to say. He was a good-looking kid, despite the stringy, long hair and Ohio Wesleyan sweatshirt that had needed laundering a week before.

"Yes," he said quickly, as if he had realized that he'd waited too long to reply.

"What did you see, Mr. Willis? Why the 911 call?" Estelle glanced around the generic room. A large nylon overnight bag rested on the dresser, beside what appeared to be a bulky camera case.

"We were just starting to unload from the van, outside there where we're parked? I was at the back door, and happened to glance back that way—" he waved in the direction of the motel office "—and saw three men talking. At least that's what it looked like. One of them appeared to collapse against the wall of the motel and then fell. The other two men drove away and left him there."

"Drove away in what?"

"A late-model car of some kind. I'm not sure what model. Maybe an Olds or a Buick. Something like that. Full-sized."

"Did you go over to check on the stricken man?"

Willis hesitated again. "No. I thought that the best thing I could do was call 911 and let the professionals do it."

The bathroom door opened and an enormously pregnant young woman emerged wearing a thick plaid bathrobe and fluffy slippers. Her thin, swarthy face accentuated the dark hollows under her eyes.

"Hi," she said, and moved to the bed, sitting down gently on the corner with one hand under her belly.

"Ms. Hart?" Estelle said, and introduced herself again. "Are you all right?"

"Yes. I'm just tired." Stacie Hart smiled wanly. "And we're kind of upset about what happened down the way. Is the man going to be all right?"

"We don't know," Estelle said. "But we're interested in what you saw."

"I was inside already. I didn't see what happened."

"Did both of you go into the motel office when you checked in?"

Stacie nodded. "Would you close the door, please?" she said to her fiancé, and Willis did so. "Yes…I went in with Todd."

"When was the first time that you became aware of any of the three men on down the way?"

"As we were turning around. I mean after we checked in," Willis said. "We went back out to the van, and we were turning around to drive down here. One of the three men was just walking down the parking lot toward the lobby as we did that. A great big guy with a ponytail. I had parked kinda close to the doors, and when I was pulling out, he took a step back and turned sideways, I guess thinking that maybe I needed the room to maneuver." Willis paused and looked at his fiancée. "He was a big guy, like I said. And he looked fit. Not fat or anything."

"He never said anything? Any gestures?"

"No. He just waited a second or two for me to move the van out of the way."

"And then what?"

"Then we drove down to our parking spot, outside here. I glanced back toward the office when we were getting out of the van to come inside our room, and another of the men was walking toward the motel entrance. He was reaching out with one hand, kind of like he was running the flat of his hand along the wall, like maybe for balance. I didn't know if he was drunk, or what."

"Where were the other two men at that time?"

"I didn't see them. I mean, I didn't look. We were busy getting our stuff from the van into the room."

"But you saw the man collapse?"

"That was a minute or so later. I went back out to get some stuff and close the van's back door, and the three of them were down by the two cars."

"Talking, arguing?"

"I couldn't tell. If I had to guess, I'd say just talking. I locked up the van, and when I turned around again, I saw the one older man sag against the wall, then fall to his hands and knees."

"What did the other two men do?" Estelle asked.

"Nothing, I guess."

"Did you see them touch the man at any time?"

Willis shook his head. "It just looked like they were talking, and like maybe the man who collapsed was walking away, around the front of the car."

"What prompted your call, then?"

"Well, I saw the old guy collapse, but then the other two just drove away and left him there. That's when I called 911."

"How long after the man collapsed was it before the other two drove away?" Estelle asked.

"Right away. I mean, right then. They didn't go over to him, or anything. They just got in the car and left. Just like that."

"And you didn't walk down to see if you could help?"

Willis took a deep breath and glanced at Stacie. "No."

Bill Gastner grunted something to himself and thrust his hands deeper in his pockets. He glowered at the young man over the top of his glasses. Estelle didn't interrupt as the old man's unblinking gaze dissected Todd Willis for a long, uncomfortable moment. "Why not?" Gastner finally asked. "Wouldn't that be the logical thing to do?"

"I thought…I thought the best thing was to call emergency," Willis said lamely. "I don't know CPR or anything like that."

"Shit," Gastner said with disgust and turned half away, his interest apparently attracted to the print of a Dutch windmill that hung over the blond oak desk.

"This is just your second stop this evening here in town?" Estelle asked gently. Willis nodded quickly as if relieved to be talking to her, rather than her elderly companion. He glanced at Deputy Taber for confirmation.

"We talked to Deputy Taber earlier," he said. "Over at the park."

"Were you thinking of staying there for the night? In the park, I mean?"

"No," he said quickly. "We just stopped there to look at the map."

"Ah. You're lost?"

He smiled and ducked his head. "No. We're not lost. Not the map, actually. We were looking through our notes and stuff. Looking through the Posadas directory."

"For?"

"Well," and he hesitated. "To see where else we might be able to stay."

"I'm surprised that the B-and-B didn't have a vacancy this time of year," Estelle said. "Where else have you tried?"

"We stopped at the B and B," Willis said, "but the owner...well, she..." He finished with a vague waffle of his hand.

"No, I meant stopped at places other than in Posadas," Estelle said. She had been watching Stacie Hart as they talked. The girl had remained silent, all her energy consumed by the effort to keep her spine vertical. "Did you stop in Deming on your way over from Cruces?"

"Actually, what difference does it make where we stopped?" Todd said, a little petulance creeping into his voice. "We haven't done anything wrong."

"I don't suppose it makes any difference at all," Estelle said. "I'm just trying to form an accurate picture in my mind of what happened here tonight."

Willis sat down on the bed beside Stacie, and her hand slipped over to intertwine with his.

"Deming has a good many motels and such," Estelle said. "I was wondering if you had tried any of them."

"We stopped at three places," Willis said. "Two motels and one B and B sort of place."

"Deming's only an hour or so out of Cruces," Gastner said.

"Well, yes, it is," Willis agreed.

"And these places that you tried…they all refused you?" Estelle asked.

Willis didn't answer, but shrugged evasively.

"That's interesting," Estelle said. She looked around the room again at the couple's possessions. "You're headed for Tucson?"

"Yes, ma'am."

"You have enough money for gas?"

"I think so."

Estelle regarded Willis for a long moment, and he blushed as if correctly reading the skepticism in her gaze.

"I mean, we were planning on just driving to Tucson, right? It's not that far. We weren't planning to stop. But then Stacie got to feeling…well, uncomfortable, and we thought we'd try to find a place to stop, and continue on tomorrow." He tried an engaging grin. "Got money for gas, or motel. Not both."

"I see," Estelle said. "Well, Mr. Patel is a most gracious person." Her eyes roamed the room, taking in the neat travel bag, the leather camera case, and the cell phone that rested on top of Stacie Hart's beaded handbag. Through the open bathroom door, she could see a spread of bath accoutrements, including a curling iron that was plugged in beside the mirror.

"Are you planning to pay your bill here when you check out? Is that the deal?"

The room fell silent, and Estelle let the silence hang.

FOUR

"LOOK," WILLIS SAID. He glanced nervously at his girlfriend. "We haven't done anything wrong. We didn't use a fake credit card, or skip out without paying. The manager offered this room, and we accepted. That's all there is to it. I'm sorry about the old guy down the way, but there wasn't anything I could do about that. I called 911, like we're supposed to. And I've answered all your questions."

"Mr. Willis," Estelle said, "I'll be happy to put you in touch with Traveler's Aid if you're having trouble." She had a momentary thought about how nice it would be to put Todd Willis under bright lights for a half-hour or so, but other matters weighed more heavily.

"That's not necessary," Willis replied.

"I didn't think it was, sir. And to tell the truth, at the moment I don't really care about your room scam." She saw his eyes narrow a little at her choice of words. "I assume that you at least *implied* that you couldn't pay when you inquired about a room?"

"Has someone complained?"

"Your evasion makes me curious."

"I'm not evading anything. I just don't have to explain…" Willis's protest faded.

"Mr. Patel just offered you a room at no charge? You didn't have to ask?"

"Well, no. Look, we haven't done anything wrong."

"I suppose that out of the charity of his heart, he saw your fiancée's condition and offered lodging. Is that it?"

Willis grimaced and fixed his attention on the bedspread.

"There would be no reason for anyone to offer a complimentary lodging otherwise…although it is the Christmas season. And you made certain that Miss Hart's condition was noticed, since in both occasions, she accompanied you to the check-in desk. That certainly wasn't necessary, was it…with it being so unpleasant out and her condition being so uncomfortable." Estelle paused, watching the flush play up Todd Willis's cheeks.

"So there appears to be some misrepresentation there," Estelle continued. "But more important, you saw a man collapse, obviously hurt or ill. You never approached to check on the condition of the victim?"

"No…I already told you that I didn't."

"Yet you called 911 to report an unattended death. That's what the dispatcher reported."

"I…"

"And you said the victim was an old man."

"Well, obviously he was. Anyone could see that."

"Really. I wonder about that when you say you observed the incident from nearly the length of the motel, in poor light."

"In the rain," Gastner added.

Stacie Hart groaned and pushed herself up straighter on the bed. "Just tell them, Todd," she said.

The young man weighed that suggestion for a moment and then shrugged. "Okay, okay," he said. "I *did* go up there. I saw that the guy was lying all scrunched up, half on and half off the curb. When I got to him, I could see that his eyes were glassy, and he was unreactive when I spoke to him. It looked like maybe he had some froth on his lips, and I couldn't find any pulse at his neck. I could see then that he was an older guy."

"And the other two men were gone by this time?"

"Yes. They drove away before I actually started walking over that way. I couldn't tell if they'd assaulted the older guy or not. I didn't see any blood, but that doesn't mean anything. They drove away in a hurry, though, after he collapsed. So I ran up there, saw that there was a problem, and called 911 on my cell."

"And then you just left him there?"

"I didn't want to move him. I mean, we're not supposed to do that, right? I thought that I'd get a blanket from the room, but by the time I even thought to do that, I could hear a siren coming." Willis took a step back and settled on the corner of the bed. "I just stayed out of the way."

"Goddamn commendable," Gastner said.

"Well…" Willis said, and gave up with a shrug.

"Why not just duck into the office and ask for a blanket? Or tell them to call the cops?" Gastner asked.

Willis looked skeptical. "Did you talk to the desk girl?"

"Yes."

"Well, then you know why I didn't try and explain to her. Miss *Like Vague*. Besides, I thought about doing that, but when I went by, her back was turned to the door and I could see that she was on the telephone."

"At any time, did you see either of the two men strike the victim before they left?"

"No."

"Did you see any contact between the three of them at all?" Estelle glanced at her watch.

"No," Willis said. "But they were out of my view on more than one occasion. Something could have happened while I was inside this room, or when I was going back and forth to the van…any number of opportunities."

"Did you see what direction they drove after leaving the parking lot?"

"No. They went around the end of the building, and I couldn't see them after that."

"What do you do for a living, Mr. Willis?" Estelle asked. She glanced again at the travel bag and camera case.

"I'm a…a writer."

"Ah. You're on assignment now?"

Willis hesitated just enough that Estelle sensed his uneasiness. "Yeah, I guess. Sort of."

"Interesting. Mr. Willis, it may be necessary for us to talk to you again. Is there a number where we can reach you in the next day or two?"

"We're going to visit Stacie's family in Tucson. That was our plan, anyway."

"Are you all right with that?" Estelle said, turning to the girl.

"I'm fine."

"You're sure?"

The girl nodded.

"When's the baby due?"

"Around the tenth," she said.

"Ah," Estelle said. "We'll need a name and number there where we can reach you, Mr. Willis."

He turned to his fiancée, but she was already rummaging in her purse. She produced a business card and jotted the information on the back, then extended the card to Estelle. "That's my sister's number in Las Cruces, too," she said.

Estelle flipped the card over and saw Stacie Hart's name printed in simple script with address, home phone, and e-mail listed. "Your sister owns the van?"

Stacie nodded. "We were out in Tucson for Thanksgiving, and our car blew its transmission on the way home. She's letting us use the van while our car's being fixed."

"A transmission? That's an expensive proposition," Gastner said.

"It's on warranty," Stacie said, and Estelle grinned at the comment. *See, we're cooperative,* the superfluous information shouted. "And that van's not much of a bargain, either."

"I hope everything goes well for you," Estelle said. "We'll be in touch. You're heading straight through tomorrow to Tucson?"

Todd Willis nodded.

"No more stops to see if there's room at the inn?" Gastner asked. "That should be an interesting story."

"No more stops," Willis said but he didn't rise to Gastner's remark.

"I hope that we won't have to bother you again tonight, but it's a possibility," Estelle said.

"I understand," the young man said. He held the door for them, nodding pleasantly. "Have a Merry Christmas."

"Indeed," Bill Gastner muttered. "You do the same." He looked hard at Willis for a moment. "This Mary and Joseph thing," he said. "I wasn't aware that they feigned indigence in order to find lodging. I'll be interested to see how you twist that around in your story." He didn't wait for Willis to answer before turning away.

Outside the stuffy motel room, Estelle saw that the county's flatbed car hauler had arrived. The decrepit Dodge was cranked halfway aboard, looking lopsided and bedraggled in the rain.

"East or west?" Gastner said when the door of Room 110 had closed behind them.

"West," Estelle said immediately. "*Unattended death.* That's interesting. The average Joe on the street doesn't use that term, sir, but Willis did when he talked with dispatch."

"Cops, EMTs, firemen, coroners, newspaper reporters—all the odd folks. It took a while, but his name came to me."

"Oh?"

"Todd Willis. It's a byline I've seen now and then in one of the Las Cruces papers. I did a long telephone interview with him once, back when I retired from your esteemed department." He huffed a chuckle. "Only a matter of time before my steel-trap memory dug him up."

"I like your theory about the story he's working on," Estelle said.

Gastner snorted in disgust. "I'm not much of a biblical scholar, but I never realized that Mary and Joseph were looking for a *freebie*."

"A plea for charity on Christmas Eve is a nice setup," Estelle said. "I'll be curious to find out what percentage refused them lodging."

"And a village named Posadas is a perfect target," Gastner grumbled.

"Mr. Patel put a dent in their statistics," Estelle said, and she moved away from the building, looked up into the night sky, and wrinkled her nose against the fine drizzle. "And that's kind of neat. But they're not our problem right now, unless Miss Stacie goes into hard labor in Room 110."

They watched as the flat bed of the car hauler thumped horizontal with its load and Stub Moore and his helper cranked the tie-downs tight. "It doesn't make any sense to steal a car back east, get this far, and then circle around and head east again." She glanced at her watch again. "Tommy was headed toward Regál, and the State Police are covering the Interstate all the way to the state lines in both directions, so those two aren't going to make it very far."

"Or they could be smart," Gastner said. "Slip south through María, work their way east toward El Paso and the border crossing there."

"They might do that. And they might have riffled through the chief's glove box and found his address, and gone over there and robbed the place blind while the rest of the folks are at the hospital." She glanced at Jackie.

"I'll check on that," the deputy said. "Tony Abeyta and I are going to talk with the other guests here at the motel, too. Just on the off chance that someone saw something. There's only a couple, but you never know."

Estelle watched the stocky woman hustle off toward her vehicle. "If I were them, I'd stay on the Interstate westbound," she said. "Rainy night, cops few and far between, they could do that and shoot all the way west out of the state. Their luck's run pretty smooth so far."

"All the way from Indiana, or wherever it was," Gastner said. "Publish all the bulletins you want, but somebody has to *read* them in order for BOLOs to do any good."

"True enough." She nodded toward her car. "I want to stop by the hospital," Estelle said. "We have two to worry about over there. I thought Bobby looked pretty wretched tonight."

"Ah," Gastner scoffed, "he's okay. Mr. Sunshine is one of those folks who makes a lousy patient, is all. I'm sure he's thoroughly tired of hurting by this point. He likes to be in the middle of things, and here he is, forced to hobble around like an old man. He's not even good competition for me."

As they drove out of the parking lot past the motel's main entry, they could see Adrian Patel and Miranda Lopez in close conversation with Deputy Mike Sisneros.

"I wonder why he came down here," Estelle said. She started the car and sat for a moment with her hand on the gearshift.

"Who, the chief? He needed aspirin," Gastner said. "At least that's what he thought he needed."

She shook her head in resignation and pulled the car into gear, turning toward the entrance to Grande Avenue.

"Eduardo always did like the café here," Gastner added. "He said they had the best iced tea in town, and he was probably right. So he was used to coming here. The lobby is always open, and he knew where the vending machine was." Gastner thumped the side of the door thoughtfully with the back of his fist. "There's no accounting for what people do when they aren't thinking straight."

Estelle's cell phone chirped, and she pulled it out of her pocket. "That includes young Mister Willis," she said to Gastner, and then acknowledged the call.

"Estelle," dispatcher Brent Sutherland said, "I tried to get you on the radio, but you must have been out of the car."

"Just preoccupied," Estelle said, and at the same time reached over and turned the volume of the radio up. "What's up?"

"Tom has the chief's car in sight," Sutherland said, and even as he said it, Bill Gastner pointed ahead of them. The bright lights of a fast-moving vehicle had materialized on Grande, and in a moment Sheriff Robert Torrez's unmarked Expedition howled past southbound, grill lights pulsing. "The vehicle is parked at the church in Regál."

"At the church?"

"That's what Pasquale says. I just told the sheriff, and he's on the way. Mike's headed out that way, too."

"Roger that," Estelle said, and she swung a wide U-turn on Grande. "Are the two suspects in sight? Are they with the vehicle?"

"Negative. Tom thinks that they're inside the church."

"What's his twenty right now?"

"He's just up the road, in the turnoff to the water tank. He said he drove past the church lot, down toward the border crossing, and saw the car. I didn't know whether or not Chief Martinez still had a scanner in his car, so I wanted to stay off the radio as much as I could," Sutherland said.

"That's good. We're on the way. Tell Tom to stay put unless they come out of the church and it looks as if they're going to take off."

"You got it."

She handed the phone to Gastner and pulled the mike off the clip.

"Three oh eight, three ten. We copy the info on Bert's Place. We're a minute or so behind you."

"Ten four." Torrez's reply in his habitual radio voice was not much more than a murmur. "Bert's Place," the radio moniker for the Iglesia de Nuestra Señora in Regál, where Father Bertrand Anselmo was the priest, was one way to keep scanner aficionados—and perhaps the two car thieves if they had a radio—in the dark about location. Torrez's voice broke the silence once again.

"Three oh two, sit tight."

"Now that's bizarre," Gastner said. He reached out and braced one hand against the dash when Estelle braked hard enough to make the tires howl as they turned onto State 56, the highway leading southwest the twenty-three miles to Regál Pass and the little village beyond on the Mexican border. "Why would two car thieves hole up in the church? That's not good news."

"No, sir," Estelle said. She accelerated hard, and far ahead of them, they could see the taillights of the sheriff's vehicle as she closed the gap between them.

FIVE

LA IGLESIA DE NUESTRA SEÑORA was one of the most frequently photographed landmarks in Posadas County, preserved on film by thousands of tourists. Most travelers found the small church charming and quaint, and they then went away relieved that they didn't have to attend services there.

Three-foot-thick adobe walls, tall and narrow windows recessed with eighteen-inch windowsills, and carved ceiling beams that had been salvaged more than a century before from an Indian ruin in northern Mexico encased the cool interior in musty silence.

Cottonwood planks had been intricately carved and painted for the altar, with a heavy communion railing polished to a soft, reflective shine by generations of hands. The same cottonwood had been used for each of the twelve stations of the cross, the carvings nestled deep in *nichos* sunken into the adobe walls.

With a little cooperative planning, the twelve straight-backed pews, six on each side of a narrow aisle, could seat sixty worshipers—nearly twice the total population of the village of Regál.

That neat package, immaculately maintained and painted so white that a blast of sun through one of the narrow windows could reflect from the opposite wall like a flashbulb, had never known a utility. For evening services, light came from beeswax candles made by one of the parishioners. Burning piñon and juniper in the plump potbellied stove that stood in the center of the long east wall chased the deep chill that settled into the building when it stood empty. The black single-walled stovepipe reached up precariously a dozen feet before piercing through the ceiling thimble.

Estelle let her memories of the little church form a blueprint in her mind as they sped southwest. There were no hiding places in the church—no attic, no sanctuary. She glanced at the clock. There was also no congregation at this hour, and for that she was thankful. Not long before, her mother and aunt had knelt within those stout walls during the 5:00 p.m. service, listening to Father Anselmo and inhaling the fragrance of juniper boughs. There would be another service at nine o'clock that Christmas Eve, and, just because Father Anselmo loved it so, another at midnight.

As they crested Regál Pass, Estelle could see a scattering of lights off to the right, through the mist and light rain. The village of Regál nestled against the slope of the San Cristóbals, facing Mexico to the south. The land fell away to the flat, empty Mexican desert, a vista of endless stunted brush, cacti, and arroyos by day, a giant black hole at night.

A thousand yards southeast of the village, the Regál border crossing was harshly illuminated by a fleet of lights. In recent months, the fence had been upgraded, the chainlink and razor wire shining in the light of the sodium vapors.

There wasn't enough traffic to operate the border crossing at night. As a concession, a large gravel-surfaced lot had been provided so that folks could park their RVs and grab a nap until the customs people arrived at 6:00 a.m. Or, they could walk a hundred yards to the church and find quiet comfort there. The *iglesia* was never locked—its mammoth, carved doors had never known a hasp.

"Nice night," Gastner muttered. "You want to lay odds on what happened?"

"What do you think?" Estelle leaned forward, still picturing the church and its parking lot.

"I think that they decided not to take the Interstate, and took the state road without knowing where the hell it went," Gastner said. "I think they're lost. The kind of genius who would steal a 1982 Dodge in Indiana as a getaway car would have trouble with a road map."

"Maybe so."

"Three oh two, ten twenty." Sheriff Robert Torrez's voice was barely audible, and Estelle reached down to turn the radio volume up.

"I'm on water tank road," Deputy Pasquale replied. "Mike's here with me." The radio barked squelch twice as Torrez acknowledged by keying the microphone.

"There's a midnight service planned?" Gastner asked.

"I think so," Estelle said. "Father Anselmo does a service at seven over in María, and then comes back here for one at nine and then again at midnight. Someone will keep the fire going."

"Emilio Contreras, probably," Gastner said, and Estelle felt a pang of worry. No church enjoyed more tender, persistent maintenance than that provided to Nuestra Señora by Contreras, himself closing on eighty years old. The old man cleaned, painted, and patched, working all day, every day, except Sundays. Despite using an aluminum walker to support a bad hip, Contreras walked the three hundred yards from his home in Regál to the church.

Before the border fence upgrade, Regál had been a favorite resting spot for illegals, and the unlocked church had been a convenient hostel. Even a hard cottonwood pew made a welcome bed after a desert crossing on foot. Various law enforcement agencies had tried to convince Father Anselmo over the years that a locked door would be a small concession. Small concession or not, no lock had marred the finish since 1826, when the door had first been hung.

Tom Pasquale's unit was parked on the gravel access road to the village water tank, high on the flank of the mountains behind Regál, with Deputy Mike Sisneros's well off the highway's shoulder. Sheriff Torrez turned into the narrow lane and stopped door-to-door with the deputy's vehicle. Estelle pulled onto the shoulder behind Mike's SUV and killed the lights. By the time she had shrugged into her slicker, Pasquale had gotten out. He rested an elbow comfortably on the spotlight housing of Torrez's Expedition.

"Nothing going on that I can see," he said. "The chief's car was parked there when I cruised through. I didn't even pull into the parking lot. Didn't want to spook 'em. You want to use my glasses?" He reached into his vehicle and pulled the bulky, military-surplus night glasses out, offering them to Estelle, but she shook her head.

"That's okay," she said. "The thing that concerns me is Emilio Contreras." She turned and looked down the hill. It was dark enough that she couldn't see smoke from the church's stovepipe, rainy enough that the faint glow from candles wouldn't illuminate the windows. "They get this far, and now they find that the border's closed."

"Not the sharpest tools in the box," Torrez said.

"Maybe they're thinking about spending the night until the border opens," Tom said.

"Maybe. We don't know if they're armed or not. We don't know if they're just sitting there chatting with Emilio, or robbing him, or what."

"So let's go find out," Torrez said. He turned and grinned at Estelle. "You up for helping an old peg leg?"

"Sure," she said. "What do you have in mind?"

"Have Bill take your unit," Torrez said. "If he stays right here, that'll cover us if they manage to make a run up the hill. Mike can cover the village, and Tom will stay loose on the highway."

A fleeting expression of impatience crossed Pasquale's face, but he didn't argue. He was in uniform, and neither Estelle nor the sheriff were.

In a moment, with the vehicle swap completed and Estelle's unmarked sedan parked on the water tank road with Bill Gastner at the wheel, Estelle and Bob Torrez drove sedately down the state highway in Torrez's unmarked Expedition.

Going on ahead, Mike Sisneros turned onto Sanchez Road, the dirt thoroughfare that was Regál's main street. In a moment, his county vehicle had disappeared in the labyrinth of corrals, barns, sheds, and dwellings. Tom Pasquale drove directly toward the border crossing and the parking lot there.

"What's the word on Chief Martinez?" Estelle asked as they neared the church.

"I don't know," Torrez said simply. "I got called away on this before I had a chance to find out. When they took him into the ER, he was still alive. That's all I know." He swung the unmarked vehicle into the church's broad parking lot, nosing upward toward the knoll on which Nuestra Señora had been built. At the same time, he reached over and turned off the radio.

The chief's brown Buick was parked away from the doorway, snuggled tight against the church, invisible unless someone knew exactly where to look. Torrez regarded the Buick for a moment. He then parked on the other side of the church, letting the dark bulk of the building hide the various non-civilian features of the Expedition should someone open the front door of the church and peer outside for a closer look.

"You suppose some bonehead from Indiana knows how much that car's worth down south?" he asked.

"I doubt it," Estelle said. She unclipped her badge from her belt and slipped it in her pocket, then leaned forward and slid her automatic as far rearward as it would go, well hidden under her jacket.

"No stealth now," Torrez said. He managed a grin, and Estelle saw that the crow's feet around his eyes had grown a bit more etched during the last month or two—and not from laughter. "We're supposed to be parishioners stopping by to see if anyone remembered to bring the fruitcake. And right about now, I wish this damn place had a back door we could just slip in."

He opened the car door and slid slowly down until his feet touched the ground, then pulled his cane loose from its position between the seats.

Estelle had just enough room between the vehicle and the building to slip through the open door, which she then slammed with vigor. "You park close enough to the building?" she said loudly.

"Hago todo lo posible," the sheriff said, and his Spanish startled Estelle. He took his time with the two narrow steps up to the church door, and grasped the wrought-iron handle. He partially opened the door inward, and stopped, turning to look at Estelle. "Did Geraldo remember about tonight?" he asked, and Estelle shook her head.

"He didn't say anything to me," she said. Looking beyond Torrez's wide shoulders, she saw Emilio Contreras standing in front of the stove, hands casually behind his back as he toasted his arthritic fingers.

"Hola, Emilio!" she called, and with her left hand held the door until Torrez had passed clear. The old man beamed widely at them, and Estelle felt a wash of relief. One of the two men was standing directly in front of the altar, as if he had been examining the ornate cross overhead. His ponytail reached almost

to his waist, and he had twisted to see who had entered the church. His welding cap was scrunched in his right hand. The other man sat sideways on the pew directly in front of the stove's alcove, one arm lying on the high wooden back, the other blocked from Estelle's view by the pew in front of him.

"We stopped by early to see if there's anything else you need, Father," Estelle said, and she closed the door, making sure the wooden latch fell into place.

"Hey, Bobby—you know what you were supposed to bring this afternoon," Emilio said. He stepped away from the stove, one hand rubbing his hot corduroy trousers against his butt.

"What's that?" Torrez said.

"Remember that load of firewood? You know," and he indicated the deep wood box off to his right. "I got what's in here, and maybe one or two more loads, and that's it. You going to bring some down?"

Torrez grimaced at his poor memory as he made his way down the center aisle. "Ah…we'll get it down here. I got too many things goin'."

"How you been?" Emilio said to Estelle as she approached. "The *hijos?*"

"They're fine," Estelle said.

"I enjoyed seeing your mother again," Emilio said. "She and your aunt were here at the early service. I was looking for you guys." His nod included both Estelle and the sheriff. His eyes were watchful, but Estelle felt a surge of relief that he was keeping perfect composure—either a tribute to his skill as an actor, or because the two car thieves had done nothing to arouse his suspicion.

"That's the way it is," Estelle said. She shied away from the stove. "*Caramba*, you have that old thing stoked up." By retreating away from the heat, she was able to step past the pew where the man sat. Medium age, medium build, heavy work boots, blue jeans and brown work jacket, no weapon visible, both hands in sight. His legs were crossed, and his right hand rested lightly on one boot.

"Nasty night," Emilio said.

"Yes, it is," Estelle agreed. "How are you doing?" she said to the man, her smile broad and warm. The big man with the ponytail glanced first at his partner, then at Estelle, then at Robert Torrez. The sheriff was making his way with painful steps toward the front of the church, his right hand running along the plastered wall for additional support. The big man rested his weight against the communion rail, arms crossed over his chest. If he carried a weapon, there was no sign. It certainly didn't appear as if Torrez was advancing on *him*...perhaps just making his way to the sacristy of the church to check on who knew what.

"These are some traveling friends from..." Emilio paused, standing near the wood box. "Where did you say you was from?"

"Over Oklahoma way," the man in the pew said. "We're just passin' through." He smiled engagingly at Estelle. "Nice place you folks have here."

"Yes, it is," Estelle said. Out of the corner of her eye, she saw that Torrez was two pews from the front of the church, within fifteen feet of the big man with the ponytail. The sheriff's hand pulled away from the windowsill at that point, and Estelle knew exactly what he intended.

She swept her hand behind her, and the automatic appeared in her hand in one fluid motion. The man in the pew startled backward, almost losing his balance.

"Both hands on top of your head," Estelle snapped.

"You too, buckaroo," she heard Torrez bellow in a tone that left nothing to the imagination. His own .45 had appeared in his right hand, the cane now abandoned against the wall.

"Hey, we don't…"

"Hands on top of your head," Estelle barked, and she motioned with the automatic. Emilio had moved away, and he now stood well off to one side, both hands on the back of one of the pews.

As large as Ponytail was, he elected not to argue with Torrez. He belly-flopped onto the floor when told to do so, arms stretched out over his head.

The middle-aged man lifted both hands, but he hesitated.

"Hands on your head, fingers locked," Estelle commanded, and snapped off her automatic's thumb safety. The man's startled expression had been replaced by wary assessment.

"I'm not armed," he said, shaking his head. "Really…" He stood up slowly, and Estelle shifted position so that the end of the next pew was between her and the man.

Behind her, Estelle heard the sharp *snick* of handcuffs and knew that Ponytail had been neutralized. The middle-aged man heard the same sound and glanced to his right, toward Emilio Contreras. With a grunt, he moved with remarkable agility, springing first onto the pew and then vaulting the back, his heavy boots crashing on the wooden floor.

Even if Estelle, or Bob Torrez now limping up behind her, had wanted to fire if they saw the threat of a weapon, Emilio was in jeopardy. The man saw the opening and sprinted toward the door.

"Wardell!" shouted the big man on the floor, but his partner was headed south. His hand hit the door and grabbed the stout rope latch, but the weight of the door, even on hinges oiled to perfection, precluded snatching it open. Hard on his heels, Estelle hit the door just as it yawned open a foot. Her momentum knocked the man sideways against the small lectern that held the visitors' book, and both lectern and man crashed to the floor.

Estelle grabbed the man's right wrist and twisted, pinning his arm behind his back, at the same time driving her left knee into the base of his neck.

"Just shoot the son-of-a-bitch," she heard Torrez shout, and beneath her, the man stopped struggling. Perhaps with the border so close, he had no idea what kind of barbed-wire justice awaited him. She remained motionless while the sheriff single-footed down the aisle, and an instant later she felt her handcuffs removed from the cuff case at the small of her back.

"Okay," the sheriff said. The cuffs snapped into place. "You can stop grindin' his face into the floor now." He stepped back and watched as Estelle hauled the man to his feet. Over the car thief's shoulder, she saw that the sheriff's face was pasty white, the sweat standing on his forehead.

Palming her radio, she pushed the transmit. "Tom, get over here ASAP." She pushed the man to the nearest pew. "Sit," she ordered, then turned to Torrez. "You, too," she said.

SIX

EARLY CHRISTMAS MORNING, Everett Wardell and Bruce Jakes would be arraigned on charges of grand larceny auto theft, interstate transportation of stolen goods, conspiracy, and resisting arrest, as well as assault during the commission of a felony. Estelle had no intention of dragging Judge Lester Hobart out of bed before then.

Sour under any circumstances, Hobart's reaction was predictable. He would dither with rage as he dealt with the ragged pair who had dared to assault one of his oldest friends on such an otherwise peaceful holiday.

Both Wardell and Jakes swore to the deputies that they had never laid a hand on retired Posadas Police Chief Eduardo Martinez back at the motel, but that would cut no ice with Judge Hobart. Whether Chief Martinez was ever going to have a chance to recite his version of the incident remained in question.

The young Las Cruces reporter, Todd Willis, whom Bill Gastner had dubbed "Joseph," remained the only witness to some of the events outside the Posadas Inn that Christmas Eve. None of the motel's other patrons interviewed by deputies had glanced out a window or strolled into the parking lot during the moments in question. And Willis was unwavering in his recollection. He had not seen the two Indiana men physically touch Chief Martinez.

Until they could appear for preliminary arraignment before

the judge, the two men could enjoy the sterile comfort of separate cells. There was no reason to doubt their pitiful tale.

Bruce Jakes had worked for an auto parts store in Hickory Grove, Indiana. The week before Christmas, his uninsured 1982 Datsun pickup truck, parked at the curb under a growing pile of snow, had been totaled by one of the Hickory Grove city snowplows. As that storm stretched on and on, the leaden skies over Hickory Grove remained bleak and oppressive, crushing the winter-weary Hoosiers.

Bruce Jakes's string of bad luck and the dismal weather finally prompted Jakes to suggest, during a long drinking binge with his unemployed pal, Everett Wardell, that the sunny climes of the Baja were just the place for two Indiana slush-kickers. Neither had ever visited Baja, but Jakes had seen enough of it during coverage of an off-road race on ESPN that it looked like heaven compared to the mounds of snow. One thing led to another.

Responsible for closing the auto parts store at noon on Saturday, Jakes had done just that…after pocketing the cash portion of the week's receipts. Secure in knowing that the store's owner was enjoying two weeks in Georgia with a daughter's family, Jakes then stole the well-worn Dodge sedan that belonged to the store owner's wife. With pockets flush and the car sort of eager, Jakes and Wardell had headed west.

They had a full day's head start. The store owner's teenaged son reported both the stolen car and pilfered store the following Monday morning. By that time, Wardell and Jakes were long gone.

When they crossed the Mississippi River on Sunday afternoon, they had outrun the winter storm. The skies cleared and they motored on, convinced that the gods were smiling on their enterprise. The Interstate seemed a safe place, and the old Dodge blended in with traffic.

The first tickle of sour luck struck Monday afternoon in eastern Oklahoma. Whether it was flu or food poisoning, a virulent bug laid them both flat on their backs, and the motel outside of Claremore became their home until they were able to stagger back onto the road.

Trading driving chores, they had made it as far as downtown New Mexico before the weather turned bad again near Las Cruces, and then a bit later the right front tire gave up the ghost—almost exactly halfway between Deming and Posadas. Bolting the silly little space-saver spare on the Dodge, the two men wobbled ever westward into Posadas, stopping at the Posadas Inn on Christmas Eve. By now road-weary, they saw the inn as a safe haven for the night. They would tackle tire troubles the next morning, if they could find a service station open on Christmas Day.

Temptation smiled on them through the drizzle that Christmas Eve. In the motel's parking lot, they chanced to pull in beside a nice, shiny new Buick LeSabre, warmed up and ready to go, with an owner who barely had the strength to haul himself toward the motel entrance. Everett Wardell had seen heart attacks before—both his father and two brothers had died of them. He could tell that the little stout man with the pale, sweaty face and bluish lips wasn't going to need the Buick much longer.

Neither Wardell nor Jakes knew anything about border crossings, but with the impulsive theft of the Buick, life was becoming complicated enough that Mexico seemed like a good idea, sooner rather than later. Arriving in Regál innocent of the realization that now they were only minutes ahead of the law, they were astonished to find the border crossing closed for the night—whoever had heard of such a thing?

That presented a problem, since both men knew from the

movies that both the big crossing behind them at El Paso and the one farther ahead somewhere in Arizona were crawling with Border Patrol and other cops at all hours of the day and night—holidays not withstanding.

The brainstorm of hiding at the little picturesque *iglesia* had been Wardell's, part of his life philosophy whose cornerstone read, "When in doubt, do nothing." Parking beside the bulk of the church, the Buick remained in the shadows, its license plate hidden. Had the headlights of Deputy Tom Pasquale's patrol unit not glinted briefly off the Buick's headlight chrome, the fugitives' luck might have held.

The inside of the church was warm and inviting, and both Jakes and Wardell relaxed, chatting with the ancient man who kept the fire stoked. Had the scene not been interrupted so rudely a few minutes later by the young man and woman who, it turned out, were far more than just a young couple, Wardell and Jakes might have been invited over to the old caretaker's house after church services for some holiday cheer.

Fifteen minutes after midnight on Christmas morning, Estelle Reyes-Guzman finished the preliminary paperwork and recorded the requisite message on District Attorney Dan Schroeder's voice mail. She cranked out a brief press release for Frank Dayan, publisher of the *Posadas Register,* knowing that the release would prompt a flood of additional questions that she either couldn't, or wouldn't, answer.

The fugitives were in separate cells in the Public Safety Building lockup, no doubt staring sleeplessly at the ceiling and thinking that this was turning out to be one of their least merry Christmases. Confirmation of their story had already arrived from the Hickory Grove, Indiana, police department.

Stopping at the small newspaper office just long enough to slip the release through the mail slot, Estelle then continued on to the hospital, where she found that the extended Martinez family had pitched camp, taking over the small waiting room beside the intensive care unit. Father Bertrand Anselmo had stayed with them.

Estelle spent half an hour with the family after looking in on the chief. Eduardo Martinez remained unresponsive amid the welter of tubes and sighing machinery. His body was there, but he was clearly no longer in residence. Having done as much as he could, Dr. Francis Guzman had gone home, leaving the ICU in the efficient care of the unit nurse.

Shortly after 1:00 a.m., Estelle left the hospital as well. The rain had stopped. She drove slowly with her window down, savoring the sharp wind from the southwest that carried a bouquet of aromas from the wet desert. She could see a scattering of stars breaking through the scud over the San Cristóbals.

Turning south on Twelfth Street, she saw that her husband's SUV was pulled into their driveway, tucked in close to the neighbor's fence so that Estelle would have plenty of space to park her county car.

Sofía Tournál's Mercedes was parked at the curb in front of the house as if poised for a swift getaway, but in truth, Francis Guzman's aunt would have reveled in the opportunity to spend a long evening with Estelle's sometimes acerbic mother and the two little boys.

If not feeling actually cheated or jealous, Estelle did feel a pang of regret that she had passed Christmas Eve investigating the exploits of two misfits from Indiana, her mood driven further into melancholy by Eduardo Martinez's illness.

She punched off the headlights as she nosed the car into the driveway. As she got out, she saw that besides the porch light, a single light burned in the living room. She pushed the car door closed with her knee so that the latch made no more than a quiet click. Standing still for a moment, she inhaled the tang of the sharp, damp air. The antiseptic smells of the hospital still clung to her, the same smells that lingered on her husband's clothing as a sort of permanent trademark.

The front door opened, and Sofía Tournál stood framed by the porch light.

"Qué noche," she said as Estelle approached the step, then switched to her elegantly accented English. "The good doctor came home about an hour ago."

"I'm sorry all of this came up," Estelle said.

"Oh, there's nothing to be sorry about, *querida.*" Sofía deftly held open the storm door with her hip and hugged Estelle at the same time. "We all have our jobs to do." She peered out toward the street. "I half expected the good *Señor Noctámbulo* to be with you."

Estelle laughed at Sofía's reference to Bill Gastner, *Mr. Night Owl.* "No, he went home. I think we wore him out. Either that, or he got hungry and went to find something to eat."

"Ah, we have plenty here," Sofía said.

"It smells wonderful." Estelle closed the door and slipped off her coat, draping it over the back of the nearest chair. "But *Padrino* is more like the old *tejón.* He comes out for a while, but then he needs to find a dark corner somewhere, away from everybody."

"Such an interesting fellow," Sofía mused. "I am very fond of this old badger, as you call him. That's most appropriate. But...," and she waved her hands in a flourish to change the subject. "What can I fix you?"

"A cup of tea would be nice."

Sofía looked askance at her nephew's wife. "Tea? Just tea, after such a night? Don't be ridiculous. Let me fix you a little something."

"No, really," Estelle said, holding up a hand. "I need to let my stomach settle a little. It's too late to eat now."

"Ah," Sofía said. "An ugly night, no?"

"Just depressing," Estelle said. She lowered herself into one of the straight chairs at the dining table with a sigh. "Sometimes I think that people lie awake nights thinking of stupid things to do."

"Ah," Sofía said again. "Well, we both know that to be true." She half-filled a saucepan with water and set it on the stove, and Estelle watched as the older woman methodically double-checked that she was turning on the correct burner. "Do I know Mr. Martinez?"

Estelle rested her head on her hand with half-closed eyes. It felt good not to move. "I think you met him the night we had the big retirement banquet for *Padrino* a couple of years ago. Short, quite heavy, a very *gentle* man in every way."

"His wife is Essie?"

"Yes. I wish I had your memory, Sofía."

The older woman chuckled. "I remember only things that don't really matter, *querida*. But I remember her. We had a nice talk that night, I remember. She was so glad that Arturo…is it Arturo?"

"Eduardo."

"Ah. She was pleased that Eduardo had retired the year before." She leaned her hip against the counter and watched the water. "I remember that she was a little bit worried about *Padrino*…that maybe he'd have a hard time with retirement." A wistful expression touched her face. "That maybe he wouldn't find enough to do."

"Not likely," Estelle said. "I think *Padrino* is every bit as busy now as he ever was."

"I think so, too. But the good doctor doesn't think it will go so well for Mr. Martinez now." The "good doctor" was her standard reference to her nephew, Estelle's husband.

"No."

"*Lo siento,*" Sofía said. Estelle watched her husband's aunt contemplate the steaming water. The lines in Sofía's face were etched a little deeper, her square shoulders a little more rounded than Estelle remembered. She knew that Sofía Tournál had enjoyed a long and distinguished career in the complex legal and political world of Veracruz by being intelligent, tough, and cool under pressure. Sofía had buried two husbands and, childless herself, had focused her attention over the years on the myriad nieces and nephews in her extended family, in particular her favorite, Dr. Francis Guzman.

The quiet worry that Estelle saw now wasn't because a man whom Sofía had met only once had suffered a heart attack…or even because she might be worried that retired sheriff William Gastner might not be finding enough to keep him busy.

"These things are always so sad," Sofía said finally. She glanced at Estelle. "But we had a nice evening. You know…," and she stopped in mid-sentence, busy with selecting just the right mug from a cabinet beside the refrigerator. With economy of motion, she filled the tea strainer with bulk green tea, then poured the boiling water. She turned off the burner and carried the cup to the table.

"There," she said. "And nothing else?"

"No, thanks, *tía*. This is fine." It was nice to be waited upon.

Sofía settled in the chair beside Estelle, folding her arms comfortably on the table. Estelle stirred the tea gently, waiting. The older woman's lips had been pursed in concentration, but now her face relaxed. She took a deep breath, her patrician eyebrows rising with the inhalation.

"I should just go to bed," she said. "Such a day."

Estelle smiled and adjusted the mug carefully on the table, lining it up with the pattern of the placemat. "But that's not what you want to do," she said.

Sofía reached out and patted the back of Estelle's left hand. "You're most perceptive," she said, and then leaned closer, her voice no more than a whisper. "Listen, *querida,* I tell myself that this is none of my business, but…"

She stopped, and Estelle took Sofía's hand in both of her own for a quick squeeze, touched at the woman's uncharacteristic reticence. Her aunt looked somehow older, more fragile. The skin of her hand felt paper thin, and Estelle felt a jolt at the realization that this amazing woman was actually *aging.* A quiet force who had simply always *been,* now for the first time that Estelle could remember Sofía Tournál appeared hesitant and unsure.

"We must talk about Francisco," Sofía said abruptly.

Estelle's heart jolted and she couldn't keep the surprise out of her expression. She instinctively knew that Sofía was not referring to Dr. Francis—any concern she might have about her nephew and his clinic she handled *mano a mano* with "the good doctor." That left little Francisco, and clearly, this was not a "boys must have a dog," "baseball through the window," or "chocolate smeared on the carpet" moment. Such things, Sofía would shrug off with an expressive roll of her green eyes. Few of life's vicissitudes appeared to dent the gracious attorney's serenity.

Giving herself time to think, Estelle turned the tea strainer around the cup, then lifted it out, holding it for a moment to catch the drips. She placed it carefully on the napkin. Sofía said nothing else, but waited as if it might be important that Estelle hold on to the table with both hands.

"It's important for me to know what you think," Estelle said.

Sofía's face softened and it seemed as if some of the tension left her.

"That's good," she said, "because I have to speak my mind even if you should hate me for it."

Estelle smiled at her aunt's formality. "I think you know me better than that," she said. "You're talking about *hijo*'s music?"

"Ah," Sofía said, nodding. "Yes. That's what we need to discuss, you and I. Your mother sat up with me until the good doctor came home. She and I talked this over." She flashed a smile. "And listen to me now. This is what I mean. Two old ladies discussing what the boy's mother and father should do. It's none of our business, no?"

"You have an interest," Estelle replied. "And you're concerned. So am I."

Sofía heaved an enormous sigh. "Tell me," she started to say, then hesitated. "Tell me what you think about this little boy of yours."

"He worries me," Estelle replied. She pushed the mug of tea to one side. "It keeps me awake at night. Here he is, six years old, so drawn to the piano, so sucked into his own private world," and Estelle collapsed an imaginary ball with both hands until her fists were clenched one over the other, "that I know exactly where he's going to be when I come home."

She nodded toward the living room. "Even Carlos…I see changes in him. He's always been enchanted with books and stories—you've seen that. And now, with his older brother composing these…these *soundtracks* to go with them, it's as if Carlos has become a permanent fixture on the end of the piano bench." She paused, surprised at the gush of words she'd released. "All of that is wonderful, but I don't know where it's going, and I don't know what to do about it, if anything." She raised an eyebrow at her aunt. "So you see, *querida*, what you think is important to me."

"Ah," Sofía said, and she drew it out thoughtfully. "Let me

just say it, then. I talked to Francisco's piano teacher today."
She folded her hands, as if passively waiting for an explosion.
"We spoke on the phone earlier, and she invited me to stop by.
I did so, early this afternoon."

"Mrs. Gracie is an interesting lady," Estelle said.

"Yes, she is," Sofía said slowly. "I was surprised when she
agreed with me."

"Agreed? About what?"

"Francisco is a prodigious talent, you know."

"Yes."

"But listen. I don't mean simply gifted. He is so much
more than that. The problem arises…," and she paused. "The
problem arises because in just a short time, there will be
nothing for him here."

"Nothing for him here? What does that mean?"

"Mrs. Gracie agrees that within the year, perhaps two at
most, Francisco will grow beyond anything that she might be
able to do for him. Maybe even sooner than that."

"She's such a wonderful musician," Estelle said.

Sofía tilted her head in agreement. "Yes, she is, *querida*. She
plays beautifully. And you know," and Estelle's aunt leaned
forward, a twinkle in her eyes that Estelle saw was tinged with
something akin to regret, "so do I, when this *arthritis* allows
it." She thumped swollen knuckles gently on the tabletop. "But
we are not Francisco."

"That's hard to believe, *tía*."

"You must believe it, *querida*."

"Perhaps she can recommend someone else, then," Estelle
said.

"Oh, perhaps she can, perhaps she can. And so can I. But
the truth we must face is a simple one: Posadas, dear little
village that it is, is not the sort of place that will—" she paused,

searching for the right words "—that will nurture the musical world of this remarkable little boy. His mind is so filled with it, you see. He *thinks* in musical terms, Estelle." She leaned forward eagerly. "Music to Francisco is simply a private language that he speaks far more fluently than English, or Spanish, or whatever you choose."

She spread her hands in front of her and waggled her fingers. "With all of that, he is also blessed with the magical coordination that allows him to speak this language of his."

Estelle sat back, the tea forgotten.

"This is a serious question," Sofía said. "And I will put it in the simplest terms. You have a son with an extraordinary gift.... It is beyond anything I have ever seen—and I have seen many gifted young musicians come and go."

"He's only six, *tía.*"

"I don't care if he's but *three,*" Sofía said with surprising vehemence. "What faces you now is deciding how that gift should be bestowed on the world."

She leaned forward again, again placing a hand on Estelle's. "The twelve years between this moment and when we start thinking of him as a young man...those are vital to his growth as a creative genius. I'm sure you know that."

The twelve years, Estelle thought, and found herself unable to imagine little Francisco as an eighteen-year-old. Worse yet, various faces of eighteen-year-olds that she'd had contact with through work paraded unbidden through her mind, like Macbeth's ghosts.

"He is so...so *dócil* at this point, don't you think?" Sofía asked.

"I know that he seems *consumed,*" Estelle said carefully. "It's as if the piano is a window for him, somehow."

Sofía nodded. "It is a rare thing, this combination. The gift up *here*—" she touched her own temple "—and the gift *here.*"

she extended her hands palms up, the fingers playing silent arpeggios in the air. "And I see..." Once more she hesitated, searching for just the right words in English. "I see a kind of concentration, a kind of ambition with no concern for time, that is most unusual in a mere child." She shrugged expressively. "But he is no mere child. Do you agree?"

Estelle laughed quietly. "He has no sense of the time of day, that's for sure. If he wasn't interrupted, I don't know how long he would sit at the piano."

"Just so. And every moment he spends there, it is as if another door opens for him. I hope you see that. The challenge is that he must work with someone who recognizes those doorways, those opportunities, and directs Francisco on this path he has discovered."

"He's only six," Estelle said again, and surprised herself with the defensive edge in her voice.

"*Only* six," Sofía replied. "You keep saying that. To him, it is an eternity since his fifth birthday. He does more in a single *hour* than the average child who is forced to plod through piano lessons does in a year. Let me tell you what we did this evening." She leaned forward with relish, both hands clasped tightly, pressed between table and bosom. "I played for him a small piece, a trifle, by Debussy. Maybe you know it." She hummed a lilting series of notes. "It is his 'Reverie,' and everyone who takes lessons on the piano plays it sooner or later. I had played no more than ten measures when Francisco dissolved in giggles...pure six-year-old, you know. He leans against my arm and says, 'He has his feet in the water.' And he swings his legs back and forth under the bench, like so." Sofía paddled her hands.

"His feet in the water?"

"That's what happens, you see," Sofía said. "When Francisco hears music, it instantly paints a picture in his little head. And then he uses the piano to extend that picture, to paint the whole image...the whole *gallery,* if you like. That—" Sofía leaned back in satisfaction "—*that* is his genius. And for him, I see no limitations."

Estelle sat silently for a long time. "My husband needs to invent a potion to keep *hijo* six years old forever."

"Ah, that would be a tragedy for Francisco," Sofía said, unamused. "He must grow into himself, and we must help him do that."

"What are you suggesting?" Estelle asked, feeling as if she'd drunk a bag of cement rather than a quarter-cup of tea.

"There is so much to discuss, *querida,* but Mrs. Gracie and I agreed, and maybe we are out of place. But I must say it. Posadas is a wonderful little village, and you and Doctor Francis have done wonderful things here...commendable things. But it is not the place for Francisco. Not now."

SEVEN

"DID YOU TWO SOLVE all the world's problems?" Even though her husband's voice was no more than a breathy whisper, it startled Estelle. So lost was she in her own thoughts that she had never felt him shift his position in bed, never sensed his waking. Her eyes ached from staring into the dark void overhead, the inky depths broken only by the single red eye of the smoke alarm on the opposite bedroom wall.

"Not even close," she murmured. She and Sofía had talked for another hour, and afterward, when she'd made her way into bed, she had fallen instantly asleep...for an hour. She turned now and squinted at the clock on the dresser. In another few minutes, the boys would be awake, excited about whatever might await them out under the Christmas tree.

Francis shifted and Estelle could feel his breath on her neck. "I don't think we're big-city people," he whispered.

"She talked to you, too?"

"'Cornered' might be more accurate," Francis said. "She's worried."

"*Y yo también,*" Estelle said, "I don't know what to do."

"Maybe nothing is the appropriate thing right now," her husband whispered.

She twisted onto her side so that she faced him, then reached up and found the side of his face, stroking the silky beard that he now kept clipped short, just enough to soften his square jaw line. "Is that the right thing, *oso?*"

A long moment of silence followed, but she knew that Francis had heard the question. She felt his touch, light and delicate, as his wrist crossed hers. With a single finger, he traced the outline of her lips.

"The right thing is for them to grow up healthy and happy," he said finally. "Anything else is gravy."

Estelle drew in a long, deep breath that trembled when she exhaled. "When she talked about Veracruz, it made me remember Andy Browers. That's not fair, but that's what it made me think of. I didn't tell Sofía that, of course."

Her husband's finger hesitated, then moved from her lips and tapped the end of her nose, his only comment.

"I know," she replied to the unspoken comment. "I know it's not the same." She knew that there was no logic to the emotions that tied her stomach in knots. Andy Browers had been an opportunistic punk who three years before had tried to kidnap two area children—his own stepchild and little Francisco Guzman, then three years old—with the notion of selling the children in Mexico. The memory of those moments had lost some sharpness around the edges, but they still haunted her.

"I couldn't send Francisco away, even if it was to live with Sofía," Estelle said. Her husband didn't respond. "Could you do that?"

He tapped the end of her nose again, and then she felt his heavy arm settle around her shoulders, drawing her closer. "Nope," he said. "And all we can do is hope that it's that simple, *querida*."

"Tell me why it isn't that simple," she said.

"Because," Francis said, as if that was that.

"Oh, *sí*." She managed to grip a few beard hairs and twisted, wagging them from side to side.

"Because Sofía would argue that a genius belongs to the world," he said, and the words came out with such finality, such measured conviction, that it startled Estelle. When she had assumed that he was sound asleep, perhaps in truth he had been staring at the ceiling, too, wrestling with his own thoughts.

"Do you believe that, too?"

"In a way, sure. That's just the way it works. I think that's what Sofía is trying to say."

"What's that mean?" she whispered, knowing perfectly well what it meant.

Francis drew in a deep breath. "It means that we're responsible for helping him find his way," he said. "Whatever that takes."

"You think this is his way, then?"

"I don't know, *querida*. I'm not exactly practiced in this."

"*Ni yo*. But he's only six, *oso*. Tomorrow he might decide that he's going to collect toys out of cereal boxes. The world's largest collection."

"Don't we wish life was that simple," Francis whispered. "But I don't think that's going to happen. He's been consumed with that piano since the moment the store delivered it. Anybody can see that. And before that, he sneaked off and practiced on the piano at school. I don't think this is a passing fancy."

"I don't think so either."

"All I know is what Sofía says," Francis said. "And what I see and hear myself…not that I'm much of a judge. My musical ability is limited to playing about four chords. I think Francisco inherited it all from you."

"*Ay*," Estelle said. "Two musical duds, and look what we produce."

"Yep. Of course, you might have some great conductor in your past, for all we know. Maybe your real last name is Bach. Didn't old Johann have about twenty kids, or something like that? Maybe some of them made it to the hinterlands of Mexico. I mean, when they were carrying those virgins up the steps of those Aztec temples to rip their hearts out, someone had to play the march music."

She ground a knuckle into his ribs. "That's it," Estelle agreed. She could have counted on one hand the times when it might have mattered to her who her parents had been. Teresa Reyes, childless and a widow, had adopted her through the church in Tres Santos when Estelle was not yet two years old.

Francis locked a hand over hers to prevent more damage. "But I think he *has* to go sometime. I trust Sofía's judgment about his genius, *mi corazón*. If Francisco had just a little bit of talent…a little proficiency, maybe, she wouldn't be making such a big deal out of all this. She'd suggest that we make sure hijo got into band in school, that he took lessons, all that stuff that kids do. She was adamant that we buy the piano, and thank God we did that."

"And when's that 'sometime'? Now what?"

"That's exactly right. Now what? I don't know."

"He's too young to go anywhere."

"Of course he's too young, *querida*. He's six. And I can hear what Sofía would say. She'd say that at age six, he's getting a late start. After all, Mozart was composing and performing in public when he was, what…four? Five?"

"And dead at thirtysomething, *oso*."

"That's the question, isn't it?" Francis said. "For all this medical stuff that keeps me off the street corners, we don't know, do we?" He pulled her touch closer. "But Mozart was a couple centuries ago, back when they thought that the heart pumped air. I probably could have kept him alive with a good dose of amoxicillin. He might have lived long enough to write *Don Giovanni,* Part Six."

"I'm serious, *querido*. I don't care about Mozart. I care about Francisco. There has to be some other answer," Estelle said.

"Sure. We could send *hijo* to New York City."

"*Caramba.* I don't think so. Anyway, he's too young for Juilliard."

"But not for the Conservatorio de Veracruz," Francis said. "*Ay.*"

"Yep. I know exactly what she's thinking. Sofía could walk Francisco the two blocks to the conservatory and back. From her condo. Every day." Her husband said it so easily, as if he could actually imagine such a thing. No doubt Sofía could, and as much as Estelle dearly loved her aunt-in-law and Sofía's wisdom, she felt a pang of jealousy.

"Carlos would be a sad little *saquito*," Estelle said.

"Not if he went, too."

She pulled his beard very hard, enough to make him gasp.

"Maybe we just moved the wrong way last time," he said, referring to their half-year in Minnesota. "And you could get a job working for the *judiciales*."

She smoothed his kinked beard, and her lips found his in the darkness. After a long moment, she pulled just far enough away that she could whisper, "I don't want to think that far ahead yet, *oso*."

"Me neither. And I like what we're doing right here in the backwaters. It's the kind of medicine I want to practice, where I want to practice it. I can't picture living in one of the busiest cities on earth. And I look at it this way…when Francisco is eighty-five and venerated around the world, with a bazillion recordings and honors to his credit, will it matter whether he began at age six or sixteen?"

"I don't think so. I tell myself that it won't."

"I don't think it will matter either. I think our job is to keep him eager, *querida*. Keep him fueled. We don't need to send him to some fancy labor camp to twist the last little bit of music out of him before he's seven." He stroked her cheek, fingers drawing down the side of her neck, "Besides, if need be, we can bring the world to him. If there's some great maestro that he needs to study under, we'll import the guy. If we have to add a music room out back, we'll do that. He can go to music camps for two weeks at a shot in the summer."

"I like the sound of that," Estelle whispered. For a long moment, they lay in each other's arms, breath matching breath.

"It's Christmas morning, you know. The boys will be up in a few minutes," her husband said.

"Then we'd better not waste time," she replied, snuggling deeper into the curve of his body.

EIGHT

WHEN THE TELEPHONE RANG at 5:55 that Christmas morning, the two boys had indeed been up for many minutes. Estelle was in the kitchen, guiding an industrious Francisco through his second major passion in life, the manufacture of enormous pancakes whose batter he poured meticulously one cake's worth at a time, dead center in the pan.

Without releasing her support of the heavy bowl, she reached across the counter and picked up the receiver.

"Guzman."

"Estelle, I need to talk to Francis," Dr. Alan Perrone said. His tone was clipped and brusque, and he didn't waste time with the usually automatic apology for the early-hour disturbance on a holiday.

"He's in the shower," Estelle said. "Hang on just a second." At the same time, Sofía Tournál rose from where she had been sitting in the living room with Carlos as the little boy narrated the photos from his latest treasure to her and his grandmother. He had received a Christmas gift book from *Padrino* that described the history and development of farm tractors...a book that Dr. Francis Guzman had joked would be set to music before the end of the day—*Concerto in John Deere Flat.*

Sofía smoothly segued into position as bowl handler as Estelle headed down the hall.

"You probably want to head down here, too," Perrone said. "Someone's going to want to hold Gayle's hand."

"Sure," she said, without actually having heard what Dr. Perrone had said. When the phone rang, she had immediately thought about Chief Eduardo Martinez, and it was only as she entered the master bedroom that it registered. She stopped short and beckoned to her husband, who appeared shaggy and wet, a towel around his middle.

She handed him the phone. "It's Alan."

"Shit," Francis said matter-of-factly. "What's up?" he said into the phone, then frowned as he listened to his partner. At the same time, he reached out and touched Estelle on the shoulder as if to hold her in place. "Okay," he said after a moment. "Yes, I think we're going to have to do that. He's stable enough now?" Again, the room was silent as he listened. "Right. Okay, that's good." He nodded as if Alan Perrone could see him. "How long was he out?" He frowned and nodded, this time more slowly. "Okay. Give me ten minutes. Estelle will probably be there before that."

He rang off. "Bob Torrez apparently had a pulmonary embolism early this morning." He handed her the telephone. "Gayle drove him to the hospital about an hour ago. Alan wants to transport him to University in Albuquerque."

"*Ay,*" Estelle whispered, but she was already turning toward the door. "I'll head down," she said. Francis nodded, and she left him to dress.

"We'll be fine," Sofía said when she saw Estelle's face. "Just go and do whatever it is that you have to do."

Without interrupting the process, Estelle bent over her industrious son and kissed him on the forehead, one hand cupping the side of his face while staying clear of the dripping ladle. "*Perfecto,*" she whispered to him, and he beamed at the huge pancake forming and bubbling. "Thanks, *tía*," she said to Sofía. In the living room, she was met with a frown from her mother.

"You have to go at this hour?" Teresa observed, knowing perfectly well that the hour of the day or night didn't matter.

"*Mamá* helps people," Carlos said, and Estelle felt a twinge at his innocent defense. She clamped a hand on his small skull the way his father did, turning his face up so that she looked directly into his dark brown eyes, so rich and deep that she could become lost in them. Neither of them said a word, and after a moment she kissed him on the bridge of his nose, squarely between the eyes.

"The sheriff's sick," she said to her mother, taking her by the hand. "I'll be back when I can."

"*Ay*," Teresa said, her expression softening. "I bet that stubborn one didn't get his flu shot."

"I wish it were that simple," Estelle said.

A few minutes later, Estelle saw Sheriff Bob Torrez's heavy-lidded eyes flicker with a touch of irritation as she rapped lightly on the freestanding partition. The sheriff lay in the hospital bed, the skimpy gown looking ridiculous on his large frame. He had kicked the sheet off, and his left leg was flexed with his foot propped up on the bed rail…a pathetic imitation of his habit of thumping a boot across the corner of his office desk.

The crowd around his bed—now grown to three people— surely was stretching Torrez's patience. Dr. Alan Perrone stood near the sheriff's left shoulder, regarding the screen that monitored the patient's vital signs. Gayle Torrez flanked her husband on the other side of the bed.

"What are you doin' here already?" Torrez asked ungraciously. His voice was husky, and he reached up and fiddled with the oxygen tube in his nostrils. An IV was taped to the back of each hand. "We were just about to wrap all this up."

"Oh, sure," the unflappable Dr. Perrone said. He smiled tightly at Estelle. "How are you doing, young lady?"

"I'm okay," Estelle replied.

"Happy Holidays," Perrone added. "Or maybe I said that last night...I'm losing track."

"And Merry Christmas to all," Estelle said. She rapped a knuckle on the bedframe as she stepped around to stand beside Gayle. "Hey," she said, and rested a hand on Gayle's shoulder.

"Some people will do anything to get out of a family gathering," Gayle said, but she didn't even try to smile. Christmas with the hugely extended Torrez family meant that Bob Torrez's mother would host half a hundred people in her modest adobe home on McArthur...and the overflow would reach Bob and Gayle's mobile home less than half a block away.

"Actually, it's pretty simple, Estelle," Perrone said, "We're in the process of explaining to this guy that there are two easy ways to find what happened...to find where that embolism is and just how nasty it might be. We can do a postmortem, or Robert can let us do our jobs without all the macho fuss."

His glance shifted to Gayle, who accepted the barb, made only partially in jest, with a nod of agreement. "We took X-rays," the physician continued, "and they don't show as much as I'd like. We're going to get a CAT here in a few minutes, but I'm willing to bet that'll be inconclusive, too. The best way to see what we're dealing with is pulmonary angiography...put in a little tracer and watch where it goes."

"I don't need to be stuck full of dye," Torrez grumbled.

"Better a little bit of dye than a gallon or two of embalming fluid," Perrone said, and Estelle saw Gayle wince. "Anyway, I want all the cards in my hand when we do that, and that means that we cart you up to University Hospital in Albuquerque." He glanced at his watch. "We're lucky. The Med-Evac flight crew thought they might get to enjoy Christmas at home, and we were able to round them up in Las Cruces. The plane will be here in a few minutes."

"I'm not flyin' to no Albuquerque," Torrez said, but the protest was without much conviction.

"Oh, yes you are," Gayle said. "Don't be so stupid."

"We've already established that you haven't been taking the meds that were prescribed," Perrone said. "That didn't take much detective work. And you haven't shown your face at physical therapy for the past couple of weeks. Mr. Model Patient, here." He snorted with impatience, reached out a hand, and patted Torrez on the arm. "We'll find a blunt needle and fill him full of happy syrup. He won't even know where he is when we're done with him."

"Like hell," the sheriff said.

"Yep," Perrone agreed. He beckoned Estelle out of the room, nodding in sympathy at Gayle as he did so. "We'll be back in a minute. Talk some sense into your husband, okay? And you should plan to go with us, by the way."

Out in the hall, Perrone walked away from the ICU. He dug in his pocket for a mint and offered one to Estelle. "Francis is on the way down?"

"He'll be here in just a minute or two," Estelle said. "What happened?"

"Well, like I told Gayle, I'm sure it's a clot that broke loose and ended up in his lung. Pulmonary embolism," Perrone said. "I'm sure of that. Gayle says that early this morning, Bobby woke up and couldn't get his breath. His heartbeat went wild, and he fell on his face when he tried to climb out of bed. Scared the bejeepers out of her. He wouldn't let her call an ambulance, and he's goddamn lucky that stupid little decision didn't kill him. She drove him down here herself."

"That sounds like Bobby," Estelle said.

Perrone leaned against the polished tile wall and regarded the grout between the tiles as if all the answers lay there. "None of this surprises me, I guess. All that surgery he had on his leg and hips, and then he doesn't take care of himself and pay attention to physical therapy. If he's not careful, he's going to end up being forty-five years old and walking like an old man of eighty-five."

"I thought he looked pretty bad last night," Estelle said. "We had a little confrontation down in Regál, and even Bill Gastner said that Bobby looked terrible."

"That sorry affair didn't do the sheriff any good, I'm sure. He's in no condition for scuffles."

"Well, sort of a scuffle, Alan. But that was more me than him."

"Ah." Perrone took off his glasses, and Estelle felt his ice-blue eyes assessing her. "And you're none the worse for wear?"

"No. I'm fine."

"Well, his nibs here isn't. At the moment, we have him on rat poison and a handful of other things to thin his blood. We need to do a full rundown and see what the hell is going on." Perrone patted his own right hip. "He's got a hell of a bruise on his thigh, just above where the break was. Gayle says that somehow he managed to smack himself with the door of his truck yesterday or the day before."

"He never said anything about that," Estelle said. "But what else is new." She glanced at her watch. In another few minutes, the shift at the Sheriff's Department would cycle from graveyard to days, and Gayle Torrez, office manager and head dispatcher, had been scheduled for duty…the first Christmas tour she'd drawn in several years, thanks to the conspiring of root canals, flu, and various other complications among the small staff.

"So if he goes to Albuquerque, what are we talking about? How long?" Estelle asked.

"He *is* going to Albuquerque," Perrone said. "He doesn't have a choice there. And it all depends what we find. Unfortunately, clots tend not to be isolated events. We'll just have to see. He's going to be out of commission for a while…and I'm afraid it's an indeterminate while just now. That's the best I can tell you. He might be back on his feet in a day or two, or not."

Estelle started to say something when her husband appeared around the corner by the Hospital Auxiliary's coffee bar.

"Ah," Perrone said. "Now we're all set."

Reaching out to take Perrone by the elbow, Estelle nodded toward the ward behind them. "How's Eduardo?" Somehow, it seemed weeks ago that she had last seen Eduardo Martinez, pale and frail, in *his* ICU bed—not just hours. If his family was still maintaining a vigil, they were cloistered away somewhere, perhaps in the ICU waiting room down the hall.

"That's the problem," Perrone said. "I'm starting to think that it might be a good idea if one of us rides on the plane with Bobby, but maybe not. That's what I wanted to discuss with Dr. Guzman," and Perrone held up his hand like a traffic cop as Francis strode up to them. "One of us certainly needs to stay here and ride herd on the chief. And to answer your question, Estelle, he's not good. He's unresponsive, and the family is trying to decide what to do. He's reached a point where the machines are breathing for him. Not good." He nodded in resignation. "Like I said, Merry Christmas, eh?"

He stepped away, yielding his spot in the conversation to Estelle's husband. "We'll talk in a bit," he said to Estelle, and then with a final pat to his associate's shoulder, he hustled back to the ICU.

"Sofía said not to bother calling Irma," Francis said, referring to Irma Sedillos, the Guzman boys' *nana* and Gayle's sister. "Everything is under control on the home front, *querida*."

"That's the least of my worries right now, *oso,*" Estelle said. "But Sofía is a sweetheart." She glanced at her watch again. "I need to swing by the office for a little bit to make sure we're covered, and then I'll stick pretty close to here, I guess. If Essie Martinez needs anything…" Her cell phone chirped and she looked heavenward. "If you end up marooned in Albuquerque, let me know, okay? If you go up there on the plane? When things quiet down, maybe we can all take a drive up there to pick you up. Sofía mentioned that she'd like to do that one day while she's here. A little vacation."

"Vacation?" Francis said, puzzled. Then he grinned and kissed Estelle lightly, first on the lips, then the tip of her nose, and then squarely between the eyes, just as she'd done to Carlos. "Love you, *querida.* Be careful. No more heroics."

Palming the tiny phone that insisted with a variety of chirps, she waved at her husband as he disappeared through the glass doors. "Guzman."

"Estelle, this is Brent," the graveyard-shift dispatcher said cheerfully. "Sorry to bother you."

"No bother. What's up?"

"Did you happen to hear from Gayle? I was kinda lookin' for her."

"I was just about to call," Estelle said. "We're all over here at the hospital. Gayle's not going to be in today, Brent. Can you stay put until I have a chance to rearrange some things?"

Sutherland hesitated just long enough that Estelle knew he'd probably made plans that he was loath to break. "Sure. You mean like the whole shift?"

"It might come to that. We don't know yet."

"Well…okay, sure. Is everything all right?"

"The sheriff's going to be going to Albuquerque for some treatment. Gayle will go with him."

"Geez, that's no good. What, for his leg, you mean?"

"Yes."

"Okay. How's the chief doing, by the way?"

"Not well."

"Frank's here, asking."

"I can just imagine," Estelle said. Frank Dayan, publisher and quasi-editor of the *Posadas Register*, matched anyone in town for long, irregular hours.

"You want to talk with him?"

"Sure."

"Just a sec."

When he came on the line, Frank's voice was quiet and concerned. "Merry Christmas, Undersheriff," he said. "You have your hands full over there?"

"Yes, we do, Frank. We're imploding."

"Look, I got your note about the arrests and about Eduardo. How's he doing?"

"Critical," Estelle said.

"But not directly because of assault, or anything like that?"

"No. I don't think so."

"Boy," Dayan said. "If the chief didn't have bad luck, he wouldn't have any luck at all." Estelle didn't respond, and Dayan shifted gears. "Look, Estelle...did you get a copy of the short list for county manager? I was going to try and talk to you yesterday—or Pam was going to. We didn't have the chance."

"I got one a while ago, Frank. I haven't looked at it. We got kinda busy around here." She knew that the county commission had called a short special meeting to sort through and qualify the handful of applications for the county manager's vacancy, but it was nothing that she had needed to attend...and Bob Torrez could be counted on to flee to the opposite side of the county from anything remotely construed as politics.

"Well, I have a copy with me," Dayan said. "I think you and the sheriff are going to be very interested."

"How many applications did they finally end up with?" As she talked, Estelle had made her way toward the front door of the hospital, and now she stood just inside the foyer where framed photos of the staff, including her husband, graced the east wall.

"Five that they're going to consider," Dayan said. "Were you planning to come in to the office this morning?"

"I'm on my way there right now." She stepped outside and saw that the skies had cleared, leaving only a small smudge of clouds to the southwest.

"Maybe we could chat for a minute, then. I know it's a bad time, with it being Christmas morning and all, but I'm trying to keep ahead of things. It'll take me all week just to wheedle a comment out of the sheriff."

"I sympathize, Frank," Estelle said. Frank Dayan's newspaper hit the streets on Thursdays, dictated more by the schedule of grocery store advertising inserts than by when breaking news was most likely…something that Estelle was sure twanged the newspaper publisher's heart in opposing directions. And the search for a new county manager was a significant story for the county in general and the Sheriff's Department in particular, regardless of Sheriff Robert Torrez's disinterest in either politics or the press. Torrez had pretty much ignored the previous county manager, leaving the attendance of county meetings and reports to his undersheriff.

"Did anybody local make the short list?" Estelle asked.

"Oh, yes." Dayan chuckled. "You and Robert are going to like this." His tone said otherwise.

NINE

FRANK DAYAN HANDED the undersheriff a photocopy that included five names. Each name was followed by a one- or two-sentence résumé. Estelle settled in her chair and smoothed the single sheet of paper on the center of her desk calendar. She folded her hands and glanced up at Frank, seeing the twinkle in his eyes as he waited expectantly for her to read the list.

"Now this is interesting," she said, and Dayan's smile widened, lighting up his narrow, swarthy face.

"That's an understatement," he said. "Did you have any heads-up about this?"

"I hadn't heard that this guy from Oklahoma City had applied."

Dayan laughed at Estelle's joke. "Oh, gosh. We're concerned about him, all right."

Estelle regarded the newspaper publisher with amusement and saw the expression that meant Dayan was sniffing for good front-page stuff. "I knew that Leona had applied," she said. She again read the short statement about the candidate who had drawn Frank Dayan's interest.

Leona Spears, B.S., M.S., Stanford University; Ph.D., California Institute of Technology; 28-year employment with New Mexico State Department of Transportation's Highway Department. Currently planning engineer, DOT District 19.

"She told me a month or so ago that she was going to apply," the undersheriff added.

"We'd be interested in what the sheriff has to say," Dayan said.

"*Ay,*" Estelle sighed. "Well, *ya veremos.*"

"Is he going to be coming in later?" He waved a hand defensively. "I know this is Christmas and all." Or maybe he didn't, Estelle thought. Dayan was divorced, and seemed to spend every waking hour hovering over his newspaper…a dedication that was seldom rewarded by the newspaper chain's corporate owners a thousand miles away. She glanced out the office door toward the dispatch island where Brent Sutherland presently commanded telecommunications. The young deputy had said nothing to Frank Dayan about the sheriff's condition, and Estelle jotted a mental note to compliment Sutherland on his discretion…and to compliment him for not grumbling about swinging a double shift.

"The sheriff is on his way to University Hospital in Albuquerque, Frank."

Dayan grimaced. "They're transferring Chief Martinez up there?"

"No. It's the *sheriff* who's being transferred."

Dayan's face went blank. "You're kidding."

"No."

"For what?"

"The possibility of a blood clot in his lung. We'll know more later today." She was almost ready to add, *That's not for publication,* but didn't. The *Posadas Register* came out on Thursday…five days away. The entire world could change by then—and at the rate things were going, probably would.

"You're kidding," Dayan said again. "He was with you down in Regál last night. That's what I heard."

"Yes, he was."

Dayan settled back in his chair. "Huh." He grinned sheepishly and nodded at the list. "This is going to cause a relapse, that's for sure."

"Well, we'll see," Estelle said. True enough, Leona Spears was a special case. A talented engineer and skillful planner when it came to asphalt, bridges, and drainage culverts, she still managed to tweak the sheriff the wrong way with her eccentric ways, right down to the bright, floral muumuus that she preferred when not in khaki and hard-hat at work.

More than that, during one memorable election year she had run against Bob Torrez for sheriff, a position for which she wasn't remotely qualified. In years previous, she had run for county commission, for school board, for village trustee, losing every election in spectacular fashion.

The other names on the commission's short list for county manager included two applicants from Las Cruces, one from Oklahoma City, and the current acting manager, a nice enough older man who had worked in the village planning and zoning office, but who Estelle knew had significant problems with both basic arithmetic and alcohol.

"The list of finalists is also the entire list of everyone who applied," Dayan observed. "Posadas County is not everyone's top choice."

Estelle nodded, but didn't volunteer the information that Dr. Arnold Gray, a local chiropractor and chairman of the county commission, had told her the week before—both that Leona had applied for the county manager's job and that he and at least two other commissioners supported her choice. As Gray had succinctly put it, "When you look beyond Leona's eccentricities, she's a good fit. She's not going to work for us for a couple of months and then go somewhere else." With their support, Leona was a shoe-in.

Evidently, Dr. Gray hadn't seen the necessity of tipping off either Frank Dayan or the sheriff himself. Perhaps the commission chairman was trusting Estelle to build some defenses for their decision…not that it mattered to them what the sheriff thought.

"Any comment?" the newspaper publisher asked hopefully. He fished a ballpoint pen and small notebook out of his jacket pocket.

Estelle handed the list back to Dayan. "They'll do what they do," she said. "I'm sure the Posadas County Sheriff's Department will offer full cooperation with whoever is selected."

Dayan grinned. "That's nice. You don't have any concerns?"

"Concerns? Lots of concerns, Frank. I don't even want to start counting them. But no. None about Leona. Not at this point."

"Ms. Spears has something of a history, you know. 'Colorful' might be a kind way to put it."

"Yes, it would." Estelle relaxed back in her chair and folded her hands across her stomach. "I've had occasion to talk with her a number of times in the past several years about one thing or another. But at the moment, we have two men in jail for grand larceny, auto theft, and assault, we have a former chief of police who is desperately ill, and Sheriff Torrez has had better days, I'm sure. And as you know from your own well-written front-page story last week, we've just started a mammoth records project to consolidate the village records with our own. That all by itself takes time and lots of manpower."

"How's that going, by the way?" Dayan asked. "We need to follow up on that."

"We've just started."

"Bill Gastner?"

Estelle nodded. "He's fine."

"No…I meant to ask if he's still heading up the project."

"Yes, he is. Thank heavens, too."

"There's a good story there," Dayan said. "I talked to Bill a little bit last week. I don't think that when the village and county voted to consolidate services, they thought about all the work involved. I've never *seen* so much paperwork." Dayan's short article had included a front-page photo that featured the five huge, old filing cabinets that held most of the records, the photo nicely out of focus in typical Dayan fashion. Standing in front of the trove of records were Gastner and his two helpers, department photographer Linda Real and Deputy Mike Sisneros.

"The village was incorporated in 1931," Estelle said, and held up both hands. "And the Sheriff's Department has records going back to 1914. Even for a little wide spot in the road, that's a lot of paperwork that has accumulated over the years."

"So what do you do with it all?"

"Consolidate it with our own," Estelle said. "Someone has to decide what is passed along to the state and to the NCIC computerized systems. If John Doe has a file with the county," and she shifted in her chair, "and also a record with the village, then all of that has to be consolidated in one comprehensive data base."

"He's going to be able to do all that?"

"He?"

"Bill."

"Frank, he's not working by himself. Mike Sisneros is full-time on the project with him. So is Linda Real…at least as much of the time as we can spare her."

"What kind of timetable are you looking at?"

"I don't know." She shrugged. "We've never done this before, Frank. We're sort of feeling our way. What we don't want to do is end up with some enormous mess on our hands. We want all the files comprehensible and electronically accessible as a useful database. Otherwise, there's no point in any of it. I've made that a priority this year."

"But you haven't actually started sifting yet?"

Estelle shook her head. "We've done a lot of preliminary work, Frank. For one thing, we moved all the files to this building so that there's some security. We've set up shop in the conference room. It's a good place to work." Estelle watched impassively as Frank jotted for a moment.

"I guess I'm going to need to talk with the sheriff, huh?"

"Eventually. That would be a good idea."

"What's he think of this consolidation thing?"

"You'd have to ask him, Frank."

Dayan grimaced. "I mean, does he think it's a good idea, generally? He didn't have much to say during the commission meetings."

"It's what the county commission and the village trustees want to do," Estelle said. "It's really as simple as that. Naturally, from an administrative standpoint, there are some advantages for us by putting everything under one roof. That makes some things easier."

"Some things?"

"Sure. Some. Not all. Nothing's perfect. And remember that it isn't really *consolidation,* Frank. That's what we all call it, but it's not really that. The village dissolved its police department, and contracted the county for services. That's a little different than consolidation."

"You're a good politician, you know that?" Dayan laughed, and pushed himself out of the straight-backed chair. "There's a bunch of things I need to do. I'll get out of here and let you enjoy your Christmas morning," he said. "Where are we at with the two morons from Indiana?"

"We're going to fit in a prelim with Judge Hobart this morning sometime. Just as soon as we can. I think that Tom Pasquale is going to handle that chore."

"What's next, then?"

"We'll be meeting with the district attorney...probably

tomorrow or Monday. We'll just have to see. There are some communications that are necessary with the folks in Indiana, too."

"You think he's going to set bail pretty high? Interstate flight risk and all that?"

"You'd have to ask the judge about that, Frank."

"Oh, sure." He took a deep breath. "That's like petting a rattlesnake. How about if I check with you tomorrow. How about that?"

"That would be good." She rose and offered a warm smile to Dayan. "I know I'm not terribly forthcoming, Frank. But we have a lot that's pending, and until some basic decisions are made…"

"I know how it works," Dayan said. "I'll be in touch. Would you holler if something major erupts?"

She nodded and stood behind her desk for a moment, well past the time when his footsteps had faded down the hall. Eventually she realized that Deputy Brent Sutherland was standing in the doorway of her office. He leaned against the doorframe as if content to see how long Estelle was planning to remain lost in her thoughts.

"*Hola, Señor Brent,*" she said, and shook her head to bring the present time and place back into focus. "Thanks for staying on. I really appreciate it."

"No problem," the young deputy said, although the resigned expression on his face said that wasn't quite true. "How's the sheriff?"

"Not so good, I think," Estelle replied. "They're going to fly him up to Albuquerque in a few minutes."

"Ouch."

"Yes, ouch." She moved out from behind her desk. "I saw on the duty board that Tommy Pasquale has switched with Dennis for the day?"

"Yes, ma'am. Sergeant Mears okayed that. Dennis wanted

to go to Phoenix to spend Christmas with his mom and dad, and Pasquale didn't have any problems about working today. Linda was coming in this afternoon anyway. She and Bill Gastner were going to figure out where to start. With her working, Tom thought he might as well do the same."

"Ah," Estelle said. "*Padrino* is a bad influence, I can see that." She speculated that holidays meant little more to Bill Gastner than just another irritating day when his favorite restaurant might be closed. A long-time widower, he didn't take the opportunity of the holidays to visit any of his own four adult children and their families.

Looking as if dispensing more good news might win him a reprieve, Sutherland said, "Sergeant Mears wired up three computer terminals in the conference room that all tie into the main server. They're all set to go. Linda was going to check everything out this afternoon when Gastner got here."

"What about Mike?"

Sutherland smiled. "He said he might duck in for a few minutes before he and Janet headed to Lordsburg to see his folks."

Former sheriff Bill Gastner had agreed to head up the records project if Deputy Mike Sisneros, a former village patrolman, worked with Linda Real and himself as a team. Estelle had agreed, even though she was loath to tie up Linda with the job, since Linda was the department's most talented photographer and Gayle Torrez's assistant office manager.

She pulled the cell phone from her belt as it chirped.

"Guzman." She could hear the thunderous roar in the background and knew instantly that it was the twin turboprops of the air ambulance.

"*Querida,* we're on the way," her husband said, his voice unnaturally loud. "I'll give you a buzz from the hospital a little later, all right?"

"Sure. And I was serious about taking Sofía to Albuquerque, *oso*. Let me know if you get yourself stuck up there. We'll come rescue you."

"We'll just have to see," Francis said. "I think they're dead-heading the plane back to Cruces after they drop us off, and if they do that, I'm going to lose my ride."

"Then let me know. How's Bobby?"

"Riding comfortably, and cranky as ever. I'm optimistic, but we'll just see how this all goes."

"Be careful."

"You got it. Love you, *querida*."

"*Y yo a ti*," she said, and rang off. Brent Sutherland had re-treated back to his world of radios, phones, and computers, and Estelle stepped out of her office in time to see Deputy Jackie Taber heading toward the staff workroom.

"All quiet?" she called, and Taber stopped short.

"I think so," the deputy said, and looked heavenward. "I escorted the ambulance over to the airport. They got off all right. I was thinkin' that a good rap upside the head might make the sheriff a little easier to manage." She patted the tele-scoping baton on her belt. "He's a real trip."

"He just prefers to be the one carrying the stretcher, rather than riding on it," Estelle said.

"Can't argue with that," Jackie said. "Being pampered ruins his Mr. Indestructible image."

Estelle laughed. "You're going to do up a sympathy card?"

"You bet," Jackie said with relish. An artist of considerable talent, the deputy enjoyed turning her pen and ink to caricatures of the department when the need arose. "Real sympathy. I started on it as soon as I heard." She propped her briefcase on one knee and opened it, pulling out a drawing tablet. She swept the tablet cover back and offered it to Estelle.

The rough pencil sketch showed the sheriff in a hospital gown that was far too short, lying in bed amid an enormous tangle of hospital paraphernalia, with various roughed-out figures gathered around the bed. Estelle recognized Perrone's slicked-back hair and large nose, as well as Gayle Torrez's trademark ponytail. The figure on the bed was recoiling in horror from the apparition who was approaching the foot of the bed…a figure who was unmistakably Leona Spears. The large woman, her muumuu flowing, carried a hospital cafeteria tray. YOU JUST NEED SOME MOTHERING, was printed in neat architectural block letters above Leona's head. Her name tag included the tiny legend, COUNTY MANAGER.

"You're cruel," Estelle said. "What a way to find out."

"He doesn't know about Leona yet? The rest of the world does."

Estelle shook her head. "I don't think so. He would have said something to me if he did."

"You want me to hold off?"

Estelle thought for only a second. "Nah," she said, and nodded at the artwork. "That's delightful. He'll treasure it, I'm sure."

Jackie laughed as she slipped the drawing pad back in her briefcase. "Treasure it all the way to reassigning me to Siberia," she said.

"To the day shift, more likely."

The deputy looked up in mock horror. "Spare me, please."

TEN

AFTER THE TURMOIL of Christmas Eve and the tense moments of early morning, Estelle savored the peace and quiet of Christmas afternoon. The skies were clear and the sun almost hot, toasting the dormant sage and yarrow underfoot as she sauntered along the narrow trail that ran along the rim of Escudero Arroyo west of Twelfth Street. She strolled with her arm linked through Sofía Tournál's. They had no particular destination, no particular agenda. Every moment that the telephone in her jacket pocket didn't ring, or the pager didn't chirp, or the handheld two-way radio clipped to her belt at the small of her back didn't squawk, Estelle counted as a victory.

Dr. Francis Guzman had called to report that the sheriff was resting comfortably, although practicing a charming combination of groggy and cranky. The air ambulance was scheduled to return to Las Cruces that evening, and would swing by Posadas to bring Dr. Guzman home.

Word was less promising from Posadas General Hospital, where Eduardo Martinez still remained in a coma.

As Estelle and Sofía strolled and talked, the two children scampered here and there in general orbit around them, chattering like squirrels.

Teresa Reyes had suggested the walk, and Estelle knew why. Not only would the fresh, cool air be a balm for Estelle's own nerves, but it would leave the house quiet and peaceful for a while…her mother's nap time.

For a brief season, the desert was relatively safe for the two boys, the risks limited to being spiked occasionally by a withered cactus or snagged by the amazing thorns of the stunted acacia. Nights were cold enough that the various fanged creatures, or even the scuttling stinging ones, were holed up, well out of reach of curious little fingers until spring. Estelle found herself watching the children, comparing their mannerisms and interests.

Carlos spent much of his time squatting on his haunches, examining the fine details of the treasures he found. He seemed particularly intrigued with the stink beetles that he uncovered. He would have loved to have brought home a pocketful, but accepted with sober resignation the logic that the little beetles were happier remaining in their own homes.

Francisco seemed to enjoy the roll and sweep of the lay of the land itself. Perhaps because he knew it made his mother nervous, he skirted the very edge of the arroyo, defying the precarious, sandy overhangs that could so easily collapse under his feet. Once in a while, Sofía would gasp as the boy came too close to disaster, but Estelle remained philosophically quiet. She saw that the six-year-old had brought his music with him, the sounds inside his head providing a framework for what he saw out on the prairie.

"This is nice," Estelle sighed at one point, and Sofía glanced at her with amusement. Estelle had stopped, and was watching Francisco, who had found an old cattle path that cut the rim. He didn't race to the bottom twelve feet below. Rather, he stepped down the trail just enough so that his head was level with the rim. The grass-high view provided an interesting perspective of the arroyo as it swept away, cutting through the flat of the prairie.

Estelle watched as her son stood still and raised his arms for a moment, like Moses parting the waters, and she saw his head bob.

"We let ourselves become so busy that we forget what we're missing," Sofía said. The sound of a snarling motorcycle blossomed behind them, and Estelle turned to watch its approach up the arroyo from the southwest.

"Hijo," she called to Francisco, and he retreated up the cow path toward them.

"That's Butch," he shouted. Fresh paint winking in the late afternoon sun, trailing a plume of blue smoke from its wailing two-stroke engine, the dirt bike catapulted up the narrow arroyo bottom, the rider fighting the loose sand.

As the biker flashed by, he attempted a wheelie, but the traction wasn't there and he executed a wild fishtail instead, then raised a hand in greeting. The two boys waved back frantically, but the rider didn't stop.

"Their time isn't far off," Sofía said, watching the bike disappear up the arroyo.

"Oh, yes it is," Estelle replied quickly, and she laughed. "I'm going to be the original ogre mom when it comes to motorcycles."

"You believe that, do you?"

"Oh, *sí.* I have a short list, you see. And motorcycles are right up there at the top."

She watched Butch Romero careen northward, the new Christmas bike freshly shed of its red ribbons and already ingesting sand and dust. The Romero family lived two doors down the street from the Guzmans, and the parade of go-carts, old trucks, and tiny, dilapidated import cars trying to impersonate street rods were a constant source of entertainment for Francisco and Carlos.

"You may change your mind as he grows older," Sofía said.

"Por supuesto," Estelle replied. "I'm sure I will. When he's forty-five, he can buy anything he wants, even a motorcycle."

They walked for another ten minutes in companionable silence. The sun was still warm, but as it sank toward the San Cristóbal Mountains, the shadows jumped out in stark relief around each clump of prairie vegetation, creating a blanket of geometric patterns.

When he's forty-five, Estelle thought. Thirty-nine more years. What a career that might be. And in thirty-nine years, she'd be seventy-seven. Her mother would be long gone—Sofía, too. Estelle glanced at her husband's aunt with affection. Then again, maybe not. Sofía, a mere seventy-one, was the same age as Bill Gastner. Estelle could picture the boys' *Padrino* and Sofía at age 108, trading barbs. She shook her head, derailing that train of thought.

The yowl of the motorcycle drifted back to them, and out of habit, Estelle glanced up to make sure that Francisco wasn't standing in the middle of the arroyo bottom, blithely waiting for Butch Romero and his dirt bike to crash into him. After a moment, Estelle stopped and turned, cocking her head to listen. On his trip north, the teenager had obviously finished his familiarization run with the new bike. Now, he was flogging it for all it was worth, the pitch of the two-stroke strained and angry.

He appeared suddenly a thousand yards away, vaulting the bright yellow bike up and out of the arroyo as he followed a cattle trail, one that would bring him to the same rim path along which Estelle, Sofía, and the two boys walked. The arroyo curved in a long loop toward the east, and the bike hurtled along the trail toward them, dodging clumps of acacia and cholla.

Fifty yards away, he backed off and headed directly toward them, and Estelle stepped off the trail, Carlos now content to have his hand locked in hers. Butch rolled the bike to a stop, balancing on his right foot, and killed the engine.

"That's quite a bike," Estelle said. "Merry Christmas, Butch."

Romero pushed up his face shield, then tore at the helmet's chin strap. He pulled the helmet off, his hair caked from sweat, his narrow face flushed. It wasn't exhilaration on his face, though.

"Sheriff—" he turned and pointed north "—there's somebody back up there." He almost lost his balance, and twisted the handlebars sharply to catch himself. "I hit her, I think." Romero was breathing so hard it looked as if he might pass out.

Estelle stepped forward and rested a steadying hand on the boy's left forearm. "A person hurt, you mean?"

Butch Romero nodded and blinked rapidly. "She's dead, I think."

"Tell me exactly where."

The teenager turned and looked back up the arroyo. "See that grove of trees way up there?"

"I see the desert-willow clump right on the rim," Estelle said. "Where you came up out of the arroyo. Beyond that?"

"Way beyond. Go to them, then turn and follow the arroyo," Romero said. "You can just see the tops of them."

"Where the section fence turns east?"

"Beyond that. Maybe half a mile." He turned back to Estelle. "There's a spot where Highland Drive comes out and ends? It's paved for a ways and then it's all like dirt and stuff? And there's all those big old trees right there along the arroyo."

"She's down in the arroyo?"

"Yeah…there's some brush there, and a couple junk cars? You want me to take you up there and show you? Or you can take my bike."

"Ah, no, as a matter of fact. Thanks anyway. We'll get someone up there." She glanced at her watch and saw that it was five minutes after four. Ernie Wheeler would have taken over in dispatch, with Eddie Mitchell and Tony Abeyta on the road, hoping to finish off a quiet Christmas Day. Estelle walked several steps away, her back turned to her family and the teenager as she opened her cell phone.

Wheeler picked up the phone after two rings.

"Ernie, this is Estelle. We have a report of a possible body in the arroyo at the north end of Highland Drive. Who's central, Tony?"

"Yes, ma'am. Captain Mitchell is down in Regál with a minor MVA. Tony's standing right here, wishing he had something to do."

"Well, he's got it," Estelle said. "I'm on foot out behind Twelfth with my family and Butch Romero. He's the one who made the report, but we're a ways downstream. I need to walk the kids back home, and then I'll be up there as soon as I can. Tony needs to lock things up for me, and as soon as Eddie's clear, give him the heads-up, all right?"

"Ten four. Ambulance?"

"Go ahead and alert."

"Ten four. Just a second." She heard mumbled voices and then Wheeler came back on the line. "Tony's on the way. Tom Pasquale came off shift, but he's still here. He's in the conference room with Linda and Bill Gastner."

"Thanks. I'm on my way in."

She snapped the phone shut and turned to Butch.

"You want me to ride back up there?" he asked.

Estelle shook her head. "We'll go back home first." Sofía had Carlos in hand on the left, and Francisco on the right, and she had already started back down the trail toward home. "Butch, we may need to talk with you again. You'll be home later this evening?"

"Yes, ma'am."

"Okay. I need to hustle," she said, and reached out to shake Butch by the shoulder.

"I can go back up there and kinda keep an eye out until the cops get there, if you want," Butch offered.

"No...I don't want you to do that, Butch. One of the deputies will be there in just a minute. He'll be there quicker than you can make it back up the arroyo. You're sure it wasn't a manikin or something like that?"

Butch shook his head vehemently. "No, ma'am. No manikin." As if having second thoughts about being caught out on the darkening prairie with a corpse, he said quickly, "I'll go back with you guys, then." Estelle couldn't tell if he felt genuinely protective, or if he was spooked. A fourteen-year-old wasn't a necessary chaperone, but the two boys would enjoy it as he orbited them with his bike, making the quarter-mile hike back home an unexpected treat.

"Thanks, Butch. I appreciate that." She turned away as he kicked the bike into life. Sofía had a short head start, and Estelle jogged after her aunt and the two little boys.

"Sorry about this," she said as she fell into step with the group.

Sofía shrugged. "That's the way these things go…but how sad for someone."

Estelle nodded and looked hard at Francisco, who had broken away from his great-aunt's grip and was zigzagging through the bushes, watching Butch and the motorcycle blast across the prairie, the scout out ahead of the pioneers. "You don't go cruising, *hijo*," she said. "Stay with us." By the time they reached the arroyo crossing and were trekking through the Parkmans' backyard toward their own house, Butch had peeled away with a wave. Estelle scooped Carlos up as the little boy lagged, the fast thousand-yard walk taking its toll on his short legs.

Francisco reached the house first, and he burst inside with enough breath left to bellow to his grandmother, "Butch has a new bike, *Abuela!*"

"I'm so pleased to hear that," Teresa Reyes laughed.

Estelle hung Carlos upside down, lowering him headfirst to the foyer floor. "I need to go, *Mamá*."

"Ah, a bad day for someone else," the old woman said, settling back into her chair. "Is that what I've been hearing?"

Sure enough, her mother's hearing was keen. Far in the distance, Estelle heard the thin, high warble of a siren.

"Sorry, *Mamá*," Estelle said.

"Such a Christmas," her mother said.

ELEVEN

ESCUDERO ARROYO ORIGINATED at the base of Cat Mesa north of the village. During rare cloudbursts several generations before, rain had channeled and excavated a scar across the prairie that dodged this way and that, the trickle of water deflected by a cholla here or a greasewood bush there until the arroyo wandered like an old drunk.

In places where several tributary arroyos had joined forces, the gash was deep, a dozen feet down through sand and gravel to the original bedrock. One such deep cut swerved due west near the end of Highland Drive, a street that, despite its pretentious name, became nothing more than a rough, washboarded dirt two-track before dead-ending at the arroyo. Several retired concrete highway barriers had been dropped haphazardly on the arroyo lip to prevent preoccupied motorists from nosing over into the sandy depths.

Escudero Arroyo north of the village was one of those eyesores that a few million dollars and a willing Army Corps of Engineers could make go away. But until then, it was part of the landscape, an opportunity for kids with .22s, kids with dirt bikes, and folks too lazy to take their junk up to the official landfill.

Estelle parked her unmarked car on the pavement a hundred yards south of the arroyo, tucking in behind two other sheriff's units and Linda Real's tiny sedan. The back door of Tom Pasquale's Expedition was open, and the deputy was in the process of unsnarling a wad of yellow plastic ribbon. Halfway back from the arroyo, Deputy Tony Abeyta jogged down the center of Highland Drive toward them, head down and watching his feet.

Pasquale paused in his efforts with the tape as Linda appeared with her bulky camera case.

"Hey, the gang's all here," Linda said, the armor of her good humor refusing dents even during the worst of times. She smiled sympathetically at Estelle. "So much for peace and quiet, huh?"

"Oh, *sí*," said Estelle. "We're sure it's not a manikin or something?"

"I think we're sure of that," Pasquale said. He glanced around the side of the Expedition. "Tony's headed back now."

"Are we far enough back here?" Estelle asked. She turned to look south, down Highland toward the intersection with Twelfth Street.

"I don't think so. Maybe we're going to want to block things off farther back before things start gettin' all scuffed up," Pasquale said.

Tony Abeyta reached them, breathing hard. "Estelle, it's an adult female. The body's partly stuffed under one of those wrecked cars." He stopped and heaved a deep breath. "If I had to make a preliminary guess, I'd say either hit in the head with something, or shot. Can't see her face, but the hair on the back of her head is caked with blood."

"*Ay.*" Estelle thrust her hands in her jacket pockets. "Okay. Tom, let's put the tape across back there," and she nodded toward Twelfth. "Maybe you'd man the door for a while until we get the rest of the crew up here."

"Yes, ma'am."

"Did someone call Perrone?"

"I just did," Abeyta said. "I wanted to be sure." Even as he spoke, an ambulance swung into view, lights flashing.

Tom Pasquale slammed the back doors of the Expedition. "Did they get lost, or what?" He shook his head in wonder. "I'll head 'em off."

"We're probably going to need Mike, too," Estelle said, referring to Deputy Mike Sisneros, who until the consolidation had been one of the village officers. "Wasn't he at the office with you guys earlier?"

"He was," Linda Real said. "He and I were working on trying to reboot one of the computers, and then he and Janet were going over to his folks for dinner."

"Maybe we won't need him," Estelle said. "We'll see." She popped the trunk of her car and picked up a bundle of small surveyor's flags, each on its own slender wire. She waited until Pasquale had backed his patrol unit out of the way, then beckoned to Abeyta. "You all set?" she asked Linda. The photographer had already unlimbered one of her 35s, and was surveying the terrain through a wide-angle lens.

"You bet."

"Right down the middle," Estelle said. She handed Deputy Abeyta a bundle of flags, keeping half for herself. "Lead on," she said, and set off behind Abeyta, placing her steps in his.

The washboards and ruts of the two-track showed fresh vehicle tracks of several types. Highland Drive was a favorite access route for hikers wanting to reach the base of Cat Mesa, or for neckers in too much of a lustful rush to find somewhere more romantically elegant.

Twenty-five yards before the discarded concrete barriers, the path widened into a casual parking lot not quite large enough to swing the average vehicle around in a single maneuver.

Estelle stopped a dozen feet shy of the arroyo edge. Along

the arroyo, the prairie was rumpled, dotted here and there with the tough, stunted vegetation that could survive on eight inches of moisture a year. Over decades, cattle had grazed the sparse bunch grass to dust.

The terrain sloped slightly, and a dozen feet beyond the last concrete barrier, a grove of elms had managed to grab hold and flourish. No one had planted the trees. Perhaps a single seed had blown in, or had been part of a load of yard debris dumped over the side. The grove now provided the illusion of shade in the summer, the illusion that this was a secluded little park that broke through the dreariness of the prairie.

What could have been a picturesque spot with a commanding view of the jagged buttress of Cat Mesa to the north was instead commanded by junk. A selection of crushed cars, some old enough that they were rusted to an even russet patina, had been pushed over the arroyo bank, providing protection against the cut and surge of storm water. The car carcasses were decorated with a selection of snagged flood detritus, as well as a scattering of old tires, stoves, barbecue grills, and enough beer cans to start a museum.

At that point, the bottom of the arroyo was fairly wide, stretching out nearly sixty feet to the inside of the corner on the other side. The seasonal waters had tried to carve the outside of the sweeping course, keeping the arroyo bottom that lay beyond the average junkster's toss reasonably clear.

"There's a path over there on the left," Deputy Abeyta said.

"Okay," Estelle said. Linda stopped and her camera clicked. Estelle saw that one of the latest automotive contributions was the engineless, doorless carcass of a 1957 Oldsmobile, one heavily chromed winged fender still recognizable. The Olds lay skewed on its top, nose down, the crumpled front end crushed over the innards of the historical layer of metal underneath. The grille, missing its teeth and the chromed front bumper, dug into the sand of the arroyo bottom. The frame was either broken or bent, the engine and transmission missing.

As Estelle moved to the edge, Abeyta touched her on the arm and pointed. "Right down there."

"I see it." From under the mess of twisted and rusted steel, a single white arm extended, the hand palm-down and the fingers spread as if trying to caress the warm sand.

The undersheriff glanced at Linda, whose camera was eating through film at a furious rate.

"I climbed down over there," Abeyta said. He pointed eastward, where he had found a narrow slip through the trash. "Or, there's a cattle trail down into the arroyo a little further up the wash."

"Let's do that," Estelle said, and she followed the deputy east, around the last of the concrete barriers, past the final grove of elms, and then another thirty yards to where the lip of the arroyo had been caved in by cattle traffic. No human shoe-prints marked the bare dirt.

She scrambled down into the arroyo, staying near the north side of the cut, the width of the dry wash between her and the body. She saw the wiggly tracks that might have been left by Butch Romero's motorcycle. It looked as if he had blasted into the corner, cutting too close to the bank and the junked cars in his path.

"Linda?" Estelle called, and the photographer looked up. "Come down the same way we did. And I need these tracks. Especially where they come close to the front of the car."

"You got it."

"The kid on the motorbike says that he hit the victim's arm when he slid by on his bike. I'm not sure that he did, but we'll see."

"I walked straight along the bank," Deputy Abeyta offered, pointing at the other side of the arroyo. "Right along the very edge under all those tree roots. I'm thinking that it's not likely anyone else would stay so close to the bank."

"Good man." Estelle crossed the arroyo toward the corpse slightly upstream of the site, stepping carefully like a cat sneaking up on an unsuspecting finch. She saw, when she stepped gingerly over Butch Romero's fresh bike tracks, that the body wasn't actually *under* the car. Rather, it had slid down along the side of the inverted Oldsmobile, then tumbled into a narrow cave formed by the bashed-in roof of a late '40s vintage sedan.

"I stepped right across there," Abeyta said, and Estelle could see the loose indentations of his boots in the sandy gravel. "I bent down to see what I could, checked to make sure that she was dead, and then backed out. Nobody's been here in between."

Estelle stood quietly, surveying the tangle. She counted the remains of at least a dozen vehicles, including several from the 1940s, the peak of the rounded fender era. The Oldsmobile appeared to be the most recent addition, perhaps toppled into the arroyo within the decade.

With one hand for balance on the projecting frame member of the Olds, Estelle knelt down. She reached out and touched the woman's wrist. The flesh was cool and soft, and Estelle's pulse accelerated. She slid her index finger carefully under the victim's and lifted gently. The hand was completely limp, with no rigor.

"Tony?"

"Right behind you," Abeyta said.

"Make sure that Perrone is en route," she said. "If he can't break away, then we're going to need someone else ASAP. Dr. Francis should be flying in, and maybe we can speed things up. Okay?"

"Got it."

She let her body sink down, releasing her grasp on the Oldsmobile and repositioning her support hand on the yawning hole where the headlamp had once been.

The marks in the sand were clear. Unless the body had been moved since Butch Romero's motorcycle roared around the corner, the bike's tires hadn't actually touched the woman's hand or arm. Close enough, but no contact. The skin was unblemished. But at one point, the fingers had flexed, drawing short, vague lines in the sand—nothing desperate or repeated, but instead a single spasm, a single gentle raking as the last breath of life escaped.

"Linda, this is going to be tricky," Estelle said. She didn't look up, but sensed the photographer's presence nearby. "These marks—" she used a pencil to point toward the ends of the victim's fingers "—not much to see, but I think she was still alive when she was dumped here."

"I can do that," Linda said.

Estelle remained on her haunches for a long time, looking at the slender, white hand, the silky blond hair on the forearm, the delicate bend of the elbow. By ducking her head, she could see the cuff of the woman's short-sleeved blouse. A single dot of blood marked the yellow fabric near the right shoulder.

Again with a hand on the Oldsmobile for support, she skirted the projecting front fender. The car rested nose-down, its massive body at a 45-degree angle to the arroyo, crushed on top of a portion of an old sedan underneath. It looked as if a hard wrench with a crowbar could topple the Oldsmobile's carcass. Gingerly, she rocked the Olds to make sure that it was secure, then bent down, letting her back slide down the flat of the other, older sedan's crumpled door. She took her time, mindful of sharp metal.

"No way," she muttered.

"You okay?" Linda's shadow appeared off to her right.

"*I'm* okay," Estelle said. "But this whole thing is a long, long way from okay. There's no way."

"No way what?"

"I'm trying to imagine how she got here," Estelle said. "This doesn't make sense." She twisted and looked back up the side of the arroyo, through the tangle of junk. Drag a body to the edge and pitch it over, and it would tumble and flop, maybe catch on the Oldsmobile's chassis, maybe thud into the pocket of the older sedan's roof.

"Oh, man," Linda said, a perfectly natural reaction. Estelle didn't look at her, but sensed her presence as she drew closer.

"Oh, man is right," Estelle said. "I need to work my way in there a little."

She glanced at Linda and saw that the photographer's round, olive-toned face was uncharacteristically pale. "You okay?"

"Maybe," Linda said, and busied herself changing lenses on her bulky camera.

Estelle scrunched down as far as she could. The small cavern formed by the two crumpled cars was large enough for only one body. She saw that the victim was wearing a pair of designer blue jeans and a yellow blouse, with short white socks and expensive running shoes. From this new angle, Estelle could see that blood soaked the blouse over the woman's left shoulder, and her sandy blond hair was a matted mess of blood and dirt. Without moving the corpse, or without moving the car, there was no way to see the victim's face. If she had moved at all, the woman had managed to crawl forward somehow, into the cavity formed by the crushed firewall of the inverted Olds and the battered hindquarters of the old sedan. Then, with nowhere else to go, she had extended her right arm through the small hollow formed by the crumpled fender and the arroyo bottom—whether by unconscious spasm or the intent of a fading consciousness, it was impossible to tell.

Linda made a little noise, a faint hissed intake of breath, as if she'd stepped on a goathead, and Estelle crunched down so that she could turn to look at her.

"Not good," the undersheriff said.

"Estelle," Linda whispered, and her breath caught again.

"What?"

"That's Janet."

"What do you mean?"

"I recognize the blouse and jeans," Linda said. "That's what Janet was wearing this afternoon when she stopped by the office." When Estelle didn't respond, Linda added, "Mike's Janet."

TWELVE

ESTELLE COULDN'T MOVE. Now that a name had been supplied, she recognized Janet Tripp, and for a long moment, the under-sheriff simply froze, poleaxed by the turn of events. She didn't know Tripp well—only that she seemed like a sober, almost dour person with a sudden, rare sweet smile who'd stolen Deputy Mike Sisneros's heart a few months ago.

Janet Tripp hadn't hung around the Public Safety Building. She hadn't been a *Here's a box of cookies and platter of fudge for the deputies* person. She hadn't written supportive letters to the editor of the *Posadas Register*. She hadn't picked up Mike when his shift ended.

Estelle had seen Janet only rarely, and now that she thought about it, could count on one hand the times she had actually spoken to the young woman. She knew that Mike and Janet had planned to be married sometime later in the spring, but the couple had kept their plans to themselves, trying their best to avoid a department gala. Only because of relaying a phone call a month ago did she know that Janet was employed at A & H Welding and Supply in Posadas.

Other than that, Estelle knew nothing of the victim, and certainly not how Janet Tripp had come to lie dead under an old car on Christmas afternoon. But the implications that included Deputy Mike Sisneros were immediate and sickening.

For a time before Dr. Alan Perrone arrived, Estelle sat on

her haunches, back against the cool metal of the old sedan, looking at the woman. She was satisfied that she'd seen everything there was to see under the Oldsmobile, down its flanks, and in scuff marks across the top of the old sedan. As if sensing that the undersheriff wanted moments to herself, Linda Real had finished several rolls of film and several yards of videotape, then retreated back up to the parking lot, where Tony Abeyta put her to work. He had isolated seven different tire prints that were worth both photos and plaster casts. Anything that might have been shoe or boot prints were no more than worthless bruises in the dirt, without definition or distinctive shape.

Perrone arrived at 5:43 that afternoon, the light already failing enough to make work difficult. Estelle didn't hear his car, and turned with a start when his shoes crunched the gravel of the arroyo to her left.

"Hey," the physician said. "This is about the sorriest goddamn thing I've ever seen." He frowned at Estelle's expression. "You all right?"

Estelle pushed herself to her feet. "How's the chief?" she asked.

"Unchanged," he said. He bent over to examine what he could see of the hand and forearm. "Actually, I'm more inclined to say 'failing.' I get the impression that his system is just kind of caving in on itself, a little bit at a time. The family's with him, and that's good." He nodded at the victim. "How the hell do folks do it?" he said, more to himself than actually expecting an answer. "Do we know who this is?"

"We think it's Janet Tripp," Estelle said. She looked up to see both Captain Eddie Mitchell and Deputy Jackie Taber in quiet, intense conversation with Tony Abeyta. Mitchell caught Estelle's glance and raised a hand in salute, then broke away from the others and strode toward the cow trail down the bank.

"Janet Tripp," Perrone mused. "Do I know Janet Tripp? I think I do."

"Mike Sisneros's fiancée," Estelle said.

Perrone grimaced and his shoulders slumped. "Oh, you're kidding. That's ugly." He waited a moment, but when Estelle didn't say anything, added, "Let's have a look."

Short and wiry, Perrone maneuvered himself and his medical bag under the old car. "Okay," Estelle heard him say, and knew he was talking into a small tape recorder. "We've got a white female, maybe thirty-five years old." He droned on as he made the awkward examination, then said, "Estelle?"

"Sir?"

"What time was the body discovered?"

She had already done the mental calculations, estimating the time it had taken Butch Romero to roar first up and then back down the arroyo. "About 4:05," she said. "That's when I talked to dispatch after the neighborhood kid reported the body to me."

"About," Perrone mumbled. "Who found her? A kid, you say?"

"One of the neighborhood youngsters. Butch Romero? He was riding his bike up the arroyo."

"Ah, he of the broken arm," Estelle heard Perrone say to himself. The doctor had his own way of remembering patients. "Was he by himself?"

"Yes, sir."

"You're sure?"

"Yes."

"This young lady hasn't been here very long, you know," Perrone said.

"That was my impression," Estelle said. She rested her hand on the old sedan, keeping out of the way.

"I'm guessing, but I'd say one shot to the back of the head. Right through the mastoid behind the ear. And small caliber. I don't think we have an exit wound, but I'm going to have to wait for that to be sure. It's kind of awkward trying to do an examination here."

He shifted position with a middle-aged grunt. "Beyond that, I don't know. I don't think there's much more that I can tell you at the moment. I don't see any other injuries other than some scuffing that the fall down here might account for."

"Could she have survived for any length of time after being shot?"

A long silence followed, and then Perrone backed out from underneath the Oldsmobile. "Estelle, I can't answer that," the physician said. He nodded at Eddie Mitchell, who stood quietly to one side, looking down at Janet Tripp's hand. "All I can tell you is that a shot like that *usually* drops the victim like a sack of bricks. Remember RFK?" He tapped his own skull behind his left ear, touching the mastoid tuberosity. "No, you don't. But that's where he was hit. Down he went, boom. Didn't move a step or two past the point where he was shot. At least that's what all the famous pictures show. But he lived for several hours…what, almost a day, or something like that?"

He carefully adjusted a strand of blond hair that had fallen across his forehead. "You can imagine any wound you want, and there will be case studies where the victim lived for a while…seconds, minutes, hours, or long enough to heal and have a happy life. It all depends on how fast the blood pressure drops to zero, and how long it stays there without intervention." He shrugged.

"It looks as if she raked the sand with her fingers, Alan."

"She might have. Maybe just some reflex. Or maybe all the way to the other end of the spectrum. Conscious and looking for a way out. You're going to bag those hands carefully, I'm sure.

But a reflex movement is certainly not beyond what we might expect." He regarded his rubber gloves. Blood smeared the one on his right hand. "Much of the blood in her hair is comparatively fresh, Estelle. However this happened, it hasn't been long."

The undersheriff calculated backward. "Janet Tripp was seen alive early this afternoon," she said. "In our office."

"Well, then," Perrone said. "There you go." He nodded at the Oldsmobile. "I'm clear, if you want the EMTs to remove the body now. Francis is headed home, by the way. Did he get ahold of you?"

"Yes. The Med-Evac is going to drop him off."

"I chatted with him a few minutes ago—maybe half an hour before this call. He says that Bobby is feeling okay. Groggy, but okay. They've got him sedated and drugged and God knows what else. His blood will be as thin as distilled water right about now." He turned and saw Linda, squatting on her haunches out in the center of the arroyo, camera in hand, waiting. "Puzzles," he said cryptically. "I'm on my way, unless there's anything else."

"Thanks, Alan." She turned to Mitchell, who hadn't moved a centimeter since climbing down in the arroyo. He regarded her, his expression expectant.

"Merry Christmas," he said.

"Sure enough."

"Where's Sisneros? Has someone talked with him yet?"

"No." Estelle heard the shift, perhaps unconscious, in Mitchell's tone. The informal "Mike" was replaced with the flat, professional reference to "Sisneros." "Linda says that he went over to his folks' place for dinner."

"In Lordsburg."

"Yes."

"Without his fiancée." Mitchell's quiet, soft voice made

it sound like a simple statement of fact, despite the obvious implications.

"Apparently."

"How long?" He nodded at the victim.

"Linda saw her at the office in the early afternoon."

"Found at?"

"Shortly after four. By a kid riding a motorcycle."

Mitchell mulled that as he watched the three EMTs approach. He moved out of the way, giving them a parking place for the gurney. Matty Finnegan, who approached the front of the Oldsmobile warily as if it might be a den for rattlesnakes, hesitated and looked at Estelle.

"Okay to go?" she asked.

Estelle nodded. "There's a lot of sharp metal there. Be careful."

The three EMTs were careful, easing Janet Tripp's corpse out of its tiny resting place. "Good thing she ain't frozen up," EMT Eric Sanchez remarked at one point, and the comment earned him an acidic glare from Matty.

"Where do you want to start?" Mitchell asked as the gurney began the final trip up and out of the arroyo.

"It's just two hours," Estelle said. "That's in our favor. From the time Janet left the Sheriff's Department until she ended up here, maybe two hours. I was going to talk to Linda and get a closer estimate from her. But regardless, that's not much of a time window."

Mitchell looked at his watch. "And now it's a four-hour head start for somebody," he said.

"Or less."

"Or less. Did you talk to Bill yet?"

Estelle shook her head. "That's ahead. We need to know who was at the office, what time they left…anything that will help us narrow this down. How well did you know Janet?"

Mitchell shook his head. "Didn't. She and Mike weren't the most public couple in the world." He heaved a deep breath. "You want me to go get him?"

"Either you or me. I don't want him to find out about this from a phone call."

"I'll run over. You have enough on your plate."

"Thanks."

"This could be just some creep passing by, you know that, don't you?"

"Yes, it could. I think we're going to have some tire prints. We know that she was shot somewhere else and dumped here."

"Maybe right up there," Mitchell said, nodding at the rim of the arroyo.

"Maybe. No blood, but that doesn't mean anything." She stepped closer to the tangle of junk. "The scuff marks on the top of this car hint that the body slid down here, and then into that opening."

"Odd to be stretched out the way she was if that's what happened," Mitchell said.

"I think she moved some, Eddie. I think she was still alive. I can't picture the killer climbing down here and stuffing her farther in. Maybe that's what he did, but I can't picture it. I see him pushing her down into the junk, and when she slides into the gap between the cars, he's going to figure that's enough."

"Maybe."

"All he needs is some time to slip away."

"Then he doesn't care much if the body is found," Mitchell said.

"That's a little something that bothers me, Eddie. The body was *bound* to be found…maybe not in hours like it was, but certainly the odds were good, over time."

"Son-of-a-bitch is confident or careless, one or the other."

"That's the scary part. Dr. Perrone said that she was popped once, behind the ear. Small caliber, execution style. That's one thing. Then she's dumped out here. If this were the swamps of New Jersey or the bay shore of Chicago, I'd say 'gangland.'"

"Huh."

"Cold confidence," Estelle said. "Shoot and dump. That doesn't leave us much."

"That's the whole point, I would guess," Mitchell said. He twisted and looked up at the sky. "Clear tonight. You want some lights out here, or go over it again first thing in the morning?"

Estelle hesitated. "There's nothing magic out here, Eddie. That's what my first impressions tell me. Someone drove up, and we have tire tracks. Someone lifted Janet Tripp out of the trunk of a car, or the back of a pickup, and lugged her over to the edge. It'd be nice if we had a clear set of bootprints, but we don't...and I don't think a set is going to magically appear, either. Her body slid down here, and that's that." She shook her head. "We need to button this up, but I'm not sure we can afford to spend more time out here tonight. If we dillydally around, the trail's going to grow cold. Jackie's on shift, and there's nobody better to sit the scene until morning. We won't lose a thing. If you go to Lordsburg right now and bring Mike back, that'll be good. We need to talk with him and connect the dots there. While you do that, I'll sit down with Linda and really nail down what she remembers. And I'll do the same with Bill Gastner. Then we'll see where we are."

Mitchell hunched his broad shoulders against the growing chill as the heavy twilight crept across the prairie. "And there's that one nasty possibility, Eddie," Estelle said. "From what I've heard, Mike and Janet were planning to drive to Lordsburg together. They didn't. Mike went by himself. Janet ended up here."

Mitchell nodded morosely. "That's what I've been thinking." He scuffed the loose sand of the arroyo bottom with the toe of a polished boot. "Are you going to call the sheriff?"

"That's next on my list."

"Make sure Gayle is right there when you do. Otherwise he'll be out of bed, trying to find a taxi home." Mitchell reached out and tapped Estelle at the base of her throat, on the hard plane of her sternum. "And put on your vest, Undersheriff."

THIRTEEN

SHERIFF ROBERT TORREZ growled what might have passed for a greeting, and Estelle imagined him as embarrassed at having to talk on the telephone while lying half-naked and helpless in bed.

"I think they're going to unplug me in the morning," he said. "They aren't sayin' much except that I gotta stay overnight." As if feeling that he'd already passed along more information than necessary, he changed the subject. "What's up?"

"Bobby, Janet Tripp has been killed. Her body was found in the arroyo out on Highland Drive." Silence greeted that announcement, and after a few seconds Estelle added, "One of the Romero boys found the body late this afternoon while riding his motorcycle."

Torrez remained silent, and Estelle continued, assuming that the sheriff hadn't simply passed into an unresponsive, drug-induced fog. "It looks like she was shot once in the head, but we don't know anything more at the moment."

"Where's Mike?" Torrez asked, his voice husky. Estelle felt a twinge of relief. The sheriff wasn't so under the weather that he failed to recognize the heart of the matter.

"Eddie went to Lordsburg to pick him up," Estelle replied, and immediately realized that that was a poor choice of words. "We think he's at his parents' place. We wanted to break the news to him in person, and then make sure he gets back here safely. I don't think any of us knows how he might react."

Torrez grunted something incomprehensible, and it sounded like he was shifting in bed. Estelle heard Gayle's voice in the background.

"Janet didn't go over to Lordsburg with him?" Torrez asked. "Leave it alone," he added, apparently talking to Gayle. "Who was the last one to see her alive?" Torrez asked, breaking off his exchange with his wife.

"We're not sure yet, Bobby. Linda said that she, Bill, and Mike had been doing some preliminary organizational work this afternoon in the conference room. Linda says that Janet showed up for a few minutes around two or so."

"Okay. And then?"

"She left right after that, apparently."

"Mike went with her?"

"No. Linda says that he worked for a bit, then after a while left.... Linda assumes it was to go to Lordsburg to have Christmas dinner with his folks. That's what he had been planning, anyway."

"Huh. They have a fight or something?"

"We don't know yet, Bobby. Mike doesn't know anything about any of this yet." The sheriff didn't comment, and Estelle added, "At least we hope he doesn't."

"How long after Janet left the office was it before Mike went?"

"It couldn't have been long," Estelle said. "She was alive at two—and Butch Romero found her body at four or so. A lot can happen in two hours."

"That's for damn sure," Torrez said. "Lemme know later tonight what you find out, all right? What weapon was used, by the way? Could you tell?"

"Perrone says a small-caliber gun. By what I could see, I'd guess a .22, held close."

"Skull damage?"

"Entry, no exit, and not a whole lot of blood. Little or no back blast."

"Could have been a .25, even .32," Torrez said.

"Whatever it was, we think she was probably shot somewhere else, and then dumped. We're looking for her car right now."

"Huh. Did you talk with Bill yet?"

"No. Not yet. I'm headed that way."

Torrez exhaled what may have been a melodious growl of irritation or a hum of deep thought. "Huh," he said again. "So where was Janet headed when she left the office, if she wasn't goin' to Lordsburg with Mike?"

"We don't know."

"Linda doesn't know anything? She's always blabbin' with somebody."

"She wasn't sure what Janet's plans were.... It's one of those things, Bobby. She wasn't really paying attention to who was going where. But it seems to me that if Mike and Janet were planning to go to Lordsburg together, Mike would have gone looking for her when he was ready to go."

"Maybe."

"He wouldn't have just driven off without her, Bobby."

"And we don't really know that, do we? Somebody sure as hell drove off without her."

"Well—" Estelle hesitated "—we'd like to think that Mike wouldn't." Hard as it might be to start a nonexistent list of suspects with Mike Sisneros's name, Estelle knew that the sheriff was right. Everyone, whether cop or not, whether friend or not—everyone had secrets stashed in the closet.

Something that sounded like a bedpan clanging against the side rail of the hospital bed was followed by Gayle's voice, this time clear enough for Estelle to hear. "You're not supposed to mess with that," she said, and Estelle smiled.

"I'll check back with you in a bit, Bobby," she said. "We need to notify Janet's relatives. Mike may have to help us with that. I don't know her family."

"She's got a sister, I think," Torrez said. "Just a second." A short conversation followed between him and his wife, the phone covered. Then he came back on the line. "Gayle says that she thinks Janet has a sister somewhere in Oklahoma or Kansas...one of those places. Bill would probably know."

"Ah, he might. I'll ask him. I'll check back with you later, okay? Behave yourself."

"Call tonight," Torrez said, and Estelle could imagine how sidelined the sheriff must be feeling.

"*Sin duda,*" she said.

"Any change yet with Eduardo?"

"Nope. I'd like to say that he's holding his own, but I guess that's not the case. Perrone says he's just lingering."

"Huh."

Estelle thought that she detected a touch of wistful regret in that single syllable. "Let me talk with Gayle for a minute," she said.

"Tell her that I gotta get out of here," Torrez said, and then Estelle heard the soft thuds of the telephone being passed.

"Hey," Gayle said. "Estelle, what happened? You're saying Janet Tripp was killed?" Her tone carried enough shock and disbelief to more than make up for her taciturn husband's gruff calm.

"Earlier this afternoon, Gayle. And that's all we know."

"How awful."

"I wanted to ask you...when Mike was working in the conference room earlier in the week, was Janet there any of the time?"

"Two or three times," Gayle said. "She's been in and out quite a bit the last couple of days."

"That shows how much I've been paying attention," Estelle

said. "Was there anything going on between her and Mike that you could tell? Any friction? Any arguments?"

"They're always lovey-dovey, Estelle. Well, in their own quiet way, they are. In fact, Bill mentioned to Mike a day or two ago that now that they've started on the project, he didn't want anybody else who wasn't actually working on it to be in the conference room. I guess Bill must have thought that Janet was going to end up sitting on Mike's lap or something. *Por Dios,*" Gayle murmured, "this is awful. Have you talked with Mike yet? How's he taking it?"

"Let her get back to work," her husband's voice groused in the background.

"No, I haven't," Estelle said. "Eddie's on the way to do that right now. And Gayle…I'm sorry to have bothered you guys by calling, but Bobby really needs to know."

"Please," Gayle said quickly. "This will give him something to stew about so he won't take it all out on the nurses. I wish I could help more with the sister, but all I know *is* that there is one, and I think she's in the Midwest somewhere."

"Mike will know. I'll call back in a bit. You guys take care."

She switched off the phone and walked outside to her car. The drive to the end of Highland Court took two minutes, and as she reached the end of the pavement, Estelle saw Jackie Taber's unit parked fifty yards off to the side, tucked under a spray of junipers that had sprung up beside the foundation of a small shed.

The sedan bumped and pitched as she idled across the prairie so she could park window-to-window.

"Need a break?"

"I'm fine," the deputy said. "It's very, very quiet."

"I brought the sheriff up to date, and we should be hearing from Eddie in a few minutes. I'm going to talk with Bill here in a little bit and then visit with Linda again. Everybody else is trying to track down Janet's car."

"If they stole her car and headed to Mexico, they're long gone."

"Most likely. But I put in a call to Naranjo's office in Asunción and passed on the information to the *judiciales*. We'll see."

Her cell phone beeped and she flipped it open. Bill Gastner's gruff voice greeted her.

"Merry Christmas, sweetheart," he said. "I heard."

"Sir, I was just setting out to track you down."

"I figured as much." He sounded weary. "You at the office?"

"No, but I can be in a few minutes."

"Let's have some peace and quiet. How about a cup of that awful tea that you drink? Over at the house. Mine, that is."

"That sounds good. But give me fifteen minutes, okay? I want to stop by the hospital and see what Perrone has for us. Linda's over there finishing up with her photos."

"That'll work. It'll give me a few minutes to finish eating and then go home and figure out how to boil water."

"Good luck with that," Estelle said. "If something comes up, I'll let you know."

"Enough's come up to last a lifetime, sweetheart. This is a goddamn Christmas Day for the record books. See you in a little bit."

Estelle switched off and shrugged at Jackie. "If you come up with any interesting theories, I'd like to hear them."

"I'm working on it," the deputy said.

Estelle drove out of Highland Court wishing that she could force herself to sit still and let the evidence roam around in her mind until something clicked. Even a flash of intuition would have been nice.

In the reserved staff parking at Posadas General she found Linda Real's tiny, aging Honda nestled in beside Alan Perrone's elegant BMW. Entering through the Emergency Room doors, she made her way downstairs. Lights were on in the Coroner/Deputy State Medical Examiner's office, but the door was locked. Estelle continued down the hall toward a set of double security doors and touched the blue pad on the wall. The doors swung open, and she saw that the morgue lights were on.

She rapped on the stainless steel door and waited, watching the small speaker by the door as if the words would somehow appear there in print.

"Yes?" Perrone sounded officious and peeved.

"It's Estelle, sir."

"Oh, good. My office is open. Get yourself duded up. Yellow cabinet."

"I'll be right back."

"Door's open," Perrone said.

Estelle returned to Perrone's office and found the tall yellow cabinet as organized as everything else in the physician's life. She donned a blue mesh cap that encapsulated her hair from forehead to the nape of her neck, a long plastic disposable gown, blue booties, and latex gloves. The stainless-steel doors opened soundlessly at the press of another "elbow" button, and she saw the similarly garbed Linda standing close beside the medical examiner, bending slightly at the waist to focus her bulky camera on something to which Perrone pointed with a probe.

"Come and look at this," Perrone said. Linda looked up from the camera and stepped back.

"How are you doing?" Estelle asked. Linda had a brave face painted on, but she was even more pale than earlier, out at the arroyo.

"Okay," the photographer said, and she shook her head. "If I just look through the camera, I do all right." She waved a hand toward Janet Tripp's shrouded body, now facedown on the table. "It's hard to believe that just a little while ago…" She let her voice trail off.

"Estelle, you'll be wanting this," Perrone interrupted. He swept a small plastic evidence bag off the stainless-steel table beside him. "Twenty-two hollow point, in three fragments." He held the bag out to Estelle. "Nothing unusual there. The bullet traveled from left to right, and the major fragment struck the inside of the cranium just above the right eye. That's an uphill trajectory, and we can assume several scenarios." He paused for breath. "First, the shooter might have been left-handed. I'm not saying he was," he added quickly. "But he could bring up the gun and shoot, and the bullet goes in behind the left ear and comes to rest over the right eye." He shrugged. "He could have been standing behind her, his gun hand a little lower than her ear. Or, she could have been sitting down, head bowed forward. The killer could have shot from behind, either right- or left-handed."

"If she'd been sitting in her car…" Estelle offered.

"That's possible. But its being a .22 is going to give you trouble. The most common round in the world. And fragmented so that marks are difficult." He beckoned Estelle closer, and the odd, cloying smell of death rose like a curtain. "The gun was held either right against her skull, or very close…a fraction of an inch. Right there." He touched the victim's skull just behind the left ear. "Some characteristic powder stippling, singed hair, nice corona."

Estelle bent down. Janet Tripp's hair was a rich blond, truly the color of clean, fresh oat straw. She had worn it short and casual, the sort of easy style that fell into place with a shake of the head. Now, the hair around her left ear was caked with blood and particulate.

The coroner glanced at Linda, who was studiously examining the far wall.

"Nothing else of interest, Estelle," Perrone said. "Nothing under her fingernails except some arroyo sand. She wasn't assaulted, or struck, or anything else. Her clothing was intact, and only as disarranged as we might expect from being carried and then dumped. The only blood on her clothing was on the left shoulder and upper left back of her blouse, along with a spot or two on the right. I wish I could hand you something on a platter, but I can't."

"We'll see," Estelle said. "Have you fixed a time of death?"

"I examined her at four forty-five. I would guess that she had been dead less than an hour."

"*Less* than an hour?"

"That's right. Butch Romero doesn't know what a lucky kid he is. If he hadn't lingered over another piece of fruitcake before going riding, he might have ridden into something pretty nasty."

"*Ay*," Estelle murmured. "That close."

"That close."

"Will you process the film tonight?" she asked Linda.

"Sure.

"And I'll get started on everything else," Perrone said. "Toxicology, whatever. I'll be surprised if anything comes up. I don't have a whole lot of lab equipment here. There's a few simple things I can do, but I think we're going to end up waiting for the state lab to mull things over. And with the holiday, don't hold your breath."

Estelle grimaced.

"Is Mike back yet?" Linda asked.

"On the way, I think." Her cell phone rang, obscenely loud in the tomblike hush of the morgue.

"Guzman."

"Estelle, it's Pasquale. We found Tripp's car."

FOURTEEN

THE MOMENT ESTELLE SAW Janet Tripp's Jeep Liberty, a small piece of the puzzle, a very small piece, leaped into focus. The little blue SUV was parked in one of the diagonal slots at Posadas State Bank, just a few steps from the automatic teller machine, the only operation of the bank that remained open on Christmas Day. The ATM was inside a small glassed-in foyer, available for foot traffic only.

If Janet had been headed for the ATM, she would have pulled in, parked, and walked across the small parking lot to the foyer. The Jeep was parked precisely as one might expect if that had happened.

Estelle's heart raced at the possibilities. She knew that ATM transactions were routinely videotaped, and if they were lucky, the small camera in the foyer might actually be working.

Deputy Tom Pasquale stood beside his unit, leaning against the front fender, arms crossed over his chest. He watched Estelle drive in and stop, but he didn't approach, giving her time to look at the scene without interference. Estelle remained in her car for a moment. She pictured the Jeep pulling into the lot, pictured Janet choosing a parking spot that provided easy access to the ATM, and then easy out. She would have reached across to the passenger seat for her purse, or perhaps unzipped a fanny pack to find her ATM card.

If robbery was the motive, the killer—if he had half a

brain—would have waited until Janet had visited the ATM, and approached her as she returned to the car with ready cash. Had he—or she—been parked toward the rear of the bank's lot, waiting for a likely candidate?

Another possibility lay in Pershing Park, just across the street, perhaps a hundred steps from where Janet had parked. It would have taken just seconds to cross the street and the parking lot, stealthily on athletic shoes. Janet might not have heard a thing.

Estelle twisted in her seat and surveyed the park. The old tank, moldering on its concrete pedestal, the wheat-colored grass, the small gazebo, the dozen elms that all depended on village water—the place was far from being a garden spot. But it did provide a choice of cover.

A second question nagged Estelle. An obvious possibility was that Janet had been assaulted for her money. The opposite possibility was that someone had assaulted Janet Tripp because of who she was.

She turned back to the Jeep. Whatever the circumstances, it was easy to imagine the bullet's path into Janet Tripp's skull from the left quadrant, and then the projectile's path slightly upward through her brain. And the attack was as cold-blooded as any underworld execution. The victim may have heard a small click or two and then...nothing.

Estelle pulled her car into gear and backed up, swinging it around to block the entry driveway to the bank's parking lot. She shut it off and stepped out. As she did so, Pasquale pushed himself away from his backrest. Despite his best efforts, a grin spread across his broad face. During his short career with the Posadas County Sheriff's Department, he had suffered plenty of uncomfortable, sometimes embarrassing, stumbles and blunders. Doing something right was always refreshing—for both him and his colleagues.

"I didn't touch anything," the young man said as Estelle approached. "I knew it was Janet's SUV the minute I saw it, but I ran the plate just to be sure."

"Good work." She took a few steps toward the SUV and stopped. "What's the chime?"

Pasquale looked puzzled. "The what?"

"I hear bells, like someone left on their lights, or the key in the ignition, or the door ajar."

"Oh. I don't hear it. Maybe they did. You want me to check?"

"No," she said quickly as he started to turn toward the victim's car. She approached slowly and stopped a dozen yards from the Liberty's back bumper, turning to regard the bank. Situated on Pershing Avenue just a stone's throw from Bustos, the main east-west drag through the village, the bank was anything but secluded. The ATM foyer, no more than ten feet square, was on the east end, nothing more than a porch enclosed with tinted glass, one exterior door, and no interior entrance to the bank proper.

Estelle looked back toward the street. Since she had pulled into the parking lot, not a single car had passed on either Bustos or Pershing. No one was in the park. The village was as quiet as only early Christmas evening could be—people full of too much food, lots of football on television, and plenty of gifts whose newness had yet to wear off. Company wasn't heading home yet.

Deputy Tom Pasquale waited quietly, in itself something of an accomplishment. "Tomás, Tomás, Tomás," Estelle said, and smiled at him even as she saw the look of uncertainty cross his face. "You didn't look inside the car?"

"I did not approach the vehicle," Pasquale replied formally, as if he were reading from one of his academy texts, shaking his head for emphasis.

She nodded with satisfaction. "I think we need to call

Sergeant Mears, Tomás." She took a step toward the SUV. "And…who do we have left?"

"Ah…"

"Exactly," Estelle said. She ran down the mental list. The sheriff was flat on his back in Albuquerque. Captain Mitchell was somewhere between Lordsburg and Posadas, hopefully with Mike Sisneros in tow. Jackie Taber was guarding one crime scene, and she and Pasquale were at another. "We need to call Tony back in. And Dennis is supposed to work graveyard tonight, right? Assuming he gets back from Phoenix in time."

"Yes, ma'am."

"Well, he can start work early if he does. We're going to need all the crew we can scrounge up, Tomás." She started toward the SUV. "Oh…and Linda. She's at the morgue right now. But the minute she's finished up there, we're going to want her over here." Pasquale nodded and turned to his unit to make the calls. "And I want this entire parking lot cordoned off. When the others get here, they can park out on the street."

The Jeep's front door was closed, but not fully latched. Estelle approached one step at a time, watching her footing on the clean asphalt. The insistent *bong, bong, bong* came from inside the vehicle, but she ignored it. It would continue until either the door was shut, the key was taken from the ignition, or the battery went dead.

Even though the sodium vapor lights around the parking lot were bright and harsh, she used her flashlight as well. Five feet from the driver's door, she saw the first dime-sized blotch of brown crust on the black tar, and breathed another fervent prayer of thanks that Tom Pasquale hadn't just clumped over to the SUV, obliterating evidence as he went.

She laid her flashlight on the pavement beside the blood

droplet and walked back the way she had come. Tom was standing by his Expedition, talking on the phone with dispatcher Ernie Wheeler, and when he glanced at Estelle, she gave him a thumbs-up. From her own car she retrieved her large field case and returned. Careful that there was nothing else to disturb, she traced a bold circle of white chalk around the blood droplet. Between that spot and the Jeep, she circled four more splotches of blood, one as large as a silver dollar.

"What can I do?" Pasquale asked. "Everyone is on the way except Collins. Ernie's still trying to get ahold of him."

Estelle remained kneeling, sorting through her options. "We need to call the State Police again and fill them in, Tomás. They were alerted that we had a homicide, but now that we've got Janet's car, they don't want to waste time looking for that. That's one thing off the list. And we might ne their mobile CSI unit. I'm not sure yet."

"Be nice if we knew what we should be looking for," Pasquale said.

"Yes, it would." She turned, looking back along the trail of bloodstains. "See the first circle of chalk?" Pasquale nodded. "We have a line of blood droplets leading from the Jeep. I'm assuming *from*, anyway, at this point. Okay?" Pasquale nodded again. "I need to know where that line of blood ends, Tomás." She reached out her arm, pointing in line with the ragged trail of five white circles.

"You think she was shot in the car and then carried out?"

"I don't know what to think yet. That's what we're going to find out."

She rose, moving closer to the SUV. The driver's window was rolled up. Estelle looked at the door critically. It was almost latched, caught on the last notch before chunking completely closed. The bell continued its gentle reminder. Nothing marred the new vehicle's paint job, a light blue against which blood smears would have contrasted like neon.

Using her flashlight to eliminate shadows and hiding spots, Estelle worked her way around the outside of the Jeep and found nothing…no marks, no dings, no dents, no bullet holes. The hood was cold to the touch, as was the tailpipe.

The killer hadn't fired through the window glass. Had he done so, it was likely that he would have had to shoot more than once. The heavy safety glass could easily deflect a .22 slug. That meant that either the window was open, or the door was. Had Janet Tripp just returned to the Jeep from the ATM, it was entirely possible that the door might be open while she fumbled with purse, keys, and seatbelt.

Without touching the door, Estelle played the flashlight around the interior, aided by the dome light. A purse lay on the passenger's seat, the top of the southwestern beaded fabric unzipped. A wallet lay on the floor in front of the seat. She saw that the Jeep had electric windows. The key was in the ignition, turned to the off position.

"Okay," Estelle whispered. This assailant hadn't just reached in and grabbed Janet's wallet from her hands…or rapped her on the head, or struggled with her in any way. From all appearances, he had padded up behind her while she sat in the car and popped her once through the brain, willing to risk a murder charge for a few bucks. The hair on the back of Estelle's neck rose.

"Tape's up," Pasquale said, and Estelle startled. "Sorry," the deputy said. "Lieutenant Adams said to let you know that he's alerted his guys. He said that if you need his CSI team, just let State Police dispatch know. And I found one more blood droplet, about four feet from the last one you marked. That's all, though."

"Good. Look, tell me something," she said.

"What?"

"Why would he shoot her here, and then bother to move the body?"

Pasquale's eyebrows furrowed quizzically. "Lots of reasons."

"If the killer was just after the money that Janet removed from the ATM, then why not just take it and be off? As quiet as it is tonight, who's to notice her car, or even if they do, wonder enough to look inside? She'd slump over and be invisible to a casual passerby."

"Well, we'd notice," Pasquale said. "There's no reason to park here at the bank. We'd kind of wonder when we went by on routine patrol and saw the vehicle, wouldn't we?"

"I hope that we would. Then, we'd call in the license and find out that the car belonged to Janet Tripp. And then, knowing that she's Mike's girlfriend, we'd shrug and let it go."

"I think that's just about *exactly* what I would do—if we hadn't found her body in the arroyo earlier."

"Exactly. You wouldn't look inside?"

"Well, I might." He nodded. "Sure...I guess I probably would, with the car parked at a bank."

"And if she's not in it..."

"I'd do what you said."

"Even if you saw her purse and what appears to be her riffled wallet lying on the seat and floor?"

Pasquale craned his neck to see past Estelle to the interior of the Jeep. "Well, sure. I'd wonder about that."

"Yes, you would. I would too. What would you do?"

"I guess I'd try to contact her on the phone to make sure that she was all right. And when she didn't answer, I guess that I'd probably call Mike. She's with him more often than not, anyway."

"Doing all that takes some time, doesn't it. And that's *if* you stopped in the first place to check the car. A unit this new might well belong to one of the bank officers, here to do a little extra work. And that's *if* you stepped out of your unit to look inside it, once you ran the computer check."

"Well, sure."

"And all that changes if we find the car, look inside, and see a corpse, right?"

Tom Pasquale laughed. "Well, sure." he said.

"So it might be worthwhile for the shooter to take the body and dispose of it to gain some time—maybe even after weighing the risks of being seen."

Another county Expedition squealed to a stop at the curb on Pershing, and a slender man in jeans, checkered flannel shirt, and baseball cap got out. "Ah, here's Tom One," Estelle said, referring to Gayle Torrez's habit of calling Mears and Pasquale the Two Toms. Sergeant Tom Mears ambled to the yellow tape that Pasquale had stretched from the front door of Estelle's sedan to the front door handle of the bank. He stopped there, and Estelle beckoned, swinging her arm in a big circle to the left that would steer Mears well clear of the blood droplets.

When he saw the chalked circles, he angled inward and stooped to examine them. "You're kidding," Mears said, straightening up and scrutinizing the small vehicle. "Kinda bizarre, don't you think?"

"Oh, *sí.*"

"If that's her blood, it kinda gives us a link," Mears said.

"I think so. I mean, it's Janet's car, it's her *only* car, and it's logical for her to have been in this spot. If she was going to Lordsburg with Mike Sisneros, then she might have wanted some cash along. But that was early this afternoon. She didn't do that. She had other plans, same answer."

"*Was* she going to Lordsburg?"

"We don't know yet, Tom. We've got conflicting versions so far. Eddie went over there to talk to him."

"He doesn't know about Janet, then. That's no good."

"No."

The other Tom made a noise that might have been a cough, a groan, or a strangled chuckle. "Unless…," he said meaningfully.

"Yeah, unless," Mears said. "But I don't even want to think about that." He glanced toward the street as one of the department's Crown Victorias rolled to a stop behind his unit. "Here's Abeyta. Let's see what our three great minds can come up with."

"There's four of us here," Pasquale observed, stepping into the trap with alacrity.

"Uh-huh," Mears said, and his thin face broke into a smile. "Process of elimination then, right?" He turned toward the Jeep. "One thing we want to be aware of right off," he said. "If she was in the car when she was shot, and the shooter was standing by her door, then…" He paused.

"Perrone said the bullet struck her just behind the left ear, low on the mastoid, and ranged forward and up, Tom. It didn't break out of the front of her skull."

"That's not surprising. The gun was close to her skull when fired, right? That's what Abeyta said." He reached out and rested a hand on Tony Abeyta's shoulder for emphasis as the deputy joined the group. "Then we want the shell casing, guys."

"What if it wasn't an automatic?" Pasquale asked.

"Then we don't get the casing," Mears said easily. "But if it was, then the gun tossed it out to the right, or straight up—unless the shooter held it Hollywood 'gangsta' style. The empty case would either glance off the back window glass, or some other part of the car, or…" He peered toward the Liberty. "Is that the ignition warning that I'm hearing?"

"Yes," Estelle said. "Key's there, door's ajar."

Mears nodded. "If she was leaning forward, like maybe she was picking something off the floor, or just looking down at her lap, and the gun was pressed to her skull, then the casing might be inside here."

"Unless he picked it up," Pasquale said.

"Stranger things have happened," Mears agreed. "Stranger things have happened. But for now, I want everything that's on the ground—under, beside, off in the brush somewhere. Don't just grind stuff into the asphalt with your big feet. Pay attention." He turned to Estelle. "Do we know how much she got from the ATM? Do we know if she even made a withdrawal?"

"Not yet. No one's touched anything inside the car. I haven't even opened the door."

"Then let's do the simple things first," Mears said. "That wallet and purse should tell us a few things. That's where I want to start."

FIFTEEN

IF JANET TRIPP HAD withdrawn money from the ATM at Posadas State Bank, there was no record of it in the Jeep. There had been no money or papers in her clothing when it was searched at the morgue. There was no cash in her wallet, no credit cards, no driver's license, no ATM receipt, no nothing. Her purse held an assortment of typical personal items of no particular value, but nothing that made Estelle pause.

"Good surface for prints," Mears said as he dropped the glossy black leather wallet into an evidence bag. "But I'll be surprised. She was hit by somebody who knew exactly what he was doing. He's not going to butter everything up with his fingerprints." He looked at Estelle, who was crouched at the passenger side, in the open door. "What?"

"I don't understand the fit," she said.

"The fit? Of what?"

"If this is a typical robbery—if someone had the ATM staked out and wanted to make a score—why choose Christmas Day, why then *shoot* the victim, and why remove the corpse, other than to buy himself some time?"

Mears shrugged. "I don't know, Estelle. Christmas Day is dull, without a lot of traffic. But maybe he figured that whoever stopped would be flat busted from last-minute shopping, and be more apt to withdraw a larger amount?" He grinned. "If you've already dug yourself a financial hole with too much

Christmas shopping, what's the harm of adding a little bit more to it? How's that for far-fetched. Hell, I don't know why. Maybe my brilliant brother has a theory."

"And we need to call him, too," Estelle said. Terry Mears, Tom's twin brother, was vice-president of Posadas State Bank.

"Shooting the victim in the head," Mears continued, "is a pretty sure way of making certain that she doesn't talk, that's pretty obvious. And you're probably as close as anybody about why he moved the body. Or maybe he was thinking that a little nasty-time recreation with her might be in order. You know how these things can go."

"Casing!" Tony Abeyta shouted. He had been working far to the right side of the Jeep, on his hands and knees close to the edge of the asphalt. He stood up suddenly, as if he'd crawled too close to a rattlesnake. Estelle saw that the single .22 long-rifle cartridge case rested in the channel between asphalt and the soil of the border garden.

Estelle looked back to the Liberty. "If that's the one, the gun ejected it right over the roof of the car," she said. "That's quite a toss."

"I have a bag," Abeyta said, but Estelle held up a hand.

"Don't move it until Linda takes the photos, Tony. And we don't know for sure if this is the one. So measure about four times, okay? Mark it with a flag, then just leave it alone."

"You got it."

Estelle moved off to one side and opened her phone. In a moment, Linda answered, her voice sounding small and far away.

"Hey," Estelle said. "Are you okay?"

"Oh, I guess so. I'm down in the darkroom."

"Ah." Estelle knew that it was one thing, out in the open with others to provide support, to deal with death and destruction, especially if the victim was family. But it was worse to watch the grotesque images appear out of the chemical bath, ghostly apparitions that gazed up out of the developer tray in the hushed and musty tomb of the lonely downstairs darkroom.

Linda Real usually handled such things with aplomb and good humor. The rules changed when violent death became personal, taking a step closer.

"I wanted to finish up the black and whites," she said. As standard procedure, she took triplicate photos, one set in black and white that she could develop herself, a set with another camera in color—film that would have to be sent out for processing, with both the attendant risks and delays—and finally finishing up with digital shots for instant reference.

"We found Janet's car, Linda. As soon as you can break loose…"

"I'm on my way."

"We're in the bank parking lot."

"Gotcha." Linda sounded as if she might revive. "I could use a little air."

Estelle returned to the Jeep. "Do you want to call your brother, or do you want me to?" she asked the sergeant.

Mears laughed. "I'll get him. He's just sitting in front of the television, anyway, fat and happy."

Estelle knew that at least half of that wasn't the case. Both Tom and Terry Mears were angular, slim, and barely average height. "I want to know if Janet withdrew anything from her account…and how much. There should be a time on the ATM slip, shouldn't there?"

"I would think so. I don't use 'em, so I can't tell you for sure. Bro's going to ask for a court order, you know."

"*Ay*, I was afraid of that. Well, tell him that we'll need to look at the ATM transaction tape, and also at the video. In the meantime, I'll go get the paperwork from Judge Hobart."

"Better you than me," Mears said. "By the way, I'll use the black light to make sure, but I don't think we have any blood spatters in the vehicle itself."

"That's surprising," Estelle said.

"Nah, not really. Not with a .22. Pops a nice hole, not much blow-back, not much in the way of bone chips on the outside. Plays hell on the *inside,* but not otherwise. But we'll see." He knelt down by the Liberty's running board and looked up toward the driver's window, then played his flashlight upward at the soft, finely textured fabric head liner.

"We might get lucky and find some powder residue on the liner," Mears added.

"And if you'll get your brother, I'll see about the warrant." She glanced at her watch, remembering her promise to former sheriff Bill Gastner. What was supposed to be fifteen minutes had mushroomed into an evening. "I was going to talk to Bill about what happened in the office earlier this afternoon, but I never made it. I'll get him to go with me to Hobart's. That'll mellow the judge down some."

"Linda's on the way?"

"Yes."

"Good. We need to impound this puppy, too. Get it over into the secure barn so nobody dinks with it," Mears said, and shook his head. "We're going to have a long, long list of folks wondering about whatever happened to their nice holiday."

"Remind them that Janet Tripp can't wonder about anything anymore," Estelle said. Far off to the north, she heard the moan of an aircraft, and her own spirits rose. As it approached fast and direct, she could tell that it was a twin jet-prop. "And that has to be the air ambulance," she said. "I need to pick up Francis at the airport."

"Merry Christmas," Mears said.

"People keep telling me that. If I hear it long enough, I might start believing it."

Back at her car, she opened the door and removed the plastic crime-scene tape that Pasquale had strung up, repositioning it to Mears's unit. Then she headed to the airport, six miles away at the foot of Cat Mesa. By the time she arrived there, the Piper Navajo had parked, its engines spooling down to idle. Estelle left her car at the chainlink gate and walked out across the tarmac toward the air ambulance. In a moment, Francis gingerly made his way down the little folding steps from the plane, turning to wave at whomever was inside. The moment he was around the wing and clear, the engines shrieked, the nose wheel cocked sharply to the left, and the Navajo surged back out to the taxiway.

"Smooth as silk," Francis said. "Flying at night is neat, *querida*."

"I'll take your word for it, *oso*." She snuggled into his arms and enjoyed her own airborne moment as her "bear" swung her around, her feet well clear of the ground.

"How's it going?" he whispered in her ear.

She sighed. "Not good, *oso*. Not good. And it's not going to improve much, either."

"What's going on? I phoned Alan, and he said Eduardo was slipping. He also said you had a homicide of some sort. We had a bad connection, and I didn't get the details."

"A homicide of *some* sort," Estelle repeated. "We have the kind where someone's been killed to death." But she didn't smile, and neither did Francis. He saw the look of misery in her eyes and lowered her until her feet touched the ground. "Someone I know?"

"I don't think so. Janet Tripp? She's Mike Sisneros's girl-friend."

"My God. This happened just this afternoon?"

"Yep." She took his hand as they walked back to the county car. "Remember Butch Romero?"

"Sure."

"He found the body in Escudero Arroyo."

"Wow."

"One gunshot to the head. Just dumped in a tangle of old cars. Nothing else. It's looking like she was attacked over at Posadas State Bank, and then dumped in the arroyo afterward." Francis tried to settle his bulk in the passenger seat and yelped as he cracked his knee against the computer that grew out of the center console in front of the radios. "Let me fold that out of your way," she said.

He thumped his left elbow against the shotgun in the rack between them. "You need some more junk in this car," he said. "It's a miracle that it has enough power to move."

"We don't get a lot of passengers up front," she said. *"A veces no está en situación de exigir nada."*

"Your mother says that," Francis said as Estelle backed the car away from the gate. "Her version of 'Beggars can't be choosers.'"

"She says lots of things. And after today, she's going to be at her acid best," Estelle said. "I haven't been home since 4:05 this afternoon, and we haven't even started yet."

"Any good leads?" Francis settled with one hand looped through the panic handle as the car accelerated hard on the highway toward Posadas.

"It's bizarre," Estelle said. "And no...nothing that sends us in any particular direction. That's the trouble." She paused as she let the car drift toward the center line as they raced around the sweeping corner, and then pushed hard through the intersection with County Road 43. "Every minute that we dawdle, the killer puts more miles between him and us."

Francis leaned over the center console equipment, gazing at the speedometer. "Dawdle has a new definition in this household," he said.

"If I could figure out a way to be in three places at once, I'd try it," Estelle said.

"Alan's doing the autopsy?"

"As we speak. I just came from there a little bit ago."

Francis looked hard at her. "Is there anything that makes you suspect the deputy? The boyfriend?"

"*Por Dios,* I hope not," Estelle sighed. "But we can't be sure. Not yet. Eddie went over to Lordsburg to get him."

"Bizarre," Francis said.

"Oh, *sí.*"

"Sofía is okay with the two terrors?"

"She's in heaven…or so she says. We were all out for a nice afternoon walk when Butch found the body. And then he found us. That ended the nice walk."

They swung into the hospital parking lot where Francis's vehicle had been left. "You going home now?" he asked.

Estelle shook her head. "I can't, *querido.* I need to talk with *Padrino* about this afternoon. He's one of the last people to see Janet alive." She glanced at her watch. "And I was supposed to do that hours ago." She rested her forehead against his, the two of them bent over the junk between their seats.

"Be hard as hell to make out in this car," Francis said.

"That's what the back seat is for." Estelle laughed.

"I need to check on Eduardo," he said, and tipped his head back until their lips met.

"Do what you can for him."

"Oh, for sure," he replied. "And I'll check in with Alan and see what he needs."

"Maybe next week sometime, we can get together for a while and pretend that we have a life."

"It's a deal." He opened the door and pushed himself out. "Be careful, *querida*."

"Love you, *oso*."

As she accelerated out of the parking lot, she watched Francis in the rearview mirror, watched as he trudged toward the emergency room entrance. She stopped at the highway and looked again. From that distance, just before he pulled open the doors, his figure in the evening light looked just like Francisco, and she felt a pang of loss as he opened the door and disappeared inside.

SIXTEEN

EVEN THOUGH SHE KNEW that she still needed to call on Judge Lester Hobart to obtain a subpoena for the bank's ATM records, and then return to the bank parking lot, Estelle still felt a soft flood of relaxation and relief as she turned onto Guadalupe Terrace. Former sheriff Bill Gastner's large, fortress-like adobe nestled in the huge cottonwoods, a retreat where it would be just too easy to welcome a mug of tea and good conversation.

The porch light was off, an old habit that Gastner had once explained away with a shrug. "A light scares away the nesting swallows. Besides, I know where the damn step is." Christmas wasn't the nesting season for the little birds, and with returning curls of clouds and a fraction of moon, it was dark enough that the single porch light would have been welcome.

She pulled into his driveway and at the same time found her cell phone, thumbing the autodial. Gastner might well ignore the telephone, too. He did. His answering machine, a gadget he loathed but kept in deference to his job as a state livestock inspector, finally clicked, and Estelle switched off before the beep to record a message.

The front door, a massive, carved affair from a mission deep in Mexico, was recessed in the small courtyard. Had Gastner possessed the faintest tinge of green in his thumbs, realtors would have described the entryway courtyard as "inviting and charming." As it was, it more resembled a fortress, plain and utilitarian.

Estelle pulled her small flashlight off her belt to navigate the short distance from her car through the gateless portal, across the courtyard to the front door, and stopped short. The small beam of light caught first a pair of boots, then corduroy trousers, and finally the large body lying half on and half off the single concrete step, head deep in a runty acacia that Gastner had allowed to grow to the right of the door as his "guard dog."

"Padrino!" she gasped, and darted forward. The acacia was a nasty little bush, and its stubby thorns and sharp, leafless twigs had cut Gastner's face in half a dozen places as he had crashed down.

Even as she checked the old man's neck for a pulse, she realized that she herself was in danger of hyperventilating. She forced herself to breathe evenly, eyes closed, as her fingers traced along the side of his neck. Responding to her touch, one of his hands lifted from the gravel a few inches, and hovered helplessly.

"Padrino," Estelle whispered. She flicked the light across his eyes, and saw him grimace and clamp them shut. Slipping her right hand behind his head, she reached across to pull a threatening acacia limb away from his eyes.

"Don't try this at home," Gastner said clearly.

Estelle couldn't have laughed if she had wanted to. Holding his head in one hand, she managed to pull her phone from her pocket and dialed 911. Ernie Wheeler answered on the first ring.

"Ernie, this is Estelle. I need an ambulance at Bill Gastner's house right now. I don't know what the problem is. Just get one here."

"Ten four," Wheeler said quickly, and Estelle pocketed the phone, reaching up to cradle Gastner's head in both of her hands. He murmured something that didn't make sense. Loath to move him, Estelle simply waited, crouched at his side with his head in her hands. His upper body lay on the ground and his hips and legs lay twisted and awkward on the broad step.

After a minute, his hand slowly lifted until he could grasp her right forearm. He held onto her with a surprisingly strong grip. In the distance, she heard the ambulance, its siren piercing in the calm, damp air.

"I don't know," Gastner said. "Hell of a thing."

His legs appeared to be straight, ankles and knees pointing in all the right directions. His breathing was shallow but regular, and his pulse was steady.

"A good argument for a porch light, sir," she said. Her own pulse had slowed enough that her heart felt as if it might not rip loose after all. Gastner raised a single index finger to acknowledge the comment without moving another muscle. She shifted her hands in an effort to cradle his heavy skull and immediately sucked in a sharp breath even as Gastner winced. Her right hand came away wet with blood.

She could hear the siren marking the ambulance's route down Grande, heard the vehicle brake hard for Escondido, accelerate again, and then slow for the sharp turn onto Guadalupe. Lights flashed across the cottonwoods, and the ambulance swung wide, then backed up toward Estelle, its own Christmas tree of lights winking.

Eric Sanchez appeared from the driver's side, with Matty Finnegan making her way around the right side of the vehicle. While Sanchez opened the rear doors, Matty knelt by Estelle.

"Did he fall?" she asked as she slipped the stethoscope's earpieces in place.

"I think so," Estelle said. "I found him lying here just a couple of minutes ago."

"I didn't fall," Gastner said with surprising vehemence.

"Easy, sir," Matty said.

"He has a wound of some kind on the back of his head."

"Hit something when he went over, I bet," Matty said brusquely. "Sir, can you hear me?" She bent close, probing with her fingers while Estelle held her flashlight.

"Stop shouting," Gastner said, and Matty laughed, grinning at Estelle. "He hasn't changed a bit," she said. "Sir, did you hit your head on something when you fell?" She looked over at Estelle and frowned. "He's got a nasty laceration on the back of his head. Eric, we'll want a good pad and easy pressure on that."

"I didn't fall," Gastner said.

"That would explain the horizontal position," Matty quipped. She slipped a blood-pressure cuff around his upper arm, and as she pumped, she turned to her partner, who had clattered the gurney close at hand. "We're going to want the backboard, Eric. Pulse is 90, BP—" she paused as she held her light to read the dial "—just about 140 over 95." She patted Gastner's arm as she pulled off the cuff. "If I didn't tell ya, you'd ask, right sir? Not too bad, though."

Sanchez handed her a neck brace, and she deftly slipped it into place as he worked to secure a temporary bandage around Gastner's head, tramping down the acacia in the process. "Nice bush," she said as the last Velcro fastener grabbed into place. "Sir, we want to move you out of the vegetation. Are you up for that?"

Gastner grunted something that might have been a "yes."

"Do you hurt anywhere else? Ankles? Knees? Hips? Back?"

"Absolutely fit," Gastner said, and this time he managed to open his eyes. "Who are you?"

"I'm Matty Finnegan, sir. You know my mom and dad."

"Of course I do. I know you, too."

"That's good, sir. We're going to try and get you on the

backboard." That took considerable muscle and maneuvering, with Estelle holding Gastner's head and the thick pad of bandage Matty had gauzed in place to cover the head wound.

Once Gastner was secured to the backboard and gurney, the three of them worked in careful unison to heft his portly carcass into the ambulance.

"Let's rock and roll," Matty said. "See you at the hospital, Sheriff," she said, and when she saw how pale Estelle's face was, she added, "He'll be okay, Estelle."

"I'm right behind you," Estelle said. She could hear Eric Sanchez on the radio, advising Posadas General of an incoming head injury. She watched the ambulance pull out of the driveway and for a moment found herself unable to move. Common sense worked its way into her brain, and she realized that *Padrino* was now in good hands—there was nothing she could do for him at the hospital.

Behind her, the house loomed dark and cold. Still wanting to follow the ambulance, she forced herself to turn and walk across the small courtyard. It appeared that Gastner had been stepping up to enter the house, miscalculated, and careened into the acacia head-first. It was the sort of simple trip that a teenager would handle with a corrective skip. Gastner, seventy-one years old, overweight, and always fighting his trifocals, had managed a full gainer.

The crushed bush showed splotches of blood, but Estelle could see nothing against which he would have torn his scalp, unless he had first struck the sharp edge of the step.

She checked the front door and found it locked. Off to the left, her light caught the glint of keys, and she stooped to pick them up, recognizing the leather key fob. That made sense. As Gastner had stepped toward the door, he'd been fumbling his keys. When he went flying, so did the keys. She pocketed them and walked quickly back to her car, where she settled into the seat with a loud sigh.

"*Caramba,*" she said to the quiet night. She leaned her head back against the rest and closed her eyes, but her hands were on autopilot, finding the telephone. She opened one eye and regarded the display, then selected Tom Mears's number.

"Mears."

"Tom, this is Estelle."

"Oh, good. Look, Terry will come over the minute we have that court order," he said. "I wish I could say that we've found a magic bullet of some kind, but we haven't. We need to know what's on that ATM receipt."

"I'm headed that way, I think."

"You think?" Mears chuckled.

"Yeah. I'm at Bill's house. He took a tumble."

"He what?"

"He tripped over his front step and cracked his head. The ambulance just took him to the hospital. I really need to go there for a few minutes."

"Yipes," Mears said. "Is he okay?"

"I think so, but I need to be there."

"Yep," Mears agreed. "This is like dominos, you know that? You think it's something in the air? We got us quite a run going."

"I hope not."

"Collins and Taber just showed up, so we can break someone free to go visit the judge if that will help speed things up."

"Good idea, Tom. You know, Jackie gets along with the judge pretty well. I think he's afraid of her," Estelle said, trying a weak laugh.

"Then she's on the way," Mears said. "By the way, Eddie and Mike are back from Lordsburg. They're going to be down in Eddie's office for a bit."

"I'll swing by when I can," Estelle said.

"I understand that. I hope things go all right."

"Thanks, Tom."

She let the telephone fall to her lap, counted to a hundred while forcing slow, even breaths, and then straightened up and started the car. As she pulled out of Gastner's driveway, she palmed the mike.

"PSO dispatch, three ten."

"Three ten, go ahead."

"I'll be ten-seven at the hospital. Call Lieutenant Adams at the State Police and ask him if we can borrow a couple of his officers."

"Ten four. He just called a few minutes ago, asking about that."

"Okay. Tell him I'd like one of his guys to patrol central, and the other to give us some help, especially on State 76 down to the border."

"Ten four."

She racked the mike and drove up Grande toward Posadas General Hospital, so lost in her thoughts that she didn't realize that she'd driven through the red light at the intersection of Bustos and Grande. *"Por Dios,"* she said aloud with a start. "Pull yourself together." Her pulse raced, partly from fatigue and partly from the grim image of her patrol car T-boning some innocent old lady out to buy a late-night can of cat food.

SEVENTEEN

FOR MORE THAN an hour, Estelle paced the waiting room at Posadas General Hospital, knowing perfectly well that there were a dozen things more productive that she should be doing, knowing that Bill Gastner would be the first person to call her silly for wasting her time just because he needed a couple of stitches in his scalp. But she couldn't bring herself to leave.

It would have been an oversimplification to characterize her relationship with the former sheriff as father-daughter, although there was a strong element of that, especially since Estelle had never known her own biological father...or mother.

Gastner had served as her mentor, confessor, counselor, friend, and perhaps most important of all he had been a true *padrino,* or godfather, for both of her children. As she paced the polished tile floor, she thought back twenty-two years, when she had come to the United States at age sixteen to live with her Uncle Reuben and attend the last two years of high school in Posadas. More than once, her uncle had talked about Undersheriff Gastner and *El brazo largo de la ley*... "the long arm of the law," and before she graduated from high school, she'd discovered that law enforcement was magical for her.

When she'd earned her first degree in criminal justice, it seemed only natural that she would seek a job that would allow her to remain close to home and her fiancé, the young doctor Francis Guzman.

Undersheriff Bill Gastner had pushed the then civilian sheriff to hire twenty-two-year-old Estelle Reyes, and she'd become the first uniformed deputy sheriff in the history of Posadas County. During the nineteen years since then, the bond between Bill Gastner, herself, and her family had only deepened. She'd even been amused at the affection between Francis's Aunt Sofía and the old lawman.

During the wait, she had come close to calling Sofía at home, but was loath do to so until she had concrete information about Gastner's condition. At 10:05, her cell phone rang, and Eddie Mitchell's calm, quiet voice brought her back into focus.

"How are we doing?" he asked.

"We are waiting," Estelle said. "They took him down to CAT scan, and we'll see."

"Huh. Look, they got the warrant from Hobart, and Mears is down there now with his brother. It looks like Janet withdrew three hundred and fifty dollars at 3:05 p.m."

Estelle frowned as she rolled the numbers around in her head, and Mitchell mistook the silence for irritation at not being told sooner. "Mears said that he'd wait to hear from you before he told you," Mitchell added. "He didn't want to bother you over there."

"I appreciate that, but bother might be better than wearing circles in the waiting room floor," Estelle said. "Three fifty. That's a nice, logical number. Enough to get her through a long weekend, and not enough to be suspicious."

"Right. At least we have a time now."

"Three oh five." *Dead center in the middle of a Christmas afternoon,* she thought. Just seven hours had passed. "Are those numbers accurate, do you suppose?"

"Terry Mears says so."

"What about a video?"

"Nothing. For one thing, it's out of service at the moment. For another, it shows only the interior of the ATM foyer... nothing outside. If the killer nailed her in the car, then it's out of range of the camera. Of course, he might have talked to her at the ATM. We don't know."

"That's about an hour between the time she was at the office and when she went to the ATM...and presumably was killed shortly thereafter."

"That's right," Mitchell said. "Mike's spending some time by himself in the sheriff's office, writing out a deposition. We had a good long talk on the way back from Lordsburg. That's primarily why I called."

"How's he doing?"

"'Basket case' might be a good description. He wants to arrest the whole world just now. I don't want him out on the street, and I don't want to send him home. I was thinking that maybe he should go back to his folks in Lordsburg when we're all wrapped up tonight."

"Maybe."

"Anyway, I'd like to go over what he said when you get the chance. We ran through it a dozen times, and now he's taking a cooler and putting it down on paper."

"What do you think, Eddie?"

There was a pause. "If he killed Janet Tripp, then he deserves an Oscar for best actor. No...I don't think he had anything to do with Janet's death. But he's the logical place to start, Estelle." He exhaled a little huffing sound that might have been the beginning of a laugh. "I need your intuition."

"My intuition," Estelle said wryly. "I might have had some, once upon a time."

"Take a deep breath and get it back in gear, Undersheriff," Mitchell said. "You got your vest on?" When she didn't answer instantly, he added, "Things like dark alleys and landfill pits should have made you a believer, my friend," referring to two previous incidents that could have gone even more wrong than they had.

"The sheriff should have had an armored butt," she laughed, knowing perfectly well that Mitchell was right.

"Yeah," he said. "Look, we'll be here for quite a while. If you get a chance to break away, we need to talk, okay? And by the way, Frank Dayan's had his scanner on again. He stopped by."

"Use your own judgment," Estelle said.

"Yeah, well. I didn't have much to tell him. But for once he's got a major story hanging with lots of time before he goes to press…a whole damn week, practically."

"I'll talk to him when I get a chance."

"He doesn't know about Gastner yet."

"He doesn't need to…Bill's a civilian, and it was a home accident. If I told Frank, *Padrino* would have my hide."

"I can imagine. We have a State Police presence, by the way. Not a good time for folks to be speeding through Posadas. The lieutenant says that whatever we need, we've got."

"Hopefully, nothing," Estelle said.

"You never know, once the bad luck snowball really gets moving downhill. The Christmas from Hell. Look, I'll catch you in a bit. You're going to be ten-seven there for a while more?"

"I think so, Eddie. I keep thinking of a dozen things to be doing, and it's like I'm stuck in the mud. I don't want to leave here until I make sure *Padrino* is going to be all right."

She saw a door open down the hall, and her husband stepped out of the emergency room, rubbing the back of his neck. "Here's Francis," she said.

"Catch you later."

"Thanks, Eddie."

Francis ambled down the hall toward her, both hands hooked

behind his head. Estelle reached out and put a hand on each of his hips, using him as an anchor. He grinned.

"A very hard head," he said. "CAT shows that he's got a hairline skull fracture, and we're a little concerned about intracranial bleeding, *querida*. That's always the joker in injuries like this. Eight sutures, and he has some area added to his bald spot now. However…" He stopped, resting his forearms across Estelle's shoulders. "You need some photos."

"I need photos? Why, for when his hair grows back?"

He laughed. "No. Whatever he was hit with left some pretty characteristic marks. Even the sutures don't cover 'em up."

Estelle looked up into her husband's dark eyes, her mind churning as if trying to find the right gear. "Whatever he was *hit* with?"

Francis nodded. "That's what Alan and I think. If I had to place bets, I'd say that someone gave him a good one from behind. The wound on the back of his head isn't like something he might suffer by hitting the edge of that stupid concrete step of his…and if it was, you'd find some hair and blood on that, too."

He shook her gently, as if correctly reading the confusion. "You had this locked in as an accident?"

When Estelle didn't answer, Francis said, "He's conscious, if you want to talk with him. Sedated a bit, but conscious. If you want photos, I'll remove the dressing for you." He turned and nodded down the hall. "He's down in OR recovery. We're going to keep him at least overnight, maybe even a day or two longer, just to be on the safe side. His vital signs are as good as we can expect from someone who thinks the cure-all for any ill in the world is a jumbo green chile burrito."

"You really think that someone *hit* him?"

"Yes, I do." He put a hand on either side of Estelle's face. "And at this point, I'd love to be wrong."

"Then let me make a call, *oso*."

To her surprise, Brent Sutherland, the graveyard dispatcher, answered the phone, working his second shift of the day.

"Brent, we need a unit over at Bill Gastner's house. Until I have a chance to get back there, I don't want anyone going in or out, or tampering with anything on the property. If the deputy sees anyone hanging around the place, or scouting it out, I want them detained." She thought for a second, then added, "In fact, pull Taber off the Highland scene, and if you can't find anyone else who's clear, ask one of the State Police to take over for her."

"So you specifically want Jackie at Gastner's?"

"That's right. ASAP. Cover Highland with whomever you can find."

"Ten four. Mr. Gastner's okay?"

"I think so."

"Okay, I'm on it."

"I'm still ten-seven at the hospital, and then I'll be at Gastner's. I'll keep you posted." She clicked the phone shut, and her husband raised an eyebrow.

"You have an explanation for all this?"

"I wish," Estelle said. "All I can say is that I've been trying to talk with *Padrino* all evening. Now I have a captive audience."

"It's not your fault that he's here," Francis said, and Estelle grimaced with irritation.

"I know that, *querido*. But if you're right—and you always are in matters like this—then it's *someone's* fault that he's here. And that's a scary thought." She set off down the hall toward OR recovery, dialing Linda Real's cell phone as she walked. Dr. Guzman had to quicken his step to keep up.

EIGHTEEN

"LET'S SEE HOW many more people we can fit in here," Bill Gastner said. He managed a weak imitation of his bulldog frown. "Your hubby is damn quick with those needles, sweetheart."

"How are you feeling?" Estelle asked.

"Like somebody used me as a doormat." He lifted his right hand, mindful of the various IVs, tubes, and gadgets, and rested the palm on the top of his head. He opened one eye. "Are my glasses around here somewhere?"

"They're in the closet with his clothes," the nurse said, and busied herself searching for Gastner's trifocals. "Ah, here they are," she said. "They're a little bit bent." She straightened one errant bow, and then slid the spectacles ceremoniously into place, the right earpiece hanging on the outside of the mound of bandages.

"Thanks," he grumbled. "Now I can see who the hell is torturing me." He squinted at the nurse's nametag. "Anna, give me a few minutes alone with the minions of the law, if you can," he said.

"You behave," Anna admonished.

"Absolutely," Gastner said. When she was gone, he looked at Estelle sheepishly. "Sorry about all this."

"Nothing to be sorry about, sir," Estelle said. "You scared the ay-ay out of me, that's for sure."

"Me, too."

"Do you remember talking to me?"

"You mean while relaxing supine on my threshold?" Estelle laughed at his exaggerated choice of words. "No, I don't remember," he added.

"You told me that you didn't fall. You don't remember saying that?"

"Well…I'm not always responsible for what I say. We've known that for a long time."

"And the good doctor Guzman doesn't think that bash on the back of your head is from falling, either." She turned as the door behind her opened. Linda Real peeked around the door without entering. "Come in, Linda. He's ready."

"Ready for what?" Gastner said. "Is this another one of those Playboy of the Month calendar shots?"

"That's an idea," Linda said.

"No, it isn't," Gastner snapped.

"As soon as my husband gets back here to manage the patient, we want to take a photo or ten of the head wound, sir," Estelle said.

"Oh." He frowned and closed his eyes. "Goddamn glad I didn't get kicked somewhere else. Look, this is what I remember…at least at the moment. I think I know my own name. Bill something. Smith, maybe. I remember clear as a bell trying to find my house keys, and wishing I had fixed that light over the door."

"I've found myself wishing that more than once, *Padrino*."

"Yeah, well, I remember that. And then, *poof*. The next image in my mind is of this angelic face close to mine, asking encouraging questions like did I hurt." He reached out a hand to Linda, and she took it. "How are you doing, young lady?"

"Fine, I think."

"You think?"

"It's been a long, nasty day, *Padrino*."

"Yes, it has. One of the worst on record."

"You don't remember falling?" Estelle persisted.

"No." Gastner released Linda's hand and turned back to Estelle, shifting his head slightly to bring the correct portion of his glasses into position. "The thought that occurred to me here a bit ago was that I had had another stroke. While I was lying here, staring up at the ceiling and ruminating, that thought occurred to me."

"We don't think so."

"I'm glad we don't," he said, amused. "Or maybe I should hope for that. It might be less bother. What, you think someone whopped me on the head, or what?"

"I don't know."

"Hubby thinks so, though."

"Yes, he does," Estelle said.

"Then that's what happened. He's not wrong very often. Maybe it will all come back to me in a Technicolor flash, especially if they make me eat hospital food." He looked over at the small wing table that held a glass of water. Looking at it with distaste, he said, "You want to go out for some dinner?"

"No, you don't," Estelle said. She rested both hands on his right forearm. "He said the head wound had distinctive patterns in the bruising, sir."

"*He* being Francis?"

"Yes."

"Distinctive how?"

"Kind of a diagonal pattern of bruises. That's why we need pictures."

"Huh. Did someone get inside my house?"

"I don't think so. The door was still locked."

"And you have my keys?"

"Yes, sir. They were on the ground. Do you remember what time you arrived home?"

"Christ, now you're stretching it, sweetheart." He pressed a hand over his eyes. "I would guess right about nine. Something like that. How's that for helpful."

"It's a start."

"Well, then." He shifted and let out a little groan. "It sure as hell hurts now, though. Down deep in my head, where the Novocaine doesn't reach. You know, I haven't had an argument with anybody in a good long time, at least not enough that they'd want to take something to my head in the middle of the night."

Francis Guzman arrived with the nurse in tow, and he immediately circled an arm around Estelle's waist. "You want to see his ugly head?"

"Sí."

The physician nodded at Linda. "Where's best for you, young lady?"

"It doesn't matter. Just so I can get close."

"I think," Francis said to the nurse, "that if we just have him roll on his left side, that'll be all we need. Linda, you can shoot from over here. Okay?"

In a moment, the nurse had removed the dressing from Gastner's skull, and she stepped back to give the others room. Gastner remained grimly silent through the procedure, lying on his side like an old whale.

A patch the size of a grapefruit had been shaved on the back and crown of his broad skull. In the center was a nasty two-inch laceration, surrounded by a spectacular bruise. The black sutures had closed the wound, but Estelle could immediately see what her husband had been talking about. Small diagonal marks crossed the wound track, like railroad ties set slightly askew.

"You think you can catch that?" she said to Linda.

"She can do anything," Gastner muttered. For a moment Linda worked in silence, trying different settings and different ways to bounce the flash, and then taking another set with available light, finishing off with digital.

"Okay," she said. "That's got it."

"Pull up one on that show-and-tell screen," Gastner said. "I want to see what you guys are gawking at."

Francis and the nurse rebandaged the head wound and helped Gastner back to a comfortable position flat on his back. When he was resituated, he held the digital camera for a long time, turning it this way and that as he scrutinized the small review screen.

"Ouch," he said finally. "Interesting."

"What do you think, sir?"

"I think somebody didn't want to discuss the weather with me, that's for sure." He turned and caught the nurse's eye, and she nodded and left the room. "Kick that closed, will you?" he said, and Linda made sure the door was fully latched. Gastner beckoned Francis close. "This is what you're talking about?" With a stubby finger he pointed at two marks that were particularly clear, even on the tiny screen.

"Right."

"You know what this reminds me of?"

"What?"

"Sweetheart, remember when Bruce Corcoran got killed out at the bridge on Highway 56? Among other horrible things, poor old Bruce got whaled along the side of his face by a piece of rebar when a load shifted somehow. Remember that?"

"Not the details, no," Estelle said.

"Well, I do. Rebar has those funny little raised whatchacallits…those little humpy bumps. Gives the concrete something to grip. Little raised ridges."

"You think someone hit you with a piece of rebar?"

"That's my best guess." He shrugged and handed the camera to Linda. "I don't think I was supposed to walk away from that.

No argument, no confrontation. Just pow. A half-inch piece of steel rod across the pate. And I take a nose-dive into the bushes. The old fart trips on his own doorstep. The only thing not in the plan was a sharp-eyed doctor ready and waiting in the emergency room." He reached out to Estelle again. "Good thing you happened by, sweetheart. Otherwise, come morning, I might have been a little bit stiff."

He took a deep breath and rolled his eyes. "And I'm talking too much."

"I need to talk to you about Mike Sisneros and this afternoon," Estelle said. She glanced at her watch. "If it is still this afternoon, and not tomorrow."

Francis touched her shoulder. "He really should rest for a bit, *querida*."

"Nah, what the hell," Gastner said. "We can give it a few minutes."

After the others had left and she was alone with the former sheriff, Estelle leaned her hip against the side of the bed and regarded Gastner intently. "I left the office, oh, maybe three-ish or so. I didn't pay attention," he said.

"How long was Mike there?"

"He left a little bit before that. Not much." He grimaced in frustration. "I wish I could remember specifics."

"And Janet?"

"You know, she came and went *sometime*. How's that. I just wasn't paying attention. She came in right after we started…that would be around two. She suggested that maybe she should go get some pizza, but we were all stoked up from lunch. Mike told her not to bother."

"Did they talk about going to Lordsburg?"

"Nope. Mike said that he had to 'go get ready' at one point." Gastner fell silent, deep in thought. "I just don't know. They might have been going together, or not…. I just don't know. It wasn't something that they talked about while I was in the room. Did they mention Lordsburg to Linda?"

"She said that Mike mentioned it. That Janet wasn't going."

"That she *wasn't* going?"

"Right."

"Well, there you are, then."

"Can you think of a logical reason why she wouldn't want to go with Mike to his parents' home?"

"It's his mother and stepfather," Gastner corrected. "I don't know if you ever met them? She's Irene Cruz now. Give me a minute and the stepdad's name might come to me, other than the Cruz part. Worked for the cable company for a while. Anyway, I don't know if Janet was close to Irene or not. Or to what's-his-name, the stepfather."

"I didn't know that," Estelle said. "I thought I had met Mike's dad once."

"You may well have. Hank Sisneros is alive and well, as far as I know. He used to work for the mine before it closed. Then he ran that little business in back of Chavez Chrysler that used to make camper shells for pickups. Then I don't know what the hell happened. He moved, like half the rest of the population. To Deming, I think."

"Ah," Estelle said, once more amazed by Gastner's gazetteer-like memory.

"Janet might have wanted to have part of the holiday with her own folks," Estelle said.

"That's not likely. They're long gone, although I don't remember the exact circumstances." He closed his eyes again, trying to remember. "Nope…can't recall."

"So as far as we know, she was free to go with Mike, if she wanted to."

"T'would appear so," Gastner said.

"But she didn't."

"Nope. She stayed home and got herself murdered. Not a good choice. By the way, do you have someone over at my place?"

"Jackie."

"Good enough. What time is it?"

"Working on eleven."

He gazed down at the various hoses and pipes that held him prisoner.

"I was thinking some chile would taste good right about now."

"Francis wants you here overnight, sir. It's a good idea, too. Just behave yourself."

"There's always delivery." He grinned at Estelle's withering look. "You been home to get some sleep yet? Stupid question." He held up a hand to stop her from leaving. "What's Mike say, by the way? You told me that Eddie went to Lordsburg to fetch him."

Estelle took a deep breath. "That's next on the list," she said.

"Leave him to Eddie, sweetheart. Talk to them in the morning. Tell Jackie what you're looking for, and let her go at it. You go home and get some sleep. And when you see her next time, tell your Aunt Sofía that I'm sorry I didn't get over there this evening. I was supposed to help finish off the *menudo*."

"I'll have her bring you a bowl," Estelle said, and saw the look of panic as Gastner jerked the sheet even farther up over the mound of his stomach.

"God, not here," he said quickly. "I'm not my usual suave and debonair self just now."

She bent down and kissed him lightly on the forehead. "I'll keep you posted, sir. Don't do anything foolish. If you remember something that you think I should know, give me a call."

NINETEEN

WHEN ESTELLE LEFT the hospital parking lot and drove south on Grande to the "four corners" intersection with Bustos, she found herself pausing at the light, even though it was green. A driver westbound on Bustos arrived at the light and looked across at her, puzzled. When his light turned green, he hesitated, and then accelerated away toward the west. Estelle watched him go. She recognized him, the sort of acquaintance seen at the grocery store a dozen times, perhaps earning a nod and smile when passing in the aisle.

The dash clock said it was just passing 11:00 p.m., an hour away from the end of that Christmas Day. What was this particular driver doing cruising the streets? Had he just visited Tommy Portillo's Handi-Way convenience store down the street, grabbing a late-night donut just before Tommy closed at eleven o'clock? Maybe he'd run out of dental floss, just when his back molars had reached their limit of packed cracks. Or was he the one who had bashed Bill Gastner on the back of the head, and now, pleased at how well that episode had played out, drove around the village looking for another easy holiday score?

If someone had actually attacked Gastner—if Dr. Guzman was right—then that person, if not simply lucky, had calculated perfectly. Bill Gastner hadn't surprised a burglary in process. He'd simply been walking toward the front-door stoop, keys in hand, ready to go inside. If the attacker had been surprised when

Gastner drove in the driveway, if he'd been scouting the home for a possible burglary, he could have melted into the darkness without attacking and Gastner would never have been the wiser. Instead—if her husband was correct—he had struck with vicious accuracy, the sort of blow calculated to kill. Had he then stepped over the body, picked up the keys, entered Gastner's home, and taken his time rummaging through the house?

The cold calculation of the crime was disturbingly familiar. Estelle gazed up Bustos toward the west. The taillights of the other vehicle turned south on Tenth.

Glancing to the left, Estelle let her foot slide off the brake and allowed the Crown Victoria to idle across the intersection. Janet Tripp had been approached after tapping an ATM machine for $350. It hadn't been a confrontation. There were no signs of argument or confrontation, just one shot to the head, like a hit man. Take the money and run. Except the killer *hadn't* run. He'd removed the body and dumped it in an arroyo north of the village. The body was bound to be found, but he'd achieved a head start, even if it hadn't been as comfortably long as he might have liked.

South Grande was deserted, four lanes of black asphalt marked with moons of illumination from the sparse street lights. Window open, cool air whispering by, Estelle drove at not much more than a fast walk down South Grande, looking and listening with one part of her mind, the other off in the darkness somewhere.

Deputy Jackie Taber had parked her unit across Guadalupe Terrace from Gastner's adobe, affording her a full view of the front of the property. Estelle let the car drift to a stop, blocking Gastner's driveway. Behind her, she heard the click of a door, and in a moment Jackie stood beside the door of Estelle's car.

"Collins is parked around behind in the pharmacy parking

lot," she said. "Nobody's going to sneak around back there."
Gastner's property had originally included five acres, but he had
given most of it to Estelle and Francis three years before. The
property now included the elegant, single-story Posadas Clinic
and Pharmacy. Gastner had been left with a large, comfortable
back lot overgrown with enormous cottonwoods, thick oak
scrub, and a dozen other varieties of plants, most falling into
the "weeds" classification.

"He's stayed away from the house?"

"I told him to stay in his unit unless he actually had to
confront somebody." Jackie smiled. "That's the extent of my
guarantee. What's the deal? Is Mr. Gastner okay?"

"He's fine. And he's lucky. Francis thinks that someone hit
Bill on the head. If this guy then went inside the house, he had
to use the house keys. I found those on the step. If he used them,
then he just dropped 'em on his way out."

Jackie remained silent.

"I haven't checked inside yet," Estelle added. "I borrowed
Padrino's keys at the hospital. There's one for the back door, too.
It's under one of those little fake rock things right under the
kitchen window. We need to check and make sure it's still there."

"Where do you want to start?"

Estelle stood quietly in the darkness, gazing at the old house.
"Right at the gate, Jackie."

The small courtyard, sheltered even from what little moon-
light or starlight there might be, was a twenty-by-twenty-foot
expanse of gravel and dirt with a flagstone walkway leading to
the front door and the concrete step. The courtyard and walk
were recent additions, built two summers before in a moment
of boredom when Gastner had run out of other things to do.

An old shovel leaned against the blocks in the corner to
Estelle's left, marking the spot where Gastner had thought

about planting a climbing rose bush. The shovel had yet to earn its keep, but he had gone so far as to mark the spot for the rose.

Estelle stopped and let the flashlight beam linger in the corner, illuminating the bent piece of rusted steel rebar projecting out of the ground at a haphazard angle. Now that she saw it, she remembered Gastner driving the length of steel in a couple of inches with the flat of the shovel, remarking that the hard-packed clay soil might grow the rebar just fine, but probably not the roses.

Keeping her feet as close as she could to the plastered wall, she crossed to the corner as Jackie added more light from the walkway.

"You think?" the deputy asked.

"I don't know." She slipped on a pair of cotton gloves, bent down, and with the tip of her index finger touched the top of the bent stake. It rocked easily in its hole, barely deep enough to sink through the crushed stone cover to the clay underneath.

"Let me get a large bag," Jackie said, and Estelle knelt beside the stake, examining the ground. The crushed stone formed a uniform, featureless expanse. A busload of people could have stood in this corner and not left a single track. Whoever had assaulted Gastner could have crouched here, just as she crouched, and the twenty-four-inch-long piece of rebar would have presented itself as an easy weapon. But why not the shovel, itself heavy and lethal?

Estelle swung the light methodically, gridding the crushed stone surface in the corner. No cigarette butts, no gum wrappers, no blob of half-dried tobacco juice. Nothing indicated that a human being had stood here, waiting in the darkness.

"Here," Jackie said, touching Estelle on the shoulder. The rebar came out of the ground with little effort. Even the rain of earlier in the day hadn't been enough to soak through the blanket of crushed stone to the dense clay underneath. Holding the steel by the last half inch of one end, she gently lowered it into the plastic bag and zipped the top closed.

"Anything on it?"

"I can't tell in this light," Estelle said. "But I'm willing to bet."

"If he wanted a weapon, why not use the shovel?" Jackie asked. "You want that, too?"

"Yes. But I don't think that's what he used. The marks on the wound seemed pretty characteristic." She examined the corner once more. "Why, though?"

"Because it's handy?"

"Sure enough it is. But if he came here planning to assault *Padrino,* why wouldn't he have had a weapon ready? Why take up the rebar as a last-minute substitute?"

They heard a vehicle turn onto Guadalupe, and in a moment Tom Pasquale's Expedition pulled in behind Estelle's unit.

"Where do you want me?" he said as he approached the courtyard gate. "Sarge said he's about wrapped up over at the bank and that I should get over here." He saw the evidence bag and shovel in Jackie's hands. "Gardening?"

"That's it," Jackie said.

"We're about to go inside," Estelle said. "I think the chunk of rebar that Jackie has in the bag is the weapon. We haven't covered the area around the doorway yet, so go lightly."

"What are we looking for?"

"Anything at all, Tomás." She pointed with her light toward the front door. "He was lying half on the step, head in the bushes there on the right when I found him. So we have some compromise already. I went right to him without much regard for anything else, thinking that he had tripped, or had another stroke, or something like that. And then the two EMTs did what they do. So I'm not sure what we'll find."

"I don't figure," Pasquale said.

"Someone came up behind the sheriff and hit him on the head," Jackie said. "And down he went. That's what we have."

"No, I mean where did you find the weapon?"

"If it is a weapon," Estelle said. "It was stuck in the ground over there in the corner. That's where it's been for a couple of months now."

"So why would he put it *back?*" Pasquale asked.

"Neat and tidy," Jackie offered. "If he just hits the sheriff with it and drops it, that's pretty obvious. Stick it back where it was, and we might go for quite a while thinking the sheriff hit his head after an accidental fall."

"Simpler just to take it along and chuck it in the bushes somewhere," Pasquale said.

"Nos vemos," Estelle said. "For now, we have what we have." She stepped toward the front door. The gravel bordering the flagstones was scuffed here and there where the EMTs had worked with the gurney and backboard. "He had the keys in his hand," she said, and paused, picturing Bill Gastner's lumbering figure as he approached the stoop. "I've seen him open this door a thousand times," she said. "He waits until he's right here before he finds the right key."

"The porch light works?" Pasquale asked.

"He doesn't use it," Estelle said. "He does have one of those little plastic boots that he keeps on the door key, so he can separate it out from all the rest. Then he fumbles around trying to find the keyhole." She played the light around the heavy, carved door with its brass hardware.

"You said that you have the keys?" Pasquale asked.

"Yes, I do," Estelle replied. "But I'm not there yet."

"This is fresh," Jackie said. She brought her light close to the door jamb. The wood was scarred, with a chip gouged out and hanging by a strand.

"*Ay*," Estelle breathed. "Look at that." She bent close and saw that the rip was indeed recent, the wood gouged right through the surface stain into the soft pine underneath. "Tomás, was Linda still over at the bank?"

"I think so. You want her here?"

"Yes indeed. Use the phone, though. Not the radio."

"You got it."

With a hand on Jackie Taber's shoulder, Estelle said, "You're about *Padrino*'s height. Let's try this." She maneuvered the deputy into position, imitating Gastner's position as he reached for the lock. "If you're bent over trying to find the keyhole, that puts you just about like this," she said. Raising the plastic evidence bag, she held the rebar out, as if clubbing the deputy on the back of the head. "And there you are. It would have been easy for the bar to strike the door jamb, maybe at the same time as he hit *Padrino*." She held the position for a moment. "Lean a little against the jamb," she instructed, trying to imitate the position she'd seen Gastner assume innumerable times as he slumped against the short wall while sorting keys.

"It's a good thing, then," Jackie said. "If the end of the rebar hit the jamb at the same time as the rest of it struck him in the skull, it might have saved his life."

"That close," Estelle whispered.

"You might get a matching impression in the wood."

"Maybe. Not in this light, though." With the sides of both thumbs, she gingerly tried the door latch, keeping her touch on the outside edge of the flat brass surface. "Still locked."

"Unless he went inside, did his thing, and made sure it was locked on the way out."

"Maybe. And then he just drops the keys. Maybe."

"Any prints, you think?" Tom Pasquale asked, returned from his brief conversation with Linda Real.

"I would bet not," Estelle said. She drew out the wad of keys. "There's also the matter of the clumsy responding officer," she said. "I picked these up when the EMTs were here. I assumed that *Padrino* had fallen, and…" She shrugged. "My prints are on them, that's for sure." She selected the key with the blue plastic marker and slid it into the door lock. It opened easily, and with one finger she pushed the door open a foot until it hit the resistance of hinges long in need of lubrication. The resulting creak was eerie and loud, a sound Bill Gastner had found amusing and friendly.

The scent from inside the house was familiar—old wood, old leather, musty carpets too long from a cleaning, the hint of Gastner's characteristic aftershave.

"Let me go in," Estelle said. She bent down, letting her flashlight beam angle across the age-polished Saltillo tile of the foyer and hallway. Damp footprints would show like neon signs. "I don't think he came inside," she said, and reached across to flip on the hall and foyer lights. Nothing appeared out of place, and she walked down the hallway toward the sunken living room and kitchen, staying close to one wall.

A half pot of coffee sat cold on the kitchen counter, a habit Gastner had cultivated in an effort to remember to turn off the coffee maker when he left the house, having burned up several in recent months. The back door leading from the kitchen out into the overgrown patio was locked.

She crossed the living room and checked the guest bedrooms, finally peering into Gastner's office. Nothing appeared out of place. An expensive Civil War musket that had been stolen and retrieved once before still hung over the east-facing window. The light gray sifting of dust on his massive mahogany desk was undisturbed. She crossed to the far corner and a four-drawer filing cabinet with a locked security rod that Gastner had purchased several years before. It was secure.

On the other side of the house, Gastner's bedroom appeared normal enough, right down to the fastidiously made bed, its corners still tucked in the military fashion.

"All clear," she said, and relocked the front door.

"You think he was scared off somehow?" Pasquale asked.

"I don't know. Maybe. I don't much like the other possibility."

"What, that somebody just wanted to bash his head in?" Pasquale said, and Estelle winced at the blunt assessment.

"Maybe that," she said.

"The sheriff still had his wallet and money?"

Estelle nodded and turned to watch Linda Real add her vehicle to the growing parking lot on Guadalupe Terrace. "Jackie, will you give Linda a hand with what we have here? Tom and I will check the garage and around back. I don't think we're going to find anything, but I want to be sure."

She was halfway to the garage, her flashlight and Pasquale's sweeping the gravel driveway, when her cell phone chirped. The sound was loud in the quiet night air.

"Guzman."

"Querida," her husband's soft voice said. "You okay?"

"Sure. Are you home?"

"No. Look, Eduardo Martinez died a little bit ago. I wanted to let you know. I set the time at 10:58."

She stopped in her tracks, and looked up at the night sky. A few stars were showing, the others obscured by traces of wispy clouds.

"You there?" Francis asked.

"Yes, I'm here," she said finally. "I'll stop by in a few minutes."

"That's not necessary. Essie and the others all went home a few minutes ago." When she didn't respond immediately, he added, "Are you all right?"

"Sure. Did you look in on *Padrino?*"

"He's fine, *querida*. He's going to be just fine. I told him

about Eduardo, and he was philosophical about it. He said he'd
get together with Essie a little later, after the family thins out
some. The hard part will be keeping *Padrino* from getting up
and walking out of the hospital when our backs are turned. You
know how he is."

"We won't turn our backs," Estelle said.

TWENTY

"STAY PUT," Captain Eddie Mitchell said, looking back over his shoulder into his office. Out in the hall, Estelle's view was blocked by Mitchell's husky figure and the door, and she stepped sideways. Deputy Mike Sisneros sat at the end of the large folding table that Mitchell preferred to a standard desk. A tape recorder rested near his left elbow, and his pencil was poised over a legal pad.

Sisneros glanced up and saw the undersheriff. The young deputy's face was pallid, and a half day's worth of scruffy black stubble did nothing to hide the exhaustion on his face. Mitchell closed the door of his small office thoughtfully, keeping his grip on the knob even after it latched. "Let's talk in your office," he said to Estelle.

"He's going to be all right by himself?"

"Adams is in there with him," Mitchell said, and grinned without much humor. "Coiled over in the corner."

"Ah," Estelle said. She didn't ask Mitchell why he had deemed it necessary to have an official witness in the room while he talked with Sisneros, but that was the captain's call. Mitchell was as careful and methodical as anyone in the department. That he didn't feel it prudent to leave the young deputy alone at this particular moment spoke volumes, especially since he had left him in the intimidating presence of New Mexico State Police Lieutenant Mark Adams, whom former sheriff Bill

Gastner had once described as having the "deadest pair of eyes this side of a corpse."

Mitchell followed Estelle into her office and sat in the straight-backed chair by the filing cabinet. He rested his head back against the wall and closed both eyes. After Estelle had settled behind her desk, Mitchell opened his left eye and looked at her. Add thirty years of wear and tear and fifty pounds in all the wrong places, and he'd be a fair Bill Gastner impersonator...except for the glacial blue of his eyes. In that respect he was a good match for Lieutenant Adams. Neither gave the impression that they would cut their own mother a deal.

"I am sooooo tired," he said, and managed a grin. "And you too, I bet."

"Very," she said.

"Our young man is a basket case," Mitchell said, and opened both eyes as he pulled away from the wall. "This is his story so far. He left here about 2:45 or so this afternoon to go back to his apartment, clean up, and then drive to Lordsburg. For some reason, and he doesn't know why, Ms. Tripp decided at the last minute not to go along. Mike claims he almost canceled the visit, but he knew his mom would be disappointed, so he went over by himself. He arrived at his mother's and stepfather's place just about four thirty. They confirm that, although they're a little fuzzy about the time. He was with them until I arrived there about a quarter to six." Mitchell shrugged. "And that's about it. It's really that simple, if he's telling the truth."

"He really doesn't know why Janet didn't want to go to Lordsburg with him? No idea at all?"

"Nope. His best guess is that maybe Janet was uncomfortable around his mother. The two of them don't hit it off much, he said. Since Mike and Janet started seeing each other back in September, he says that Janet and his mother haven't spoken more than once or twice." Mitchell bent his right index finger and studiously examined the short, blunt fingernail. "That's not anything that surprises me, Estelle. I mean, some folks just don't care for each other. But there are a number of little things that trouble me."

Estelle waited, giving Mitchell time to frame his thoughts. "Number one," he said without looking up, "it appears that Janet Tripp was killed sometime after 3:05 p.m. That's what the ATM receipt shows, and we have no reason to suppose that she waited around in the parking lot for any length of time after making her transaction. There's always the chance that the killer took her ATM card after shooting her and did the transaction himself."

"I can't imagine that," Estelle said. "He'd have to have her PIN number, for one thing."

"That, and other reasons. Number one, why take just $350? The single transaction limit is $500 a day, Mears tells me. And second, once the shot is fired, I would think that the killer would be motivated to split. I can't see him casually walking over to the ATM, with her lying there, shot and bleeding."

"He took the time to pull her out of her car and dump her into his…trunk, back of an SUV, whatever it was."

"Sure, he did. But if we use a couple of minutes after 3:05 as the time of the shooting, that gives us a window of opportunity there. It might be easier if we had a stopwatch timing everything, but nobody pays too much attention to the fine details. The only time we're sure of is what's printed on the ATM slip." He raised his head to look at Estelle. "3:05. She does her business, walks back to the Jeep, and pop."

"And at that time, Mike isn't even on his way to Lordsburg yet. He's still in town," Estelle said.

"Correct. But…," and Mitchell leaned forward, shifting his weight on the small chair and pulling at the bottom of his vest where it chafed his belly. "I would be willing to bet every penny that's in my enormous pension fund that Mike Sisneros didn't kill Janet Tripp. I talked to him in Lordsburg, and tried to lay things out as gently as I could. I might as well have hit him between the eyes with a baseball bat. And if it was an acting job, I'll hang up my spurs."

"What's he have to say, then?" Estelle asked. "Did Janet have enemies, or does Mike think it was just a random thing…a crime of opportunity?"

"I'm not sure he's thinking straight at all. *Desperate* might be a good word. He'd like to wrap his finger around the trigger and put the killer in his sights. If anything, we're going to have trouble keeping him from mucking around and getting in our way with this thing. He and Janet were closer than I thought, I guess. He said that they were planning to get married this spring sometime."

"*Ay.* That's rough. I'd heard that rumor, but they were keeping their plans close to themselves."

"He said that he almost decided not to go over to his mom's, but Janet talked him into it. Mrs. Cruz is ailing, and Janet said that Mike should spend some holiday time with her."

"Generous girl."

"I've only met her half a dozen times, but I liked her," Mitchell said.

"And what was she going to do?"

"Do?"

"For the rest of her holiday? She evidently wasn't in the apartment to see Mike off. Was she going to see relatives of her own? Does Janet have folks nearby? I know about the sister out east somewhere."

"Mike says not. Her mother died a while ago. Dad walked out

on the family when Janet was just a kid, and who the hell knows where he is. Maybe the sister knows. Mike says that Janet told him that she had some errands, and then was going to spend a quiet evening in their apartment. Mike planned to be home by ten or so." He shrugged. "Finish out their holiday together."

"Not to be," Estelle said, more to herself than Mitchell. She glanced at the wall clock, then at the captain. "That's all?" With it pushing midnight, it wouldn't have taken Eddie five hours to round out Mike Sisneros's simple story…even to the point of double and triple checking times with whoever might have an accurate guess about what might have happened when.

"No," Eddie said. "We have a few bullet fragments from Tripp's brain, but I kinda doubt that we're going to match much of anything. I'm sure it's a .22, and so is Mears." He paused, looking down at his hands again. "I asked Mike if he had a .22 of some kind. In point of fact, he has two. Actually, I should say, *had* two."

"Had?"

"One's missing."

Silence hung heavy for a moment.

"You mean stolen?"

"I don't know what I mean," Mitchell said. "And neither does Mike. The last time he saw it, the gun was in a dresser drawer in their bedroom. It's not there now. The plastic box is there. The gun isn't."

"What about the other one?"

"He showed it to me. It's a .22 conversion kit that he bought to fit his duty gun. Kind of a slick little deal. Take the barrel and slide off the .45, and just slip on the replacement .22 kit. Go plink on the cheap. The kit's clean as a whistle. It hasn't been fired in a while, unless Mike did the job and then came home and diligently cleaned up."

"But you said a second gun is missing."

"Yup. A .22 Ruger .22/45, one of those heavy barreled things that's supposed to sort of match a 1911 in heft. He says that he's had it for quite a number of years."

"He didn't loan it to anyone?"

"Says not."

"Janet didn't use it?"

Mitchell shook his head. "She wasn't much of a gun fancier. What bothers me is that Mike can't account for how it might have gone missing. He says that he knew it was in its case, in the drawer. No doubt Janet did too, although he says that she would never use it for anything. He says that he once tried to talk her into carrying a little something for protection, but that she wouldn't do it. So he doesn't think she took it. And it doesn't make sense to me that she would."

"Somebody did."

"Sure enough, somebody did," Mitchell said. "The apartment was locked, with no sign of forced entry. It's on the second floor, so no one busted in through a window." He took a deep breath and let it out slowly. "Nothing else is missing, as far as Mike can tell. And we really looked."

"Just the gun."

"Yup. And Mike claims he doesn't know how, why, or when. I have trouble with that, Estelle. A gun is not the kind of thing most folks misplace."

TWENTY-ONE

ANOTHER HOUR SPENT with Deputy Mike Sisneros produced nothing that the investigators didn't already know. Estelle let Captain Eddie Mitchell's steady, methodical pressure on the young deputy continue uninterrupted. No one in the department knew Sisneros any better than did Mitchell. As the time dragged into the early hours of the morning, small bits and pieces of information dribbled in, but Estelle knew, as that awful Christmas Day finally slipped into yesterday, that they'd reached an impasse.

A State Police officer in Lordsburg reported that a careful search of Mike Sisneros's personal vehicle, still parked at his mother and stepfather's house, had produced nothing out of the ordinary. It would have been physically impossible to cram a body the size of Janet Tripp's into what passed for a trunk in the Mustang without leaving traces behind. Samples of human hair on the upholstery were taken, and Estelle had no doubt that they would belong to Mike and Janet. Further search had revealed the usual junk lodged under the seats—popcorn, two wrapped mints, pennies, one dime, an empty .45 ACP casing without even a hint of burned powder aroma, and a broken windshield scraper.

Other than the ATM records and a single .22 long-rifle cartridge casing found in the parking lot, Janet Tripp's vehicle produced nothing but questions.

The arroyo where the young woman's body had been found was telling no stories.

Estelle had chafed at the delay, but she knew there was nothing she could do about it. Her one contact at the lab who might have considered coming into the state office to work on a holiday was out of town visiting relatives. The wheels of forensic laboratory work ground to a halt on Christmas Day, further hampered by the holiday's falling on a Saturday. But there was little that the lab could tell them anyway, short of an unexpected curve ball when the toxicology reports came back.

Alan Perrone had called the office earlier with the news that Janet Tripp's body bore no other wounds or marks that weren't consistent with being roughly transported and then dumped into a tangle of rusting cars and arroyo gravel. She hadn't struggled with anyone…her short fingernails were clean with the exception of a small amount of grit from her death spasms in the arroyo. She hadn't flailed about, grabbing her assailant's hair, or gouging flesh from his face or arms. Instead, all signs pointed to her sitting in her car in the bank parking lot, head bowed forward as she tucked money and the ATM receipt into her purse. And then…*pop*. Unconsciousness, if not death, would have been instantaneous.

An hour after Estelle had given Tom Mears the rebar, Bill Gastner's house keys, and the shovel, the sergeant's report confirmed what she had expected. There were no prints on the rebar, none on the shovel. Her own—and Bill Gastner's—were on the bundle of keys and the tiny penlight joined on the ring.

Linda Real's photographs clearly showed the eruption of dirt around the hole in the ground where the rebar had first been jerked out, then returned to its place.

Beyond that, nothing.

Shortly after two in the morning of December 26, when no new ground could be pawed over, Lieutenant Mark Adams ran out of patience and overtime. He offered to drive Mike Sisneros home, and Estelle watched the young officer leave Mitchell's office, his shoulders bowed like an old man's. She wanted to find a quiet, dark corner and talk with Sisneros by herself, but was too tired at the moment to frame coherent questions and strategy.

"Shit," Eddie Mitchell said succinctly. He stretched far back in his chair with a creaking of leather, arms straight over his head, fingers entwined. He held that position for a long time, then slumped with his hands in his lap. "You got any bright ideas?"

"I wish that I did," Estelle said. She rubbed her face wearily. "I need a great big sign in neon letters that says, 'Go this way.'"

"Copy that."

She grinned at Mitchell and his curt military style, even though the dark circles under his eyes were probably just as deep as hers. "I wonder if we're missing something obvious just because of the way we're looking at this."

"And how would that be, Undersheriff?"

"If we go all the way back to the beginning of this miserable holiday, to what is now the day before yesterday, I responded to a telephone call from Chief Martinez on Christmas Eve." She paused. "That seems like a year ago, now."

"Okay, he called you from the motel."

"And then he goes out in the rain, to sit in his car, to do what, we don't really know. What we know is that he did not do what my husband told him to do—sit down and wait for medical help. We know he did *not* say, 'Okay, Dr. Francis, I feel terrible. Treat me. Here I am, waiting at the motel. Take me to the ER and make this all go away.'"

"Most people aren't so rational, but okay."

"And we progress from there," and she chopped the air in a line with her hand. "First one event, then another. We have the two kids in the motel trying to make some lame point about modern generosity with their Mary and Joseph thing...or whatever it is that they were doing. A nice way to spend Christmas Eve. Then the next day, on Christmas afternoon, a kid on a motorcycle finds Janet Tripp, dumped in a trash heap in the arroyo, the victim of a bizarre robbery. And then later that night, when he and I should have been having a meaningful and productive conversation, I get tied up in work and someone else takes the opportunity to club Bill Gastner over the head...but this guy, or gal, doesn't take anything. He doesn't take Bill's wallet, or his keys, or go inside and ransack the house. It seems clear to me that the *target* was Bill."

"Some old enemy, maybe," Mitchell offered.

"There may be some of those. I don't know what cases he's working on at the moment, except he's got some guy from Montana who keeps trying to bring horses into New Mexico without any paperwork...who knows why."

"Or a burglar who thought he was trapped when Wild Bill drove up. He hides behind the wall, and when the old man's back is turned, he grabs a weapon and swings."

"But why?" Estelle said. "What sense does that make? He could just have huddled there in the dark for a minute until *Padrino* went inside and then slipped away as easily as can be— or just darted off when Bill's back was turned. There isn't going to be a foot chase, that's for sure." She ran fingers through her short black hair in frustration. "For us, all these events seem related." She chopped her hand through the air again. "But maybe only because one comes right after another. That's what's confusing me."

"If you don't see a connection with all these things, I'm with you there," Mitchell said.

The room fell silent, and from out in the hall, they both heard the quiet cadence of dispatcher Brent Sutherland passing information over the radio. Mitchell had turned down the volume of the speaker on his desk, and he reached across now and turned it up just far enough that Estelle could hear Deputy Tom Pasquale's clipped delivery.

"We have three officers on the road for the quietest night of the year," Mitchell said. "Taber's out there, Pasquale's running every plate he sees, and Mears is poking around who knows where. Adams has two State Police officers in the county. The Border Patrol has a heads-up, along with every Sheriff's Department in southern New Mexico. We have lots of eyes out there. And you and me are sitting here wishing we'd get smart." He leaned forward and let his head fall, forehead resting on his hands. "Sleep would feel good. That might be the smart thing."

He jerked upright. "The trouble is, we have some woodchuck out there with a gun who thinks killing a girl for a few bucks is a fair trade, and we got another creep who tracks down an old man and whacks him on the head with an iron pipe. They're good company for our two creeps from Indiana who figure it's fair to steal a car from an old man dying from a heart attack."

"I keep circling around to that," Estelle said.

"To what, Wardell and Jakes?"

She nodded.

"You want to tell me why?"

"I don't know why, Eddie. Maybe just because that's where all this started."

"Huh." He toyed with a pencil. "Eduardo deserved better than he got, that's for sure," he said after a minute. "It's going to be interesting to see what charges Schroeder will agree to file against those guys." He dropped the pencil. "I'm going home," he said, and pushed his chair back, standing abruptly. "Roberto is coming home later today." He looked at the clock as if to ascertain that it was after midnight, and officially Saturday. "Did I tell you that earlier?"

She shook her head. "You talked with Gayle?"

"Yup. His sister is going up to Albuquerque to pick the two of them up after Bob's released. Gayle said he isn't a happy camper. He's got this whole regimen of therapy that he's supposed to do several times a day, and a locker full of drugs. You can imagine how all that sits with him. He'd rather just go off by himself, hunting somewhere."

"We have lots of hunting he can do," Estelle said.

Mitchell snorted what might have been a laugh had he not been so tired. "He'll like that." He watched Estelle push herself out of the chair. "You need to go home," he said. "Switch all this off for a while." Estelle grinned. Eddie Mitchell still managed to sound very much like the chief of police he had been before the village and county had consolidated departments.

"Yes, sir," she said, and managed a limp salute.

Moments later, as she walked out of the building to her car, she realized that she was bone tired, but wide awake. At home, Francisco and Carlos would be snoozing soundly, their world incomprehensibly simple from an adult point of view. If Dr. Francis wasn't home yet, he would be soon. He would tumble into bed and be asleep before his head settled into the pillow.

Estelle paused with her hand on the door handle of the Crown Victoria. If she went home now, she would lie in bed staring at the ceiling, kept awake by the cacophony of images swirling in her mind, trying to discover answers in the mess. There certainly should be something more productive than doing that, she thought.

She knew who else would be awake, his insomnia honed by long years of practice. The Don Juan de O-ate Restaurant was long closed, so she couldn't bring former sheriff Bill Gastner one of his beloved burrito grandes as a middle-of-the-night snack, but at least she could bring him a puzzle or two.

TWENTY-TWO

THE YELLOW PLASTIC CONE that announced caution on one side and cuidado on the other was placed dead center in the hospital's main hallway, and behind it, Stacy Cunningham guided the floor polisher in gentle, sweeping arcs. He allowed the pad to nuzzle right up to the rubber wall trim on one side, then with a little shift of weight and pressure on the handlebars, encouraged the machine to float back the other way.

Cunningham saw Estelle enter and out of reflex looked over his shoulder at the large clock.

Taking two seconds to wait for the machine to complete its arc to the left, he then shut it off, letting his weight settle on the handles as if he had been expecting exactly this old friend to walk through the doors. "Hey, Merry Christmas," he said cheerfully. "But I guess officially it's over."

"A whole new day," Estelle said, and paused near the cone.

"Oh, you can walk on it. It's dry. I'm just giving the final buff."

"Thanks."

"I was sorry to hear about Chief Martinez. He was a cool old guy."

And you would know, Estelle thought. Stacy Cunningham had been one of those high-school students whom most teachers had fervently hoped would drop out and go away…the sooner the better. He had done neither. Estelle had had a number of conversations with Principal Glenn Archer and Police Chief

Eduardo Martinez over the years about various students who had somehow run afoul of the law, or gotten themselves killed when their cars slammed to a stop before they did. Stacy had been the subject of conversation more than once, but somehow he had managed to survive the pitfalls.

"We'll miss him," Estelle said. "He was a good man."

Stacy shifted his weight on the handlebars of the floor polisher. "Yep, he was a cool old guy," he said. "I wish I'd taken more time to talk with him." Estelle looked at him with some surprise. With the wash of freckles across his angular, homely face, the unkempt red hair, and too-thin body...and his history...it was easy to dismiss the young man as an empty vessel stuck with a job that no one else had the patience or inclination to do.

"Yes, he was," Estelle agreed.

"He never threw his weight around, you know what I mean?"

"I know *exactly* what you mean," Estelle said.

"He could've," Stacy reflected, and Estelle wondered what incident he was remembering. His face brightened. "Big chief in a small town. But he didn't."

"No."

"Do you know when the funeral is going to be?"

She shook her head. "No, Stacy, I don't. That's something that the family will have to decide."

"Yeah, that's right," he said philosophically. "I'd like to go, you know? No special reason. But I'd like to. He cut me some slack a few times when he didn't need to."

Estelle nodded, and felt a pang of regret. On several occasions, she had lost her patience with Eduardo Martinez, and more than once had thought—even if she had never voiced it—that Eduardo was content as long as his school zones were enforced. With a kid like Stacy Cunningham, Eduardo had managed a delicate balance that most cops wouldn't take the time for, keeping the leash just long enough that the kid had survived his howling teens without serious damage to himself or anyone else.

"Your husband's already left," Stacy said as Estelle stepped around the coil of yellow extension cord.

"I hope so. That's what I should be doing, is leaving."

Cunningham grinned, showing faultless pearly whites that lit up his face. "We got 'em all, don't we?" He saw the puzzled look on Estelle's face. "I mean, I was here last night when they brought in Sheriff Torrez, but I guess he went to Albuquerque. And Mr. G is down there in 112."

"Ah," Estelle said. "Mr. G?"

"Sheriff Gastner. He's another cool old guy. I was talkin' to him a little while ago. I don't think he was supposed to be up, but he decided to cruise the hall for a little bit. We talked for a while. Can't believe somebody socked him in the head like that."

"There's all kinds, Stacy," Estelle said, wondering how much information Stacy gleaned from his informal conversations.

"He's cool, though."

Apparently the two categories were "cool" and "uncool," Estelle thought. She noticed that current Sheriff Robert Torrez hadn't yet been categorized.

"I'll get out of your way," she said. "Good talking to you, Stacy."

"You take care," he said. As she continued down the hall, the soft swooshing of the polisher resumed.

The nurse's station at first looked abandoned, but a head appeared as Estelle reached the Plexiglas window. The young nurse, homely and overweight with heavy features and too much makeup, was in the process of picking up the contents of a folder that had spilled on the floor.

"I'm just stopping in to see Mr. Gastner for a bit," Estelle said, reading the girl's nametag. "I know it's a bad time, but it's important."

"We're going to need to tie him down," Tabitha Escudero said gruffly, tapping the folder back into compliance. She evidently knew who Estelle was, not surprised in the least that, at two in the morning, Bill Gastner would have visitors. Tabitha's expression hardened just a bit into that look of control that the medical staff assumed when a civilian was tampering with the hospital's due process. "But if he's finally asleep, I hope you won't wake him."

"Absolutely not, Tabitha. Thanks. I'll just peek in."

The nurse fluttered her fingers in dismissal, turning toward a box stuffed with more folders.

The door of 112 was ajar a finger's width, and Estelle nudged it open far enough to see the bed. Gastner lay with the unpunctured arm up on his pillow, hand resting on the top of his head. As the door moved, she saw him turn just enough to be able to see her.

"Hey," he said, and jerked his arm down in that reflex motion to pull the sheet higher up. "What the hell are you doing nosing around at this time of the goddamn night?"

"Trying to think, sir," she said.

"Well, that's not a bad thing. Any success?"

"*Trying* is the operative word."

"So who the hell did you arrest for giving me this headache?"

"Nobody yet."

"Ideas?"

"I was hoping you'd have a list of grudges," she said. She rested her hand on his, tapping the back of it with her fingertips.

"We need to get out of here and go to work," he said.

"I was party to one of those escapades a few years ago, as you'll remember. I don't think I want to do it again."

"Escapades, hell," Gastner said. "There's no profit in any of this if the hospital can't keep me here until my insurance pays all it can pay, you know. It's all just a scam."

"Yes, sir. The scam the last time, as I remember, was whether to do a heart bypass on you, or let you stumble out of here so you could go chase bad guys until you fell on your face."

"And as I remember, it worked out pretty well," Gastner said cheerfully. "Not so good for the bad guys, but good enough for me." His fingers drifted down to where his pajamas covered the thick scar from the bypass. "They had the chance to carve on me eventually. But…," and he pushed himself up in bed a little, dragging the tubes and wires with him, "I don't want to talk about me at whatever it is in the morning. And you don't either."

"Some interesting things, sir." She turned and pulled one of the white chairs closer, then hesitated. "Mind if I use your bathroom?"

"Why would I mind that?" Gastner said, and waved toward the small cubicle. In a moment, Estelle returned, tucking in her blouse.

She draped the heavy Kevlar vest over the back of the chair and sat down. "That feels better."

"Put it back on when you leave," Gastner said.

"You sound like Eddie," Estelle replied, and held up a hand to stop his rejoinder. "I know, I know."

"They never made one of those things that works with someone my shape," Gastner said.

"Me neither."

He laughed hard, and then grimaced, holding the top of his skull. "Don't do that." He rubbed his head, fingers straying down toward the bandage. "Son of a bitch sure hit me hard enough."

"He used that piece of rebar that you had in the corner of the yard, sir. The one for the roses? He used it, and then put it back."

"No shit? That was goddamn thoughtful of the son-of-a-bitch."

"We think he swung, and when he hit you with it, the tip of

the rebar also hit the door jamb. It took a deep gouge out of the wood." Estelle used her right index finger to represent the length of rebar, and the palm of her left as the jamb. "If that hadn't absorbed some of the energy, you'd really have a headache."

"Or not," Gastner muttered. "Did somebody tell you that Eduardo died?"

"Yes, sir. Francis called me."

"Makes me feel positively mortal," Gastner said. "How's Bobby, as long as we're checking the list of the lame and useless."

"He's okay. He'll be home later today. His sister's driving up to Albuquerque to pick up him and Gayle."

"He's chafing, I imagine."

"That's putting it mildly, sir." She leaned an elbow on the side of his bed, and it felt comfortable enough that she could have closed her eyes and dozed off. "There's a window of opportunity during which Mike could have shot Janet before driving over to Lordsburg."

"He didn't do it."

"No, I don't think he did. But the timing is right. And there's one other thing. He owns a couple of .22 pistols. One of them is missing. He can't account for it."

"Stolen, then?"

"Maybe."

"Why maybe?"

"For one thing, it was in the dresser drawer of his apartment, which is usually locked. He told Eddie that Janet knew it was there, too. What's interesting to me is that the gun was gone, but the plastic case that it comes in? That was still there."

"Huh. I'm not sure that means much. A thief can grab the gun and stick it under the waistband of his pants. Tough to do that with a bulky plastic case. Mike thought the gun was there until when? When you guys checked his apartment?"

"Right."

"So it was taken recently, then. If it was taken at all."

"I think so."

"By who, then?"

"I don't know. Mike says he doesn't, either."

"Janet wouldn't have, I don't think. But she lives with him, so there you are."

"Yes."

"So what's the point?" He scratched his head tentatively. "I like things that go from A to B to C to D," he said. "Nice relationships. I've been lying here thinking, and my brain's about as responsive as tapioca pudding." He held up an index finger. "Eduardo has a heart attack, exacerbated by a couple of penny-ante thugs who decide his new Buick would be a nice thing to have. Bobby doesn't pay attention to *his* doctors, and damn near ends up on the slab, through no one's fault but his own. Then, some cold son-of-a-bitch shoots Janet Tripp in the head so he can take her cash, and dumps her body in the arroyo as if she's some bag of household trash. God, that makes me mad." His eyes narrowed as he glared at the ceiling tile.

"And it's in the air," he continued. "Here I am, minding my own business, trying to let myself into the house, and somebody bends a piece of my own rebar across my own skull."

"They didn't take anything, sir. Nobody went inside your house."

"I figured that out for myself, sweetheart. If it had been a burglar, he could have just waited, and left when I surprised him." He lifted his hand up and regarded his fingers. "Nah. Someone had a grudge of some kind." He let his arm relax on the sheets and looked steadily at Estelle. "I suppose I've made my share of enemies over the years. None recently, as far as I know."

"That's what I wondered."

He waved his hand again in dismissal. "I don't think so. But, hell, I don't know for sure. All kinds of fruitcakes in this world. We just happened to hit the season right this time. Maybe whoever tried to dent my hard head will hear that he didn't do the job right, and come back for a second try." He nodded at the clipboard fastened to the base frame of the bed. "I'll have him sign in when he does."

"That's not funny, sir."

"Well, then go home and bring me back my .45. I'll keep it under my pillow, here."

"Nurse Tabitha would like that—you waving that cannon around, especially without your glasses."

"She's something, isn't she? Damn near uglier'n me." Gastner folded his hands on his belly. "Pretty sad deal," he said finally. "Janet, I mean. You know, I didn't really know her all that well. Hell," and he shrugged, "I guess I didn't know her at all. I've been thinking about that a lot, too. Mike's a hell of a good kid, and what, the couple of times I've met her? Janet seemed like a pretty steady sort."

Estelle smiled at the use of the word *kid*. His thirtieth birthday was past history for Mike, and Janet hadn't been far behind. Bill Gastner had four decades on both of them. She regarded Gastner fondly, amazed once again at his seemingly inexhaustible reserves.

"You have to wonder why that son-of-a-bitch picked on her," Gastner said. "Other than just the roll of the dice."

"Maybe that's exactly what it was," Estelle said.

"And then again…" Gastner added, then stopped, thinking. "The whole arroyo thing doesn't square with me," he said. "Not for an ATM robbery. Why not do what the other guy did to me? Once up behind the head, grab the money, and run. What's so hard about that?"

"But, you see," Estelle said, "whoever hit you didn't grab the money and run. He wanted to kill you, sir. That's all there is to it. He didn't go into the house. He didn't take your wallet. He didn't take your .45. He didn't go into the garage and steal your Blazer."

Gastner shifted in the bed so he could look more squarely at her. "That's interesting."

"What is, sir?"

"Janet's assailant didn't have to kill her to take the 350 bucks. He could have wrestled it away from her, or threatened her, or bashed her head against the door. Any of that would have been enough. But he *executes* her, for God's sakes. That's what he did. He goddamn well *executed* her, didn't he. And then he took the money and whatnot, and her body. Why the hell do that? And my guy…he wraps a steel bar around my skull, one good shot that would drop an elephant, and then just leaves." He fell silent, lips pursed.

"Here's what you need to do, sweetheart," he said after a moment. "You know that filing cabinet in my study?"

"Sure."

"The top drawer, first section, includes all the current stuff I'm working on. It isn't much, and I don't think you'll find a damn thing. But maybe it'll give you a name or two. I haven't gotten cross-wise with anyone in a long, long time. Anyway, do that. And it wouldn't hurt to put Janet Tripp's background under glass, either. As many years as she lived in town, you'd think I'd be able to come up with something in the old memory. But it's blank. I don't know her, I don't know her folks." He waved a hand in disgust. "The minute Bobby gets home, drop this whole thing in his lap. Give him something to do. The more good minds we have working on this, the better. In the meantime," and he folded his hands again, composing himself corpse-like, "I'm going to lie here and think great thoughts. If I come up with something, I'll give you a call."

"That would be good."

"Don't be a stranger." He hadn't bothered to open his eyes, and his speech had taken on something of a slur. She sat quietly and watched him. After a few moments, she saw his lower lip sag just a little as sleep finally came. She patted the back of his hand, rose, and collected her vest. As her hand touched the door, his voice caught up with her. "Merry Christmas," he said.

"You too, sir."

"Put that on. It doesn't do any good draped over your arm."

"Yes, sir." As she shut the door, she almost collided with Tabitha Escudero. The nurse held a small tray of tiny paper cups filled with medications.

"Is he going to need something to help him sleep?" she asked.

Estelle shook her head. "I don't think so, Tabitha. I wore him out."

TWENTY-THREE

ESTELLE AWOKE TO BRIGHT light bouncing off the tile floor as sun streamed in through the bedroom window. As if at a great distance, she heard the incredibly soft, gentle piano music, and for a moment she lay without breathing, listening.

By moving her head a fraction, she could see the clock on the night stand. She had finally given up at 3:00 a.m. that Sunday morning, stumbling into bed and falling asleep so quickly that her husband had never stirred. Perhaps she had only dreamed of his rising at six, perhaps she had actually drifted close to consciousness when he brushed her cheek with his lips.

For five blissful hours, the phone hadn't rung—or if it had, she hadn't heard it. She watched the clock flick its little digital window over to 8:04 a.m.—five hours more security for Janet Tripp's killer and for the would-be killer who'd dented Bill Gastner's head. If they had left town, those five hours would have put another 375 miles between their back bumpers and Posadas, New Mexico.

Combine those minutes and miles with the hours immediately after the crime, until the time Estelle had finally gone to bed exhausted with frustration, and they could be crossing the Mississippi or dabbling their toes in the Pacific...or be speaking Spanish somewhere south of the border.

She knew perfectly well that the county was patrolled as well as it could be—State Police, her own deputies (including at least two who were working double shifts), the Border Patrol, even the New Mexico Department of Game and Fish. Every badge and agency within five states, and beyond by computer entry, knew that Posadas County was looking for a killer...or two.

Estelle groaned with a mixture of fatigue and irritation that she'd slept away too many hours.

From the front of the house, she heard Sofía say something to Francisco, the older woman's voice little more than a whisper. In response, the little boy spent ten seconds trilling two notes, a soft tinkling sound, some small adjustment in this magical world he had discovered. And clearly, Sofía Tournál knew exactly which entry keys were the ones to help the little boy continue opening one door after another.

Estelle turned onto her stomach and buried her face into the heart of her pillow, leaving both ears above the surface.

"You wake?" She could feel the butterfly of her youngest son's breath on her arm.

"Yes," she said without moving.

"Do we get to go see *Padrino* today?"

"Maybe, *hijo*." She turned her head and was eye-to-eye with the four-year-old. "Would you like to do that?"

He nodded. "*Papá* said somebody hit him on the head," he said soberly.

"That's right. Somebody did."

"Why did they do that?"

"I don't know, *hijo*."

"Are you going to catch 'em?"

"If I can get out of bed."

"Okay." At least there was no doubt in his mind, Estelle thought. Carlos grabbed the blanket and backed away, pulling it half off the bed. She reached down and yanked it back, and a tug-of-war ensued that ended up with Carlos on the floor, wrapped in the blanket like a mummy. Estelle picked him up and dumped him on the bed and piled the pillows on top of him.

In response to the shrieks and giggles from Carlos, the volume of music out in the living room increased, reached a crescendo, then abruptly ceased.

"Ay," Estelle said to the squirming mummy. "Reinforcements." By the time the war was finished five minutes later, both boys lay trussed on the bed like cocoons. One foot, already plenty large for a six-year-old, stuck out unprotected, and Estelle sat down on the bed, grabbed Francisco's ankle, and played spider on the bottom of his foot, holding him firmly against his laughing convulsions.

After a moment she stopped, and helped the two of them out of the wadded bedding without ever releasing her grasp on her eldest son's ankle.

"You're too strong, *Mamá*," Francisco gasped. He tried to pry her fingers loose.

"Way too strong for you, *mi corazón*. What were you playing?"

"*Tía* gave it to me yesterday for Christmas," he said. "It's by Bach." He exaggerated the guttural *ch* of the composer's name. "He's a grump."

Christmas. What was that? "A grump?"

"*Un gruñón*," Carlos chirped.

Estelle looked over at the little boy in surprise. "Where did you hear that funny word?"

"*Tía* said he was."

"Ah. *Tía* said. Bach the *gruñón*."

"You want to hear?" Francisco asked.

"Of course I want to hear. Then I have to get dressed."

She wrapped herself in a white terry-cloth robe and followed the two out to the living room. Teresa Reyes already had taken up court in her large rocker, and she held a small mug of coffee in both hands, looking expectant. Sofía Tournál looked up from the kitchen sink as Estelle appeared.

"Finally, you get some rest," she said. She held up a peach, impaled on a small paring knife. "These are no good this time of year, but we'll make do. You have time for some breakfast?"

"Sure. First I promised to listen to *el gruñón.*"

"Ah, that." Sofía waved the knife toward the living room. *"Hijo!"* she called, and somehow Francisco knew exactly which *hijo* was under orders. He slipped from the piano bench and trotted to the kitchen.

Sofía held up a bent index finger. "Give them time to talk," she said, and then fluttered her fingers together in the universal sign of people jabbering. *"Están parloteando, mi hombre.* Let them have their say. Let's see how well you can do it now."

Francisco nodded and made a face as he returned to the piano. Apparently this was serious, since Carlos didn't slide onto the piano bench with him, but instead took up a post on the sofa nearest his grandmother. Francisco sat for a moment, regarding the piano keys, and Estelle leaned against the right arm of her mother's chair.

"Six hours of this," Teresa grumbled. "You're lucky you have something to do outside the house." She wasn't altogether successful at keeping the pride out of her voice.

What followed, even to Estelle's untrained ear, seemed to be a conversation between two or three people—at times it was impossible to tell how many. One hand took a melody, then handed it off to the other, and even though Francisco started out precisely and almost methodically, before long he lost it in a burst of giggles, driving the invention into manic *parloteando,* a musical jabbering that made no sense.

"See what happens?" Sofía said matter-of-factly. "No

wonder the composer is so *gruñón* when he hears you play like that. You make him tumble end for end in his grave."

Each successive attempt dissolved into a musical intersection whose traffic light was out of order, but Estelle enjoyed it nevertheless.

"He's not ready to be an old man," Teresa observed dryly after Francisco abandoned Bach's original time signature and ventured off on his own.

"That may be a good thing," Estelle said.

"Come and eat something," Sofía called, and Estelle couldn't help noticing that her aunt had waited for an auspicious moment when it was clear Francisco was having trouble searching for something else to slaughter. The concert stopped as abruptly as it began.

"I'm impressed," Estelle said as she settled at the kitchen table. She looked at Francisco. "Tell me what you hear when you play that piece by the *gruñón, hijo.*"

The little boy craned his neck, looking out the window behind Estelle. He pointed outside. "When the jays come," he said. "They all fly in and argue about the seeds. Nobody listens. They all just jabber, jabber, jabber."

Estelle laughed. "Bird feeder music. I wonder if Bach fed the birds."

"No," Francisco said without hesitation. "They didn't *have* birds like that back then."

"*Por Dios,*" Sofía said. "Where he gets these ideas." She placed a large bowl of honeyed fruit on the table, along with a platter of English muffins. Teresa tottered to the table after a trip to the coffee pot.

Estelle turned to Carlos, who was already industriously buttering one of the muffin halves. "And what do you hear?"

He shrugged. "I like the other one better," he said, and before

Estelle had a chance to ask *which* other one, he added, "Can we go see *Padrino* now?"

"I can't this morning," Estelle said. "Bobby is coming home today, too. I need to talk with him."

"He's a *gruñón* too," Francisco observed. "A scary *gruñón*."

"That may be, *hijo*. And maybe he has reason to be, no? It was a scary day yesterday."

"Do you want me to take the boys by the hospital?" Sofía asked.

Estelle was about to refuse the offer, but thought better of it. Things put off had a nasty tendency to turn into regrets. The gouge in *Padrino*'s door jamb came to mind, the gouge that had absorbed just enough of the blow that the old man's eighth or ninth life had been spared. "If you would, I think that would be wonderful," she said. "He'll bitch and complain, but he'll appreciate the visit, *tía*."

"You come, too," Carlos said.

"I can't right away, *mi corazón*. I talked to *Padrino* just before I came home last night, and he understands."

She ate so little that she earned disapproving looks from both her mother and aunt.

"Take something with you," Sofía said.

"No. I can't." Both boys were within reach, and she took Carlos's left hand and Francisco's right, bringing them together until she could cover both hands with hers. "I need to go. When you two are with *Padrino,* you be careful, you understand? He doesn't feel well. Don't make it harder for him."

"Somebody hit him," Carlos said, as if maybe his older brother hadn't heard the previous conversation. Estelle didn't add to the remark, but just sat quietly for a moment, then released their hands with a final squeeze and excused herself from the table.

She showered quickly, brushed her short hair just enough to restore some semblance of order, and then dressed in one of her tan pants suits. She was in the process of putting her Kevlar vest on over her blouse when she realized that Francisco was standing in the doorway.

"What's that?" he asked, although Estelle was certain that he already knew.

"My vest," she said. "It fools the bad guys, *hijo*."

"Does Bobby wear one of those?"

"Sure he does." She didn't bother to tell the boy that Bobby hadn't been wearing a steel ass-protector when the .223 rifle bullet had drilled him through the rump, making hash of a pound or two of muscle and mixing it with chips of hip bone.

"Does *Padrino*?"

"Sometimes."

"Not on his head, though, huh."

"Nope. Not on his head."

"You know those helmet thingies that knights wear?" Francisco stretched his hand far up, emulating the plume on top of the helmet.

"Maybe we should have those, too," Estelle said. She watched her son's eyes stray downward to the stubby .45 automatic in its black holster at the small of her back, and to the handcuffs beside that. An eyebrow flickered, but he didn't say anything.

"When you come home for lunch," he said, with implications far more refined and pointed than his years should have allowed, "I'll play that piece just the way old *gruñón* says, okay?"

She picked him up in a fierce hug. "Promise?"

He nodded, knocking the knuckles of his left hand against her vest.

"I love you, *hijo*. You know that, don't you?"

"I know that," Francisco said with a grimace. He seemed fascinated by the hard edge of the vest, and as she held him, Estelle realized how heavy and solid he was. She boosted him up and held him even more fiercely.

"Don't make *Padrino* laugh too much, *hijo*. He's got a sore head."

He beamed, and she crunched him one more time before letting him slide to the floor. She had just time to slip on her suit jacket before Carlos catapulted into the room for his hug, and he felt tiny and fragile to her in comparison to the robust six-year-old.

"Thanks, Sofía," she said on her way to the front door, and then she detoured to her mother, who was back in the rocker. "Are you going with them to the hospital?" she asked.

"Oh, I don't think so," Teresa said. "Hospitals…" She let it go with a wave of her hand in front of her nose, fending off the odors. "That makes you look fat," she said, nodding at the vest. "But I'm glad you wear it."

"It's easy to forget," Estelle said. "Eddie gave me a hard time."

"As well he should," Teresa said. "You just be careful and take your time with this nasty thing you're working on. *Con paciencia, se gana el cielo,* you know."

"I know, *Mamá*." With patience, you can reach the sky. As she went outside to her car, she wondered what Janet Tripp's killer was thinking. And she wondered what the man who had clubbed Bill Gastner was thinking. She turned the ignition key, and as if she somehow shared in the jolt of voltage, realized that it made sense to her that the two attackers were one and the same.

TWENTY-FOUR

SHE LISTENED TO THE telephone's pulse as she drove. After eight rings, she was about to disconnect when Mike Sisneros answered.

"Yes." His voice was flat and mechanical, and Estelle, at once relieved that he *had* answered, now had the mental image of him wrapped around a bottle, his face unshaven, with dark bags under his eyes. No one would have blamed him.

"Mike, this is Estelle. Can we talk?"

"Sure." Again, no emotion, no rise.

"Have you had breakfast?"

This time there was a moment's hesitation. "No, I guess I haven't."

"How about if I pick you up?"

"Okay. If that's what you want to do."

"Give me five minutes."

"Okay."

Estelle switched off the phone. If not wrapped around a bottle, Sisneros sounded as if he'd been zapped with one too many sedatives, uncomfortable with any decision more complicated than "yes" or "no."

The apartment complex, a homely brick box divided into three apartments downstairs and two above, fronted on Third Street, across from the high school's athletic field. Through his front window, Sisneros could watch high-school football games from the comfort of his easy chair. The rear of the building was separated by an alley from Posadas Lumber and Hardware on Grande.

Estelle parked in the empty spot reserved for the deputy's Mustang that had been stranded in Lordsburg when Mike was picked up by Eddie Mitchell. As she got out of the car, she heard a door above and looked up to see Sisneros putting his keys back in his pocket. He came down the outside stairway with a methodical rhythm that bobbed his head with each step. He wore fashionably faded blue jeans and a STOLEN FROM THE UNIVERSITY OF NEW MEXICO ATHLETIC DEPARTMENT T-shirt that was two sizes too large and not tucked in. Even though it was barely fifty degrees outside, he wore no jacket. The T-shirt did nothing to hide the holstered automatic on his belt.

"Ma'am," he said with a nod.

"Did you get any sleep?" she asked.

"Nope."

She reached out and touched his arm, nodding toward the Crown Victoria. "I wish I knew some way to make this easier," she said.

"Can't think of a way," he said, and settled into the seat. He swung the door shut too gently, like a man with a migraine who was afraid that his head would shatter. He tried again. "At least I'm still ridin' in the front." He glanced at Estelle to see if she'd caught his reference to the fenced-in back seat. "This is so…" He ran out of words. She guessed that he had been up all night…at least he *smelled* as if he had been.

"Can you eat something?"

He shrugged. "I guess."

"Don Juan?"

"Sure. Anything."

The restaurant was less than a dozen blocks away, and by the time they had reached the Don Juan's parking lot, Mike

Sisneros had slumped even farther, shoulder against the door, head resting on his right hand, gazing off at nothing.

JanaLynn Torrez, one of the sheriff's innumerable cousins, greeted them inside the restaurant, managing to conceal most of her surprise at seeing Estelle without her customary restaurant companion, Bill Gastner.

"Booth in the back?" JanaLynn said brightly. She looked from Estelle to Mike, doing a creditable job of pretending that nothing was wrong that green chile couldn't fix. The Posadas grapevine was amazingly efficient at spreading information, correct or otherwise. JanaLynn would have heard about the murder of Janet Tripp, perhaps even the head-bashing of Bill Gastner, one of her favorite patrons. If she was eager to ask questions, she showed great self-control.

She led them to Gastner's booth. "How's this?" A hand reached out and brushed Mike's shoulder—just a light touch that carried a world of sympathy with it.

"Perfect," Estelle said. Tucked toward the rear of the restaurant, the booth had a fine view of the parking lot, and was blocked from the rest of the dining area by one of the serving stations.

"I heard Bobby was coming home this morning," JanaLynn said. It was always safe to stick with family.

"We hope so," Estelle said. "Now the trick will be getting him to behave himself."

"Gayle will see to that," JanaLynn said. "Either that or his mother." She smiled sweetly. "Menus?"

"Please."

"Oh," she said almost as an afterthought, and her expression grew sympathetically serious. "I heard Bill is going to be all right?"

"Oh, sure," Estelle said. "He's got a hard head."

"Oh, boy, does he," JanaLynn agreed. "I hope you find out

who the burglar was and hang him by his heels in Pershing Park." She left without a word or question about Janet Tripp, or an expression of condolence to Mike. Her touch had said it all.

As soon as JanaLynn was out of earshot, Estelle pushed her napkin and silverware to one side. "Mike, I realize that Eddie talked with you at considerable length yesterday, and then he and I had a go later. I know some of this is going to be repetitive for you."

"I know the drill," he said.

Estelle traced the patterns in the plastic tablecloth for a moment, considering how best to begin. JanaLynn arrived with menus, giving her another couple of minutes.

"I guess just coffee," Mike said, and JanaLynn frowned.

"That stuff will burn a hole in your stomach if you don't have something to eat," she said. Estelle glanced up at that, hearing a little more than just polite waitress in JanaLynn's tone. If Mike Sisneros caught the message of compassion, he gave no indication. "How about a nice omelet?"

"Yeah," Mike said. "Okay. That's fine."

"Green chile? Bacon? What would you like?"

"Just whatever," he said.

JanaLynn nodded with satisfaction and turned to Estelle. "How about you?"

"I guess a green chile breakfast burrito."

Surprise flickered briefly on JanaLynn's pretty face. "Tea with that?"

"Please."

"So," Estelle said when they were once more alone, "let me just tell you what I think, Mike." She regarded him thoughtfully, looking for some sign of interest. He had changed out of the clothes she'd seen the night before, when Mitchell had brought him home from his mother and stepfather's Christmas dinner.

Why he'd bothered, she couldn't guess. He hadn't forgotten the gun, though.

Sisneros didn't respond, but sat quietly with his hands down on the seat of the booth, as if he needed the two props to hold himself up. Maybe he did, Estelle thought.

"I think the same person who killed Janet also attacked Bill Gastner."

His eyelids flickered. "How do you figure that?"

"It's just a guess, at this point. Look," she said, and slid one hand across toward him, palm up. "What happened to Janet tells me that there's someone out there who set out to see her dead...I don't buy that it was a robbery. If it was a robbery, the killer wouldn't have moved the body. He would have just left her there, slumped in the car."

Mike turned and gazed out the window. "Why'd he take her?" he asked, voice no more than a whisper.

"I don't know, Mike. Maybe he... I don't know. We could speculate all day, and not know for sure."

"Mitchell said she wasn't assaulted," the deputy said.

"No. She wasn't."

"Then why take her?"

"I don't know. Maybe just to gain some time, Mike. There was a good chance that her body wouldn't have been discovered for days. Maybe he didn't want to take the time, or the chance, to actually bury her somewhere. If he'd done that, we might *still* not know where she was." She saw Mike's eyes narrow. "It didn't turn out that way, anyway. Who could predict a kid riding his Christmas bike up the Escudero."

"One more interruption," JanaLynn said tactfully from several paces away. She placed a mug and carafe of coffee in front of Mike, and a pot and teacup by Estelle's place. "The food will be out in a minute."

"Thanks, Jana," Estelle said, and the waitress ducked away. "Look, Mike," she continued, "the shooting isn't something that stemmed from a confrontation at the ATM. You stand there with a fistful of money, and you're a prime target for a snatch and run. Janet wasn't a big girl, she wasn't some ninja, she wasn't armed in any way. A teenager could have menaced her out of that money. It doesn't make any sense to me that someone would sneak up behind her and *execute* her." She paused for a minute. "I'm sorry, Mike, but that's what happened."

His dark eyes held hers, watchful and alert. "Why take the money at all, then?"

"It's there, it's easy, and maybe he figured it would lead us off in the wrong direction. Mike, we're not looking for a simple thief. We're looking for a killer. And that's what got me to thinking. Whoever hit Bill Gastner *didn't* confront him, like someone with a grudge. There were no words exchanged. No threats. Bill had no warning, never saw it coming. Just one very hard blow from the back, and if the weapon hadn't struck the door jamb at the same time, that would have been it. It would have done the job."

"If it was the same person, why didn't he just use the gun?" Mike's speech cadence had picked up a notch as his mind engaged.

"If he had, that would have connected the two, for sure. No doubt. And who knows? Maybe the killer *did* plan to use the gun. Maybe he crouched in the dark on that patio, gun in hand. Maybe he had second thoughts. Maybe he had time to think about the noise out in that quiet neighborhood. Maybe he tripped over the piece of rebar while he waited, and that changed his mind. Maybe it was one of those bright ideas at the last minute."

One eyebrow twitched, but Mike remained silent.

"But see," Estelle persisted, "it was the same sort of simple attack. One blow, and that was it. We both know that if they'd met face to face, he would have *had* to use the gun. Bill's a tough old guy, even pretty quick on his feet when he's not thinking about it. The killer didn't hang around to argue, to gloat, or for that matter, to ransack Bill's house. The keys were right there. He could have gone inside with no problem. But he didn't. One blow, and he's gone."

"Someone local, then," Mike said. "It wasn't just someone down off the Interstate who saw an opportunity and robbed Janet. He'd have no reason to wander around town until he stumbled on Gastner coming home."

"That's exactly right," Estelle said. "It's someone local, and it's someone who doesn't want to be caught. That's the only thing that makes sense to me."

TWENTY-FIVE

JANALYNN ARRIVED WITH the food, but didn't linger. The burrito, thoughtfully reduced in size from the dish that would have brought a grin of anticipation to Bill Gastner's face, rested fragrant and daunting in front of Estelle. She had ordered it only to encourage Mike Sisneros to eat, and now the idea of trying to work her way through its ten thousand calories cramped her stomach. The omelet parked in front of Mike Sisneros could have nourished a small army.

"Tell me about her," Estelle said as she started to unwrap one end of the burrito, exposing the filling without having to eat the thick tortilla or the blanket of cheese that held it all together. The request prompted silence. "Mike, look," Estelle said. "You're a good police officer. You know what we're up against. We have a victim. We have precious little forensic evidence. We have no one who has stepped forward and presented himself as a suspect. There's a missing gun in the picture. The gun belonged to the victim's fiancé. Do you want to quote me some statistics about domestic violence?"

"I'm the most likely person to have killed her," the deputy said dully. "That's what the statistics say."

"That's right. That's what they say."

"Captain Mitchell didn't arrest me last night, and here I am, trying to stuff my face this morning. The undersheriff hasn't arrested me either, so I guess I'm off the hook, huh?" He almost managed a tired smile. "For a while, anyway."

"So it appears. But you're a good cop, Mike."

"That's what you said."

"So you tell me where we should start." She pushed her plate to one side. "Mike, *I* don't know anything about Janet. Let's start that way. I haven't met her half a dozen times in the last six months. I know she worked at A & H. Doing what, I don't know. And I sure don't know why anyone would want to kill her."

He shook his head slowly, the omelet growing cold after the initial explorations. "I went to school with her," he said, and Estelle could see that he wasn't seeing the designs his fork drew in the omelet's crusty surface. "Well, sort of. She was a year behind me. I didn't hang out with her or anything. She was one of those kids that...well, that nobody really notices. She had her friends, I had mine. She went to work for the welding shop right out of high school. I know that, 'cause my father's a welder and taught me how, and we used to buy supplies and stuff like that over there. I'd see her once in a while."

"When did you start going out with her?"

He heaved a sigh. "Remember that nasty fire over at the Popes' place a couple of years ago?"

"Of course."

"She was one of the ones who helped round up some of the horses and donkeys that got loose after that. She lives in that trailer park right there when you turn off from Grande to Escondido? I mean, she *did*. Anyway, she broke her ankle that night. Stepped crooked or something, walking back home along the road. I was the responding officer to that."

"Ah." *A damsel in distress does it every time,* Estelle thought.

"We got to talking, and it just kinda grew from there. At first, she didn't seem too excited to have anything to do with a cop, but she came around." A ghost of a smile touched his face.

"She was never married before?"

"No. Kinda took our time, didn't we?"

"I wouldn't call thirty-one over the hill, Mike."

"I'm thirty-two. She's a year younger."

She grinned. "Well, then. *That's* over the hill. I speak from painful experience. She has family?" The night before, Mike Sisneros had been vague about Janet Tripp's relatives.

"She has one sister." Sisneros frowned at the table. "She lives over in Kansas. I know Janet has her address and number in her little book. But they don't talk much."

"Parents?"

"I…well, her mom died ten years ago or so. They were divorced. I know that. Her dad just walked out on 'em one day a long time ago. Left 'em high and dry. Janet doesn't like to talk about it. So we don't. I mean we didn't."

"Sometimes this is a hard time of year for folks with family problems," Estelle said.

"Yep. That's what the textbooks say." He glanced up and shook his head. "Sorry."

"Why didn't she go with you to Lordsburg on Christmas Day? Wasn't she planning to originally?"

"Maybe. Yeah. I guess she was. But I know that sometimes she's a little uncomfortable around my mom. It's one of those things—she has to kind of work up to it, you know? My mom is…well, she's bossy. And she doesn't like it much that I'm living with a white girl. And not married to boot. Mom is the Catholic of all Catholics when it comes to things like that."

"A white girl?"

"What can I say. To Mom, there's Indian, and there's white, and never the twain."

"She's Hopi?"

"Zuni."

"And your dad?"

"My stepdad is Zuni. My dad-dad is just plain old Mexican. That's white as far as Mom is concerned." He grinned but his eyes didn't go along. "Maybe that's where all the problems start, huh? A psychologist would have a ball."

"So Janet decided not to go over to Lordsburg at the last minute?"

"Yep." He worked the fork into the omelet until the utensil could stand upright by itself. "That was something that we were going to have to work out."

"Your mom, you mean?"

"Yep." He gave the fork a twist and withdrew it and put it down on the tablecloth. "I don't see it," he whispered. "Who'd want to do…"

"Who had access to your apartment, Mike?"

"Access?"

"I'm talking about the missing gun. People don't just *lose* guns, Mike. And I'm not suggesting that your gun was used as the murder weapon, either. But it's a loose end. Do you see? We have a weapon missing that's similar to what might have been used in a homicide."

"Janet had a key for the apartment. She was living with me."

"I understand that. And I find it hard to believe that Janet took the gun."

"She didn't take it. She didn't like guns."

"Well, then. *Someone* did, unless you took it out of its plastic case, diddled with it, and then put it somewhere else and forgot about it." She grinned. "Somewhere safe where you wouldn't lose it."

"*Diddled* with it?"

"*Con permiso,* Mike. I'm sorry. I have two little boys." She smiled at the deputy. "Sometimes these things slip out."

"I didn't put it somewhere else, Estelle. I kept it in the original box. I never shot it much."

"How long have you had it?"

"I got it for my twenty-fifth birthday. My dad gave it to me."

"Ah. This is Mr. Cruz?"

"No. Not my stepdad. My *dad*. Hank."

"And he lives in…"

"Deming. He moved there about fifteen years ago when him and my mom split up."

"You get over to see him a lot?"

"No." He didn't amplify, and Estelle saw the muscles of his jaw twitch. She hazarded a guess.

"The pistol was a peace offering of sorts, then? From him?"

"A *peace* offering?" He shrugged. "Yeah. I guess you could call it that. He gave it to me when I signed on with the village PD."

"It didn't work, though? It didn't work as a peace offering?"

"No, it didn't work. I was going to sell it, but I never got around to it. It just sat in the box in the back of my drawer. I maybe took it out once or twice. I haven't shot it for five years."

"But you still kept it."

"Well, it was from my dad."

Estelle took a small, tentative sample of the burrito's aromatic filling and chewed thoughtfully, letting the essence of the green chile waft up through her sinuses. "What was the deal between you and your dad?"

"We don't have to go there," Sisneros said.

She hesitated. "You know we do, Mike." She let him have a moment to think. "What was the deal?"

"The *deal* was that he's a drunk, Estelle. Was and still is. He made my mom's life a living hell, that's what the deal was. You've rolled on enough domestics that you know the story. Well, my dad's one of the statistics. Let me put it that way. Just about classic. He'd be the example in every chapter on family disputes. Drink, and a temper to light it with."

"So you don't see him much now?"

"I don't see him at all."

"You must have seen him when he gave you the gun, what, about six or seven years ago?"

"Yeah. I saw him then. For all of maybe five minutes. I told him at that time that I didn't need to have him in my life."

"But you kept the gun."

"It wasn't quite like that. He left it behind. I didn't notice that he'd done that. And yeah, I should have taken the trouble to return it. I didn't. I just shoved the case in the dresser drawer, and that's that."

"Does your dad have a key to your apartment?"

He frowned with surprise. "Of course not. Why would he?"

"Is this because of your mom?"

"Is what because of my mom?"

"The reason you don't talk."

His face darkened. "I don't see how that would have anything to do with any of this."

"Does he ever talk to your mom? Do you know?"

"No." His answer was out almost before she had finished her sentence.

JanaLynn appeared by the serving station, hesitant to intrude. Estelle looked at her and nodded, and she stepped up to the table. "Not much in the mood for eating, huh," JanaLynn said sympathetically. Both dishes looked as if an ambitious mouse had attacked one corner. "How about a take-home box?"

"That'll work," Mike replied.

"How about you?" JanaLynn asked Estelle.

"Sure. Why not." The plates disappeared.

"When was the last time your mom talked to your dad, Mike?"

"I have no idea how I would know something like that. You'd have to ask her." His tone was clipped and contentious, and Estelle hesitated.

"What year were they divorced?"

"Nineteen ninety-two," he said without hesitating to calculate.

"Long time ago."

"Yeah, it's a long time. Life goes on."

Yes, it does, Estelle thought. "Tell me about Janet's friends," Estelle said. "She's lived with you for how long now?"

"A couple of months."

"And in that time, who's come over to the apartment?"

"Oh, she has a couple of friends that we see now and then. Nobody that has a key."

"No one she'd lend a key to?"

"What for? You don't just lend house keys, do you? And there's the timing thing, too. I don't know for sure when the pistol went missing. I told Mitchell that, too. I don't take it out and fondle it on a regular basis, you know. It could have been taken yesterday, or last week, or last month…even last year."

"Do you have anyone come into your apartment on a regular basis? Cleaning lady, someone like that?"

"Mitchell and I went over every inch of that. No, I don't. I can't afford a cleaning lady. The gas guy reads the meter from the outside. So does the electric company." He grinned and, except for the fatigue, might have looked five years younger. "The Jehovah's Witnesses knock once in a while, but I don't let 'em in." He took a long swig of coffee and grimaced. "The last person in the apartment, other than me and Janet, was Tommy Pasquale. He borrowed the Mustang to take Linda out for a swank dinner in Las Cruces. He didn't want to take her in his Jeep."

"When was that?"

"I don't remember exactly. Sometime in early December. I told him that he could just let himself in and toss the keys on the table when he came back."

"And that's what he did?"

"That's what he did. Said 'Howdy' to Janet, and went on his way. And if I can't trust him, then the whole damn world can just come to a stop for all I care."

"Sure enough," Estelle agreed, and then she sat back abruptly. A realization stabbed through Estelle's head like a mini-stroke, so simple and obvious that she felt the surge of blood up her neck. She hadn't blushed in years, but her face burned now. Everyone was tired, everyone had worked too many hours, everyone—well, *she*—was preoccupied with a dozen other things, and it all boiled down to missing the obvious.

She pulled her cell phone off her belt and punched the speed dial for Sergeant Tom Mears.

TWENTY-SIX

"YOU HAVE REACHED voice mail for Sergeant Tom Mears. If this is an emergency, please dial 911. Otherwise, leave a message at the tone."

"And your call is important to us," Estelle said to the robotic voice. She punched another set and waited.

"Posadas County Sheriff's Department. Sutherland."

"Brent, this is Estelle. Do you know where Sergeant Mears is right now?"

"I think he's home, ma'am. I'm not sure. He worked most of the night, I know. He logged out this morning about four or so."

"How long have you been up?"

"Oh, I don't know," Sutherland said. "But Ernie is coming in a little later to relieve."

And he's the swing shift, Estelle thought. The department organization was going to pieces. "Okay, thanks."

"Captain Mitchell just came in a few minutes ago. Do you want to talk to him? He's standing right here."

"Sure."

In a moment Mitchell's quiet, soft voice greeted her. Estelle had always thought that if voices were all that mattered, Edward Mitchell would make a great physician, handling patients over the phone. He could make *Take two aspirins and call me in the morning* sound as if it really might work.

"Eddie, we need to check Janet Tripp's keys. Tom Mears had

them in an evidence bag, and he was going to run prints, but we need to know if her *apartment* keys are on the ring."

"You mean the keys to the place she shares with Sisneros?" Mitchell asked.

"Right."

"Is Sisneros with you?"

"Yes, he is. We're at the Don Juan."

"Okay. Hang tight. Tom was downstairs with Linda a few minutes ago. I don't know if he still is or not. Give me a minute to track things down."

"We're headed back to the office right now," Estelle said. As she switched off, Mike nodded and slid out of the booth. He accepted both doggie boxes from JanaLynn.

Estelle dropped a twenty-dollar bill on the table, thinking immediately of the countless times she'd seen Bill Gastner do exactly the same thing, whether he'd had a dinner or just a slice of pie and coffee. "Thanks, JL," she said.

"You guys take care," JanaLynn said, and the look she gave Mike Sisneros would have been comical under other circumstances. She didn't quite reach up and pinch her nose shut against the aroma, but her reaction was close. Oblivious, the deputy headed out of the restaurant toward Estelle's car.

"Is he going to be all right?" JanaLynn whispered to Estelle as Mike slipped through the inner foyer door.

"We hope so," Estelle said. "A little more sleep, a lot less beer, and a very long shower."

It took a minute and a half to drive back to the Public Safety Building, straight east on Bustos through the heart of Posadas. The two of them rode in silence, Estelle content to leave the young man alone with his thoughts. Mike Sisneros appeared to have pulled himself out of his personal morass, and his eyes flicked from one side of the street to another as if the answers to all his questions were about to step out in front of the county car. Estelle could see that he was thinking, not just puddling. That was progress of a sort.

Inside the Sheriff's Office, Eddie Mitchell stood near the dispatch island, and as Estelle and Mike entered, he extended a plastic evidence bag toward Estelle. "They're still downstairs," he said.

"Still?" She looked up at the wall clock as she and Mike followed Mitchell to his office.

"Still. It's the new schedule we talked about. Thirty-six hours on, two hours off. That way, we'll be able to cut back to a staff of two. Leona Spears will be ecstatic."

Estelle looked quickly toward the front doors and the foyer, where the line of plastic chairs awaited visitors. Leona Spears, the potential county manager-to-be, was nowhere in sight. "She was here?"

Mitchell raised a skeptical eyebrow. "Paranoid, are we?"

"No…not paranoid, exactly. I just want to have time to prepare for the challenge," Estelle said. Mitchell closed his office door, and Estelle spread the plastic bag out on his desk so she could look at each key. The fob was bright blue plastic with the A & H WELDING logo in gold. "Which one goes to the apartment, Mike?"

Sisneros took the bag, glanced through the set, and shook his head, then looked more carefully. "It's not there."

"She did have them, though?"

"Well, of course she had them."

"As far as you know, she had them when you two last saw each other? What, that would be yesterday some time?"

"I suppose so. I didn't ask." He hunched his shoulders. "Who ever asks somebody if they have their keys? I mean, do *you* have your house key on your key ring?"

"Yes."

"You're sure?"

Resisting the temptation to check, but now keenly aware of the weight of her own key ring in her pocket, she plunged doggedly on. "But as far as you knew, Janet had her own key to your apartment and she had it with her. It was on *this* key ring, not some separate one? She didn't have it on a separate special one or something?"

"Yes, I said." A flash of irritation flushed his face. "It's just the one key." He enunciated the words as if talking to little Carlos. "It's one key, and it fits both the inside door by the stairwell, and the outside door. That's the one door we use most of the time. We don't come and go through the house. We use the outside stairway."

"You always lock the apartment when you go out?" Mitchell asked.

"Yes. I mean, we forget once in a while, but yeah…we lock it as a matter of course."

"Leave an extra key with somebody? The manager, someone like that?"

"No. Mrs. Freeman might have one. I suppose she does. I never asked her."

"Let me see yours." Mitchell held out his hand and waited while the deputy dug the wad of keys out of his hip pocket. "Which one?"

Sisneros held the apartment key by the blade, the rest dangling. Mitchell took them and looked again at the keys in the evidence bag.

"Okay," he said slowly, and looked up questioningly at Estelle. "Keys don't just come off key rings all by themselves. And you're sure she didn't keep it on a separate ring."

"I know she didn't."

"So where did it go?"

"I don't know, Captain." The use of rank as a name wasn't lost on Eddie, who gazed thoughtfully at Sisneros.

"We have two choices that make sense," Estelle said. "Either Janet gave it to someone…to anyone—"

"Why would she do that?" Sisneros interrupted.

"You'd know that better than we would, Mike."

"Well, I don't know it."

"No idea? All right, then. The other choice is that someone took it. Let's suppose for a minute. Suppose that the killer took it off the ring."

"What would he want with it?" Sisneros asked. "The killer, I mean. If he took it."

"Good question. Obviously to get inside her apartment…either then or to use at some point in the future. He knew where she lived. Or he found out one way or another." She held up the keys in the bag, looking at them again. "It doesn't take a rocket scientist to figure out which one is for the apartment." She counted them off. "Jeep keys, this one looks like it's for a small suitcase or night bag, we've got a safety deposit key for Posadas State Bank, and I'd be willing to bet that this big Yale key is for A & H Welding. Who knows what the little Brinks key is for…some little padlock somewhere."

"That's to her storage unit over on Escondido, by the trailer park. Where she used to live."

"Fair enough. Somebody wasn't interested in gaining entry to that, evidently. Is anything else missing from your apartment?" Mitchell asked.

"Anything *else?*" Sisneros replied. "I mean, *nothing*'s missing. I was there from the time you dropped me off until the undersheriff called this morning. If something was gone, I would have noticed."

I'm not so sure of that, Estelle thought. The way Mike Sisneros had looked when she first saw him plodding down the stairs suggested that a bulldozer could have driven through the apartment and he wouldn't have noticed or, if he had noticed, wouldn't have minded.

"Other than your .22 pistol, I think he means," Estelle said. "Janet's personal effects were all there?"

For the first time since breakfast, the young man's face crumpled with agony, and he leaned against Mitchell's desk, jaw slack. "Christ," he whispered. "Yeah…they were there. They're still there. I walked into the bathroom and her comb and brush and everything…" He choked it off. "Still there," he murmured. "Just like she stepped out for a minute and was coming right back." He rubbed his face with both hands. "I can't believe this."

"The gun was gone," Mitchell said mildly, repeating the obvious. His heavy-lidded eyes assessed Mike Sisneros without a trace of expression.

"I don't know when that happened," the deputy said. "I've said that a dozen times."

"*Could* it have happened yesterday?"

"I suppose it could," Sisneros said, exasperated. "And it could have happened a year ago, too. But what sense does that make? He shot her, then took her apartment key, went to the apartment and stole my gun? That's sort of backward for that little scenario, don't you think?"

"What if Janet didn't have her key with her yesterday." Estelle voiced the possibility and waited.

"If she lost her key, why wouldn't she have said something to me when she came here? Wouldn't that have been the logical thing? Especially since I was going to Lordsburg, and she had decided not to. What's she going to do, sit in the apartment all day?"

"But she didn't do that, did she?"

Mike's temper rose again. "What are you getting at, anyway?"

Estelle held up the evidence bag. "The apartment key is gone. That's what I'm getting at. We don't know why it's gone. We don't know *when* it went missing." She dropped the plastic bag back on Mitchell's desk. "I'll feel better when I know the answers."

"Well, so will I."

"I'm glad to hear that. You ready to go back to work?"

He didn't look ready for anything, but Estelle saw Mike Sisneros's spine straighten a little.

"What do you want me to do?"

"Now that we know the key is missing, I want you to go back to your apartment and really *look*, Mike. Look through everything. All your papers. All your stuff. And Janet's too. I know it's hard, but you'll know better than anyone what should be there and what's not. Look at *everything*, Mike." She paused. "When you're going through Janet's things, get the telephone number and address for her sister. We'll want to talk with her."

"Okay. I know where that is. You want me to call her?"

"I'd rather do that, Mike." She nodded at the evidence bag. "And if I were you, I'd have the locks changed today."

"A burglar's not going to get much in my place," he said.

"I'm not worried about burglars, Mike."

TWENTY-SEVEN

WHEN ESTELLE ENTERED the hospital, the hustle and bustle of the day shift had overtaken the halls and offices. Medicine didn't pause for rest on Sundays. There was no sign of the nocturnal Stacy Cunningham and his floor polisher.

In his room, Bill Gastner stood in front of the window, gazing out into the bright December morning. A small bandage covered the back of his skull behind his left ear. Estelle rattled the door knob so he wouldn't startle, and he raised a hand without turning around.

"I saw you drive into the parking lot," he said. "Goddamn gorgeous day, you know that?"

"Yes it is."

"Have you taken any time to enjoy it yet?" He turned and grinned at her. "You missed Christmas, you know."

"Actually, I have, *Padrino,*" Estelle said. "And you look like you're ready to go." She had almost said *huggable,* since his brown Hush Puppies, russet corduroy trousers, and plaid flannel shirt made him look like a comfortably rotund teddy bear.

"*That's* for sure," Gastner said emphatically. He looked at the hospital bed with distaste. "Thanks for agreeing to play taxi."

"I bet you're hungry," Estelle said.

"Of course I'm hungry," he replied. "Let's go get a little something."

"I just spent a half-hour with Mike Sisneros at the Don Juan, so..."

"Without me? How *could* you? I'm crushed."

"Well, we could have used your touch, sir. JanaLynn says hi, by the way."

"God, the love of my life," Gastner said.

"I ordered a breakfast burrito, and didn't touch it. We can go back to the house and nuke it for you."

"Sounds good. Although their breakfast menu leaves a little something to be desired in the size department. But that's a good start." He went to the closet and pulled his jacket off the hanger. "Let's get out of here before they show up with that damn wheelchair." He patted his pocket. "And I have enough drugs to go into business."

"Should I ask if the doctors actually checked you out?"

"Of course they did," Gastner said. "Francis was here and left. That's the same thing. I asked if I could get dressed, and your hubby agreed that was a good idea. I translate that as my ticket to freedom."

A few minutes later, as they walked across the tarmac toward the car, Estelle noticed the care with which Gastner placed each step. As he reached the back fender, he stretched out a hand and stopped, leaning against the car. "The best thing about being stuck in that place is the getting out," he said. "The only thing I'm going to be able to smell for a week is spray cleaner and bleach."

A few minutes later, when Estelle turned south on Grande, Gastner looked puzzled. "I thought we were going to your place," he said.

"You're not ready for that yet," Estelle said. "And we wouldn't get anything done."

"I appreciated the troops stopping by my room earlier this morning," he said. "Sofía brought the urchins."

"They were excited about getting to do that. They worry about you, *Padrino*. You know that?"

"Rodgers and Hammerstein," Gastner mused. "How are they doing?"

She nodded noncommittally, and he reached out and closed the cover on the center console computer as if it might be listening. He leaned his elbow on it, slouching sideways in the crowded seat.

"You're allowed to brag on 'em, you know," he said. "Hell, *I* do."

"Oh, sure!" Estelle laughed, well aware of Gastner's aversion to inflicting photos of relatives and tales of their innumerable accomplishments on the unwary.

"Well, I would if the opportunity presented itself," he added. "You worried about 'em?" That took her by surprise, and he reached out to point at Escondido when it appeared that she was going to drive right by the intersection. "I live down there."

She braked hard and turned.

"You know, I have a granddaughter who plays the piano," he said. "I think I told you that. Camille's youngest? Sherri goes to the keyboard, and the rest of the family hightails to the woods. She absolutely has a *passion* for playing the piano...and she has absolutely no talent whatsoever. Go figure. Her mother does, but not the kid." He shrugged. "I worry about number one son, though." He turned and regarded Estelle. "Francisco, that is."

When Estelle didn't respond, he added, "It's not going to be easy for him."

"No, it's not," she said, and pulled to a stop in front of Gastner's adobe. She pushed the gear lever into Park. "I'm not sure what to do, *Padrino.*"

He relaxed back against the door, showing no inclination to get out of the car. "You have a list of options?"

"I suppose we do."

When she didn't elaborate, he beckoned with his fingers.

"Sofía made a suggestion that scares me," Estelle said, her voice dropping almost to a whisper.

Gastner cocked his head. "Scares you how?"

"She suggested the Conservatorio de Veracruz."

His heavy brows beetled a little. "For just him, you mean? Or the whole clan?"

"Either way. But I don't think…," and one of her hands fluttered hopelessly.

"Don't think what?" he said bluntly, refusing to let her off the hook.

"I don't think that I could send Francisco away," she said. Once the words were out, they sounded silly to her. "For one thing, I can't imagine Carlos home all alone. He and Francisco are the next best thing to Siamese twins, sir."

"Tough stuff," he grunted. "So what are the options? All of you could go, right? I mean, whether it's Veracruz or Juilliard in New York doesn't matter much, does it?"

"It matters a *lot,* sir. But yes. We all could go. We're not going to, but we *could.*"

"You think hard on what an opportunity that is, sweetheart," he said, lurching around so he could reach the door handle. "Hell, there's sick people in every corner of the world. It can't matter a whole hell of a lot where hubby works. Sick is sick. With Sofía's influence, the whole bunch of you would have to get used to living in grand style. Hell, you could get a job working for the *federales,* or some such."

Estelle laughed. "That's what Francis said, sir."

"Well, listen to somebody, sweetheart. Hey, look," and he leaned back toward her. "I've been around a while, and when my wife was alive, we went to concerts and stuff like that. Best one I can remember was that opera guy, what's-his-name? The Mexican."

"Plácido Domingo?"

"Yeah, him."

"The 'opera guy.'" She laughed. "He'd love that."

"Well, he is. Anyway, we saw him in concert in Houston, back when he was younger. You know, he spends a lot of his time working with young musicians. Anyway," and he paused and reached up to pat the bandage on his head. "What was I trying to say?"

"That you've been around, sir."

"That's it. And anyone who hears the little wart play, or who *watches* him make love to that damn piano, or watches the way he tells stories with it…hell, anybody will tell you the same thing. He isn't some little kid who should be stuck with once-a-week piano lessons in some backwater place out in the desert. What a goddamn waste to the world that would be, sweetheart." He stopped suddenly and thumped the computer lid. "It's none of my business. Except it is my business, because he's family." He shrugged. "So there it is. Do what you got to do, sweetheart. Don't let it wait."

"Francis and I need to talk about it some more. Right now we're leaning toward bringing the world to him, instead of vice versa. Let the rest of the world find out that there really is a Posadas."

"What a concept," he said brusquely. "And a damn good idea, too. I could have come up with that if I had half a brain." He opened the door and struggled out of the car. "Stop letting work interfere with your home life. That's my advice for the day." He shot her a wide grin. "Notice how effortless it is to say asinine things like that."

He stopped in front of the door and regarded the sad little acacia by the step.

"Ruined that, didn't I." He twisted and looked back at the corner of the patio where the piece of rebar had been found.

"Either I was preoccupied, or deaf, or stoned," he said. "Not to hear someone crunching across that gravel behind me." He frowned and turned to the door. "I can't remember if I was in the process of turning, or not," he added. It took him a minute or so to find the right key, and then to find the keyhole. "Don't get old, sweetheart. That's my best advice."

He swung the heavy door open. "There we go, then. Let's eat. And you can tell me what you've found out about Janet Tripp. I've been lying in bed thinking about her a lot lately."

TWENTY-EIGHT

"MIKE SISNEROS WENT to school with Janet," Estelle said. "Sort of. He was a year ahead of her. He didn't go out with her or anything like that, but he knew her. That's all."

"Infatuation from afar?" Gastner asked.

"I don't think so. He just knew who she was, that's all. And then over the years, he had occasion to see her once in a while at A & H Welding. Just a familiar face. He was the officer who provided initial treatment when she was hurt the night of the Pope fire. She stepped in a ditch and sprained or broke her ankle."

"Ah," Gastner said. "I didn't remember that." He scooped another generous load of burrito, deftly wrapping the strand of cheese around the loaded fork. "She lived over at the trailer park on Escondido. I recall that. See?" He held up the morsel. "Feed the brain, and off you go."

"She's been with Mike for a while now," Estelle said.

"Now, yes. But when she was on her own, that's where she lived."

"There's a sister, too. Mike says that she lives over in Kansas. He's going to find the number and address for me."

"No one's contacted her yet about Janet?"

"No, sir. Do you remember anything about the sister?"

"Not a damn thing." He frowned. "That may require several more of these." A tiny fragment of green chile lay at one end of the empty platter, and he speared it with his fork. "Her folks," he mused, and shut his eyes. Estelle wondered what mental process it was that sifted through half a century of memories and associations, searching for a single face or a single name. Bill Gastner had once described his memory as being like an enormous walk-in closet filled from floor to ceiling with trivia scribbled in fading ink on millions of 3 x 5 cards, a true ROM.

"Terry Tripp used to work for the electric company," he said after a moment. "The mother. I *think* that's where she worked. If it wasn't too long ago, Kevin Tierney could tell you for sure. I don't recall who was manager before him." He closed his eyes again, perhaps watching the cascade of file cards. "She died of cancer. God, how long ago? I have no idea. Ten, fifteen years? Something like that?"

"How about Janet's father?" Estelle asked. Gastner had pushed the plastic take-out box away, and she scooped it off the counter and put it in the sack of trash under the sink.

Gastner rested his chin in his hand, elbow on the counter. "This is interesting," he said. "I haven't thought about any of these folks for a long, long time." He turned just enough so he could see Estelle. "You know, when Janet came into the Sheriff's Office for the last time, whenever it was? Christmas afternoon? God…that's yesterday. Anyway, I thought of her mother. I guess in part it's because they looked a lot alike. I'm sure that at one time, I knew who Mr. Tripp was." He shrugged and one hand sought out the bandage on the back of his head. "But that's too long ago."

"Ancient history," Estelle said.

"Be careful with that *ancient* stuff," Gastner said. "Mike didn't know?"

"No. Eddie and I are both going to talk with him again today sometime."

"*His* dad was a piece of work," Gastner said. "Mike's, I mean. A joyous drunk might be a good way to put it. He was one of those guys who just plain loved alcohol. A real love affair with old Nancy Whiskey. And you know what? I don't recall a single time when he was actually arrested for DWI, or public intox, or anything like that. You ask Bobby Torrez. There's never been a cop who had it more in for drunken drivers than Bobby. You know that. But even he never managed to nail old Hank for anything."

"Careful, or lucky, or both. Mike says his old man had a fine temper."

"Well," Gastner said, hunching his shoulders, "probably." He sighed. "But he and Irene split up eventually. Mike's mom. Irene? She dumped him, he dumped her, I guess it doesn't matter. Old Nancy got in the way, is all."

"And a few other issues, Mike says," Estelle added.

"No doubt." He squinted at the opposite wall. "She is Native American."

"Zuni."

"I knew that." He frowned. "Brad Tripp," he said suddenly. He pronounced the name and then fell silent.

"The father? Janet's dad?"

Gastner nodded and his gaze shifted to the coffee maker. After a moment, he pushed himself off the tall kitchen stool and approached it. He leaned on the counter with one hand on each side of the Brewmaster as if trying to decide a strategy.

"Ask Bobby about Brad Tripp," he said finally, and he smiled broadly at the memory. "Remember the old office, back before the county built the annex? Maybe that was before your time."

"No. I was here then."

"Well, Bobby hauled Brad in for something…. I don't remember what it was. All I remember is that it involved Brad spending the rest of the night in the slammer. They were going up the stairs to the second floor, and old Brad decided that it might be a good idea to take a swing at Bobby." Gastner turned around and leaned against the counter, arms crossed over his belly. "No one could figure out what Brad thought that might accomplish, including Brad, probably."

"I remember the time," Estelle said. "Everyone was talking about it the next day. I'd forgotten that's who it was."

"That's it," Gastner said. "A huge crash, and Brad lands at the bottom of the stairs in a crumpled heap. The dispatcher at the time was Miracle Murton, and he about jumps out of his skin. Murton asks Bobby what happened. 'He fall down, go boom,' is all Bobby would tell him. Miracle worried for days about whether he should be writing reports about what happened. He was afraid old Brad was going to sue Bobby, the county, and every living soul within shouting distance."

He turned back to the coffee maker. "Goddamn good thing Brad didn't break his neck. But he was drunk enough that he bounced pretty well. No injuries that showed." He frowned at the coffeepot again. "Little squirt of a guy. I have no recollection what the incident was all about." He shook his head with frustration, then hauled the bag of coffee beans out of the cabinet above the counter.

Estelle watched him go through the process of measuring and grinding the potent beans, and then filling the machine with enough water to supply coffee to a dozen troops. Everything accomplished without disaster, he stood and regarded the gadget thoughtfully. "Helps," he said aloud, and flipped on the power switch.

He turned back to Estelle. "You want some tea or something?"

"No, thanks."

"It's still a puzzle," he said, and watched as the first thin stream of coffee gurgled out the bottom of the filter basket. "I don't remember what became of old Brad—assuming I ever knew in the first place. And all this ancient history isn't getting us very far."

"I think that the same person attacked both you and Janet," Estelle said, and Gastner looked at her with surprise at the sudden change of subject.

"That's interesting," he said. "What makes you think so? I mean, other than that this is a tiny town…and that makes the odds a gambler's choice that violent episodes in one day are connected."

"Same MO, for one thing," Estelle said.

Gastner frowned at that, but took a moment to slip out the filling carafe and pour a partial cup.

"In both cases, the intent was to kill," she said, and saw Gastner's eyebrow drift upward. He dumped too much sugar into his cup without bothering to stir it. "One shot to Janet's head, execution style. One blow to yours, darn near in the exact same spot."

"He didn't shoot me, though."

"No. I think he changed his mind at the last minute. Maybe he figured that if he shot you, that would tie the two events together for sure. He's working on being pretty clever, sir. The assault on you is obviously a grudge motive—hit and run, no robbery, no burglary of the house, no auto theft. Someone from your past, making the score even."

"And Janet?"

"It's supposed to look like a robbery at an ATM—not the most imaginative thing. But then I think he changed his mind again somehow. He shoots Janet, makes it look like a robbery, and then for some inexplicable reason, takes the body and dumps her in the arroyo."

"It makes sense if he wants to buy some time," Gastner said.

"And that fits, sir. The key to Mike's apartment was gone from her key ring. We don't know how or why. And on top of that, there's this: Mike owns a .22 pistol. It's missing, and he can't account for that."

"Well, shit," Gastner mused. "He's missing a weapon?"

"Just the .22. An odd coincidence, maybe."

"But see, none of those pieces fit. If the killer took the key…that's what you're thinking?"

Estelle nodded. "There's that possibility, sir."

"If he took the key, he wanted to use it. So he disposes of the body, which by his bizarre thinking might give him some extra time. He goes to the apartment. How does he know that *Mike* won't be there?"

"I have no idea. Maybe he didn't care. Maybe he talked to Janet before he shot her."

"And maybe dumb luck," Gastner observed. "You don't have a lick of evidence that she talked to anybody in that bank parking lot. And after he does that, and then steals the gun, which he didn't need to kill Janet, by the way, he comes over to my house and clubs me on the head." He looked at Estelle skeptically. "I don't know, sweetheart." He sipped the coffee and out of thirty years' habit as a smoker, his left hand drifted to his left shirt pocket, searching for a phantom cigarette.

After a moment, he leaned back. "You don't actually have anything that ties the two incidents together, though. Am I right?"

"*Nada.*"

"If you're right—and I'll be the first to admit that your intuition has a pretty good track record—you're saying that somehow there's a connection between Janet Tripp and myself. Something in common."

"It would appear so, sir."

"Well, you know my shadowy past pretty well, sweetheart. The next step is to find out what you can about Ms. Tripp. Some little thing. What's Bobby say about all this?"

"He comes home today, *Padrino*."

"Well, he's got a good head on his shoulders, and he's got a hell of a lot of good connections with all kinds of dark little corners around the county. Go poke around and see what you come up with."

"You'll be all right?"

"Of course I'll be all right." He patted the smooth maple of the chopping-block counter. "I'm in my castle now."

"Maybe you'd like to come over for dinner later tonight?"

"Sofía already invited me," he said with a grin. "She promised something with a name about this long," and he held his hands a yard apart. "Something that involves red snapper and chile. How bad can that be?"

"Ah, *huachinango a la veracruzana*," Estelle said. "She's been planning that for a while. She complains that there's no fresh red snapper in Posadas."

"This is surprising?" Gastner laughed. "Let's see how the day goes, sweetheart. We all know what happens when we try to plan something." He rose and stepped to the coffeepot to refill his cup, and Estelle slipped back into her jacket.

"I'll let you know what Bobby says."

"Do that," Gastner said. "I'll be home all day, and after that, I'll be over at Twelfth Street as chief taste-tester for the *chinchang*."

"*Huachinango, Padrino*." He accompanied her to the front door.

"It's a good thing you guys aren't going to take her up on her suggestion to move down there. I can just imagine my North Carolina tongue trying to wrap itself around that Aztec language," he said.

"Mayan, *Padrino*."

"But you're Aztec, aren't you?" His warm eyes took in the outlines of her face with affection. "You wouldn't fit in down there, anyway. Wise decision."

"*Nos vemos,*" she said with a resigned shrug. "There's a whole world of things I have to think about. One step at a time. Right now I'm working on making it through to dinnertime."

TWENTY-NINE

THE EXPRESSION ON Robert Torrez's face jolted Estelle to a stop at the doorway of the sheriff's tiny, bleak office. He was always master of the threatening glower, whether there was any bite behind it or not, and the dark storms on his broad, handsome face were now classic in their proportions.

He looked up so slowly it appeared that his neck muscles were actually a set of smooth hydraulic pistons. His skull clicked to a stop as his eyes locked on Estelle's.

"Welcome back," Estelle said, although she could plainly see that words of welcome were wasted on the sheriff. Whatever orders the Albuquerque physicians might have given to their patient, it didn't surprise Estelle that the sheriff had headed for his office the moment he arrived home in Posadas.

"Yeah," Torrez said. He flipped a piece of peach-colored paper across his desk toward her. "What the fuck is this?" Almost never profane, especially when he knew that women were within hearing range, the sheriff startled Estelle with his word choice.

She picked up the paper as she sat down on one of the military surplus steel folding chairs, immediately recognizing the style of the author. Leona Spears was adept at losing elections, true enough. She'd lost every one she'd tried, including the one against Bob Torrez years before. But Leona was a meticulous planner, never—ever—leaving something to the last moment if it could be planned out, organized, and strategy-checked beforehand.

The paper, perfectly organized onto a single page for maximum effect, was titled "Preliminary Needs Assessment and Budgetary Planning, Posadas County Sheriff's Department."

Torrez sat like a lump, glowering, while Estelle read the paper. She understood it immediately, and had to agree that Leona's logic was unassailable. If Leona was to be considered for the county manager's position, then it made sense to scope things out before she faced the county commission. What did each department manager or supervisor need or want in order to effectively manage his turf? Leona would have no way of knowing unless she first asked, and then later observed and judged performance for herself.

But Estelle knew that it wasn't the planning that irked Robert Torrez. Being asked how many new patrol units he anticipated needing for the coming year was not radical. There was no implication that whatever he asked for, he was asking for too much. Asking what kind of units was perfectly logical. Asking the sheriff what he thought to be the weak spots in his organization was eminently practical, and just good management.

Estelle read the paper again. Nowhere on the sheet was there the faintest hint of direction or suggestion from Ms. Leona Spears. It was impossible to judge what Leona thought by what she asked on the paper.

"I got two and a half dead people on my hands," Torrez said, but there was nothing amused in his tone. "First I find out that Eduardo died, then Janet Tripp gets herself killed, and then Bill Gastner has his skull split open by some whacko with a grudge. I get sidetracked up in the city while a hundred doctors jam needles into me and drain half my blood."

"Bobby, please…"

"Jesus, Estelle. *Leona Spears?*" He fairly shouted the woman's name. "What the hell is going through their little pointed heads?"

"Whose heads?"

"You know whose heads, damn it. The commission. Didn't you go to the meetings?"

"Yes." There was nothing to be gained by pointing out to the sheriff that nothing prevented him from attending as well.

"Leona Spears…can *not* be county manager," Torrez said emphatically. "That's just the way it is."

"She can and will be if the commissioners vote that way, Bobby."

"Bullshit." He shifted his weight and rapped his shin against the unforgiving military surplus desk, and he slammed the offending drawer shut with one swift kick of a black boot. "I mean, look at this thing." He picked up the paper again. "She's got something against white paper, for Christ's sakes?"

"Maybe she ran out," Estelle said, amused.

"Why doesn't she spray it with perfume while she's at it. What are they thinking?"

"Well, I talked with Dr. Gray a while ago…I don't even remember when it was. But a majority of the board is leaning toward giving Leona the job. She has a final interview with them on Tuesday. I suppose that's the rationale for this." She nodded at the paper. "It won't hurt her case if she does some preplanning—if she finds out what we want and need. How long has that been lying on your desk?"

He ignored her question. "Gray said all that, or is that what you think?"

Estelle hesitated, then shrugged. "Bobby, so far, it hasn't mattered much to us who the county manager is. Kevin was good," she said, referring to the previous manager, "but the one before him was an idiot. They come and they go. We both know that."

"Leona Spears needs to go, not come."

She laughed. "We'll see, Bobby. Besides, Leona is local, for one thing."

"*Loco,* you mean."

"Well, maybe. But that's important to the board, at this point. They don't want some stranger coming in who doesn't have some sympathy for the way we do things down here. Maybe they have a point. There's no one who knows the county better than Leona does, except maybe yourself or Bill Gastner. I can see why they're willing to give Leona a chance. She's a professional planner, she's good at working through budgetary matters, and she has to be pretty good at managing people, or she wouldn't have been with the Highway Department as long as she has."

"She's nuts," Torrez said.

"Maybe. She cornered me last week sometime and asked me a couple questions that didn't sound too crazy."

"Like what? She never talked to me."

Small wonder. "For one thing, she wanted some figures on how much it would cost to have enough vehicles for the deputies to take the units home when they were off-duty."

"You know we can't afford that."

"Leona wants to investigate applying for grants. That's one of her specialties, I guess. Anyway, Bobby, I liked the sound of what she wanted to do. With the county having to provide coverage for the village now, it made sense to me to have each deputy with immediate access to a vehicle. If Leona Spears can make that happen, I'm all for it."

Torrez flipped the paper off to one side in contempt.

"You want me to go through that and write up some answers?" Estelle asked. "She isn't asking a lot…and there's only a day or two left now to put together an answer that might do us some good." She refrained from adding, We could have talked about this last week.

"If you want to do that, go ahead," Torrez said. He made no move to hand her the paper, and she reached across and retrieved it. "So fill me in. What's going on, other than Leona Spears? Christ."

As succinctly as possible, Estelle reviewed their progress, and he listened without interruption, feet now propped up on his desk. When she'd finished, he let one leg slip off the desk, his boot thumping on the floor.

"Mike stopped by," he said abruptly. He picked up a 3 x 5 card. "Janet's sister lives in Kentland, Kansas. Monica Tripp-Baylor. I was going to call her…give me something to do."

"Okay. When you do that, I'd like to know something about the parents."

"She died."

"The mother? So I've been told. But Mike says that Brad Tripp just sort of walked out on the family. I'd like to know what the real story is."

"That's what happened," Torrez said. "They didn't get along, and he moved out. Lived in town for a while, then hit the road."

"I was trying to recall the incident of him on the stairway in the old building," Estelle said.

Torrez actually smiled. "He'd been tearin' up Pike's Saloon. Remember that place down past the Don Juan that burned a year or so later?"

"Sure."

"Just a bar fight," the sheriff said. "I happened to be cruisin' by, and took the call. When I brought Tripp back to the office, he decided to take me on. Didn't work," he added with some satisfaction.

"And that's it?"

"That's it." He shrugged.

"And after that incident?"

"Don't know. I didn't see him all that often. Eduardo would know, but he ain't talkin'," Torrez said bluntly.

"Well, sure, Bobby."

"No doubt about it. Probably wasn't a soul in the whole town that Eduardo *didn't* know."

"Agreed. But, as you say…"

"We need to sit down and talk with Essie, if you think you need to know something about Brad Tripp."

Estelle mulled that for a moment. Essie Martinez was living through the least merry Christmas of her life. Digging through what she recalled of her husband's tenure as police chief would be painful and, under the best of circumstances, of suspect accuracy anyway. But the sheriff was right. It was another angle, and at this point, any angle could help.

"How about if I do that," she said. "I'll take Bill along—he and Eduardo worked together for years. He might think of something to nudge Essie's memory."

Torrez glanced at his watch. "This afternoon?"

"Sure. Why not? Bill was going to come over to the house for dinner anyway. We'll swing by Essie's first. You'll be home?"

"Home or here," Torrez replied. "I got to pay attention to my *therapy* now, you know." He said the word with so much venom that Estelle laughed, and that only deepened his glower.

THIRTY

Less than an hour after Estelle left Sheriff Robert Torrez's office early on that Sunday afternoon, her phone chirped. She had just parked the county car in her driveway after running several errands, and Francisco was halfway across the front yard toward her.

"Guzman," she said, and held out a hand to her son. She was surprised to hear the characteristic monosyllabic greeting from the sheriff.

"Hey," Torrez said, and the one word didn't carry a flood of good will and holiday cheer. The intervening hour hadn't improved his mood. "Where you at?"

"I just pulled into my driveway," she replied.

"You got a few minutes?"

No, I don't, she almost said. *I'm going to spend the rest of this Sunday with my family.* "Sure." She reached across the seat and grabbed the two plastic sacks of groceries with her right hand, and handed them to Francisco, whose small hands deftly twined around the tops. "Give those to *tía, hijo,*" she said.

"We got us a problem," Torrez said. "I'm in my office." The connection broke.

"I thought *Padrino* was coming," Francisco said.

Estelle sighed. "He is, *hijo.* After a little bit. Right now, *Roberto el Gruñón* needs to see me."

"He could come over here," Francisco said. "*Tía* and *abuela* have been baking all day." His face beamed, and she saw the trace of powdered sugar near the left corner of his mouth. "There's lots to eat."

"Bobby's not hungry right now," Estelle said, and almost added, *and that's not the way* el gruñón *works.* "You save some for *Padrino.*" She closed the car door. "I'll be right back, okay?"

The little boy stepped back. "Okay." The resignation in his tone was heavy, and he didn't turn toward the house, waiting as if there were a chance his mother might change her mind.

"These things happen, *hijo,*" she said.

Her son's expression was almost comical. Had he been old enough to frame the right words, he would have muttered, "Don't make it a habit."

As she drove back to the Sheriff's Department, impatience prompted Estelle to run down her mental inventory of potential problems that might have reared their ugly heads, and she found herself centering on Mike Sisneros—if ever there was a lost soul, Mike was the very definition. With no clearcut direction for the case to go, nothing positive for him to pursue, all he could do was pace in circles and fume. The weekend even made it worse.

The sheriff's office door was open, but Estelle paused at the counter of the dispatch island, where Gayle Torrez was busy organizing and straightening after two days of unplanned absence. As if the sheriff had been lying in wait for the first sounds of his undersheriff's footsteps, his voice interrupted her greeting for Gayle.

"Hey?" His command was easy to interpret: *If you're there, get in here.*

"Neanderthal man summons," Gayle said, and beamed at Estelle. "You want to go out for some late lunch and leave him?" She knew her husband too well to be intimidated by his moods.

Estelle laughed. "Uh," she grunted in reply, bending over and dangling one arm like an ape. She straightened up. "Did you see Jackie's cartoon, by the way?"

"The one with Leona visiting Bobby in the hospital?"

"That's the one. Has he seen it yet?"

"Ah, no. Jackie showed it to me yesterday." She made the okay sign with index finger and thumb. *"Perfecto,"* she said, and then glanced toward the sheriff's office door and lowered her voice to a conspiratorial whisper. "Linda said we should save it for the calendar."

"That's just what he needs," Estelle agreed. The annual calendar project had become legendary, with photos of the Sheriff's Department staff snapped during the year—some gorgeous portraits with stunning New Mexico scenery in the background, some loaded with pathos, some comic shots of deputies caught during unguarded, less than complimentary moments. "It'll make a great cover."

Torrez appeared in his office doorway, and for a moment his eyes narrowed at the tête-à-tête, obviously called at his expense. "Hey," he said again, with somewhat less command.

"Uh," Gayle grunted, a fair imitation of Estelle's first reply. She reached out and hugged Estelle's shoulder. "You have a good day," she said.

"You bet."

"You seen this?" Torrez said by way of the only greeting Estelle could expect to hear. He held up a folded copy of a metro Sunday newspaper.

"No. I forgot it was even Sunday," Estelle said. "Are they giving Frank Dayan ulcers again?" The *Posadas Register* publisher lived in constant apprehension that the large metro dailies in the state would make his struggling weekly look foolish. Most of the time, it wasn't difficult to do.

"I don't care about Dayan," Torrez said, which Estelle knew was no understatement. In fact, she was surprised that Bobby had bothered to read anything but the sports pages and the comics of the Sunday paper. He turned to go back inside the office. Estelle glanced back at Gayle, and the sheriff's wife waved a hand in dismissal. Estelle took the proffered newspaper as the sheriff settled carefully behind the desk, and Estelle saw a flinch of pain cross his face.

"We made the front page," he said. "Did you know he was going to do that?"

"Who, and do what?" Estelle asked. She flipped the paper over and saw the headline, neatly centered over four columns at the bottom of the page.

Posadas Not So Peaceful
Murder, Assault Stalk Village Over Holiday

She frowned at the byline. "Todd Willis. That's interesting. He didn't go to Tucson after all?"

"Willis?"

"The young man who played Joseph at the motel on Christmas Eve. Friday night. The reporter who wrote this whatever it is."

"I'm not worried about him and his dippy stories," Torrez growled, and he grunted to his feet, crossed the small office, and closed the door. "What I want to know is who the 'source' is, if it ain't you."

Estelle settled in one of the chairs, holding up a hand to fend off further comment until she had read the story.

Posadas, NM—Investigation continues in Posadas County today into the death of a former Posadas Chief of Police after the man suffered an apparent heart attack on Christmas Eve after a confrontation with two travelers at a local motel. At the same time, officials are investigating the violent death of a Posadas woman on Christmas afternoon, and the assault on a former Posadas County sheriff only hours later.

Although refusing to say whether or not the three incidents are linked, Sheriff's Department officials are not ruling out any possibilities.

Sources in the department said that the death of former village Police Chief Eduardo Martinez was announced late on Christmas Day. Martinez had apparently suffered a heart attack on Christmas Eve that may have been exacerbated by a confrontation with two men at a local motel.

In that incident, Bruce Jakes, 43, and Everett Wardell, 54, both of Hickory Grove, IN, were arrested and charged with multiple counts of assault, auto theft, and resisting arrest, sheriff's officials said. Jakes and Wardell allegedly took Chief Martinez's personal vehicle after the retired law officer collapsed in the parking lot of the Posadas Inn following an apparent heart attack. Martinez, 74, collapsed after talking to the two men, witnesses said.

Jakes and Wardell were apprehended shortly afterward in the border village of Regál by Posadas County Sheriff Robert Torrez and Undersheriff Estelle Guzman.

Less than twenty-four hours later, Posadas resident Janet Tripp, 30, was found shot to death late Saturday afternoon, her body discovered in an arroyo north of Posadas by a youth riding a motorcycle, police said.

Sheriff's officials said that Tripp apparently had been killed by a single gunshot to the head, and that robbery appeared to be a motive. Police said that Tripp was killed after making a withdrawal from the Posadas State Bank's ATM. In a bizarre twist, Tripp was reportedly the fiancée of one of the Posadas County Sheriff's Deputies, officials said.

Within hours of the murder of Janet Tripp, police said that former Posadas County Sheriff William K. Gastner was assaulted near his home. Gastner was hospitalized for treatment of a head wound, officials said, and is listed in stable condition.

Officers refused to speculate on whether the killing of Tripp and the assault on Gastner were related.

"Sheriff Gastner has information that we're currently processing," a Sheriff's Department official said. "It appears that he may have information that may help police identify his attacker."

The undersheriff looked up at Bob Torrez. "See what I mean?" Torrez said. Estelle quickly scanned the rest of the article, but found nothing new.

"Let me show you the press release that I wrote yesterday," she said, and started to get up. "I think it was yesterday."

Torrez waved a hand impatiently. "Forget it. Just tell me the parts of this shit that you *didn't* write," he said.

"I never said anything about a relationship between Janet Tripp and Mike, Bobby. That's nobody's business but theirs— at least at the moment. And I *certainly* never said anything about Bill being able to identify his attacker. I said that he had been assaulted near his home, and that was it. I also never said that we were investigating any relationship between the incidents."

"Did this Willis guy talk to somebody in dispatch? Where'd he get all this crap?"

Estelle shook her head. "I'll ask...don't think he did. I'd be surprised. You know as well as I do that they have standing orders not to discuss *any* aspect of a case over the phone with anyone outside the department. Every one of them knows Frank Dayan, and they've all been over this ground time and time again. They aren't going to start blabbing just because it's from some big out-of-town paper. They won't read a police report or any other piece of public information over the phone to a reporter. They might read the call log, but that's a summary that's written for public consumption anyway. If there's a question, they always say the same thing: 'You'll have to talk to the sheriff.'"

"And then I always say, 'Go talk to Estelle.'" Torrez managed a tight smile.

"Yes, you do." It was the first sign that Bobby's blood pressure might be returning to something near normal, and Estelle was relieved.

"Did Bill talk to this guy? Willis what's-his-name?"

"That's a possibility, I suppose. Not likely, but possible. We both know that Bill's not the blabby type…. He's been in our shoes as long as both of us put together. If he said something, especially without talking to us first, he had good reason."

"Reason or not, I want to know," Torrez said. "Just because I want to know, that's all. There ain't much we can do about it now, but we don't need somebody goin' off and playin' the Lone Ranger on us."

"That's simple enough, Bobby. I'll ask *Padrino,* and he'll tell me if it was him. We were talking earlier this morning, and he's coming over for dinner later on. Right now, it makes sense to me that we should dig a little deeper into Janet Tripp's background. There's just too much there that we don't know, too many things about her death that don't make sense as a random robbery-gone-bad."

"That's what I was thinking," Torrez said, and Estelle knew it wasn't just gratuitous agreement for the sake of taking credit. He shifted on the uncomfortable chair. "Me and Eddie are going through the files, Estelle. First thing we did was check our own records—and as far as we're concerned, Janet Tripp was clean. Not even a speedin' ticket. Nothin'. The village files are somethin' else. They're a mess, for one thing. But Eddie was going to give it a try. We know there's no rap sheet on her. No obvious file." He shrugged. "But it's worth lookin'."

"I just don't think that her murder was a simple robbery, Bobby."

"You said that before."

"Well, there's just too much…" She hesitated. "I don't know. Just too many circumstances that don't make any sense to me."

"So where you goin' with it? Gastner?"

"His attack is linked somehow. I really believe that, and I couldn't tell you why, except for the unlikelihood of coincidence. There's something there that we're missing. Bill agrees."

"Huh." Torrez stared off into space for a moment, chewing his lower lip. "So what's next?"

"You said you and Eddie already made an end run on the files, and that's a logical place to start. Anything and everything that's even tangentially related to Janet Tripp—or anyone related to her. And anything that ties her to Bill Gastner."

"If there's something, it's in the village files," Torrez said.

Estelle nodded and tossed the newspaper on Torrez's desk. "Have you talked any more with Mike?"

"Some. About Janet's background, stuff like that. Eddie's run through it with him again. There just ain't nothin' there. Just that she didn't like Mike's mother very much. Some friction there." He shrugged. "But Irene Cruz is over in Lordsburg—was over in Lordsburg all day. So that don't much matter."

Estelle looked at the sheriff for a long time, mind churning.

"You're gettin' together with Bill today, then?" Torrez asked.

"Yes. I don't know what he was thinking, if he's the one who leaked that information. Maybe he thinks he can flush the attacker out, force him to try again."

"That's like grabbing a stock fence during a lightning storm," Torrez said. "It ain't too bright."

"I'll talk to him," Estelle said.

"When you do, you might remind him that he ain't sheriff anymore, either," Torrez said, and Estelle was surprised by the sudden gentleness in his tone. "Anything that goes to the newspapers about what we do goes through your office. No other way."

"I think he's well aware of that," Estelle said. "But he gets kind of stubborn about certain things. And as I said, he might have had good reason."

"Yeah, well," Torrez said philosophically. "I guess I can understand that. It's his skull that got cracked."

THIRTY-ONE

WITH BOTH HANDS raised to shoulder level, Bill Gastner backed away from his front door.

"I'll go peacefully," he said.

"It may come to that, *Padrino,*" Estelle replied, and she stepped into the dark warmth of the former sheriff's home as he moved to one side. The heat was turned up unusually high, contrary to Gastner's habit of liking his house about the same ambient temperature as a cave. "Did you see the Sunday paper this morning?"

"No…but by the tone of your voice, and the fact that you're back to visit my humble abode, I imagine that you did. And probably our good sheriff, too."

"Ah, yes," she said. She looked him up and down affectionately. Other than being dressed as if he might be called to go out in a blizzard, with heavy corduroy trousers, Wellington boots, and weighty flannel shirt, he appeared ruddy-cheeked and healthy. "How are you doing? You look great."

"Oh, I'm fine. My noggin still hurts, but then again, it hurt earlier today, too. And still will at dinner tonight." He flashed a bright smile and closed the door deliberately, pushing it against the jamb until the latch clicked. "But the newspaper? Chalk it up to senility," he said, and turned to gesture down the hallway. "Come on in. I was just in the process of doing nothing and thinking great thoughts." He paused halfway down the foyer. "You in a hurry? Are we going somewhere?"

"I wish that we were."

"Well," Gastner said philosophically, "I know exactly how dead-end streets feel." His eyebrows lifted as he accepted the newspaper clipping from Estelle. He smoothed it out on the counter, and took his time finding his glasses and settling them on his nose. After a minute, he tapped the copy. "I was afraid he'd take that." He straightened up, leaving the clipping on the counter. "Willis—that kid from the newspaper? He called me at the hospital. I'll give him this—he's resourceful."

Gastner regarded the ceiling, hand stroking his chin. "As I remember, it was late…some odd hour when I wasn't expecting to have to think. How he got past the hospital switchboard, I didn't think to ask. Reporters have their own bag of tricks, I suppose…. He proved that at the motel, didn't he? I didn't bring his Joseph scam up again, and maybe that's what he was fishing for—to see if we were going to do anything about that."

He shrugged. "What the hell. Anyway, he asked me something about Janet Tripp, and I recall mumbling something about this particular crime hitting us hard, since she was the fiancée of one of the deputies." He grimaced with embarrassment. "I remember thinking that I shouldn't have said that in the first place, but that maybe I could claim that as off the record, for a number of reasons. But I don't remember if I actually said so or not." He regarded the clipping again. "Obviously, I said *something*."

"It probably wouldn't have made any difference," Estelle said.

"Maybe not. Now the other…" He held up his hands in surrender. "I'm a little more paranoid than before. I don't turn my back on dark corners anymore, sweetheart. I can tell you that. I must be a fast study. It only takes one wallop on the head to make me pay attention." He thrust his hands in his trouser pockets. "That reporter caught me at an odd, fuzzy moment, I guess. Maybe I thought the bastard who bent that rebar over my head would like to try again."

He stepped over to the coffee maker, which was obviously loaded and primed. He glanced into the basket to remind himself of what he'd already done, then flipped the power switch.

"It's an ego thing, I think. Psychologists would have a field day explaining why my common sense and usual good-natured restraint slipped so badly. But the second time somebody tries to crack my skull, I'll be ready. That's a little childish, I admit. But that was my thinking. And if nothing else, him making a second try might give you something else to go on."

"I'll pass on that, sir," Estelle said. "We don't need that kind of help. Your head, or anybody else's. You know what you'd say if you were in my shoes. Or Bobby's."

He toyed with the newspaper clipping absently, folding it this way and that without reading it again. "Bobby was a little pissed, eh? I assume that in part is the reason for this second delightful visit." He grinned and beetled his brows. "'Tell 'im he ain't sheriff no more,'" he said, sounding remarkably like Robert Torrez. "Did he say something like that?"

"Pretty close, *Padrino*."

"Angry, huh?"

"Briefly. But this too shall pass, as my mother likes to say. Maybe it was good for him. It gave him something else to think about. Between you and Leona Spears, he hasn't had much time to dwell on his blood clots."

"Oh, my God. Don't put me in company with the Crazy Lady," he said, clutching his chest dramatically. "I would have liked to have seen Bobby's face when he heard about that."

"I assume then that you heard?"

"Oh, sure. In fact, I could rub Roberto's face in it a little by telling him that I saw it coming quite a while ago. Not long after

we lost Kevin, in fact. Somebody realized that maybe Leona
might fit right in, working with the rest of the nut cases. Ou
sheriff got a little bent, did he?" He laughed again.

"*Apoplético* might be an accurate description, *Padrino*. BF
maybe 300 over 250."

"I bet. And he's back at his desk? That's dumb."

"Yes. Just for a while, though. Gayle's staying close. I think
that right now he's with Mike. There's a memorial service for
Janet planned for Wednesday at two. At the VFW. Bobby is
helping set that up."

"I had forgotten that."

"Forgotten that?"

"That Janet was in the service. Army, wasn't it." It was a
statement, not a question. Estelle nodded, watching Gastner's
face. His eyes had that distant look as he focused on memories
here and there, associations that connected who knew how
many souls, names, and dates. "I need to stop by and see how
he's doing. Both of 'em, in fact."

"You should, sir. I know that Bobby doesn't like standing in
the corner, feeling useless."

"Can't fault him for that. Did someone get ahold of Janet's
sister, by the way?"

"Mike did. I have her name and address as well."

"Is she able to come for the service?"

"I think so."

"A fountain of information you are." Gastner laughed at the un-
adorned answer, and then his face sobered. "Too many goddamn
funerals," he said. "Rosary for Eduardo is at four tomorrow afternoon. I think Mass is Tuesday morning at All Saints."

"Ten o'clock," Estelle said. "*Mamá* wanted to go."

"You're going to take her?"

"I think so. I'd like to see what faces show up."

"Ah," Gastner said, nodding. "Mind if I tag along?"

"Of course not, sir. Essie will appreciate it."

"Maybe so. And speaking of Essie," Gastner said, "I've been thinking. We need to talk to her, sooner rather than later." He leaned forward on the stool, with one hand on the counter, looking as if he was about to put his head between his knees. He twisted as he bent, backbone letting out a symphony of satisfying cracks. "We don't know what they talked about, you know."

"They?"

"Essie and Eduardo. In the wee quiet when they couldn't sleep. In unguarded moments. You know, Eduardo was just as willing to turn a nasty investigation over to us as not. He didn't worry about turf, and I don't think that was a weakness. But you know, not everyone saw it that way, fair or not." Gastner reached out and picked up the clipping again, scanning through the story. "I'm curious what he would have said about all this."

"Which part?"

"All of it, sweetheart. I wonder what he knew about Janet Tripp—beyond that she was Mike's flame. And I wonder..." He looked up from the newspaper. "I just wonder, is all. Eduardo knew this town, Estelle. Make no mistake about that. He wasn't an aggressive cop, and he didn't put himself in people's faces. He was more apt to let someone off with a gentle warning than a ticket. He considered it a successful day when all the teenagers were home by nine o'clock. But he knew the town. He knew the people. And in that sense, it's probably a good thing that some of our beloved hot rods like Tom Pasquale and Mike Sisneros broke in with him. I'm not sure I'd have had the patience."

"Not likely, sir."

"Well," and he waved a hand in self-deprecation. "It was different. I roamed the county like some old dog who couldn't fall asleep. I know every rancher, every back road and trail. But the village was Eduardo's turf. He lived with 'em every day. Saw 'em in church, talked with 'em at the service clubs, all that stuff. Everybody in town was his neighbor, in some way."

"Maybe he didn't talk with Essie much about his day."

"Maybe so. Maybe not." Gastner ducked his head in agreement. "Maybe Janet Tripp was just a name to him, nothing else. You know, I've been racking my brain about her, and my file is damn near empty. I can remember vaguely that she was in the army, but hell, I don't remember if she lived here before that, or after, or what. I remember that her folks were in town for a little while, and then moved—I don't know to where. I'm not sure when." He got up and fetched a cup from the cupboard above the coffee maker. "Want some?"

"No thanks, sir. Bobby says the village files are a mess."

He nodded and closed the cupboard door, then filled the cup slowly. "Yes, they are. But there's good stuff there for the finding. You think that there's some connection between Janet's murder and the attack on me." He paused and spooned in three heaping teaspoons of sugar. "I would have liked the opportunity to talk with Eduardo about that. 'Cause we sure as hell don't have anything else." He turned to regard Estelle. "Do we."

"You want to talk with Essie?"

"Yep." Gastner settled onto the stool. "That'd be a good thing to do, something constructive to do in an otherwise totally frustrating case, sweetheart. We need to take those files apart, piece by piece. We have only one name so far—Janet Tripp." He shrugged. "Hell, it's kinda ironic, in a way. Little place like this, and nobody knows nothin'. Unless *you're* withholding secrets."

"I wish I were," Estelle said.

"It's like one of those thousand-piece jigsaw puzzles," Gastner said, thumping his hands onto the counter a couple of feet apart to form a frame. "You have this huge, yawning hole in the middle and you can't find a single piece to get things going. Then one drifts into place, and before you know it, you've got this neat island that grows and grows." He grinned. "You've probably heard me say all this before."

"It bears repeating," Estelle said, and Gastner laughed.

"God, that's what I love about you," he said. "You help the mantle of senility rest so gently." He patted his belly. "I get goddamn poetic when I'm hungry. Do you have time right now to go over and have a chat with Essie? I think it would be worth our while. Tomorrow's going to be tough on her, with the Rosary service and all." He frowned and glanced sideways at Estelle. "Listen to me. I sound like I'm still working."

"You are, sir," Estelle said. She tapped her right temple. "And you're right. We need connections, *Padrino*."

"Don't hold your breath on my account," Gastner said. "And here I am, rattling along, and I never asked you why you came over, other than to chew me out about this thing." He nodded at the clipping.

"I wanted to talk with Essie," Estelle said. "And I wanted you along. Nobody is going to be able to prod her memory any better than you."

"And you're one step ahead of me, as usual. I'm flattered you asked me along, but like I said, don't hold your breath. Essie might remember yesterday, but I'm having more and more trouble remembering where the next meal is coming from."

"What makes me doubt that, sir? Do you want lunch before we go?" She glanced at the wall clock and saw that it was after two. "Late lunch? Something to hold you until dinnertime?"

"Nah," Gastner said halfheartedly. "I eat, and then I'm going to want to take a nap. Hunger keeps me sharp. Let me take this mug of coffee along. That'll be enough."

"You're sure?"

"Of course not." He waved her toward the front door.

As they drove through Posadas, up Grande to Bustos, then west to Sixth, and then south toward the modest, flat-roofed adobe Martinez home, Estelle found herself scrutinizing every passing car or truck, every pedestrian, even every loose dog.

"I don't think he's still in town," Gastner said, as if he could read her mind. They saw the fleet of vehicles parked along Sixth Street, and Estelle slowed the county car. "And I don't know why I say that," he added. "You ever had a feeling like that?"

"*Por supuesto, Padrino.* That's what I'm living with at the moment."

"I just don't know what to do about it." He surveyed the Martinez's front yard, now more of a parking lot since there was no sidewalk to define where the street ended and the brown grass began. "Quite a crowd."

"When you have eleven grown children and their families all under the same roof, that's a crowd," Estelle said. "I called her earlier and asked if we could meet with her for a few minutes. I didn't know if she'd be willing at this point, or not. She's got enough to think about. But she agreed."

"I think you'll find that Essie Martinez has a steel rod in her spine," Gastner said. "She always reminded me of one of those Schmoos from the cartoons. But that's only until you talk with her. She's got a tough streak. Of course, with eleven children, I guess she'd have to."

They parked behind a Volkswagen Jetta with Wisconsin plates, and by the time they had gotten out of the car and were walking across the gravel toward the front door, Essie Martinez had appeared from inside, purse in hand, obviously on her way somewhere. Behind her, Estelle could see a number of people, and for a moment the chief's widow turned to speak with someone in the shadows. She nodded emphatically and held up a hand, cutting off the conversation.

"Is this a bad time?" Estelle said. She extended a hand, and Essie took it and squeezed hard, in no hurry to let go. Still holding on to Estelle, she reached out and took Gastner by the elbow. With an escort on both sides, she walked toward the county car, biting her lower lip and obviously close to tears. Estelle realized with a start that Essie had been waiting for their arrival, and was making a clean break.

"*Caramba*," Essie said when they reached the car. "You came just in time. Such a houseful!"

"Here," Gastner said, taking the car's door handle. "You sit in front."

"No…my goodness. You'll never fit back there," she said, then saw all the equipment in the front. "Maybe not here, either. Look at this. How do you squeeze in there?"

"Like a cork," Gastner said. He held the back door for Essie.

"I think that's why Eduardo always drove his Buick," she said as she settled onto the hard bench seat. "Do you two mind this, after all? I suppose we could find a corner somewhere in the house, but I need to get out for a little bit. I really do. Love 'em all, but *por Dios,* when they're all hovering…" She reached out and tugged tentatively at the wire screen that separated the front seat from the back. "The smell of the beer was getting to me. I never liked that stuff, you know."

"Mrs. Martinez," Estelle said, "would my office be all right with you?"

"Just wherever you want to talk, that's fine with me," Essie said. "I don't know how I can be of any help to you, but we'll see." She reached out and again touched the cage behind Estelle's head. "Eduardo thought highly of you, you know. Both you and that husband of yours." Estelle glanced in the rearview mirror and saw Mrs. Martinez tuck her hands in her lap. Other than a little redness in her eyes, her expression was serene as she watched the village roll by.

As they turned into the Public Safety Building's parking lot, Estelle saw Jackie Taber and Linda Real standing on the back step.

"You know, years ago," Essie said, "it would have been un-think-a-ble," and she drew out the word, her accent heavy and thoughtful on each syllable, "for a woman to be a police officer. And now look." She waited until Estelle had parked and Gastner pulled himself out of the car to open her door. "What do you think of that, Bill?" she said.

"I think times change, Essie," the former sheriff said.

"They sure do," Essie Martinez said. "That's what Eduardo always used to say. 'The times change.'" She shook her head sadly. "And the things that happen these days. I can't imagine what goes through people's minds, can you?"

"No, ma'am, I can't," Gastner said. "That's why we need all the help we can get."

"Even from old widow ladies," Essie said. She managed a brave smile.

THIRTY-TWO

"EDUARDO WAS VERY...*proud* of what he did," Essie Martinez said with great deliberation.

"He had every reason to be," Estelle said.

"He was chief of police for twenty-seven years," the older woman said. "Twenty-seven years. That's something, you know." She dug a tissue out of her purse, but only clenched it in her hands as if she needed the soft padding. She lifted both hands and then settled them into her lap, composed and expectant. "The way village boards come and go, elections and all that—to stay for twenty-seven years is quite an accomplishment."

"Essie," Bill Gastner said gently, "let me lay this out for you." He rubbed the back of his head. "Somebody whacked me a good one, and someone killed Janet Tripp. We're thinking there's some connection somehow, but I gotta tell ya, we're up against a hard place with this business." He leaned toward her. "What we were hoping is that you might have some recollection of something that Eduardo might have said to you, or reminisced about, or worried about...any little something. Any time he might have mentioned Janet, or her family. Or even Mike."

"You mean from this past week, before..."

"Recent stuff, sure. Anything at all. But also anything you can remember from way back when. From the Stone Age."

"Me oh my," Essie said, as if to herself. "How would I even know where to start?"

"Janet Tripp and Mike Sisneros were engaged," Estelle said. "Let's start there. Mike worked for the chief as a part-timer a few years ago," Estelle said. "Do you remember Eduardo talking about him?"

"I know that Eduardo *liked* Michael," Essie said with emphasis. "And he is such a nice young man. We were happy when Chief Mitchell hired him on full time. Eduardo said that he should, you know. He told Eddie that on several occasions. If there had been an opening before, Eduardo would have done it himself." Her eyebrows lifted as she pulled in a deep breath, then let it out in a sigh. "That wasn't always so, you know. There have been some who worked for the village who…who didn't work out so well," she said diplomatically.

"Oh, *sí*," Estelle agreed, and Deputy Tom Pasquale's sturdy face came immediately to mind. "Did you ever meet Janet?"

Essie shook her head so quickly it seemed as if she had been expecting the question. "I know who she is…that's all I know. If I saw her in the grocery store, I might recognize her."

"That's about where we are," Gastner said. "Did Eduardo ever talk about her?"

"Oh…" She regarded her tissue for a moment, smoothing one small corner against her thigh. "I don't recall any time, but that doesn't mean there wasn't one, you know." She smiled, her round face lighting. "These old heads, they're not good for much." Her smile faded. "Let me ask you something, and if it's none of my business, well, you just say so. Is Mike in some sort of trouble over this whole mess?"

"No," Estelle said without hesitation. "Your husband's estimation of Mike Sisneros was exactly right."

"I'm working with Mike on the records deal, Essie," Gastner added. "Combining village and county? He's a good man. He's had good training. Eduardo started him out right when he was a part-timer."

"Yes, he did," Essie agreed. "I don't think that young man has always had it so easy."

"In what way?" Estelle asked.

"His mother was nice. I always liked her, back when they lived in town. She was Acoma, I think. I think. I'm not sure. Maybe Laguna or Zuni. One of those. But she's moved. Years ago. Maybe Arizona or something."

"Lordsburg," Gastner prompted.

"Ah. Okay. I didn't know that. But I liked her. Irene, her name is. So pretty. Now, I know that Eduardo didn't have much use for Michael's father." She frowned at the floor. "They were divorced, you know. The Sisneros, I mean. Hank and Irene."

Gastner nodded. "Eduardo had dealings with Hank Sisneros sometimes? If that's the case, he wasn't alone. I crossed tracks with him a time or two myself. Old Hank liked the bottle, and he liked the back of the hand." While he waited for Essie to reply, Gastner drew out a small spiral notebook from his left breast pocket, along with a ballpoint pen, and made a brief notation. "I'm sure Eduardo had far more dealings with him than I did."

"I don't know," Essie said. "I just know that Eduardo didn't care for Hank. You can tell sometimes, you know? And Eduardo…he was a funny one. When there was something bad to say about someone, he talked to himself. So I suppose he had his secrets."

"There must have been a time," Estelle said. She watched Essie's face, wondering if something bubbled beneath the surface of her memory. For Essie to recall clearly that Eduardo didn't like Hank Sisneros hinted that she would know something about why.

Essie's eyes narrowed, but she seemed reluctant to open the door on indiscretion. "When Hank Sisneros moved out of town, Eduardo said that was a good thing. He thought that maybe Mike would have a chance to make something of himself. But I don't know what the relationship was between Mike and his father."

"Hank went to Deming?"

"I don't know where he went. Just that he *went,* you know. For a long time, Mike worked at the hardware store, out in the lumberyard. He was still in high school. He took such good care of his mother." Essie looked wistful. "She remarried, of course."

"And moved," Gastner said.

"You know, you ask me what Eduardo talked about. That's easy. The thing that Eduardo just *hated,*" Essie said vehemently, "was going on domestic dispute calls. He just *hated* that."

He sure did, Estelle thought. Before Chief Mitchell took over, if there had been ten domestics in a month, the Sheriff's Department routinely handled nine of them.

"That Hank Sisneros…he and Irene—they were like oil and water. I don't know how they ever got linked up in the first place, but what a mess. Hank, now, he had an eye for the ladies. That's what Eduardo used to say. What they saw in him, I don't know. It's fortunate," and she drew the word out, "that Mike takes after his mother in the looks department. The way I heard it was that finally, Irene just gave up and the church looked the other way when she divorced him. The best thing. When he moved out of town, that was a relief." She heaved another sigh. "And that's what I know about that."

"We still have our fair share of folks like that in town," Gastner said.

"Any town does," Essie said.

"Mike and Janet were happy together, though," Estelle said abruptly. "Did you ever meet her, or did Eduardo ever talk about her? Maybe she and Mike weren't seeing each other that long ago."

"I don't think so. Like I said, I don't think I know her beyond just a face in the store, you know. That sort of thing. But what a shame, no? A young girl like that."

During the next few minutes, Estelle tried every avenue to explore what Essie Martinez might know about her husband and his relationships, and got nowhere. By and large, Chief Eduardo Martinez kept his own personal thoughts to himself. Or, if there had been long sessions of "pillow talk" between the two of them, Essie guarded those chats closely. And the pressure would have been considerable to be less than discreet when enjoying gossip with the other ladies from the church.

The undersheriff looked up from her notes with annoyance when a loud rap on her office door interrupted her thoughts. "Yes?" she said, but the door was already opening.

Sheriff Torrez leaned heavily on the knob. "Hello, Essie," he said. Behind him, Estelle saw Eddie Mitchell in the hallway. "Bill, you got a minute?"

"Me?" Gastner said with surprise. "I have all kinds of minutes."

Torrez nodded at Estelle. "I need a couple of 'em with you guys," he said. "Essie, they'll be right back." He made an effort to sound pleasant and conversational. "Thanks for comin' down."

"You just go ahead," the older woman said, favoring Torrez with a nod of approval.

A moment later, the four of them crowded into Torrez's office, and the sheriff made a point of latching the door behind him. "You got your keys with you?" he asked Gastner.

"Sure." The former sheriff hauled his keys from his pocket and held them out toward Torrez, letting them dangle from the ignition key of his Blazer.

"The key to the conference room?" Torrez asked.

Gastner fingered through the keys. After looking through twice, he stopped, puzzled. "It's not there, Roberto." He looked again, and the silence was so heavy in the room that the metallic *tink* of each key turning against its neighbor sounded loud and harsh. "Nope. I don't have it." He frowned. "What the hell did I do with it?"

"You're sure *you* did something with it?" Mitchell asked.

"Hell yes, I'm sure. Otherwise it would be here."

Estelle pulled out her own keys and held the conference key out to Gastner.

"I know what it looks like," he snapped with unaccustomed impatience. "It's not here."

"Now we know what he was after," Torrez said.

"What?" Gastner said. "Who?"

"Whoever assaulted you with that bar maybe wanted you dead," Mitchell said. "Or maybe he just wanted your key."

Bill Gastner whispered an expletive, then shook his head. "That's nuts, Eddie. For one thing, how would he know which one of the goddamn collection is the right one?"

Mitchell extended his hand, and Gastner thumped the bunch into his palm. "This is the ignition and door-lock key for your Blazer, right? This Kwikset is the front door of your house, maybe the back, too. This little Sergent is the key to your wine cellar." He grinned, but his eyes remained sober. "You got a safety deposit box key here. They're easy to recognize, especially with Posadas State Bank stamped on the head. This little fart is to a suitcase or something like that. And this is the ignition key and door key to the state pickup that you drive." He paused, and looked closely at the last key. "I don't know what that one is, but it isn't one that fits any doors in the county building."

"That's to my house," Estelle said.

"Oh, there we go," Mitchell said. "We're looking for a big Yale, one that is stamped DO NOT DUPLICATE on its face. Convenient, huh?"

"Did you have the conference room key on your ring?" Torrez asked. "On this ring here?"

"Sure."

"Did you take it off?"

"Don't think so. Why would I?" Gastner glowered at Torrez, then at Mitchell. "Do you guys take keys on and off your rings?" Estelle felt the intense *déjà vu,* remembering their talk with Mike Sisneros about his own keys.

"Nope," Eddie said, as if to say, *And that settles that.*

"So that poses a goddamn interesting question," Gastner said. "Number one, if we assume that in the heat of the moment, in the goddamn *dark* of the moment, this guy can even *see* to figure out which key is which, that he then— number two—takes the key before dropping the rest of 'em in the bushes."

"Something like that," Mitchell said gently. "It could happen. And nobody is going to be the wiser. At least for a day or two. Somebody knew what Janet's apartment key looked like, too. Right?"

Gastner looked skeptical. "He whacks me, and takes my *conference room key?* Interesting that he'd know what it's for." When silence ensued, he turned to Estelle. "When you found yours truly lying on the front step like a goddamn drunk, did *you* check my keys?"

"Ah, no sir. I picked them up and put them in my pocket. And then sometime later, after Jackie and I checked out your house, I put them in your trouser pockets in the closet of your hospital room."

"This is nuts," Gastner said.

"But it would explain why he hit you, and then *didn't* enter your house. If it was the key to the conference room that he was after, he found what he came looking for, didn't he?" Mitchell said.

"Nobody's been in there, though," Torrez said. "If he wanted the key, he ain't used it yet."

"You're sure about that?" Gastner said. "Hell, busy as you gents have been? In and out and around in circles?"

"Dispatch would have seen that," Mitchell said. "It's right across the hall."

"Even if dispatch left his station for a minute to take a crap?" the older man asked bluntly. "You can't cover something like that every minute of the day. Slip in, then slip out."

"I don't think so," Mitchell said doggedly. "There's nothing in that room that you could get in and out."

"The files?"

"Even if you knew what to look for, good luck finding it," Mitchell said.

"Then he's waiting for a chance," Gastner persisted. "Maybe later on, when he has time to search. And the next question is *why*. If he took my key…" He hesitated. "We're going to look pretty foolish if I go home and there it is on my nightstand."

"Where you always leave stray keys," Estelle said, and Gastner shot her a withering look. "But that's interesting," she continued.

"What is?" Gastner asked.

"Janet's killer took her apartment key. Why would he do that?"

"There's something in her apartment that he wants," Gastner said.

"Mike's apartment also, sir."

Gastner stood with his fists on his hips, feet planted…the pugnacious stance Estelle had come to know so well over the years. "Maybe he thought Mike had a key to the conference room, and kept it stowed in the apartment."

"Mike *doesn't* have a key to the conference room," Mitchell said. "The sheriff has one, Estelle has one, and you *had* one." It was his turn to receive the withering look, and he shrugged.

"That doesn't make sense, though—for the same reason. If Mike had a key to the conference room, why would he take it *off* his key ring and leave it in the apartment? Nobody would do that. We put keys on our key rings, and they stay there."

"Then what was the killer looking for in that apartment?" Gastner said. "We don't know if he was. We don't know for sure that it was him who took the key from Janet's ring in the first place. Or mine, for that matter. We don't know if he was even there. Mike says nothing is missing from his apartment, nothing is messed up."

"There's something someone wants that he thinks are in those files," Torrez said. "That's the only thing that makes sense to me."

"Related to what?" Gastner asked.

"Wish I knew," the sheriff replied.

"Janet Tripp," Estelle said, more to herself than anyone. "Number one, I can't believe that her murder, and the assault on *Padrino*, were unrelated. The timing is just too close, and I see similarities. Number two, we think that whoever killed Janet took her apartment key…Mike's apartment key."

"And you don't know that for sure," Mitchell observed.

"No, I don't. But it makes sense to me. As you say, keys don't jump off key rings. Especially not *two* keys, from *two* key rings, within a few hours of each other. That means there was something in her—Mike's—apartment that Janet's killer was after. That he thought might be there. And as you say, Mike didn't *have* a key to the conference room files."

"The killer wouldn't know that," Torrez said.

"Maybe not. But if he thought Mike had a key, it makes no sense to go through Janet to get it, does it? Mike would have it on his key ring, just like Bill had his." She held up her own keys. "Just like I have mine, and you have yours. It makes sense to me that he wanted something that Janet had...and not the key. That's number three." She held up three fingers. "And that's what I can't get past."

"You think she knows the killer somehow?"

"Maybe."

"Huh." He gazed at Estelle, eyes narrowed. "Where the hell do we go with that. There's nothing in the county rap sheets that mentions Janet."

"And I haven't found anything in the village files," Mitchell said. "Going back to the year she was born—1977."

"She was born here?" Gastner asked, surprised.

"Yep."

"I'm surprised I didn't know that."

"No reason you should," Mitchell said. "One of your hobbies isn't memorizing birth announcements from each year, is it?"

"Not hardly," Gastner said. "I have enough trivia clogging my arteries."

"What's Essie say?"

"Nothing," Estelle said. "She's worried about Mike."

"Aren't we all," Gastner said. He started to head around Torrez's desk toward the chair. "Whoa," he said, and stopped, looking down at the desk without seeing it. "A thought occurs to me," he said slowly, then continued around the desk to sit in Torrez's remarkably uncomfortable swivel chair. He spent a long moment rearranging things on the sheriff's desk. Finally, he folded his hands and looked at the others, one at a time. "Who are the old farts in all of this?"

"Means what?" Mitchell asked.

"Who are the old farts," Gastner said again, "who would be apt to know what's in the village files from way back?"

"Chief Martinez," Torrez said, then added, "and you."

"And me. Exclusive club, compared to all you youngsters." He pushed his glasses up, and peered across at Estelle. "If you had something in those files that you'd just as soon not see the light of day, that you'd just as soon not be remembered and dug up, wouldn't you be just a little nervous when you saw the article in the newspaper about consolidation? How we were going to merge all those nifty files? How yours truly here was heading up the job? Frank Dayan did a good job with that story, didn't he."

"No one attacked Eduardo," Estelle said.

"True enough. But what happened? He had a public heart attack, and the whole town is bound to know. It was in the metro papers…at least the one from Cruces. It might have made the news on the Cruces or Deming radio. And there's our own speed-of-sound grapevine." He held up a thumb. "There's one down. *Eduardo* knows what's in those files. Pardon me. *Knew*." He turned the thumb and jabbed himself in the chest. "And I've been around for a while. Maybe somebody thinks that I know something."

"The key?" Estelle asked.

Gastner shrugged. "Don't know, sweetheart. Unless it's as simple as this: with Eduardo gone, and me gone, Mr. Slick knows that the playing field has been leveled a little, as politicians like to say. The old farts who might remember something from way back are out of the picture. And with a little luck, nobody'll notice the missing key for a while, and he'll have the chance to slip in and do a little file removal. Think on that."

"Janet," Estelle said abruptly. "If the files have to do with *her,* she's out of the way, too."

Mitchell chuckled. "Wonderful," he said. "And if all of this is out in left field somewhere, we're back where we started." He held up a hand. "What's to lose."

"I'll get the locks changed today," Torrez said, but Gastne shook his head.

"Don't bother, Roberto. It might be kind of interesting to l 'em in. See who it is, and what he wants."

The sheriff gazed at Gastner for a moment, and the crow feet at the corners of his eyes deepened a little. "If he thinl someone's going to recognize him, maybe he'll be a little r luctant anyway," he said.

"Could be that," Gastner said.

"We need to talk with Mike again," Estelle interrupted.

"What do you want to know?" Chief Mitchell asked. "F and I have been over this ground so often we've dug ruts."

"I want to know everything there is to know, starting fro 1977," she said. "For one thing, there's one obvious little deta nagging me. Mike's .22 pistol was stolen, and he can't seem account for when that happened. For some reason, he goes Lordsburg without Janet. He claims that Janet doesn't get alor so well with his mother, and maybe it's that simple. On top that, Mike is on the transition team, but he doesn't have his ow key…we limited the number of those floating around." She fe silent while the others waited, hating to voice the thought. " Mike has himself a key, no one in dispatch is going to wond when he goes in that conference room."

THIRTY-THREE

"So," Bill Gastner said as he followed Estelle back to her office. "What can I help with?" Eddie Mitchell had taken Essie Martinez home, and the sheriff had remained in the conference room, his wife hovering, while he rummaged through files.

"I want to go through our files *and* the village files again, *Padrino*." She opened the top drawer of one of her own office cabinets, riffling quickly through until she found the orange folder that contained the personnel records for Mike Sisneros. "I want you to retrieve any files from that memory of yours, too. About Mike, about Janet…about all their relatives back to the dawn of time."

"You don't know what you ask," Gastner said. "And why the relatives? We've got nothing that shows there's a connection with anything in the family album."

"Because," Estelle said. She sat down at her desk with the personnel folder. "Statistics say that the majority of violent crimes are rooted in the family."

"Ah." He shrugged. "But that's true, isn't it?"

"And that's the only door I see that's open, *Padrino*. We don't have prints. We don't have tire tracks. We don't have DNA. Or a convenient witness. And we don't have a weapon… other than the tantalizing little itch that at one time Mike Sisneros *had* a .22 pistol, and now it's missing—and it's *his* girlfriend who was shot with that same sort of weapon." She held up her hands helplessly. "I have two things I can do. I can sit here and wait for something to happen, wait for something to show itself, or I can poke around. I don't know where else to poke, other than family."

Gastner sat quietly, regarding her thoughtfully.

"I know that there's a Hank Sisneros," she said. "But I don't know where he is…except maybe this vague 'in Deming' that I keep hearing. I know he was a heller in years past."

"And a drunk."

"That, too. He leaves town, and even his own son isn't on speaking terms with him. When Mike talks about his father, I can see this steel door drop down behind his eyes." She made a chopping motion. "All that makes me curious. We have mama living in Lordsburg with a new husband. And Janet? What do we know about her? That there's a sister over in Kansas. I need to call her today." She looked up at Gastner. "And her parents? Her mother died, and her father took off for parts unknown. I don't like any of this. Vague is bad, *Padrino*."

"None of that means there's a connection with some thug working in the dark."

"When he shot Janet, it wasn't dark, Padrino."

"True enough."

She leafed through the folder, trying to force the dry notations to form an image of a living, breathing human being, dimensions beyond what Estelle thought she knew about Mike Sisneros already.

The contents of the folder painted a portrait of a level-headed, small-town kid who hadn't strayed far from the nest. His high-school record was average, heavy on sports and without any AP or honors courses. He had never failed a class—at least any that were listed. During four years of high school, Michael Sisneros had achieved only two A's outside of physical education classes: one in American history and the other in consumer math.

"It says here that Mike worked part-time at the hardware and lumber yard since his freshman year in high school."

"I remember that," Gastner said. "I think."

"And then he enlisted in the United States Army in 1992."

"I guess he did," Gastner said. "It seems to me that he was overseas for a while."

"Germany," Estelle agreed. "He finished out his tour with the military police unit at Fort Bliss."

"And then came back home."

"So it would seem. He joined the Posadas Village Police Department in 1998 as a part-time officer and attended the state law enforcement academy in 1999. Eddie hired him full time for the village that fall." She shuffled through a selection of copied diplomas, certificates of attendance, and certifications. "All the usual stuff. There's nothing there," Estelle said, and tossed the folder on the desk.

"I didn't think Mike was the one at issue," Gastner said.

"He's not, at least as far as I'm concerned. I was hoping I had missed something." She rose and the two of them went back to the conference room. Eddie Mitchell had returned, and he and the sheriff were seated at the long table, a litter of village files and documents spread out in front of them.

"Mike was in the service from 1992 through the spring of 1995," she said. "What years was Janet in the army? Do we know for sure?"

"I was lookin' at that," Torrez mumbled. He leaned forward and shifted papers. "Enlisted in January of '95. Medical discharge September, '96."

"That was in our file? I thought we didn't have anything on her."

He shook his head slowly. "Nope, we don't. I asked Virgil

Hardy at A & H for her employment records. He didn't much like bein' bothered on a Sunday afternoon, and it turns out he didn't have much on file anyways. Apparently Janet printed up this résumé when she first applied for the job. Eddie just picked it up." He turned the single sheet of paper and shot it across the table to Estelle. "That ain't what's interesting."

She scanned down the brief form. It was perfectly typed, but so brief that Virgil Hardy could have memorized it in an instant if he had felt the need. "It doesn't say what the medical discharge was for."

"Nope. Maybe old Virgil didn't need to know. Welding rods and bookkeeping don't much care about things like that."

"I'd like to know, though," Estelle persisted.

"I know a guy who knows a guy who knows a guy," Gastner said. "Getting anything out of military records is like digging a hole in a lake, but let me give it a whirl." He motioned toward Estelle's office. "Use your phone?"

"Of course. Who can you find on a Sunday?"

"We never know," Gastner said, and left the room.

She turned back to Torrez. "So she and Mike didn't serve together?"

"Nope."

"It doesn't hurt to hope," Estelle said.

"A coincidence, but that's about it," Mitchell said. "Their military service gave 'em something to talk about when they were dating, maybe. And speaking of playing the odds," Mitchell said, and shifted a boot where it rested on the mahogany table. "Let me fill you in on what we were talking about before you and Bill came back in." He held up a document that had seen better days, including a ring of coffee stain on the lower left quadrant.

"In 1990, Hank Sisneros was arrested for DWI for the fourth

time." He handed the folder to Estelle. "Interesting little file he has. Eduardo was the arresting officer. It's also interesting that there's no disposition of the case. I don't guess that it was ever prosecuted." He reached out and touched the corner of the slender folder as Estelle spread it open. "Nothing in here says that it was, anyway."

"That's been known to happen," Torrez growled. "Eduardo was from the 'escort 'em home' school of drunk management."

"Well, he'd know the way," Mitchell said. "Sisneros's home address is listed as 412 South Sixth Street. That ring a bell with anyone?"

"Next door to the chief," Estelle said, looking up quickly. "Eduardo's place is 410. Did Hank Sisneros have a rap sheet? I don't see one in this folder."

Mitchell laughed. "You're kidding. The chief didn't bother with summary paperwork, Estelle. At least not back then. We got what we got, which isn't much. It looks like the chief's habit was to make an incident report, file it, and that was that."

Those incident reports showed that Hank Sisneros had tried Chief Eduardo Martinez's patience half a dozen times for various petty complaints before his arrest in May 1990, for DWI. That arrest was the last one recorded in the folder.

"This is it? Nineteen ninety is the last entry? Fifteen years ago? What does the county have on him?"

"Absolutely nothing," Mitchell said. "I checked. Unless Bill remembers something."

"Just a vague recollection that Hank was both a drinker and a fighter. He must have moved to Deming about then, or what?" Estelle asked. "This is the last entry. He suddenly starts on the straight and narrow after this DWI arrest in 1990. Either that, or he moves."

"Something like that," Mitchell said. "I don't know the details. All this is before my time."

"And I don't remember," Torrez said when Estelle looked his way. "Ask the walking directory," he added, nodding in the direction of Bill Gastner's exit.

"I will, when he comes back from his call. So...the Sisneros family were the chief's neighbors. That's interesting. When I was talking to Essie Martinez, I wondered why she should remember so much about Hank Sisneros. She knew that Hank didn't get along with his wife, for instance. With Irene."

"At least half the town would have known that," Torrez said.

"I suppose that's true. Not the half I live in, though." She shrugged. "But it makes sense if Hank and Irene Sisneros lived right next door to the Martinezes. They'd hear every word."

"Essie didn't volunteer that they were neighbors. That's kind of interesting."

"No, she didn't."

Mitchell made a face. "How discreet." He pursed his lips and whistled tunelessly. "Maybe there are other things that Mrs. Martinez conveniently didn't notice or remember." He pointed at the folder. "Take a look at the fence incident. About the third item from the back."

"The fence incident?" She replaced the 1990 DWI report and leafed backward.

"That one," Mitchell prompted. "Also 1990, by the way."

Chief Martinez had been economical with words, with one brief paragraph written in tiny, neat block letters that used only a small portion of the space that the Uniform Accident Report form allowed:

Operator says he had borrowed dump truck from Wilton Griego, and was attempting to dump load of fines on driveway. Operator said parking brake failed, and vehicle rolled across the street and into fence and corner of tool shed at 407 South Sixth Street. Vehicle undamaged. Altercation with owner of shed. Counseled both operator of truck and owner of shed. Owner of shed says he will file with insurance company. Photo attached.

Estelle turned the report sideways so that she could examine the faded instant photo that had been stapled to the bottom of the form. The older-model dump truck had been moved by the time the photo was taken, and was parked at the curb. It appeared from the chief's diagram and notations that Hank Sisneros had backed the loaded dump truck into his driveway, parked, and gotten out to release the tail gate prior to engaging the dump box. The old truck had lurched out of gear, ambled down the slight gradient of the driveway, bumped across the street and over the curb, and nosed into the neighbor's decorative fence and the metal storage shed.

"'Owner of shed,'" Estelle read, and looked up at Mitchell. "Brad Tripp."

"Ain't that interesting?" he said.

"Yes, it is," she said. "'Altercation with owner of shed.' I like that."

"Really descriptive, isn't it?" Mitchell said.

Bill Gastner thumped into the room, and Estelle could see by the scowl on his face that he'd been less than successful in finding a short cut to Janet Tripp's military records.

"Long shot," he grumbled. "I called a sergeant buddy of mine who just retired. He's got connections, still. He says that if I send in an official written request and call again a week from whenever, there might be someone who knows something who isn't on vacation until the end of winter."

He stopped short when he saw the three silent faces. "What?"

Estelle held out the accident report and he took it, taking a moment to shift his trifocals so be could read the tiny print.

"This is the goddamnedest thing I've ever seen," he said after a minute. "'Counseled both'? Christ." He shook his head. "But Eduardo was good at that. Counseling."

"Did you know that at one time, all three lived door-to-door?" Torrez asked. "The chief, Sisneros, and the Tripps?"

Gastner's face wrinkled in perplexity. "I'll be goddamned," he said. "No, I didn't know that. What's Essie say?"

"No mention."

"Let's ask her again," Gastner said, and handed the accident report back to Estelle. "And ask the Tripp sister. What's her name?"

"Monica. We haven't talked to her yet," Mitchell said.

"I'm not sure I'd wait until tomorrow," Gastner said. "And I'll be the bad guy and bring this up.... Mike didn't mention any of this either."

"On its own merits, there's not much here to remember," Estelle said. "This long ago, maybe there's no bearing on anything that happened this weekend. Why *would* he remember this stuff?"

"That's one way of looking at it. I'll talk to Essie again, if that's what you want," Gastner offered. "It might turn out that she really does have a bum memory for things that happened fifteen years ago. And maybe not."

"I'll go with you," Estelle said.

Torrez pushed himself to his feet with a painful grimace. "You do that. In the meantime, I think we need to find Mike," he said to Estelle. "In 1990, he would have been a teenager. A kid's memory is usually pretty good."

THIRTY-FOUR

"LET US HAVE a moment," Essie Martinez said, patting her oldest son's hand. Ray Martinez looked skeptically at Estelle and Bill Gastner, then shrugged.

"If you need anything…," he said, and Essie patted his hand again.

Essie watched him leave the kitchen, and Estelle could see the quiet pride in her eyes. In everything but years, Ray was a copy of his late father.

"He's doing so well now," Essie said, and Estelle nodded, although she had no reference to what the "now" implied—whether the chief's eldest son was a late bloomer, or had had his own share of troubles, or had experienced any number of other snarls that can alter the best laid plans. "Please," the chief's widow continued. "Sit." She beckoned them to the kitchen table. "What can I get for you? You see?" She gestured at the laden countertops. "We have enough food for an army."

"Nothing, thanks," Estelle said. She glanced at Gastner and saw that the former sheriff was eyeing a particularly dramatic layer cake that had already been sampled, but he grimaced and turned away. "Essie, we need to talk with you again."

"But I've told you all I can remember."

"Maybe I can help," Estelle said. "We'd like to hear what you recall about the spring of 1990."

Essie did a fair job of looking blank. "That's fifteen years ago," she said. "*Por Dios,* how would I remember something like that." Her eyes flicked toward Bill Gastner, then off into the neutral distance. When Estelle didn't continue, Essie's gaze wavered uncertainly. *It's there,* Estelle thought.

"You had some interesting neighbors at that time," she said after a moment. "The Sisneros family lived next door. You didn't mention that when we spoke earlier this morning."

Essie drew in a long, deep breath, leaning back in her chair with both hands braced against the table. "Well," she began, then stopped. She pulled a wadded tissue out of her pocket and dabbed at her left eye. "Just Hank," she corrected. "He bought that little house a couple of years before, when the Estancias moved out. He was going to fix it up as a rental, I think, but most of the time it just sat empty. When he and Irene divorced, he moved in and stayed there. Just for a few months. Irene, she wouldn't have anything more to do with him. And then she went to Lordsburg and married that guy."

"But that was years later," Estelle prompted.

"I guess so." Essie waved a hand in dismissal. "Mike, he went in the army a little bit after that, you know. Three or four years." As if her two visitors hadn't appreciated the fact, she added, "That was a long time ago. But are you sure when that was? That was 1990?"

"We're sure," Estelle said.

"I suppose you are." Essie's resignation was tinged with a little bitterness. "So long ago."

"Essie," Estelle continued, "At the same time, at the same time in 1990, the Tripps lived across the street. Am I right?"

The older woman pursed her lips and regarded Estelle thoughtfully, long enough that the undersheriff got the impression Essie was not simply trying to remember, but was calculating how much to say.

"You know, that was a real mess," she said. "And so sad, I think."

"In what way?"

"Well, I don't know all the details," Essie said, and the tone of her voice made it clear that she certainly *did* know the details. "But Olivia...you knew her? Olivia Tripp?"

Estelle shook her head. Gastner sat silently, his face impassive, like an old bulldog dozing with his eyes open.

"Well, they had their troubles, too. They didn't live here too long, I know that. They broke up, Brad and Olivia did, and Olivia took the two girls. Brad, he stayed in that house for a while by himself. But then *he* moved away. For a while there, we had nothing but bachelors around us. A couple of lost men."

"Do you know where Brad went?"

"No idea whatsoever," Essie said with finality. "That was kind of funny, too. He packed up, and Eduardo thought that he was putting things in storage. He was really in a mess when Olivia left him." She almost smiled. "Eduardo said that it was going to take a bulldozer to clean out all the beer cans."

"Brad Tripp had a drinking problem?"

"Oh, yes."

"And apparently Hank Sisneros did, too."

Essie nodded in resignation. "Awful, isn't it? Eduardo used to say that half the time, he felt like a rehab counselor with those two. Fight, fight, fight. You know," and she nodded at the memory, "it was a good thing that they lived across the street from each other. If they had lived side by side, no telling what might have happened. Fight, fight. They'd *yell* at each other...," she tsked. "When that truck got away from Hank, we were sure World War Three was going to break out."

"Tell me about the truck."

"Oh, that," Essie said dismissively. "That old thing shouldn't even have been on the road. That's what Eduardo said. The brake failed, or some such silly thing."

Estelle opened the folder containing Hank Sisneros's history and scanned the report again. "Nothing much came of it all?"

"What do you mean?"

"Your husband said there was an altercation."

"That's for sure." She smiled, and her eyes grew sad. "Eduardo broke it up."

"What did Tripp say when the truck crashed into his yard, do you remember?"

"I just don't remember," she said. "A good thing that no one was hurt."

"It wasn't long after that incident when Eduardo arrested Hank Sisneros for driving while intoxicated. Do you remember that?"

Essie heaved another sigh. "I suppose so." Her eyes drifted down to the report that Estelle held. "May I look at that?"

"Sure."

She took her time, occasionally bringing the report closer to scrutinize her husband's tiny handwriting. "You said this was the last time?"

Silence enveloped the office for a moment. "No. I didn't say that," Estelle said.

"Well, I think it was. You know," and she reached across and handed the folder to Estelle, "Eduardo and I used to talk about these things. We were so fortunate, I guess."

"Fortunate?"

"Our children were such a joy to us. It was hard to imagine it any other way. You know what I mean with those two dear little ones of yours. And you," she said to Gastner. "You have four grown ones, with grandchildren." She smiled when Gastner didn't respond. "You know, Eduardo and I didn't disagree very often." Estelle found it hard to imagine the two gentle souls raising their voices about anything. "But we argued that night."

"About what?"

"Eduardo came home that night and I could tell that something had happened. You know, I didn't like to intrude, but we sat in the kitchen for a long time. I remember that. We sat and talked. Eduardo wasn't sure that he had done the right thing."

"And what thing was that? You mean when he arrested Hank?"

"That was only part of it," Essie said, and then fell silent for a moment. She looked up at Gastner. "This is like scratching open an old cut," she said, and hesitated. "You didn't know about this?" Gastner shook his head. "Eduardo never talked to you? He said that he would…."

"Not about any of this," Gastner said. "It's not like he's going to come to us about every DWI in the village. And for every one that makes it into the file," and he nodded at the report folder, "there's probably a thousand drunk drivers that make it home without incident. That's why they always figure that they can, Essie."

"This wasn't about a drunk driver, Bill," she said, and added with finality, "Eduardo wouldn't lose any sleep over a drunk driver." She reached out and tapped the folder sharply with an index finger. "This was about a deal."

"A deal?"

"Yes, a deal. And I told Eduardo that he shouldn't have anything to do with it. But you know, he liked to keep things…" She made a smoothing motion with her hands.

"Tell us what happened, Essie," Estelle said, but the expression on Essie Martinez's face said that the telling wasn't so simple.

A long moment of silence followed, and Estelle could see the moisture forming at the corners of the older woman's eyes. "When Eduardo stopped him, Hank Sisneros had the Tripp girl in the car with him," Essie said, and her hands settled in her lap as if in relief. "Janet...the older one." She took a deep breath as if to say, *There, I said it.*

"Janet Tripp."

"Yes."

"She would have been what, about fourteen then?" Gastner asked.

"I think so."

"What did Eduardo do, Essie?" Estelle asked.

"He thought that they had only been drinking together," she said. "At least that's what he hoped. That's what I think. He hoped. But he knew better. I know he did. Anyway, Hank Sisneros offered to move away if Eduardo wouldn't press charges against him. If he wouldn't tell Brad Tripp. Or Olivia—except that she wasn't living with Brad at the time. Maybe Janet had come over to see her dad. Maybe something like that." She looked up at the ceiling. "Oh, can you just imagine what that old drunk Mr. Tripp would have done if he found out that his neighbor across the way had his little girl...."

"And Eduardo agreed to that?"

Essie nodded slowly. "He agreed. And he never should have. If you ask me, that Hank should have ended up in jail. But Eduardo thought that wouldn't do any good."

"And Hank *did* move away shortly after that?"

"Yes. He did."

"And the Tripps?"

"You know, I don't remember. But Brad Tripp moved away, too. I know that. He moved things into storage and then he went away. And Hank, he moved away too, just like he said he would. And that was that."

"Essie, do you know whether or not the Tripps ever found out about the incident?"

"I don't know. I really don't. All I know is that after a while everyone went away. And after that, it was a much quieter neighborhood. But you know, I've often wondered..." She let it hang unfinished. "We'll never know, I suppose."

"And maybe just as well," Gastner said, pushing himself out of his chair.

"A small world," Essie said. "Eduardo thought the world of the boy, you know. Of Mike. That boy is nothing at all like his father. But I worried a little when I heard that they were going together... Mike and Janet. Do you think Mike knew about his father and the girl?"

"I don't know," Estelle said. "Kids are sometimes pretty good at keeping secrets from their parents—it works the other way around, too."

THIRTY-FIVE

ESTELLE'S FIRST EFFORT to reach Monica Tripp resulted in a busy signal, and even while she was reacting with a grimace of irritation, the cell phone on her belt chirped.

"We're at Mike's apartment," Sheriff Torrez said without greeting. "Are you finished up?" He didn't bother to elaborate.

"I just tried to reach Monica Tripp, with no success. I'm going to drop *Padrino* off so he can pick up his truck," Estelle replied. "He claims he has work to do." She glanced across the office at Bill Gastner, who shrugged in apology. "We left Essie's a few minutes ago. What she remembers jibes with the reports. I think it boils down to something pretty simple—she didn't want to embarrass Eduardo. Or at least tarnish his memory. So wait for me. I'll tell you about it when I get there. We may be barking up the wrong tree, Bobby."

"Yeah, well," the sheriff said, obviously not awash in sympathy. "Swing this way, then. And keep the old man with you."

"I'll tell him you said that," Estelle laughed.

"See you in a couple of minutes," Torrez said, and there wasn't any responsive note of humor in his tone. "You on the way?"

"Yes, sir." The phone connection broke without further comment from Torrez, and Estelle snapped her own unit closed. "Bobby wants you over at Mike's," she said to Gastner, whose shaggy eyebrows lifted in surprise.

"Moi?"

"*A ti.*"

"What'd I do?"

"I have no idea, sir. It sounds like he's talking to Mike right now. So we'll see. Can the State live without you for a few more minutes?"

Gastner laughed. "Oh, I'm sure. They can live without me for months and years at a time, no doubt."

A moment or two later, just beyond Posadas Hardware and Lumber, they swung onto the broken macadam side street that eventually wound behind the high school's athletic field. Before they reached the school property, they saw two county units pulled into the Mesa View Apartments parking lot, on the far side of the building, out of sight of Mike Sisneros's red Mustang—and the apartment window above it with the commanding view.

"He looks terrible," Gastner said, nodding in the sheriff's direction as Torrez slid down from the driver's seat of the Expedition, moving slowly as if the slightest jar when his boots touched the pavement would send shock waves up through his system.

"Agreed," Estelle said. "The more people who tell him that, though, the more stubborn he gets."

"You know," Gastner said as he pulled himself up and out of Estelle's sedan, "when he married Gayle, I was willing to bet that she'd be able to reform him in about a month. No dice. Not even in five years. Not a dent."

"It's when Gayle turns grumpy that I'm going to start worrying," Estelle replied.

"Hey." Bob Torrez's standard greeting was augmented by an expression that Estelle couldn't differentiate as a smile or a grimace. If he had overheard Gastner's comment, or hers, he gave no indication. Moving slowly to the front of Estelle's Crown Victoria, he settled his left hip ever so gingerly on the front fender. He glanced at Estelle, and she saw his gaze fix for a brief instant at the base of her throat, where the black margin of the vest showed.

With one hand braced on the fender, Torrez turned and nodded at Gastner, pointing with his free hand at the tangle of gray chest hair that peeked out around the top button of the older man's plaid shirt. "Vest," he said.

At the same time, Eddie Mitchell slammed the back door of the Expedition and appeared holding a large, well-used vest that he extended toward Gastner. "This was still in the equipment room," he, said. "It has your name on it."

"And I'm sure it still fits," Gastner said agreeably. He took the vest and laid it on the hood of Estelle's car, then shucked his own jacket. With practiced ease, he slipped the vest over his head, pulled it down so that it covered at least a portion of his belly, and slapped the Velcro stays in place. "So," he said, patting the center of the vest's reinforcement pocket. He slipped the jacket back on. "What's up? Where's Mike?"

"We don't know," Mitchell said. "That's what's up. That's his car, but no Mike."

"Not upstairs in his apartment?"

"Nope." Torrez said. "Eddie went up and rapped on the door. No answer, and the door's locked." His dark brown eyes were locked on the shadow where the interior foyer opened to the sidewalk. "I don't like it much. He could just be sittin' inside."

Or worse, Estelle thought. "Or he might be out for a Sunday stroll, Bobby." She touched the phone that hung on her belt, but Torrez had evidently reached his own decision. "We found out why Janet didn't want to spend Christmas with Mike's mother and stepfather."

"No shit?"

"It looks like years ago, Eduardo cut a deal with Hank

Sisneros, back in 1990. The chief caught Hank and young Janet together, half sloshed. And maybe doing more than just drinking. The girl was fourteen at the time."

"Essie said this?"

"She remembers it well. Apparently Eduardo cut Hank a deal. Hank offered to leave town, and the chief didn't pursue the charges. Hank must have been persuasive."

"Christ," Torrez muttered. He moved slightly, shifting his weight from a trouble spot on his hip. "Hank Sisneros." He said the name and fell silent, staring at the pavement. "That's one person who wouldn't want an old piece of paperwork to go public."

"But Chief Martinez didn't make a report," Estelle said.

"Hank wouldn't know that, would he?" Torrez said. "And he probably doesn't know that the statute of limitations puts him in the clear, the dumb shit. It's just like I said." He turned to glare at Bill Gastner. "The two old guys would remember, and that's what he's afraid of."

"One of 'em, anyway," Gastner said. "I didn't."

"And he don't know that," Torrez persisted. "Only thing we don't know is how Mike figures in all this. I can see that daddy wouldn't want the son to find out who's been bangin' the kid's fiancée." He jerked his head toward the apartment building. "We were waiting on you." He patted his jacket pocket. "We have the paperwork to go in upstairs."

Pushing himself off the car, the sheriff reached out and locked a hand on Gastner's left shoulder. So rarely did Robert Torrez ever reach out physically to anyone that the gesture startled Estelle. "Until I know where he's at," Torrez said. "Until we know what the hell is going on, I want somebody with you."

"I don't need a babysitter," Gastner said affably. "And I

don't think Mike Sisneros is a threat to anyone." He paused and cocked his head, looking askance at the sheriff.

"It's beginnin' to sound like it ain't Mike that we got to worry about," Torrez said. "And as far as threats go…well," and he let the rest of the sentence hang as he removed his big paw from Gastner's shoulder. "We don't know, do we? Mike's car is here, and he ain't. We don't know where the hell he is. He ain't in Lordsburg with his mom, and if he's in town…well, we ain't found him yet. And we've been lookin', too. He might be sittin' up there," and he nodded at the stairway, "holdin' a shotgun on the door. Or maybe he's already used it on himself. No way to know."

"Who talked to him last?" Estelle asked. "I had breakfast with him this morning, about nine or so. Did anybody see him after that?"

"Don't think so," Torrez replied.

"Does he have a bike or something? Maybe he went for a ride. To clear his head."

"He don't ride a bike," Torrez said impatiently. "That's Pasquale does that."

"Look," Eddie Mitchell said, "it's his weapon that's missing. It's his girlfriend who got whacked with a gun of the same caliber. And Bill's conference room key was taken…. Mike didn't have one of his own. And now we know something about his daddy that we didn't know before. Maybe Hank's made a deal with his son. 'You get those records for me, and we're square.'"

"And it's entirely possible that Mike doesn't know about his father and Janet Tripp," Gastner said. "Hank would have known that Eduardo would never put a minor's name in the report—if he wrote one in the first place. And *Janet* sure as hell wouldn't tell Mike."

"Let me go up there, then," Estelle said quickly. The idea of

Mike Sisneros and weapons at the ready obviously was already front and center in Torrez's mind, despite the newest revelations from Essie Martinez. Estelle didn't believe it for a moment...except for the awful possibility that events had pounded the young cop down into such a deep depression that he had sought the quick way out.

"Let's find out," she said. "If Eddie covers the inside stairs, then you and Bill can back us up from down here. Is there an upstairs back window in his apartment?"

Torrez nodded.

"Then one of you in the back, and one out here," Estelle said, glad that the stairway was enough of an obstacle that Torrez was content to cover from below—not that either he or Gastner would be of any use if a foot chase developed.

Two and two halves, Estelle thought. She reached into the car and unlocked the shotgun. "You want this, sir?"

"I don't think I need that," Gastner replied.

"Take it anyway," she said.

"Why, sure," he said agreeably, but she could see the set in his eyes. "I'll take the back." He nodded toward a large air-conditioning unit that sat on a concrete slab at the end of the building. "I can watch the window from there, and you, too."

"You've already tried calling him?" Estelle asked Torrez.

"Yup. No answer, no answering machine. No page. No nothing. Collins and Mears are both cruisin' likely spots, and they ain't found a thing. It's like he just slipped off somewhere."

"Then let's take a look and see what we have."

They kept close to the building as they moved down its length, Estelle and Eddie Mitchell moving quickly, with Gastner bringing up the rear. Torrez limped to a spot directly in front of the Mustang, and leaned against the wall beside the entrance to the inside stairwell.

The stubby .45 automatic felt bulky in Estelle's hand as she moved up the outside stairway, keeping her body against the faded siding. The air was quiet enough that she could hear a vehicle pull out of the parking lot of Tommy's Handi-Way convenience store three blocks away. Across the alley, in full view of the stairway, the lumberyard was Sunday-afternoon empty.

She was still several steps from the door when her radio, turned down just one click shy of silent, carried Eddie Mitchell's velvety soft voice. "I'm here," he said, and Estelle reached down and touched the transmit button once, sending the shortest burst of squelch as a reply.

Reaching out with her left hand, she twisted the doorknob. It turned and then stuck. She jiggled it gently back and forth, then turned hard, rocking the knob at the same time. The latch released. *Oh, sí,* Estelle thought. *This is supposed to be locked?* She glanced down and saw Bill Gastner's rotund figure. He raised a hand. Estelle looked back at the door, trying to visualize the apartment. She'd been inside once before, and nothing about the place had struck her as out of the ordinary. The door opened inward to the right, stopping against the kitchen wall. To the right was the living room and its window that fronted the parking lot. Farther down the hall was a single bedroom and a bath.

The door outside of which Eddie Mitchell waited after climbing the interior stairway opened into the far end of the living room.

From his vantage point, Bill Gastner would be able to see several feet into the apartment beyond the door. She pointed at her eyes, then to Gastner, then to the door, and he nodded, shifting position slightly. With the toe of her boot, she pushed the door as hard as she could, drawing back instantly. The door yawned open, and she glanced back at Gastner. He stretched as tall as he could, peering through the open door. He held up a hand uncertainly, then motioned all clear.

Diving past the opening, she regrouped on the opposite side of the door, sifting through the brief image she'd seen.

"I'm clear," she said into the radio, and a second later heard the other door slam open.

Estelle stepped inside, stopped, and listened. She saw Mitchell in the shadows by a large entertainment center just inside the interior door, doing the same. It took them no more than a moment to ascertain that the apartment was indeed empty.

"You need me up there?" Torrez's voice sounded tired over the radio, maybe disappointed.

"I don't think so," Estelle replied. "He's not here."

"Now what?" Mitchell said, holstering his own weapon. He was standing in the doorway of the bedroom.

"I don't know, Eddie." She surveyed the living room, then moved into the kitchen. Lived in, on the verge of sloppy, with the owner preoccupied with far more important things than a clean carpet or washed dishes—Mike Sisneros's home was exactly what a bachelor apartment might be expected to look like after a couple of days of neglect. The sink included a fair collection of unwashed dishes, glasses, and cutlery.

She bent over toward the trio of glasses still on the counter and sniffed.

"I didn't think Mike is much of a drinker," she said as Mitchell entered the kitchen behind her.

"He isn't. Actually, I don't think that he drinks at all."

"Did Janet?"

"I have no idea."

She pulled a pair of latex gloves from her jacket pocket, worked her fingers into them, and then lifted a glass gingerly by the very bottom. "Someone does."

Mitchell crossed to the sink. Estelle placed the glass back where it had been, and he bent down and sniffed all three. "Somebody does," he repeated. "One's had whiskey in it, or something similar. The others don't."

"Was the front door locked?" Estelle asked, and Mitchell shook his head. "You didn't try it earlier?"

"I came up the outside," he said.

"That one sticks."

"Apparently," Mitchell said. "I jiggled the knob, and when it didn't turn, I assumed it was locked. Assume, assume."

"So," Estelle said, surveying the room. "Where's our man? His car's here; he's not." She stepped close to the glasses again, inhaling the aroma deeply, then straightened up and methodically opened one cabinet door after another. Mitchell did the same, working from the other side.

"No booze," he said, and opened the refrigerator. "One six-pack of beer, two missing."

"Maybe down in the car," Estelle said. She pulled the trash can out from under the sink and rummaged for a moment. "Not in the trash." She straightened up. "Interesting possibilities, Eddie." She stepped toward the living room and surveyed the simple quarters, then stooped down and looked under the table and the old sofa. No empty bottles lurked in any of the logical places where a drunk might cast them away. She stood for a moment, listening, looking, and smelling.

The image came to mind of Mike Sisneros trudging down the alley in an alcoholic shuffle, shoulders stooped, the bottle of whiskey hanging from unresponsive fingers. That didn't work. But Hank Sisneros came to mind, and the image fitted.

She turned and looked back at Eddie Mitchell, and when their eyes met, she knew that he was thinking the same thing.

THIRTY-SIX

"GAYLE, I WANT AN address for Henry Sisneros," Estelle said when the sheriff's wife answered the phone at the sheriff's office. "Call Deming PD and have them find out where he lives and what kind of vehicle he's driving. We think he's in town."

"*Ay*," Gayle said, and that was the extent of the time she wasted with surprise. "I'll get back to you."

"As soon as you have a vehicle or tag number, we need a BOLO. Make sure that everyone is on their toes."

"Do you want me to wake up some faces?"

Estelle thought for a moment. "Yes. Every single body you can find. If it's a false alarm, I'll be ecstatic."

Other than the single glass holding traces of whiskey, the apartment yielded no answers. Mike Sisneros's uniform hung neatly in a bedroom closet, as did the heavy Sam Brown belt and its plethora of equipment. Although uneasy about its absence, Estelle was not surprised that the deputy's department-issue .45 automatic was missing from the holster.

"I hope Mike's the one holding that," she said. He had been wearing the weapon under his T-shirt when she met him for breakfast.

The .22 pistol case in the dresser drawer was still there, and still empty. If Janet Tripp had owned boxes of memorabilia, she'd stored them somewhere other than Mike's apartment. A single photo album rested on a coffee table in the living room, only three of its pages filled with recent photos.

Estelle sat down on the well-worn sofa and leafed through the photos. In one, Janet and Mike sat together on a stone wall in front of an imposing church ruin that Estelle recognized as Gran Quivira National Monument, far to the north near the village of Mountainair. The shadow of the willing tourist who had snapped the picture for them marked the lower corner of the photo.

In all, there were twenty photos of the two young people, including one Janet had evidently taken of Mike, the deputy posed proudly with one hand on the fender of his patrol unit. His smile was broad and sincere, and Estelle felt a pang. Happier days.

She surveyed the pages again. The album began with photos not more than a year old. No parents allowed. No past history. No military photos. No first boy- or girlfriends.

"I want to talk to her sister," Estelle said suddenly.

"The one in Kansas?"

"Yes." She walked back to the kitchen. "Mike doesn't have a phone in this apartment?"

"Makes do with the cell," Mitchell said.

"I want a land line," Estelle said. "I don't want to be halfway through a long-distance conversation and lose it." She turned in place once more. "I don't think this is going to tell us anything."

"Nope. We need to hit the road and find this kid," Mitchell said. "And if his nutzo father is in town, we need to find him, too."

"Yes, we do," she said emphatically, and glanced at her watch. "In about ten minutes, Gayle will have every person we have out looking for both Mike and Hank. I'll go back to the office and make the call to Janet's sister. That'll only take a few minutes, and I'll make sure Bill gets home. I want Mears to process this glass, too." She held up the clear plastic evidence bag and examined the whiskey glass again. "Be interesting to know," she said.

There were others who wanted to know as well. When Estelle walked back into the sheriff's office, she saw a bright Post-it note stuck to the front of her mail slot with Gayle's elegant writing. "Dayan wants you to call him," the note said, and Estelle saw Bill Gastner grin.

"I'm sure he does," Estelle said. "Maybe someday." She crumpled the note and tossed it in the wastebasket. "No interrupts for a while, Gayle," she said.

In her office, she settled back in her chair, the slip of paper with Monica Tripp's phone number smoothed out on the desk calendar. "Bets?" she said to Gastner.

"No bets," he replied.

She dialed and waited for the circuits to link New Mexico and Kansas. After four rings, the connection popped. A male voice answered, polished and practiced.

"Good afternoon. Baylor residence. This is Max speaking."

"Mr. Baylor," Estelle said, jotting down the name quickly. "This is Undersheriff Estelle Guzman calling from the Posadas County Sheriff's Department in Posadas, New Mexico."

"Oh," the man said. "Yes, okay. Just a minute."

The phone was covered with a hand, and Estelle could hear mumbling. *We're expected,* she thought.

"Yes?" The woman's voice was small, with a quaver of emotion.

"Good afternoon, ma'am," Estelle said. "Is this Monica Tripp-Baylor?"

"Yes."

"Mrs. Baylor, this is Undersheriff Estelle Guzman calling from Posadas. I believe Mike Sisneros contacted you earlier today?"

"Yes. He called earlier this morning."

"He told you about Janet?"

"Yes, he did."

Estelle waited for elaboration, but when none was forth-coming, she added, "Mrs. Baylor, we're sorry for your loss, but we'd appreciate any background you can share with us about Janet. Had you heard from her recently?"

"You're a sheriff? This Mike works for you?"

"He is a sheriff's deputy, yes." *This Mike?*

"I didn't know him," Monica said. "I didn't know anything about him, other than that he was a year ahead of Janet in school."

"You and your sister didn't correspond often?"

That brought a sniff that could have been amusement. "We didn't correspond at all, Sheriff."

"You're a couple of years younger than Janet, is that correct?"

"Four years. We weren't close. Look, I don't understand how she died, officer."

"What did Mike tell you?"

"Just that Janet had gone to the bank on Christmas Day, and someone shot her while she was standing at the ATM." What might have been a choked-off sniffle punctuated the sentence.

"That's basically what happened, ma'am. Any information you can give us about her background, about anything you might know, will be a help."

"I haven't seen her since she was in the army," Monica said. "We were never close. We never really wrote. She didn't do e-mail, or anything like that." She hesitated. "I have my family here. My life's here."

"I see. You're coming over for the funeral, though?"

"I told the deputy that I probably would, but I don't know for sure. The service is Wednesday, isn't it? There's a lot going on. I'm not sure that I can get off work."

"If you could…Mike said you might be able to come over tomorrow. There are some estate questions that I'm sure will come up. Mike and Janet weren't married, and you're the nearest relative for her estate."

Monica responded with a sigh.

"Are either of your folks still alive?"

"No. I don't think so."

Estelle frowned. "You don't *think* so? There's some question?"

"My mother died a few years ago. I don't know where my father went after he and my mom were divorced. And I'm not sure that I really care a whole lot, officer. He isn't part of my life now."

"Do you remember when your folks divorced?"

"Of course I remember. A long time ago," Monica said. "Look, those things happen. Mom was really, really hurt by the whole thing. She divorced him, and then he just left. Just left. So as far as I'm concerned, that's that."

"'Hurt by the whole thing,'" Estelle repeated gently. "What whole thing would that be?"

"Look, it's ancient history. That part of my life is over. I just don't care anymore. And I didn't talk with Janet much over the years, but I think she felt the same way. Look, officer, some families are just really close, you know? Huggy huggy close. We weren't. She wasn't my best friend, or anything like that. That's as simple as I can say it. Did you need anything else?"

"I need to know what the 'whole thing' was, Monica."

"The whole thing?"

"Why your mom and dad were divorced."

"I think…I think it would be easiest just to say that they didn't much like each other any more," Monica said. "That's just about the size of it."

"When your dad lived over on Sixth Street in Posadas, in that little yellow house? Were you with him then?"

"No. He bought that place after the divorce. He was going to fix it up, but then he just left. He wasn't there all that long.

No goodbye, no nothing. Just up and left. Janet told me that he put stuff in storage and then left."

"Stuff?"

"Well, you know. His furniture and stuff like that. Maybe he was going to come back for it later. I don't think he had much over there. I know that Janet visited him a few times, but I never did. Mom wouldn't let me."

"So you never saw the inside of that place."

"No."

"Did you ever know Mike's parents?"

"Mike? Oh, the cop, you mean? Janet's boyfriend? No, I didn't know them. I didn't even know him, let alone them. What was their name?"

"Sisneros."

"That's right. No…I didn't know them. I *don't* know them."

"Did you know Hank Sisneros? That would be Mike's father."

"No, I didn't. I didn't have any reason to know him. Look, are you guys going to find the person who killed my sister?"

"I certainly hope so, Mrs. Baylor. And we appreciate your help. When you come to Posadas, you need to stop by the sheriff's office. There will be some civil paperwork for you to deal with. As the nearest relative."

"The cop can't do that? This Mike guy?"

"No, he can't." *Even if we knew where "the cop" was.* "Sergeant Bishop is our civil affairs officer. Ask for him. He'll take you through it one step at a time," Estelle added. "I'd like to talk with you again at that time."

"I suppose."

Estelle left her name and number, and when she hung up, Bill Gastner shifted restlessly in the chair. "That sounded productive."

"*Ay,*" she said. "How dare Janet interrupt their busy life by dying."

Gastner heaved himself to his feet. "You can't always tell by a phone voice," he said. "Lots of barriers go up." He looked at the clock. "If you're finished with me, I need to go home," he said. "I have a few things to do. Then I need to get cleaned up for an evening soiree."

"Sorry, sir," she said. "Someone once taught me that once things get rolling, there's no letup. I don't think anybody's going to be relaxing much until we find Mike—and his father."

"You don't need my help for that." Estelle heard the fatigue in his voice. "It's five fifteen now. What time do you want me to show up? Or do you want a raincheck?" He frowned at her. "You going to take some time to eat?"

"*Los hijos* are expecting, you, *Padrino*."

"Ah," Gastner said. "They just want a music critic."

"No doubt, sir. How about six thirty?"

"I'll pencil it in on my busy calendar. You're sure there's nothing you need me to do?"

"I don't think so. Right now, it's hide and seek."

"It's a small county. You'll find 'em."

"I hope so, *Padrino*."

THIRTY-SEVEN

"SEE YOU IN a little bit," Bill Gastner said. He paused, car door open and one boot out on the gravel of his driveway as he sifted through his keys for the one that fit the front door of his house. "Take a breather now. Give it a rest for a few minutes. Collect your thoughts. You've got every cop in the state on pins and needles now. Let them earn their pay." He grinned. "God, I'm good at giving advice."

He turned and looked at Estelle, and the grin broadened. "You're wired, sweetheart."

"Wired?"

"Wound up. Poised for the chase. Ready to go. This doesn't bode well for a relaxed dinner with family." He glanced at his watch. "Six thirty. You got an hour to stew."

"Yes, sir. You, too."

He pointed at the front door. "I am home. No stewing for me. I gave that up a long time ago." A grin twitched the corners of his mouth and he reached out and patted Estelle's forearm. "This is going to work out."

"One way or another," Estelle said. "It's harder when it's family."

"Ain't that the truth." Gastner's hand tapped the doorsill as if he had something else to say, but then thought better of it. "Mike has a good heart," he said. "Trust him a little bit."

She nodded.

"Be careful, sweetheart."

"You bet." He got out and shut the door, lifting his hand to the brim of his baseball cap in salute. Estelle watched him trudge toward the front door. The headlights weren't much use in the late afternoon dusk, and she swiveled the spotlight this way and that, peering into dark corners of the courtyard. He keyed the massive, carved front door, and then turned to nod at her again. When the door closed behind him, she backed the car away and headed out on Guadalupe.

At the intersection with Escondido, she turned right out of habit, letting the car drift east on Guadalupe through the winter twilight toward her husband's medical clinic and pharmacy. The swing-by had become habit after two attempted break-ins during the past year. Situated in the quiet, dimly lit south end of town, on the back side of a five-acre lot that Bill Gastner had given to the Guzmans, the clinic and pharmacy could be an attractive target—at least until intruders ran into the heavily barred, small windows and comprehensive alarm system.

One of the attempts had been made by a forty-seven-year-old vagrant who had been passing by on the Interstate, huge knapsack laden with all his worldly possessions. He had paused at the Posadas exit to work his STRANDED, WILL WORK FOR FOOD, GOD BLESS sign for a couple of hours, and later told the deputy who'd arrested him that he'd seen the clinic's sign through a thin copse of elms. Nothing ventured, nothing gained, he had told the deputy as he was handcuffed and loaded into the back of the Expedition, his knapsack and sign crammed in behind the seat.

Estelle pulled into the spacious macadam parking lot and swung around, her lights flashing on two vehicles. One was the new Subaru Outback that she knew belonged to Lonnie Duarte, the pharmacist whom her husband and Dr. Perrone had hired a month or two before. That Lonnie would be working at the drug store an hour after closing time on a Sunday afternoon wasn't surprising.

Parked beside Lonnie's Subaru was a contractor's late-model pickup, with heavy side boxes and a headache rack that supported two ladders and a selection of PVC pipe sections. Estelle stopped, her first thought being that the clinic had managed to operate only a month between visits from a plumber before something went wrong again with its copper and plastic innards. The new building had proven about as healthy as an overweight sixty-year-old on nine different medications.

Swinging into the next space, she pushed the car's gear lever into Park and activated her cell phone. "Ernie," she said, when Wheeler answered at the Sheriff's Department, "I'll be at the clinic for a few minutes with Lonnie." She was pleased to hear the sound of his voice. Maybe Gayle had been able to talk her husband into going home for a while.

"Ten four," the dispatcher said. "You coming back in here tonight?"

"Probably—after dinner sometime. Why?"

"Just wondered, is all."

She was about to break the connection when she hesitated, her tired brain finally interpreting what she was seeing. Posadas had at least two reputable plumbing contractors, and Drs. Guzman and Perrone had always made a point of hiring them. Why would they then call—or ask Lonnie to call—a contractor from Deming, especially for a nighttime emergency?

"*Ay,*" Estelle whispered. Deming. She gazed at the truck for a long moment. What was the nature of coincidence? Deming, less than forty miles east, was the nearest city of any consequence.

She glanced at the dashboard clock. At 5:36 p.m., the pharmacy had been closed for more than an hour.... If a contractor passing through had stopped for a refilled prescription, or a bottle of aspirin, he would have been long since on his way. That someone had found a plumber who would respond to a call on Sunday afternoon was in itself remarkable.

"Ernie, run a plate for me, okay?"

"You got it. Go ahead when you're ready."

"I'm looking at New Mexico November Charlie Thomas seven one one."

"Just a sec," Wheeler said, and then in the background she heard another call, this one on the radio. "Stand by, three oh two," Wheeler responded.

"Don't make him wait," she said. "I'm in no hurry."

"Yes, ma'am," Wheeler said, and for the next few seconds he and Deputy Pasquale exchanged numbers, Pasquale snooping into dark corners and working traffic on State 56 just south of the village.

After a moment, the dispatcher came back on the phone. "Estelle, November Charlie Thomas seven one one should show on a commercial vehicle, a white 2003 Chevy three-quarter ton. It's registered to Bruce Wilcox, doing business as Peerless Plumbing and Heating." He rattled off the address. "Negative wants or warrants."

"Thanks, Brent. I'll be with the owner of that vehicle at the clinic. Apparently he's inside with Lonnie."

"Ten four."

She pocketed the phone, picked up her heavy flashlight, and switched off the car, locking it behind her as she got put. Walking on the narrow sidewalk, she skirted the building and arrived at the front door. Through one of the narrow, grilled windows, she could see the top of Lonnie Duarte's round, fuzzy-haired head back in the pharmacy. The rest of the store was dark. Lonnie reached up and made a notation in a large ring binder that lay on top of the counter. He was obviously alone, intent on his work.

Estelle retraced her steps to the clinic's side entrance, a plain, windowless door marked EMPLOYEES ONLY. In a moment, she found the correct key and let herself in.

Lonnie's head appeared around the corner, and a broad smile of recognition lit up his pleasant features.

"Well, hi there. Did you forget something?" he asked.

"No, I don't think so." She closed the door behind her. "You're working late."

"Always, always," Lonnie said. "It amazes me how much paperwork there is, all the time."

Estelle nodded agreeably. "There's a truck parked outside, next to your car."

"There is?"

"A plumbing contractor's truck. Was he in here earlier for something?"

"No. No one like that. At least I don't think so."

Estelle frowned. "He could have come in earlier..." She let the sentence trail off. If the plumber *had* come in earlier, he'd be gone by now. If the truck had broken down, someone would have towed it away.

"Just wondered," she said. "I was just swinging by and noticed it."

"I don't know what to tell you," Lonnie said. "Maybe it's a Christmas present from a grateful patient."

"Don't you wish. You have a good night." Estelle left the same way she had come, and stood for a moment on the sidewalk, regarding the truck. Frowning, she backed away, moving out into the parking lot for a different perspective. With an electric jolt, the memory flooded back. This wasn't the first time she had seen this truck—or at least one very much like it.

At the Posadas Inn motel, a white utility truck had been one of the vehicles parked outside the rooms…just a few spaces down from Todd Willis's battered loaner van.

Moving quickly, Estelle returned to her own vehicle, dialing the office as she did so.

"Ernie, are you clear for a minute?"

"Yes, ma'am."

"Check the Deming phone directory for a listing for Bruce Wilcox, and also Peerless Plumbing and Heating, please."

"You got it."

She could hear him humming tunelessly as he scrolled through the electronic pages. "I have a Bruce and Alma Wilcox on Rincon Drive. Is that the one? It's the only Bruce Wilcox listed."

"We'll see." He gave her the number, as well as the two listings for Peerless Plumbing and Heating. "Thanks, Ernie. What's Tom's twenty now? Still south of the Spur?"

"He's out at mile marker thirty-one on State 56. A confused tourist, I think. He was going to head on down and check both the saloon and a couple of places in Regál when he finished up. He says that one of Mike's buddies lives down that way. Art Sanchez?"

"Okay. When he's clear, have Tomás start up this way."

"Where do you want to meet him?"

"I'm not sure yet. Just have him stay central until I get back to you."

"You got it. Captain Mitchell is right over on Bustos. He and Lieutenant Adams are checking all the alleys and stuff. And Jackie's over making sure the school complex is clear."

"That's good," Estelle said. "I'll let you know." When she dialed the number for Wilcox, the phone was answered on the second ring by an answering machine, and then almost immediately that was cut off. A brusque voice said, "Yup?"

"Mr. Wilcox?"

"That's right."

"Sir, this is Undersheriff Estelle Guzman over in Posadas. I'm sorry to bother you so late."

"In Posadas, you said?"

"That's right, sir."

"Well, what can I do for you?" He sounded as if he was eating something while he talked, and Estelle could hear a television in the background.

"Sir, let me make sure I have the right party. Are you owner of Peerless Plumbing and Heating?"

"Sure am."

"I was curious about one of your trucks that's parked over here in Posadas."

"I beg your pardon?"

"One of your trucks, sir."

"Marko, turn that thing down," Wilcox shouted without bothering to cover the telephone mouthpiece. "Now, say again?" he said to Estelle.

"One of your trucks is parked at a business here in town, and the driver isn't with the vehicle. Does one of your staff live over here, or were they over here shopping? Something like that?"

"I don't think so," Wilcox said.

"How many employees do you have, sir?"

"Just five of us at the moment. We're a little short-handed. But listen, I don't understand this thing about one of my trucks."

"A white 2003 Chevy three-quarter ton, sir. License November Thomas Charlie seven one one. It's got toolboxes on the side of the bed, a couple ladders, and a small load of PVC pipe. It looks like somebody's doing a job over here or something. Except no one's around. The truck is untended." She stepped out of her car, and walked the length of the white pickup. With a great deal of care, she reached out and opened the driver's door. "It's also unlocked," she said. She leaned inside without making any contact and inhaled deeply. The smell of whiskey was pungent. As if her response was triggered by that aroma, she closed the truck's door and then turned quickly in place, surveying the shadows of the parking lot.

"Huh," Wilcox said, and then there was silence for a heartbeat. "Oh...," and he chuckled quickly. "I'm sorry—this just slipped my mind. One of the boys borrowed that to pick up some stuff over there the other day." The relief at solving the mystery was palpable in his tone. "Hank had a couple of errands he needed to run up that way, and I loaned him the truck. He said he had some furniture to move. Something like that."

"Hank, sir?"

"Hank Sisneros." He laughed again. "He used to live over that way, I guess. He asked if he could use the truck, and with the holiday and all, I thought, 'What the hell.' No big deal."

"Ah."

"But you said the truck's abandoned? I don't understand what that's all about."

"Well, parked, sir. At a local business that's closed. No driver."

"Well, I don't know about that. He'll turn up, I guess. Old Hank, he likes the bottle. You might check one of the watering holes."

"I'll do that, sir. Thanks for your help."

"No problem." *Oh yes, it's a problem,* Estelle thought. "You know what he looks like, dontcha?" Wilcox said. "He's short, kinda wiry. Mexican fella, I think. No wetback, though."

"An older man?"

"Well," and Wilcox laughed again. "That depends on your point of view, Sheriff. I would guess that he's about fifty-five. I don't consider that to be particularly old anymore. You sound like you might, though."

"Thanks for your help, sir."

"No problem. I guess the good news is that if he's wrapped himself around a bottle somewhere, at least he isn't driving my truck."

"Yes, sir."

"If you run into him, tell him to bring my truck the hell back here. We got jobs to do in the morning."

"I'll do that, sir." Estelle switched off and stood quietly beside the truck. She reached up with her left hand to rub the back of her neck, and realized the odd feeling was the hair on the nape of her neck standing erect.

Her heart thumping in her ears, she returned to the car and looked through her log. On Friday night, Tony Abeyta and Jackie Taber were the deputies who had been assigned to talk with the rest of the motel's patrons.

She punched in Jackie Taber's number, and the deputy answered promptly.

"Jackie," Estelle said. "On Friday night, when you and Tony talked with the other patrons at the motel? I need to know about the owner of the white contractor's truck that was parked there." She leaned her head back and closed her eyes, forcing her memory. "Willis's van, then the sports car, and the white truck. Down a few spaces."

"Nobody was in that room," Jackie replied. She hesitated. "We didn't talk to 'em."

"No one there, but the truck was?"

"Yes, ma'am."

"Do you remember how the plate came back?"

"Just a sec." Estelle could hear the rustle of paper. "The tag was November Thomas Charlie seven one one. Appears on a white 2003 Chevy three-quarter ton. Registered to Bruce Wilcox out of Deming."

"*Ay,* he was there," Estelle whispered.

"Beg your pardon?"

"Hank Sisneros was driving that truck," Estelle said. "I've got it over here in the pharmacy parking lot. Just the truck. No Sisneros."

"I'm on my way," Jackie said.

"I'm not sure what's going on," Estelle said. She could hear the sound of the deputy's vehicle in the background. "But I think I've got an idea. Silent approach, Jackie. Stop at the trailer park on Escondido. Okay? He doesn't know we're here, and I don't want him to know."

"Copy that. I'm on my way."

THIRTY-EIGHT

WHAT WAS NOW the parking lot of the clinic had formerly been a tangle of choked undergrowth. Guadalupe Trail curved around the five acres that had been Bill Gastner's backyard, but now asphalt replaced the stunted oak, thistle, New Mexico olive, and ragged juniper. A narrow hedge of those unruly plants, perhaps fifty feet wide, separated the back border of the parking lot from the weeds around what had once been Gastner's flagstone back patio—before he had stopped trying to keep up with the invasion.

Estelle stood between her county car and the plumber's truck, surveying the parking lot, listening to the gentle breeze and the occasional hiss of traffic on the Interstate a block to the north. Through the hedge, Estelle could see the faint glow from Gastner's kitchen window. She dialed dispatch again.

"Ernie, I'll be out of the car at Gastner's for a few minutes. Is Tom clear yet?"

"He is. He's inbound now."

"Thanks. I'll talk to him. You'll hear him say that he's headed to Regál for a few minutes. Just acknowledge that, Ernie."

Estelle clicked off and redialed. In a moment, Deputy Tom Pasquale responded.

"Tomás, this is Estelle. How far south are you?"

"About four miles, ma'am."

"Okay. Expedite north, but silent approach. I'm at Bill

Gastner's, and I think something might be going on. I'm not sure what. When you pull into Guadalupe, don't turn down Escondido, all right? I don't want any extra traffic around Bill's house. Just wait by the driveway of the trailer court on Guadalupe. Jackie's already there."

"Got it."

"And you need to radio dispatch and tell Ernie that you're headed toward Regál."

There was a second or two of silence. "You lost me," the deputy said.

"If someone has a scanner, I don't want them knowing where you are, Tomás."

"Oh, sure. Got it."

Estelle turned off her phone and slipped it in her jacket pocket. Bill Gastner *did* have a scanner in his kitchen, although he rarely turned it on. It served as a handy flat surface to cover with pocket junk. Someone else might find it handy indeed. If Hank Sisneros had come to Mike's apartment and either cajoled or coerced the young deputy to go with him to Gastner's, knowing there was a flood of cops outside wasn't going to help matters.

Skirting the back wall of the clinic, she cut across to the east side of the parking lot, well away from the sodium vapor light near the clinic's back door, staying in the dark shadows along the thicket. The vegetation was musty, and once she heard the rustle of something in the dead leaves. She wanted badly to turn on her flashlight to make sure that she wasn't about to stumble over a skunk, but resisted the impulse. The thick vegetation blocked whatever light might have strayed into the thicket from the quickly darkening sky.

She followed the perimeter of the parking lot until she was directly behind Bill Gastner's house, the kitchen window now clearly visible as a yellowish patch through the brush. She stopped. A hundred times, she had either looked out through that kitchen window, or stood on the back patio, or even walked through the thickets. Now, with only the parking lot light behind her and the faint light from the kitchen in her eyes, the fifty feet between her and the house was a formidable barrier.

She closed her eyes for a moment, concentrating on what she remembered. Off to the left of the kitchen window was an enormous cottonwood, its limbs lopped and pruned over the years so that when one dropped it wouldn't crash through the roof of the house.

Taking a deep breath, she started toward that tree, one easy step at a time. She felt the ground ahead of her with the toe of her shoe, slipping each footstep into the dry vegetation.

The cottonwood loomed ahead of her, and she reached out a hand, touching its rough bark, reconnecting her balance with the sturdy, friendly trunk. She waited until her breathing eased and her pulse slowed. A dozen paces away, the back wall of the old adobe was a black shape against the tree-laced evening sky. Through the kitchen window, bare of curtains, she could see the top of the refrigerator and the wall cabinets beside it.

Like an old Mexican fortress, the adobe's windows were all small and set high—no picture windows that opened the house and its occupants to view from the outside world. Keeping her steps short, Estelle moved across the patio, staying out of the light from the window. She rested against the wall of the house, one hand spread on the rough adobe as if taking its pulse. A loud thump from inside the house jerked her body bowstring tight. She could hear what might have been voices, but the thick walls were effective insulation.

Still holding her breath, she moved closer to the kitchen window, keeping her hand in contact with the wall. Her left foot touched what she hoped was a loosely coiled garden hose, and she hesitated, then felt her way around the tangle. She ducked under the window, turned, and straightened up slowly, staying out of the light.

To the right of the kitchen was a laundry room that Gastner never used, preferring instead to let Kealey's Kleaners take care of his needs. That door was routinely closed. To the left, the kitchen opened into a large, formal dining room through an open-topped island—the countertop of which was the only table that the old man ever used. The dining-room table, a huge Mexican antique with enormously ornate carvings, could seat a dozen people—and most of the time was covered in a mess of newspapers, magazines, books, and mail, topped off with whatever hat Gastner might have been wearing last.

Beyond the dining room, a sunken six-sided living room and library was insulated with stuffed bookshelves.

Estelle sucked in a sharp breath. By standing on her tiptoes, she could see that half of the books were a mess, some lying open on the shelves, obviously many on the floor. The lamp-shade of the antique floor lamp hung bent and askew. She heard another loud thump, this time followed by a bellow of rage, and a broad back heaved into view, erupting up from in front of the leather sofa. Arms flailed, and Estelle saw a hand holding a pistol clamped in a grip that covered all but the last inch or two of the weapon's barrel.

Drawing her own .45, she reached out and touched the knob on the back door. The door was closed, but one of the small panes was broken, the door's locks unsecured.

The kitchen door opened inward, and she stayed close to the jamb. Another crash and a curse came from the living room. So focused were the two combatants that they took no notice of Estelle's entrance. She quickly scanned the room and saw no one else.

Bill Gastner's face was nearly purple from exertion, his teeth clenched as he struggled with a smaller, more slightly built man. They were wedged in the narrow space between the leather sofa and the huge, slate table, and Gastner was using his considerable weight to advantage. Both men were slippery with blood, but despite the flailing limbs, kicks, and punches, Gastner was obviously concentrating on only one thing— control of the weapon.

On his back on the floor, the man had his arm hooked around Gastner's neck, hand on the older man's chin as if he could twist the retired sheriff's head backward. The muscles of Gastner's shoulders bulged with effort, and the two men lay quiet for a moment, breath coming in rasping gasps.

As Estelle moved across the kitchen, Gastner couldn't see her, but his assailant could. With a violent wrench, he twisted, driving a sharp elbow into the side of the retired sheriff's head. At the same time, he jerked his arms downward, driving Gastner's wrists into the sharp edge of the table. Jerking free with one hand at the same time that he elbowed Gastner's face again, he almost flung the gun toward Estelle as he yanked the trigger.

The automatic roared and the heavy slug caught the edge of the countertop, exploding upward in a shower of Formica and chipboard fragments. Stung in a dozen places by the shrapnel, Estelle dodged backward. The man brought the gun down hard on Gastner's head, rolled sideways, and slithered out from the cover of the table.

Estelle used the corner of the refrigerator to steady her own weapon, and as soon as the man dove out from between the sofa and the table, away from Gastner's humped form, she squeezed the trigger. Crouched and scrambling for his balance, trying to focus on the new threat, the man was a moving, dodging target. The .45 round took the man in the side of his right knee, buckling it out from under him. He fell with a crash, cursing, twisting toward her.

Just a hundredth part of a second from pulling a second shot, Estelle saw Gastner's large form materialize from the left. He crabbed the two steps on his hands and knees, reaching the man just as his assailant swung the gun to cover him.

Gastner's huge paw enveloped the automatic, and for a heartbeat, Estelle expected to hear another shot, even as she hurtled across the kitchen, down the steps, and across the living room.

She saw her opening. Gastner had both hands on the gun, twisting it and the hand that held it down toward the floor, the muzzle down and away, the barrel wrenched back out of battery so the pistol couldn't fire. The man's other hand was wrapped around Gastner's head. Things froze for a moment, and she tore her cuffs off the back of her belt and with a quick stab, slammed them around the man's right wrist. Using the other half of the cuffs and the chain connector as a wrench, she twisted hard, driving the steel deep into the man's wrist. At the same time, she dropped her left knee into the hollow of his neck and shoulder.

He bellowed something incomprehensible just before her driving knee crushed off his wind and blood supply. He thrashed, disregarding the bite of the handcuffs on the one wrist, or Gastner's powerful twisting on the other. One leg lashed out, the boot coming down hard on the floor in punctuation to his cries.

Estelle shoved the stubby barrel of her own .45 into the man's right eye.

"Drop the gun." She jabbed the barrel so hard blood welled up from his lacerated eyebrow. "Drop it or I'm going to spread your brains all over the floor."

Estelle could feel the man's body freeze, and she twitched the gun barrel again. "I mean it. Drop it."

"I got it," Gastner grunted, and the pistol flew across the room.

"Let go of him," Estelle commanded, and she twisted the cuffs again. The man's hand opened, and Gastner shook his head free. One of Gastner's burly arms was wrapped around the man's elbow, dislocating it forward while the other crushed his thumb backward.

Close as she was, Estelle could smell the liquor, heavy on the man's breath.

"Give me the other cuffs," Gastner panted.

"You're breakin' my arm," the man squealed as Estelle backed a little of her weight off his neck, and he tried to writhe away from the pain. With one of Gastner's legs braced and driving his considerable weight downward, there was nowhere the man could go.

"We'll break more than that, you son-of-a-bitch," Gastner panted. With one hand still locked around the man's thumb, he twisted even harder, then released the elbow long enough to take the cuffs Estelle thrust toward him. He snapped them around the man's other wrist. "Gimme that." He pushed himself up a little, reached around with surprising agility, and grabbed the other set of cuffs that secured the man's right arm. Pulling hard, he brought the man's wrists together and snapped the open cuff home.

"My eye," the man whimpered. "My knee."

"Lucky you still got a head," Gastner said. "Let's get me up." Once more on his feet, drawing deep breaths, he shook his head at Estelle. "You okay?"

"Yes."

"Got a nylon?" He took the long nylon security tie from her. "Shoot him if he moves," he said, and he made sure that Estelle had a tight grip on the cuffs being used as a tether.

After sucking in air for a moment, Gastner pushed himself

away, turning just enough that he could grab first one ankle and then another, pinning the man's legs with his own. In a moment, the man was hobbled. Gastner stood up and wiped his face.

"You okay?" he asked Estelle. "You're sure?"

"*I'm* fine," she said.

"My eye," the man said again, this time with considerably less fight in his tone.

"You'll get over it," Estelle said, not changing position. She pulled the .45 away, but just far enough that, when the man's vision cleared, the yawning muzzle would fill his whole universe. "Sir, will you take the radio? Tom and Jackie are just around the corner."

Gastner reached down and pulled the hand-held out of the holster at the small of Estelle's back.

"Three oh two," he snapped. "Officer needs assistance at Gastner's. The front door is unlocked. And ten fifty-five. Two down."

"Three oh two," Pasquale responded instantly. "ETA ten seconds."

That brought an attempt at a smile from Gastner, but his expression immediately fell serious. "Mike's down the hall," he said, and stepped away, retrieving the automatic. "This is his gun." He looked at it with disgust, then popped out the magazine and jacked the loaded round out of the chamber. For just a moment, he glared at his prostrate attacker. "And this is Hank Sisneros," he said. "Shoulda just drowned him with the rest of the kittens long, long ago."

Estelle hadn't seen much resemblance between the man on the floor, covered with blood and with a couple of extremities pointing the wrong way, and the man in the instant photo tacked to the accident report in Hank Sisneros's file—a man standing beside the old, errant dump truck, looking foolish.

"I'll see what I can do for Mike," Gastner said. "You all right?"

"Just fine," Estelle said. "We're comfortable," she added, and tapped her prisoner's eyebrow with the muzzle of the .45. "Aren't we? You're getting more of a chance than you gave Janet." The words were hardly out of her mouth when the front door burst open and Deputy Thomas Pasquale entered, gun drawn. He moved quickly to his left, out of the doorway.

"Over here," Estelle said. She moved back, lifting her knee but not relaxing her grip on the handcuffs. Pasquale holstered his own weapon and stepped around the table. Grabbing the man by the cuffs as Estelle moved him away, Pasquale turned him on his side, and then, with one hand on the cuffs and the other on the man's belt, dragged him out away from the furniture. At the same time, Estelle heard someone at the kitchen door. Deputy Jackie Taber appeared, weapon ready.

Moving so deftly and quickly that the man only had time to cough out the restriction in his throat, Pasquale recuffed him with his hands behind his back. The deputy handed the extra set of cuffs to Estelle. "Christ, what'd you do to his knee?"

"I put a .45 through it," Estelle said. "Maybe he's lucky I'm not used to the new gun yet. And you probably shouldn't move him any more than you have to until the EMTs get here."

"Shoulda aimed for his head," Pasquale said.

"I wanted to be able to hear what he has to say," Estelle said. "First, we need to tend to Mike."

"Sisneros?"

"He's down the hall with Bill. Keep an eye on this one."

"Yes, ma'am."

"How am I supposed to walk," Hank Sisneros said, finding his voice.

"You don't walk anywhere," Pasquale said pleasantly. "You just lie there and bleed."

"Towels," Gastner called from the hallway. "In the bathroom there on your right. I need some towels."

The wall near the hallway and the first bookcase were blood-spattered, and Estelle tried to avoid any of the marks and stains on the polished wood floor as she ducked into the bathroom, emerging with a pile of clean towels.

"He didn't duck fast enough," Gastner said, holding out his hand for a towel. "He tried to break away." He pressed the towel gently against Mike Sisneros's chin, his other hand steadying the younger man's shoulder. The deputy lay with his back against the wall, eyes closed, breathing in short, shallow gasps that burbled blood into the towel from the mess that once had been his chin. "You're going to be okay, Mikey," Gastner said.

"Here," Estelle said, and reached across with more padding. "Under his head." It appeared that the bullet had struck from the back, raking across the young deputy's neck and throat, exploding out through the point of his chin, a grazing shot that had done a spectacular amount of damage.

Estelle and Gastner knelt silently for a minute, waiting. In the distance they could hear the approaching sirens, a symphony that blended from three different directions. The injured man tried to bring his knees up, and one hand lifted off the floor. Estelle took Mike's hand in hers, and was surprised at the strength of the grip.

"They're on the way, Mike. Just hang on." As she reached to rearrange one of the towels, she saw more blood dripping on the wood, this time from Bill Gastner. He saw her expression and shrugged nonchalantly.

"Nicked me through the fat under the arm," he said. "Got by a corner of the vest, I guess. Not to worry. Hurts like a pup now, but that's a good thing. Everything works."

"How about sitting down," Estelle said, and Gastner didn't

argue. He slumped back against the opposite wall of the hallway, lifted his left arm, and peered at the damage. Estelle reached across with a towel, but he waved it away.

"Why bother ruining another one," he said, and sighed heavily. "That son-of-a-bitch brought Mike over here…they broke in the back. They were waiting for me, Estelle. I came in the house, and they were waiting for me. I guess it was supposed to look like Mike and I took care of each other. Do that, and it sure as shit would look like Mike killed Janet."

"He told you that?"

"He didn't say a damn thing. He might have, if Mike had given him the chance, liquored up as he was."

"I didn't hear the shots," Estelle said, cringing at the thought of what had been going on in this house while she'd been checking the pharmacy next door.

"You could fire a howitzer inside here, and you wouldn't hear it outside, at least not with you sitting in a car. He just fired the one time, though…when Mikey made a break for it down the hallway. I think he could see I wasn't getting anywhere with diplomacy. I tried my best." He shrugged painfully. "That's when we went hand-to-hand." He shook his head ruefully. "Tough little squirt, even drunk."

The sirens turned into Guadalupe, and in a moment Tom Pasquale reappeared, leading three paramedics. Estelle heard more doors slamming outside, and in a moment Eddie Mitchell and Robert Torrez appeared.

"Jesus," Torrez said when he limped into the living room. He moved carefully through the scatter of books and knick-knacks, blood and gore until he was standing near Mike Sisneros's feet. "How is it?"

"I think it looks worse than it is," EMT Matty Finnegan said. In a moment, Sisneros was IVed, gurneyed, and whisked out of the house. Matty turned her attention to Gastner. "Oh, you look good," she said.

"Don't ruin the shirt," he said.

"It already is, Bub," Matty replied. "How many times did he hit you?" She industriously scissored his shirt away from his shoulder. "Oh, nice," she said, pausing when she saw the damage to the vest. "Now, aren't you the lucky one?"

"Luck has nothing to do with it," Gastner grumbled. His luck had nearly run out when one round skipped past the armpit margin of the vest, plowing a path through the pad of fat under his left arm before being stopped by the back side of the vest.

Matty bandaged him quickly, and motioned for the second gurney.

"I don't need that thing," Gastner said.

"Oh, yes you do, honey," Matty chirped. She had untangled the lines from an IV bag and paused, frowning at him. "You want to fight me for this needle?"

"No, ma'am." He relaxed back against the wall, and closed one eye. "My head hurts."

"No doubt," Matty said. "You keep letting people batter it. But we'll get you all fixed up. You going to mind riding in the same ambulance as Mike?"

"I'd be honored," Gastner murmured.

THIRTY-NINE

HANK SISNEROS GROANED from his puddle on the floor as the gurney whisked past him with his son's quiet form lashed on board, followed almost immediately by former sheriff Bill Gastner.

"Second unit is on the way," Matty Finnegan said. She knelt beside Sisneros, glancing dismissively at the blood around his handcuffed wrists and the obviously dislocated thumb. She cut away his trousers, revealing the nasty blue-black-rimmed hole just behind his right kneecap, and the quarter-sized exit wound that had torn right through the large posterior ligament at the back of the joint. "You just lie still," she said unnecessarily, but there wasn't a lot of warmth and nurture in her tone.

Estelle Reyes-Guzman knelt beside the wounded man, and reached out with a towel to dab a bit of blood that threatened to run into his eye. He was breathing heavily, as if he'd just charged up a long flight of stairs.

"Why Janet?" Estelle said. He looked up at her quickly, but didn't reply. "After all these years, did you think that she was going to tell someone about you and her? About that night in the car when the chief stopped you?" His eyes narrowed, but he was concentrating too much on the pain to speak, pain that was quickly chasing him sober. He let his weight carry him over on his left side until his forehead was touching the floor.

"What did Bill Gastner ever do to you?"

"He had to know," Sisneros mumbled, but it was obvious he was having trouble forming the words. Between the slosh of alcohol in his veins and the shock from the ruined knee, it was surprising he was coherent at all. "All the old guys. They talk. They was all set to gang up on me. She woulda told 'em."

"She? You mean Janet?"

Hank gurgled something unintelligible and then tried to straighten up. "I tried to explain it all to her. All she had to do was help me a little bit. Just a little bit. But she was too good for that…."

"Estelle?" She turned and saw Bob Torrez standing near the front door. "Bill wants to talk to you before the ambulance takes off."

She rose quickly and went outside. Gastner's gurney was still on the gravel as the EMTs loaded Sisneros.

"I don't think he's going to say much," Gastner said, when Estelle appeared at his side. "This part's simple. Like I said, he figured that it would look like Mike and I took care of business. That would really fix the blame for Janet's death on Mike." He shrugged. "He tried to talk Janet into helping him, but she wouldn't do it. I think…I *think*…that maybe she threatened Hank. If he didn't leave her alone, she was going to Mike with the whole story about what happened when she was a kid. That's as far as I got with him. He isn't much for conversation."

Gastner reached up and touched his own forehead. "Something's really loose up here with him," he said. "Then Mike made a break for it, and that set him off. I got damn lucky, that's for sure."

"It all goes back to that night in 1990," Estelle said. "It has to. When Chief Martinez caught him and Janet together. She was in the car with him."

"That might be, but Christ…," Gastner said, and he reached

up and patted her hand as he felt his own gurney start to move. "Keep digging. Statute of limitations ran out on that sort of monkey business a long, long time ago."

She went back inside just as the second ambulance arrived. The bandaging that padded Hank Sisneros's wrecked knee was brilliant red, soaked through. His face was ashen with shock, his eyes half-closed and glassy. Sheriff Robert Torrez stood nearby, impassively watching the man try to find a less-than-agonizing way of supporting his battered body.

"They're going to need the cuffs around front for the gurney," she said, and Torrez nodded.

"We can do that." He started to bend over, and Estelle touched his elbow.

"Let me," she said. She bent close to Hank Sisneros, smelling his fetid breath, smelling the alcohol, smelling the blood. For several seconds, she just stared into his bloodshot eyes. "Why did you dump her?" she asked finally, her voice not much more than a whisper.

Sisneros was having trouble focusing, and his head lolled with each panting breath. Estelle reached out and caught him by the chin, forcing him to look at her. "Why did you dump her in the arroyo, Hank?"

A quick jerk of his lips might have been a smirk. "Hell," he mumbled.

"Why, Hank? Why did you do that?"

"Figured she might as well be with her old man," he said, and Estelle froze in place, her hand still locked on his chin, trying to force his eyes to focus on hers. "That's where he ended up." He coughed violently. "What's good enough for him is good enough for the likes of her."

"What'd he say?" Torrez said from behind her.

For a moment Estelle remained kneeling, supporting Hank

Sisneros under the chin. Then she pulled her hand away, and
the weight of his head ruined what little balance he had. He
sagged back to the floor, weight against his cuffed wrists.

"I know where Brad Tripp is," she said.

At FIRST LIGHT on Monday morning, the cavalcade of vehicles,
including a county dump truck pulling a flatbed trailer and
backhoe, rumbled out of Highland Court to the arroyo,
stopping short of the two county sheriff's units that were
parked near the edge.

Within an hour, the jumble of old cars, appliances, and other
informal flood-control structures had been spread out and separated, and the first traces of human remains had been discovered under the massive rump of what had once been the inverted
'57 Oldsmobile "chrome king."

"It wasn't being caught with Janet that bothered Hank,"
Estelle said as she stepped to the edge of the arroyo and looked
down at the gravesite. "Maybe Janet had an inkling what
happened to her father, maybe not. But Hank figured that with
the records being opened up and reviewed, and with Janet dating
Mike, the whole sorry mess would come to light somehow."

She looked across at Bob Torrez. "The old guys would
remember too much," she said. "Or maybe he thought that
Janet knew more than she did. Whatever it was, I think Hank
Sisneros started stewing that if the records came to light, everything would lead back to Brad Tripp's disappearance. He
didn't care about Janet. When Eduardo Martinez collapsed,
Hank heard about it. He was at the motel, in town figuring to
talk to Janet one more time. I'm willing to bet what happened
to Eduardo is what gave him the idea. One down and a couple
more to go. Eduardo and Bill Gastner are the only two old
enough to remember anything. With Eduardo gone, knock off

Bill Gastner and Hank would be home free…especially if he could get his hands on the records that he was so sure existed, and especially if he could focus blame on a son he didn't care enough about."

"That's why he wanted the keys," Torrez said.

"One brilliant idea that didn't work. He thought that he could get into the Sheriff's Department conference room himself, maybe." Estelle turned to gaze back down the dirt lane. "Or more likely," she said, "he was trying to talk Janet into one last favor for him. It's a possibility that Brent or one of the other dispatchers wouldn't pay a whole lot of attention to her if she came into the building."

"Wouldn't work," Torrez scoffed.

"He might have thought it would. If he thought Eduardo had kept a file on that incident between Hank and Janet, then what's to lose? Janet might have been just as happy to see the file go away as anyone." She shrugged. "That's a thread cut, Bobby. If nothing about Hank's little recreation with Janet came to light, then the odds are better that nobody is going to wonder about another drunk who just skipped town one day. Nobody cared enough about Brad Tripp to wonder one way or another. It reminds me of the vagrants we see working the Interstate interchanges with their 'gimme money' scams. Who's going to miss them if they don't turn up one exit farther down the road?"

"She wouldn't do it," the sheriff said.

"Evidently not. He took her key, thinking that she might have stashed some records or something in the apartment."

"That didn't work, either."

"No, it didn't. If Hank had known more about the chief's re-cordkeeping habits, he wouldn't have bothered in the first place. The odds are that if Hank Sisneros had just stayed in Deming, and kept out of his son's affairs, none of this would ever have come to light. Monica Tripp thought her father had just left them. It wouldn't surprise me if Janet thought the same thing."

"Well, he did leave 'em, so to speak," Torrez said. "I wonder if Brad Tripp found out about his daughter and Hank."

"Maybe. Or maybe it was just a continuation of a fight over a piece of decorative fencing mowed down by an old dump truck. When Hank sobers up, he'll talk."

Torrez made a wry face. "Don't bet on it. He ain't that stupid. It's one thing to have a body," and he nodded over the arroyo edge where Tom Mears and Eddie Mitchell were working with Dr. Alan Perrone. "It's going to be somethin' else again proving what happened here."

"Hank Sisneros doesn't have to know that," Estelle said. "When he knows that we have Brad Tripp's remains, he'll sing." She watched as Linda Real maneuvered for another shot as Mitchell rearranged the body bag to collect the pathetic jumble of bones and rotted clothing.

"Interesting," she said. "Hank managed to accomplish exactly what he was trying to avoid." She turned away. "Have you been in to see Mike this morning?"

"No," Torrez said. "Not yet."

"He's going to need some company. I was going over now for a little bit."

"You're going to take the deposition from Bill?"

"Yes. Later today. I want to let him get some rest first. He took some nasty thumps, and he was floating in sedative last night. Plus he's irritated at being stiffed for dinner."

"As long as you're headed that way, take care of him, too," Torrez said, nodding behind them toward the street. Estelle turned to see Frank Dayan's little blue compact car turning onto the dirt. "He finally has his big story on a Monday morning."